THE STRICKEN

THE STRICKEN

MORGAN SHAMY

CamCat Publishing, LLC
Fort Collins, Colorado 80524
camcatpublishing.com

Hardcover ISBN 9780744307696
Paperback ISBN 9780744307887
Large-Print Paperback ISBN 9780744307900
eBook ISBN 9780744307894
Audiobook ISBN 9780744307917

Library of Congress Control Number: 2023941674

Book and cover design by Maryann Appel
Artwork by Lyubov Ovsyannikova / Anastasiia Kurman / vidimages / DavidGoh

5 3 2 4

For Aaron,

Without you, none of this would be possible.

1

Clean Slate

My footsteps pounded down the sidewalk, my heart pumping fast. Wind bit my cheeks, and gray clouds roiled overhead, heavy in the sky. I glanced at the town clock.

The Storm would be here any minute.

People scattered from the sidewalks and streets, tending to their own business. Children darted around their mothers' legs, murmurs low in the air.

Like always, they had no idea it was coming.

I pushed my way through the crowd and dashed into the restaurant where Mom worked. Soft lights lit the room; the tables were full, though no one spoke. Complete silence. Mom was behind the bar, wiping the counter.

"Mom!" I yelled.

The sea of customers didn't flinch. They ignored me, like always, looking through me as if I were a pane of glass.

You're not going to make it.

I gritted my teeth together. "Wanna bet?"

I crossed the restaurant, welcoming the wave of warmth his voice sent through me. Even though urgency thrummed through my veins, the feel of him inside my head was like chocolate. Smooth, comforting.

It isn't safe for you to be out. You can't do anything for your mother.

I shook my head, shoving his voice to the back of my brain. I had lost Dad to the Storm—I wasn't going to lose Mom, too.

I dug my fingers into Mom's shoulder and forced her to face me. The usual look of confusion traveled over her before her eyes lit up in recognition.

"Clara, what are you doing here?"

"No time to talk." I dragged her from the restaurant like a mad bulldozer, ready to flatten anything in my path.

It's here, he said, his voice clear in my mind. *Clara, you need to run.*

I looked over my shoulder and froze. The familiar dark cloud moved toward us, gliding down the street. It crawled over the sidewalk, its tendrils stretching like poisonous claws. It surrounded cars, swallowed up buildings, circled around the clock in the middle of the square in dark wisps.

No one ran. No one screamed. The people on the street stood frozen, waiting for the dark storm to overtake them.

I gripped Mom's wrist and yanked.

"Come on!"

We raced down the sidewalk, our car parked up ahead. Every inch of me buzzed as the feeling of the Storm seeped into me. It was too close.

I shoved Mom into the car, my hair standing on end. Within seconds, the dark fog immersed us, the chaos churning, curling along the windshield. Outside, people stopped. Faces slackened and eyes went blank.

"Clara, what are we—" Mom broke off and crumpled like an empty soda can. My stomach hollowed at the look on her face. She was fading, just like Dad right before he disappeared. She couldn't take too many more of these attacks.

I wrenched the car into gear and floored it. The car screeched down Main Street, speeding through the dark haze. I swerved around the lifeless people still trapped in the chaos. I took turn after turn, zooming through the streets, until the Storm lightened. The road disappeared beneath our wheels, and houses stretched on either side of us, gray sidewalks lining dead grass. Air blew in from the open windows, cooling the sweat off my neck. The dim clouds departed fully, and the sun streamed down.

It was over.

For now.

My fingers relaxed on the steering wheel.

The Storm never affected me. I didn't know why. The worst it did was leave me with a bad headache. The Storm came every day, erasing the short-term memory of everyone in town, slowly taking away their sanity until they disappeared.

Completely.

I hiccupped, Dad's handsome face flashing to mind. The way his eyes creased when he smiled. The way he always enveloped me in a warm hug. The way he'd laugh and tell corny jokes. No. I wouldn't think of him now. The sunlight was bright as I continued to drive, my heart slowing. I peeked over at Mom, sunbeams sparkling on her golden hair. She stared out in front of her, her eyes blank.

The car rumbled to a stop as I pulled into our driveway. Our old white house towered over us, our lawn dried and brown. Mom groaned, her eyelids fluttering. She'd be all right for now, but I cursed myself for not getting to her sooner. I'd maneuvered her around the Storm for months. Life had started to come back into her eyes, and now I had lost the ground I'd gained.

It isn't your fault, Clara.

I jerked, the sound of his voice startling me. Even though he had been with me for as long as I could remember, sometimes his presence surprised me.

"Yes, it is," I said. "It is my fault."

I wish you wouldn't be so hard on yourself. You're doing the best you can. You're saving your mother from the Storm. You're keeping her safe.

"It's not good enough," I mumbled, my throat thick.

He fell silent.

He always went silent when he disagreed with me. I closed my eyes and wished for the hundredth time that I knew his name or why he spoke to me—but every time I asked, he'd disappear for days, leaving me scared he wouldn't return. I'd learned to enjoy whatever time I had with him.

The thought of being crazy had crossed my mind but then fizzled because I was saner than anyone else in this town. I also rationalized that having him inside my head had become a part of me. Even though he was just a voice, he was more real than any physical person I had ever met.

I linked Mom's arm around my neck and hefted her up our front steps. She looked high, with a dazed, goofy expression on her face. I cursed myself again for not getting to her sooner. Our schedule had been working. The Storm came at the same time every day, and since Mom's memory was shot from the daily storms, it was easy to lug her around the town, staying just enough ahead of the brain-eating monster. The rest of the town wasn't so lucky. They were so far gone, caught in the routine of their daily lives, they never realized when the Storm came.

Cobwebs hung from the ceiling, stretched out over the peeling wallpaper. The wood floor creaked beneath our feet as I helped Mom into her bed. The pillows squished out around her, and I pulled the covers up to her chin.

"There you go," I said, fluffing her pillow. I lingered for a moment, my hand hovering over her shoulder. Her body relaxed into slumber; her lips parted slightly. How much time did I have left with her? When would the Storm take her completely? Tears burned the backs of my eyes, but I blinked them away and glanced up at the ceiling. I would be strong. Dad would've wanted me to be strong.

I tiptoed across the floor and took one last glance at her before I shut the door quietly.

Only twenty-three hours.

Twenty-three hours until the next Storm came.

2
Girl Interrupted

I moved back down the hall and into the kitchen, past the garbage that spilled from the can, a putrid smell hanging on the air. I crinkled my nose and peered out the window at the forest that lined our backyard. Deep shadows filled the spaces in between the branches, and a mesh of pine boughs and leaves scattered the area. Forcing myself to exhale, I snatched my journal off the counter and stepped outside.

I headed through the forest, my feet crunching on sticks and leaves. The towering scent of pine tickled my nose, and I let it fill my lungs. This was my safe place. My haven. I'd never seen the Storm come out here.

Though I was never safe from myself.

Sometimes, when I was alone, a darkness snuck in, filling my heart. It swirled inside my chest, heavy, like my own personal storm. Sometimes I felt as if the darkness would burst from my fingertips, right before it would swallow me whole.

I didn't know what this darkness was, all I knew was that whenever I felt it, I wasn't myself. I felt angry, depressed, and I didn't trust my own mind.

It's why I cared about *him* so much.

He gave me a light and peace no one else did. Like he filled the wound in my chest, calming the storm and spreading warmth through my veins.

If only I knew who he was.

If only he knew how I felt about him.

I continued to walk for a time, reminiscing about the times we'd had together. He'd first visited me when I was seven. The storms weren't as bad then, but he'd still been my constant companion. The adventures we had together: him teaching me how to climb trees, him teasing me about how uncoordinated I was, him comforting me when I was sad.

But then my feelings changed. As I grew older, I knew he meant more to me than a friend.

I clutched my journal tight in my hands.

Today was the day.

I would tell him how much he meant to me. If Mom disappeared, he'd be the only person—only thing—I had left. He needed to know how I felt.

I moved deeper into the forest, weaving around the large pines. My usual rock sat up ahead, tucked against a shaded tree. I lowered myself onto the ground, my back pressing up against the cool boulder. I set the journal on my lap, my fingers digging into the leather binding.

He was the reason I'd been late getting to Mom. I'd gotten so caught up in writing about him, I'd lost track of time.

A breeze drifted over my face, and the air seemed to change, to move somehow—and he was there, hovering like a shadow in my head.

How are you holding up?

My shoulders relaxed, and the immediate comfort he carried washed over me.

My mouth twisted at the corners. "You really need to ask that?"

His presence shifted from one side of my head to the other. *You're doing the best you can. You shouldn't be so hard on yourself.*

I held quiet for a moment, nodding. "Well, I don't want to think about that now." My fingers continued to dig into the leather journal. "I want to play a game."

His presence stirred. I could sense his discomfort.

"I need a distraction," I said. "Please."

The energy in him softened. *What do you have in mind?*

"There's so much I don't know about you," I said. "And every time I've asked, you've shut me down. Can you be real with me? Just for today? Then we can go back to our usual routine."

His demeanor changed. It almost felt as if he were . . . smiling.

All right. What do you want to know?

"Your name," I blurted out. "You know how many times I've asked you."

He paused, still hovering, but then he relaxed.

It's Cael.

My heart jolted, and I straightened against the rock. Cael. Like kale. I rolled the name around inside my head. I didn't think he'd actually tell me.

My turn, he said.

"Your turn?" I asked.

You asked me a question, now I get to ask you.

My eyes widened. Another surprise.

"Okay," I said tentatively.

What's your favorite color?

I blinked, my brows drawing together. "Seriously? That's what you're going to ask? My favorite color?"

I've always wondered.

I held back a smile. "It's blue. Like the ocean. Though I've never seen it." I'd never left this town. "My turn again?"

His presence shifted up and down, like he was nodding.

"What is your dream?" I asked. "I mean, everyone wants something in this life. What do you wish you could have more than anything else on the planet?"

He stilled, frozen inside my head. It took him a long while to answer.

I'd like to undo a mistake I made years ago. It's haunted me ever since. I'd like to go back in time and fix my wrongdoings.

An uncomfortable silence settled between us. I didn't expect such an honest answer. It was the first real thing he'd ever told me.

"What did you do?" I whispered. My mind was spinning. I'd known him for years, and I'd only felt goodness from him, but did he actually have a past? One that I should be worried about?

My turn, he said quickly. *Same question to you. What do you wish you could have more than anything else on the planet?*

I peeked down at my journal. That was an easy question, but did I have enough courage to be honest? I ran a hand over the front cover.

I decided to be brave.

"A kiss," I said before I could stop myself. "I've never been kissed. I want to know what it's like. And . . . and I want *you* to do it."

He became deathly still—so still my own thoughts froze for a moment.

"You had to have known," I whispered. "We've spent all this time together. How did you not know that I had feelings for you?"

He remained quiet, a statue in my mind.

"You need to know how I feel, Cael." My hands shook as I peeled the journal open. I cleared my throat and began to read. "He's the only real family I have." I turned another page. "I feel something *more* than family to him." I turned another page. "I wish I could touch him, see him, be with him—"

Stop!

I clamped my lips together. His voice was clipped, angry, fiery in my head.

I don't want to hear anymore. Just . . . stop.

"No," I bit back. "I know you're real. Somehow. Please, I'm seventeen and I've never been kissed." I hated the desperation in my voice. "You *have* to feel something for me, too. Why would you have stayed around all these years?"

Heat burned inside my head, growing, expanding.

This game is over.

I felt him shoot out of my mind, leaving a sudden hollowness.

I sat motionless for a few heartbeats, embarrassment sweeping through me. I sagged against the rock, clenching my eyelids shut. How could I have been so *stupid*? I'd ruined everything. He'd probably never come back again. What would I do if I lost him? What if I never heard from him again?

I kept my eyes sealed closed, the sun hot and red through my lids. Anger surged, and I slammed the journal shut before I chucked it out in front of me, not seeing where it landed. Humiliation and regret and insecurity all coursed through me. I would never leave this spot. I couldn't. I could never face him again.

But in an instant, everything went dim behind my eyelids, like someone was standing in front of me, shading me from the sun. I stiffened, my back pressing harder against the rock.

Someone was there. All my humiliation fled, replaced by fear.

Leaves crackled on the forest floor as this person approached. Was it him? No, impossible. He didn't have a body, did he? But somehow, I knew it was him. He lowered himself down in front of me, but I still couldn't open my eyes. Fear held me paralyzed, except for my heart that was beating in my throat. He drew closer, until his breath skimmed along my cheek. I still couldn't move. What was happening? Why couldn't I open my eyes?

Was I in danger?

And then a strange pressure pushed on my lips. Tingles prickled on my skin, and I held pressed against the rock, a rush of warmth surging through me. He hovered in front of me for a few seconds, a net of power pushing and pulling between us. I wanted it to be Cael. Was it Cael? It had to be. But then the presence disappeared.

My eyes shot open.

My heart pounded.

The darkness lifted.

I was alone.

3

Face to Face

Our town high school stood tall against the sky, gray clouds moving fast behind the towering structure. Kids filed in like zombies, backpacks slung over their shoulders, eyes glued straight in front of them. They marched into the building, faces slack, not aware of one another.

Mortification still stung in my chest. I hadn't been able to shake the feeling of regret and embarrassment from yesterday. It burned heavy in my heart, sinking deeper into my stomach with each passing hour. Cael hadn't spoken to me since. The conversation played over and over again in my head.

I want a kiss.

I don't want to hear anymore. Just . . . stop.

Wind blew my hair over my face, the strands tickled my skin, and I focused back on the school before me. I came here whenever I needed to have the illusion of normality. I remembered when school had been a place of learning, back when the storms weren't as bad. The memories were faint, but I remembered when my peers' eyes sparkled with life, when I laughed with them, when I talked with them. But now, it's been years since I've had any human contact.

Once again, I had successfully carted Mom around the Storm today, staying just ahead of the massive cloud until it dispersed. She was now back at home, mindlessly going through her routine. I squeezed my eyes shut, her delicate features in my head. More angst built up within me. Any day now could be my last day with her. Were my efforts to keep her safe only prolonging the inevitable?

I rubbed my hands together. Students brushed past me, some bumping into my shoulders. An itch tickled in the middle of my back, and I spun around, peering across the street. About a block away, a few kids hovered outside a coffee shop. One kid, Daniel, wearing baggy jeans and a hoodie, chomped on the same blueberry strudel he did every morning. Sometimes, when I looked at his face, he seemed familiar—like someone I knew more personally than just another student at school. The girl next to him wore the same pink shirt she sported every day. They chatted, though it was most likely the same conversation they had yesterday. Their minds were so far gone, they weren't aware of the conversations they were having.

Angela Cummings headed up the steps in front of me, her black braids swinging over her smooth, dark skin. Her mom had disappeared yesterday. I knew because she walked her dog down our street every morning. She hadn't been there today. Did Angela have any idea? Would she ever see her again? Would I ever see my dad again?

The thought of Dad only reminded me of the family we'd once had: Mom, Dad, and me. Right before the storms got bad, Dad told us he had a child from a previous marriage. The kid was going to come live with us. I was excited. I'd always wanted a brother. But then Dad disappeared, and I never met the kid. I always wondered where he was, if he was okay, and if the Storm had gotten to him, too. I blinked away the memory.

Angela passed by, zombielike, and I sighed, following into the school after her.

Inside, the hallways stretched long and dark. Someone had forgotten to turn the lights on again. Bodies moved mechanically, lockers slammed, doors opened and closed. I flipped the light switch, and no one flinched. They continued onward as if nothing were out of the ordinary. I hefted my backpack higher on my shoulders and headed to my first class.

I'd be able to think here. I'd find some peace after the disaster yesterday. I could pretend I was in school, and for a moment, everything would be fine.

The door creaked when I walked in.

Mr. Tompkins sat at his desk, nose in a book, a few water bottles scattered around him. He was more like an accessory to the classroom than a real teacher. He was young—mid-twenties—with tousled hair and wire glasses. Muscles stretched through his collared shirt.

The regular kids were there, backs stiff, eyes glazed over. My gaze swept over the room and stopped on the dark-haired girl in the corner. She was small—maybe five-foot-nothing, with a pointy nose and thinly muscled arms, wearing the same purple tank top she wore every day. My eyes lingered on her for a moment. Like Daniel, she seemed different from the rest of the kids here. Sometimes, I felt as if her eyes were on me, like two invisible weights pressing onto my skin, but they never were. Whenever I looked at her, her head was straight forward, face bland.

I slid into the wooden desk at the front of the classroom and allowed the silence to settle in my chest, but it didn't help. Embarrassment still filled me. I lifted my fingers and traced my lips. There'd been *something* in front of me yesterday. And I had felt some sort of pressure on my lips.

Had I been kissed? What if it *was* Cael?

Maybe things weren't horrible between us. But the anger in his voice had been palpable. He might not *ever* come back. I groaned and covered my face with my hands. Mr. Tompkins slammed the book down onto his desk, and I flinched.

"The concept of parallel lives is a tricky one," he said, picking up a piece of chalk. He approached the chalkboard and drew two circles, one on top of the other. "Many believe if you are rich now, you lead a parallel life in which you are poor. If you are happy now, in your other life you are lonesome."

I froze.

What?

Mr. Tompkins hadn't taught a class for years. And he was a *math* teacher.

"Sleep is considered a parallel life," Mr. Tompkins went on. "In fact, a lot of cultures consider dreams a myth. What if our spirits do walk to another life while our bodies sleep?"

I gripped the desk. He *couldn't* be talking about something different from math. I'd never heard him venture off topic. This wasn't real. A tickle ran down my spine, and the dark-haired girl's gaze pressed in on me again. I slowly forced myself to turn around, uncurling my fingers from the desk. Was she also aware that Mr. Tompkins was speaking? She stared straight ahead, face empty, but I swear I saw her jaw clench.

"Maybe we transport to one life or the other when our bodies sleep. Is it possible that we are either in one life or another?" He looked at me for a moment before he glanced away. My lips parted. Did he just look at me? With *coherency*?

"For those who believe in parallel lives, it is said there are Noble bloodlines assigned to keep the knowledge of these two lives hidden—for the protection of each life. These Nobles have the power to travel back and forth between their lives at will, while the rest of the population doesn't."

I couldn't rip my gaze away. Mr. Tompkins was *talking*. He appeared as if he were coherent. And he had made eye contact with me—while talking about Noble bloodlines and parallel lives. My mind couldn't keep up. Too many thoughts clashed with one another. But something in his words began to resonate deep within my bones, like a forgotten memory on the verge of realization. Something about his words woke something in the back of my brain, which didn't make any sense.

A movement at the door caught my attention. Through the opaque glass, a silhouette hovered outside. My pulse spiked, thinking of *him,* but a young man walked in dressed in ratty jeans and a T-shirt. The guy was thin, bone thin. Long greasy hair hung around his face, framing a crooked nose. He marched right up to me, stopping in front of my desk. I started, leaning back against my chair.

"Which is why," Mr. Tompkins said, his eyes connecting with mine again, "I've brought Robert to connect you to your other life, Clara."

A jolt shot down through me, and I blinked. "E-excuse me?"

"It's time," Mr. Tompkins said. "We've waited long enough. Robert, go ahead."

Robert's dark gaze connected with mine, gripping me. I'd lived so long without any real human contact, I simply sat there, stunned.

"No!" The dark-haired girl in the corner jumped up from her seat. "It isn't fair. Not like this."

"Ricki," Robert growled. "You know how much I need this."

Ricki's mouth tightened and crimson rose high in her cheeks. "I know," she said. "But she should at least have a choice."

"We *can't* wait any longer," Mr. Tompkins cut in. "Do it. Now, Robert."

I whipped my gaze to Robert. The second our eyes locked, the classroom turned hazy in my peripheral vision. Ricki screamed something, but her voice was distant, fading away. Fear stampeded through me as I tensed, my mind teetering precariously over the edge. Images I had never seen flashed through my mind. I saw myself with my hair cropped short while I drove through big city traffic with a car full of friends. The picture changed to me in a cheerleader outfit, waving pom-poms on the sidelines of a football game. I saw myself flirting with several boys, the center of attention. It wasn't until I saw myself in a hospital room with that kid Daniel sick in bed that I slammed my lids shut and yelled, "Stop!"

"No!" Robert roared. "Keep your eyes open!"

A crash ricocheted through the classroom, and I peeked an eye open. Ricki threw herself on top of Robert, and they rolled on the ground before she straddled him, her tiny hands linked around his throat.

"Run!" she yelled to me.

I jerked.

"Run!" she yelled again.

Adrenaline kicked in. I bounded from my seat and bolted for the door, but Mr. Tompkins was too fast. His face popped in front of mine, and he pressed me against the wall. The look on his face scared me.

"Clara, you need to trust us," he said.

Robert threw Ricki off of him and she slid across the floor, crashing into a desk. The kids around us sat still, unaffected. Robert charged toward me, his eyes as dark as his long, scraggly hair.

Ricki screamed and threw out her hands. A flash of green light sailed through the air. The building shook and pieces of the ceiling fell, smashing into the ground. The lights flickered. A chunk of tile hit Mr. Tompkins on the head, and he bellowed, crouching down.

I bolted.

The cool spring air bit my cheeks as I sprinted to the car. Dark clouds hovered overhead.

I fumbled madly with the keys, my hands shaking as I unlocked the door. Robert rushed from the building, and he turned his head rapidly, looking around the parking lot. His face, with his deep-set eyes and pale complexion, looked gaunt, skeletal, in the waning light as the clouds closed in on the sky.

I yanked the door open and ducked inside, wrenching the car into gear. I hit the accelerator, leaving the school, Mr. Tompkins, and the strange kids behind me.

4

Thin in the Middle

I burst through the front door and ran down the hall.

"Mom!" I yelled.

I peeked inside the empty living room, then rushed to her bedroom, but she wasn't there.

"Mom!"

I sprinted into the kitchen, and Mom sat at the table, staring out the window. Her eyes were glazed over, her mouth was slightly parted. I set a hand over my heart. She was okay. A breeze stirred the lace curtains, and it was quiet, except for the cuckoo clock ticking on the wall. My heart had calmed, but adrenaline still pumped in my veins.

"Mom," I said, my voice soft. I lowered myself down across from her. "I think . . . I think we need to go."

Where we would run to, I didn't know. The Storm affected all the other nearby towns—I knew from trying to run before. I thought about calling the police, but they were as mindless as everyone else.

"Mom? Did you hear me?"

She stayed frozen, her eyes unmoving, the clock still ticking on the wall.

"Mom," I tried again.

Nothing.

"Mom! Do you even *care*?" I slapped my hands down onto the table and stood. My eyes burned and I pinched the bridge of my nose. I would not cry. I needed to be strong. I needed to think.

I quickly locked the back door, then headed into the hallway before plopping down onto a couch in the living room. I didn't know what to do. I just needed to think. Maybe Mr. Tompkins, Robert, and Ricki weren't a threat. Maybe they'd just had a lapse from the Storm's effects and everything would be back to normal tomorrow.

But what had Robert done when he'd looked into my eyes?

I slunk downward into the couch, groaning.

Then, like a punch to the chest, the darkness that sometimes built up within me surged into my core. It stretched through my veins and filled my body with a heavy warmth that ate me from the inside out. I could never predict when the dark feeling would come, but when it did, it overtook me. I held my breath, waiting for it to pass. It lingered for a moment, heat gathering, a rush of hate filling my mind. I *hated* the Storm. I *hated* my life. I *hated* that I was stuck in this existence all alone, ready to lose it any day. My fingers dug into the couch cushions.

It'll be okay, Clara. I'm here.

I sat up in a rush. My heart hammered, and I put a hand to my chest. The darkness immediately dissipated and peace settled over me.

"You're back," I said quickly. "You came back."

I'm sorry I left. I had some things to attend to.

"What things?" I knew he hinted at having a life outside of my mind. I just wished he'd tell me what it was.

You don't need to worry about it. Just breathe. You're safe.

I sat back on the couch. I decided to let it go. He was here. That was all that mattered.

"I thought you'd never return," I murmured. "Not after what happened yesterday."

His presence slid from one side of my head to the other before stilling in the middle.

I care about you, Clara. Trust me, I care. More than you'll ever know.

I slowly sat up again. "You do?"

His presence shifted once more.

If you knew who I was, you would be disappointed. I don't ever want to hurt you. But I'm . . . attached to you.

I swallowed, absorbing his words. The warmth in his voice swirled inside my head, then moved down my body. "Cael, I could never be disappointed in you." My throat tightened. "Please don't leave me ever again."

He was silent for a moment.

I'll try.

I stood up from the couch and paced in front of the empty fireplace. The floor squeaked as I moved back and forth. I shook out my hands.

"I have to leave," I said. "I can't be here any longer. Would you—" I paused. "Will you come with me?"

It seemed like an eternity before he answered.

It isn't safe for you to leave town. You need to stay here.

My mouth tightened. "What do you mean? What do you know? What's out there?"

Just trust me. I promise that I'll keep you and your mother safe.

I shook my head. "No, I need to know more. What's out there?"

Just stay put. It'll all be fine soon.

He flitted away, leaving my brain suddenly cold. I wrapped my arms around my middle and started to pace again. I wanted to trust him, I wanted to do what he said. And maybe in the past, I would've. But things had changed with the incident at the classroom. What if there was a greater threat than the Storm? Ricki had told me to run. What could Cael do to protect us? It was only a matter of time until Mr. Tompkins and Robert found me again. And the Storm was always a threat.

My heels dug into the beat-up rug, and I paused. I didn't need to rush. I needed to be smart. Tomorrow I would find out more. Cael clearly knew something. There was something out there. And I was going to find out what.

After I'd helped Mom around the Storm the next day, I headed through town, weaving through people doing their daily routines. Some shopped, some chatted outside coffee shops on the street, some worked—washing windows, sweeping the streets, selling goods. Everyone mindlessly went through their day, not realizing how similar each day was. It was as if their lives were nothing but muscle memory.

They were all people. *Good* people. People I had grown up with. I remembered when Mrs. MacDonald used to deliver homemade bread to our home every Sunday. Mr. Peterson had helped install a sprinkler system in our yard one summer. I'd been friends with the kids in town. We used to play night games and have sleepovers and spend days at the park.

Until the Storms got worse.

The Storms used to come once a year, and they didn't really affect anyone's memory. People thought it was just the crazy weather. Then it started happening every couple of months, then once a week, and now once a day. People didn't really know what was happening at first. Every day, the news would report on a different storm touching down in another place around the world. At first, there'd been fear. But then minds faded, eyes glazed over, faces became blank.

And I was the only sane one that I knew. It didn't make sense why I was special. Or cursed. Sometimes I wished I were one of the mindless, then I wouldn't have to feel the heartache of seeing them every day. I'd do anything to save them from this fate if I could.

I continued to head through town, a slight breeze tickling the back of my neck. I wore my blond hair up in a high ponytail, and it swished back and forth as I turned off Main Street. This part of town was quieter, secluded, where businesses had been abandoned.

My footsteps were quiet as I walked down the center of the street. Some of the buildings were boarded up beside me, windows broken, trash littered on the ground. I wanted to circle the town, get a view of the border from all sides. A deep forest surrounded the entire town, and I'd never fully scoped it out.

Another breeze whooshed in again, pushing me forward. This area of town was shaded, and I rubbed my arms, goosebumps rippling over my skin. I tried to settle my racing thoughts as the image of Mr. Tompkins, Robert, and Ricki replayed in my head. Mom and I weren't safe here. We needed to leave. But I needed to know what was out there first.

I reached the end of the street, bits of forest stretching out before me. I was heading out of the town when a hoarse cough sounded to my left. I paused and turned.

Daniel, the kid I saw every day across the street from the school, sat on the bottom of some cement steps that led up to a vacant building. He didn't notice me, only sat with his eyes unfocused. His skin had a sickly pallor to it, deathly white. Bruises showed up along his collar, with several on his arms. He groaned, sweat on his forehead.

My brows pinched together. "Daniel?"

He continued to stare at nothing, letting out another cough. Once again, a sense of familiarity swept through me. I didn't have too many memories of him here, but he did feel . . . *different*. And I'd seen him when Robert had stared into my eyes, which was strange. I slowly crept toward him, another set of shivers running down me. I never meddled in people's lives here. It was too hard emotionally to see them brain-dead after knowing them before. But I moved forward anyway, leaning in close to him.

"Daniel, can you hear me?"

He continued to stare out in front of him, his dark hair hanging over his forehead. I sighed and stepped back. I wondered what he had been like before the Storm. I vaguely had memories of him laughing with Angela Cummings, a twinkle in his eye. Once again, I wished I could do something for him.

I headed back down the street and turned a corner, walking straight into the forest that circled the town. I hadn't been out to this part of the forest; I usually just stuck to the woods behind my house. Thick trees shot up into the sky; the smell of pine tickled my nose. Leaves crackled underneath my feet.

I walked for a time with just the sound of my breath for company. Bits of sunlight peeked through the tree canopy, casting funky shadows on the forest floor. I weaved around trees, not sure how far I should investigate. I didn't know what I was looking for, exactly. I just knew that Cael didn't want me out here, which meant that something *had* to be out here.

I traveled for what felt like an hour before the tops of my thighs started to ache. I spotted a small boulder tucked up against two pines and I headed over, then plopped myself down. I massaged the tops of my legs.

What was I doing out here? Maybe I was wasting my time. What did I expect to find? A genie lamp that would allow me to wish my town back to sanity? I groaned and covered my face with my hands.

What are you doing?

I jerked and lowered my hands. Of course he was here.

"You know what I'm doing," I said.

Heat ignited inside my skull, and I felt his anger build.

I told you to stay put. Now go home.

"You know I can't do that," I said. "Mr. Tompkins and Rob—"

Aren't a threat to you. They'll have to go through me to get to you.

"But you can't do anything!" I burst out. "Maybe you're not even real." I sprang up from the rock, my pulse thumping. "Maybe you're not real," I repeated. I grabbed the sides of my head and walked deeper into the trees.

A heavy feeling settled in my chest, my blood hot in my veins. I'd always believed he was real. But what if he wasn't? Maybe the truth had been there all along. Maybe the Storm *did* affect me, and this was how I was going crazy. I believed Cael to be real. He still hovered with me, following me.

"Leave me alone," I said. I picked up my pace, heading farther into the woods. The trees covered the sun, and the air cooled a few degrees. But he still traveled with me inside my head.

Clara, stop. Please.

I shook my head, pushing myself to go faster. I cleared away branches as I walked, my feet stomping into the earth. I was sick of accepting my fate. Perhaps if I got out of this town, Cael would leave, and I'd have peace in my mind—my mind would sort itself out and I'd be safe from my insanity.

I kept walking until something lit the trees up ahead. I squinted. A light shimmered between the branches in front of me. My brows scrunched together, and I peered farther into the shrubbery. There wasn't any sun—the clouds still covered the sky.

Clara, I'm warning you. Turn back now.

It didn't matter if Cael was real or not. Something was ahead of me. Something different. Something I had never seen before. I started jogging, trying to block out the feel of Cael inside my brain. I pushed away more branches, ducking around the foliage, weaving around more trees, until I stopped dead.

A tall white fence stood in front of me—it was at least twenty feet tall, looking more like a line of defense than an ornamental railing. I blinked, taking in the sight. The white iron posts seemed to glow, pulsing in the dim forest. I tentatively stepped forward, shielding my eyes from the white glow, but still able to see the finely carved flowers and vines that ran down each post. I tried to see past the fence, but saw only a bright light.

I stepped closer, the white railings towering above me. There *had* to be something beyond this ornate fence, something important, but suddenly I was too numb to think. My life had been on repeat day after day for so long, this unexpected find was jarring.

I slowly continued forward, my footsteps crunching, my breaths heavy. A warmth gathered in my chest, an invisible energy that pushed between the gate and me. Almost without my will, my arm lifted, and I reached my fingertips forward to touch it.

Clara! Don't! Cael's voice screamed in my mind.

I stumbled back, gripping the sides of my head. "Get out!" I said.

You don't want to step any closer. Back away, and go home. That's an order.

"An order?" I shook my head. "You can't order me!" A sudden wave of emotion hit, and moisture built in the backs of my eyes. I swallowed, my throat thick.

Cael shifted from one side of my head to the other, the way he always did when he was thinking.

All right. He paused for a moment. *All right. I need you to not panic. I . . . I don't want to do this, but clearly I must. You need to believe that what you're about to see is real.*

I lowered my hands, still staring at the pulsing fence. "What are you talking about?"

Turn around.

A twig snapped behind me, and I froze. Awareness tickled along my back, and goosebumps formed on my arms.

Someone was there.

I held still for several moments. What was happening? But somehow, I knew, and my heart picked up the pace again. I slowly forced myself to turn around.

Before me, a shadow shifted out from the trees. A dark figure emerged, a long shadow underneath the branches. He was nothing but a silhouette, not too tall, around my height, and lean. He moved forward, the shaded outline of his features coming into view. His eyes were black, two deep chasms pouring into me. As his chest rose and fell, dark wisps flowed in and out of his mouth.

Sunlight filtered down, shimmering through his outline. My mouth fell open. He wasn't human. Or was he? But people weren't shadows.

People weren't *see-through.*

"Hello, Clara."

My mind screamed. This couldn't be real. Was it *him*?

"Don't be afraid."

That voice.

The voice I had loved more than any other voice on the planet. There was no mistaking the distinct lilt that accented his tone. But it *wasn't* inside my head. His words rolled outward, echoing out into the forest.

"Cael?"

We stood there, staring at each other, power and life flowing between us. I edged back a step and tripped over a rock before I fumbled upright.

He lifted a hand, as if motioning me to stop. "Don't be afraid. I won't hurt you."

"I know you won't," I said quickly.

He was real? I wasn't crazy. All this time, I hadn't been crazy. *Or was I imagining this?*

"How—" I started.

The wind picked up, tossing leaves and dirt into the air. A chill swept through me, and I wrapped my arms around myself. Dark clouds began to move in fast over the sky, and Cael's head shot upward.

"We don't have much time," he said, still staring at the clouds. "They're coming. They don't want you here at the gate either." He turned his head back to face me. "Maybe you're right. Maybe it isn't safe for you to stay home."

"They? Who's they?" I asked. My mind was still reeling.

"The Diviners. They're captive souls who feed off memories. You know them as the Storm."

I stared blankly. "*What*?"

"There's no time to explain. Go to your mother. I'll hold the Storm off here and meet you back at your home. We'll come up with a plan there."

But my feet stayed rooted. He wanted me to leave? *Now?* I'd just found out he was real, and now he wanted me to leave?

I shook my head. "No, Cael, I can't. You and me . . . we . . ." I swallowed.

He leveled his dark gaze with mine. "I care about you, too, Clara. I promise, we'll figure this out."

I shook my head again, peered up at the fast-moving clouds, then looked back at him. The Storm had already come that day. It didn't make sense.

"Clara," he said, more urgent this time. "The Diviners will find you out here. You need to leave. Now go!" His chest rose and fell fast, his dark shadowy stare boring into me.

Another gust of wind tossed my hair over my face. Dark clouds began to roll in above the treetops, bits of dark mist snaking toward the ground.

"See? It's coming!" he said.

My eyes darted between the oncoming Storm and him.

He was right—it was coming.

"Go!"

I jerked to attention, the fear in his voice cutting through me.

"Go!"

Without another thought, I took off, sprinting through the forest, leaving Cael and the dark Storm behind.

5
Tribal War

I raced through the forest, my chest pumping up and down. My throat burned, but I wouldn't stop. The fear in Cael's voice scared me. He told me to get to Mom. I needed to get to Mom. He was coming—he said he'd be right behind me. But what was the Storm, really? Cael said they were Diviners. Captive souls who fed off memories? That didn't make any sense. That couldn't be true.

But I trusted Cael with my life. I'd always known I could trust him. He wouldn't lie to me.

Now I knew that he was *real.*

I continued to run, and thoughts of his shadowy presence drifted through my mind. He was nothing but a shadow. Dark wisps had flowed in and out of his mouth, and the way his dark eyes had stared me down . . .

I left the forest and ran into town. Night began to settle over the sky, the streetlamps flickering on. Every part of my body ached, but I wouldn't stop running. Get to Mom. I needed to get to Mom.

Finally, I hurried up my driveway and tried to push open the door, but my shoulder rammed into the solid wood.

The door was locked.

What? I rattled the knob. Mom never locked the door.

A scream ricocheted from our backyard, and I quickly backed away from the door, stumbling down the front steps.

"Mom!" I raced around the side of our house and into the backyard.

Mom stood frozen in the middle of the yard, peering into the dark forest behind our house. Moonlight illuminated the area, highlighting her pale face. Her whole body trembled, and she slowly lifted a finger and pointed.

Within seconds, a layer of dark fog emerged from the wood. I stopped, digging my feet into the ground. The black cloud slid toward us along the forest floor, crawling slowly, deadly.

Mom wasn't moving. She just stared into the black fog. It shot toward her, spreading up and over her in a swell.

"Mom!" I sprinted forward, but the Storm engulfed me, and I stopped again, waving my arms out in front of me, trying to clear it away. I glanced around frantically for Cael. He said he'd be here. "Cael!"

I coughed, waving my hand over my mouth. My vision wavered. The fog thickened, swirling around my head. A high screech pierced through the air.

Chaos erupted.

The backyard filled with shifting forms and shouts.

Heavy drops of rain plopped, and lightning veined the sky. Dozens of shadow figures—like Cael—rushed from all directions as they closed in around me. I gasped, and the fog choked me.

Like Cael, the shadow people had no features. They were dark—nothing but silhouetted bodies. Lightning exploded and shimmered through their outlines, making them appear nearly transparent. An electric current zipped through me, sour on my tongue.

The ground rumbled, and I waved my hands through the air, trying to clear the fog.

"Help!" I yelled. I still couldn't breathe. "Mom! Cael!"

A blast of wind whooshed into me, blowing leaves and dirt into my face. I spluttered, falling onto my hands and knees. Rocks bit into my palms.

I opened my eyes wider, and dark flashes zoomed in and out of my vision. The fog began to clear, pulling apart from itself.

My lips parted as realization struck.

The dark cloud wasn't a cloud at all. It was a series of flying wraithlike things whirling in and out of one another. Like muddy ghosts caught in a tornado. They flew around me, darting through the lightning-veined sky.

And the shadow people—whatever they were—were fighting these ghosts. Each figure had a sword, a shadowy extension of their arms, slicing through the air, aimed at the cyclone of creatures. One figure lunged forward, the tip of his shadowy sword pierced a being, and the thing vanished in a cloud of dust.

I gaped, scrambling backward.

It was a battle. I was witnessing an all-out *battle.*

The shadow army moved like poetry, the way they twisted and turned in tune with one another, their motions fluid and controlled, as if they were moving through water.

Sanity was peeling away from me, my brain cracking apart like an eggshell. I blinked, unable to look away. The shadow army pierced being after being, continuing the dance.

Then I saw him.

The moonlight flickered through Cael's lean frame. He also had a sword, moving as if he were made of oil, sliding in, out, and around the enemy. He was different from the rest—he had a strength about him the others didn't.

An air of command.

The rain continued to pound down. I couldn't look away. Every cell in my body ached to watch him.

As if Cael knew I was looking, he turned his head, and the eerie, dark hollows of his eyes washed over me. Something passed between us—and all the fear fled. He was protecting me. Protecting me and Mom like he said he would. He stood staring at me, and it was as if he had taken a breath and drawn me into him.

Then reality snapped back.

Cael disappeared into the chaos, and a fresh onslaught of panic surged through me. *Where was he?* He was in danger. If anything happened to him . . .

I pushed my way forward, speeding to a run, knocking the ghost-like things out of my way. I couldn't let him out of my sight. I couldn't lose him.

Mom screamed, and I spun around. I glanced back to where Cael was, but then turned back to Mom. I threw myself in her direction, searching blindly, my lungs seizing tight, until she came into view. Several ghost creatures surrounded her, circling above her head. One dove down, shooting toward her, and I leaped forward. I shoved her onto the ground and planted myself in front of her. The creature looked like a stretched-out piece of black cloth, its eyes and mouth hollow as if someone had cut a hole right through its face. The thing sped straight at me.

I clenched my eyes shut, waiting for its attack, but everything paused. The thing shrank away, and with a sudden rush, the fog lifted, and the sounds of battle diminished, the ghosts swirling away. The rain slowed to a stop.

It was over so quickly.

I stood panting, my heart hammering. The shadow figures still circled my yard, their swords lowered to the ground. Mom sat a few feet away.

"Mom!" I bent down and patted over her body, trying to wake her, but she lay like a rag doll, eyes blank, jaw slack. "Mom!" I shook her again.

She's still here, Clara. She hasn't disappeared yet. She still has a chance.

I whirled around, searching for him. Cael had saved us. He was okay.

Cael was a short distance away, long and dark, standing in front of the shadow army. He faced them, seeming to be the commander. He paced in front of them, his hands linked behind his back.

The soldiers remained lined up and alert, and he continued to pace, his dark head tipped downward, head cocked in thought. He finally paused and spoke low and quick, an unfamiliar language flying though his lips. It was thick, heavily accented, like Russian. The shadow army bowed their heads and disappeared, vanishing like smoke, except one figure who still hovered a few feet away.

I blinked. Then blinked again.

Cael didn't waste any time.

"We need to leave." He strode toward me.

"W-what?"

He marched up to me without a word and gripped my arm, pulling me to my feet. "You were right. You do need to leave. We need to get you somewhere safe. I thought hiding here was what was best for you, but the Diviners have shown themselves, which means the Divining Masters aren't too far away. Come on."

My mind was reeling. I shook my head and planted my feet into the forest floor. "That's the second time you've mentioned them. You mean those ghost things really are Diviners? It's not a storm after all."

He nodded once. "They're followers of the Divining Masters. Divining Masters are Nobles who have turned evil."

"Nobles?"

Cael turned to the soldier who lingered off to the side. "Take Clara's mother to the Stricken camp. See what can be done for her there."

"What?" I wasn't sure what to focus on. Mom, the Diviners, Divining Masters, Nobles, the Stricken camp.

The soldier bowed, reached down, and lifted Mom into his arms. I opened my mouth to stop him, to say something, but the soldier took off into the forest, disappearing—with Mom—in a flash. The leaves rustled behind them, and a breeze brushed over my face. I shrank back, wrapping my arms over my stomach. I felt as if one of my limbs had been chopped off.

"What did you do? Where did she go?" It was barely a whisper.

Cael slowly turned, and I swear his shoulders relaxed.

"Your mother has suffered years of Diviner attacks, Clara. Only time will tell if she'll make it."

I swallowed. "You mean disappear, like my dad?"

He nodded.

I closed my eyes and inhaled deep. It was so strange to hear his voice spoken instead of inside my head. I forced myself to focus. I should've been freaking out more, but I'd lived my whole life in an unstable world with unbelievable things happening. What was one more thing?

"Tell me more about these Diviners," I said. "Why do they attack innocent people? Why do they feed off memories?"

"Their goal is to destroy Desolation. They want to take Desolation to create their own brain-dead army so they can take Khalom for their own."

"Khalom?" I asked. "Desolation? What are these names?"

Cael heaved a sigh, and he took a soft step toward me. "It won't make sense until you see it. Khalom is a city, beyond the white gates. You saw the gates today."

"Okay . . ." I said. "And Desolation?"

"Desolation is everywhere outside of the city. You've been trapped out here since you were seven."

I shook my head.

"I've grown up here. What are you talking about?"

Cael took another step forward, and his presence hovered over me like a dark blanket. "Again, you won't understand until you see the city."

"Cael." My throat welled up tight. "I've waited my whole life for answers. Do you know how hard it's been to be *alone*?" My voice choked on the last word, and suddenly every emotion I'd ever felt tumbled forward. "I can't do this anymore. I . . ." I hiccupped. "You've been here, but secretly, I doubted my sanity. Even now, as you're standing in front of me, I don't know whether to believe that you're real. My mind keeps flipping. I can't trust myself and I . . ."

"Clara." Cael sighed, and a dark swirl of air exhaled from his mouth. "I'm real. Here, touch my hand." He slowly lifted a hand toward me, and I stared at his shadowy palm.

Did I dare? What if he really wasn't real? I'd never recover. He moved closer, his hand still extended. I continued to stare.

I was going to have to find out. I slowly lifted my hand forward, and my pulse throbbed in my ears. Every inch of me buzzed, like electricity was flowing through my veins. I peeked up at his face again, and his hollow features poured into me. I looked back at his palm, and I licked my lips. I started to lower my hand, but the back door to my house swung open and light spilled out into my yard.

"Clara!"

Robert and Mr. Tompkins rushed from my house and raced across the grass. Cael planted himself in front of me and stiffened.

They found me. It was only a matter of time.

The two men skidded to a halt in front of us. Robert's beady eyes stared through the dark strands of his hair, and Mr. Tompkins's eyes peered intently from behind his wire glasses. Then they saw Cael, and they stumbled back a step.

"I know what you want," Cael said. "And I won't let you take her."

Sweat beaded on Robert's greasy brow, but his eyes connected with mine.

"I need you," he said. "Please, you need to trust us."

Mr. Tompkins straightened his glasses. His eyes shot to Cael before returning to me. "What are you doing with this Stricken?" His lips twisted. "Clara, he can't do anything for you. But me? I've been with you every day since you've been here. You can trust me."

"So have I," Cael said sharply. He kept his body in front of mine.

Mr. Tompkins's brows furrowed. He stared Cael down.

Cael turned to me smoothly, ignoring them. "It's time to go to Khalom. It's time for *Death* to return."

Death?

Before I could say a word, Cael snatched my hand. It was cool but solid in my own. I glanced down, and my lips parted. The world suddenly blurred, and my eyes caught Robert's.

"Clara, no!" he yelled.

The last thing I saw was shock flit across his face, and then we were gone.

6
Rewritten

Cael kept his hand in my own, his fingers wrapped tight.

It was the only steady thing I had.

The forest raced on either side of us, the trees blending together in a green hue. Dim flashes zoomed in and out of my vision, but I couldn't blink. I kept my eyes open, transfixed by the speeding world in front of me.

We were moving. Except I wasn't running—I was standing, but we were traveling at an impossible speed, the tree branches brushing past my face. My grip tightened in his.

"How are we moving so fast?" I yelled.

"It's called Celerating. It's the way Nobles travel."

"Nobles?" He kept bringing up that term.

He nodded, and the world continued to flash by around us. "You're one of them, Clara. One of the chosen few who were born in Khalom. You are part of a royal bloodline—all Nobles are royal, born to protect the city. Khalom is the link to all lives, to all worlds. If Khalom is destroyed, then all lives will cease to exist. It's why the Divining Masters want it for their own: they want to control both worlds."

Was this real? Was I really traveling at an impossible speed with Cael? And did Nobles and Divining Masters and Khalom exist?

"Why do the Divining Masters want the city?" I asked.

"Power. And eternal life," he said. "When they were first appointed, the rulers of Khalom were given the gift of immortality. All Nobles live extended lives, but only the Mhystic, the rulers of Khalom, live forever. The Divining Masters were once Nobles, but they gave up their nobility in their quest for power. The prospect of eternal life is enough for the Divining Masters to give up their Noblehood in order to build an army, take the city for their own, and rule over both worlds—forever."

This was all so hard to believe. How was I tied to all of this? Cael said I was a Noble, which didn't make sense. I'd know if I were one, right? I'd never had a life in Khalom. I was born in Desolation. If I believed all of this . . .

I shook my head. "Where are we going?"

"I told you, to the city."

Cael abruptly let go of my hand, and the world jolted. My feet hit hard earth, and I staggered, my vision blurring. I stumbled a few feet away from Cael, my feet crunching on sticks and leaves. I slowly straightened, taking in my surroundings.

"Are you all right?" Cael asked. He stood a few feet away, his shadow looking like an extension from the trees. If I hadn't been focusing on him, I wouldn't have seen him.

"Yeah." I set a hand to my forehead. "I think."

"Good. Follow me."

Cael turned and moved deeper into the wood, his feet silent. I tentatively followed, but with each step away from my home, a piece of myself chipped away bit by bit. I needed to get to Mom, but she'd been taken . . . to the Stricken camp? More questions.

The farther I traveled, the colder I felt. Mom was the only thing I had left. For years, all I wanted was for my family to be back together again. I would've done anything to see my dad laugh again or to see his eyes light up once more, but since he was gone, all I had was Mom. And now, I've failed to keep her safe. I was alone.

"How much farther?" I asked.

Cael didn't say a word, just continued walking. His footsteps were soft, catlike, while mine crunched heavily.

I tried not to think about everything that was happening. I tried to block Mom out of my mind and pretend she was fine. I tried to ignore the panic that was sneaking up in my chest. I just needed to see this city Cael was talking about, and then I could come up with a plan.

The muted colors of dawn peeked through the trees, and I peered deeper into the forest. Several shaded figures followed alongside us, and I shivered. Those were his warriors. Mr. Tompkins had called Cael a Stricken—was that what they all were? Why were they only shadows? What had happened to them? The sight of them made me feel as if I were being guarded. I shivered.

I focused on Cael again, and early morning light glistened through his body. It was hypnotizing, distracting, the way the light played off his dark form. Cael stopped abruptly. I nearly rammed into him.

"What? What is it?" I asked. Every inch of me stiffened, like the Diviners had found us and were going to attack again.

But Cael only stepped aside, sweeping a hand forward.

We were back.

It was the fence, but at a different location. The same white glow pulsed along the white iron, but here, golden leaves were painted along the bars, sparkling in the morning light. The glow seemed to throb, the brightness pulsing out into the air. Cael stepped up next to me, his shoulder brushing mine.

"Welcome home, Clara."

I slowly moved forward, shielding my eyes.

The last time I was here, Cael didn't want me anywhere near it. Now, he had willingly brought me. I peered into the brightness, still trying to see beyond the gates. Cael stayed close to me.

"You'll be safe inside," he said. "For the most part. Some people here might not have your best interests in mind. But you'll be safer inside than out."

I shook my head, trying to clear it. "You said I needed to see the city and then I'd understand. Well, I'm here, and I'm not understanding."

Cael slowly turned, and his hollow eyes met mine. "This isn't going to be easy, Clara, but I need you to focus. What I'm about to tell you will be very difficult to understand. But it is essential that you understand. Do you trust me?" The leaves rustled behind him, and a chill swept down my back.

I did.

Of course I did—that hadn't changed. All the feelings I'd had for him over the years welled up inside of me, burning in my heart. Now that he was here, now that he was real, it took everything in me not to throw my arms around him. I wanted to hold him and never let him go. Breathe in his scent and let it wrap me up. But he stood unmoving, like a dark statue, his gaze drilling holes into me.

"I trust you," I whispered.

Cael abruptly stepped away and started to pace, his head tipped toward his feet. I watched as he moved back and forth, several other Stricken hiding inside the woods around us. He kept his head down, as if he were thinking, but then stopped. Another chill swept through me.

"Do you remember what Gherald Tompkins taught you in class yesterday?" he asked.

My forehead creased and I thought back. I rewound the events in my mind to what Mr. Tompkins was talking about before Robert arrived. My brows shot upward.

"He was talking about parallel lives," I said. "What does that have to do with any of this?"

Cael shifted his stance and peered back into the city gates. The white glow from the fence glimmered through his being.

"Parallel lives are real, Clara. What Gherald Tompkins was teaching you was real. You're a Noble, which means you should have full knowledge of your two lives, but you've been out here in Desolation. You don't know who you are. You were taken from the city before you could discover your other self."

I blinked, then blinked again. "*What*? No, that's insane. People don't have two lives. That's ridiculous—" But then the visions I had when Robert invaded my brain came to mind. I'd seen myself living another life. I'd been a cheerleader. I'd been with friends. I'd been . . .

Happy.

I shook my head. "There's no way I have two lives."

Cael kept his gaze fixed forward, silent. He always went silent when he disagreed with me.

I exhaled. "So, is my other life inside the city then? Is that what you're telling me?" I twisted my lips.

"No," he said softly. "Khalom isn't your other life, it's just a city here—a city that exists in the middle of Desolation. Your other life—your Cursed life—your physical life . . . well, that you'll have to discover on your own."

Pain throbbed in the middle of my forehead. I pressed a knuckle to my temple and began to rub. "Then what does the city have to do with any of this? If parallel lives are real. I mean, you're telling me that I was a Noble, that I used to live in the city, but I don't remember that? And I *also* have another life, a parallel life that I don't remember? Cael, how can you possibly think I'd believe this?"

Cael slowly turned to me again. Another breeze blew in, and the trees swayed behind him. He kept absolutely still.

"I've known you for a long time, Clara. You've always known there was more to your life than what you've had. You've always believed that you were special, that you were different, and you are. This life—everything you've known—isn't where you're supposed to be. Khalom is your home. And now I'm giving you answers. The answers are just beyond that gate."

I swallowed; my heart fast in my throat. The seriousness in his voice struck me. But it was too much. How did Cael expect me to believe this?

But I'd always trusted him. He'd always been the comfort I needed when the darkness hit. But I couldn't just go into the city—not when Mom was out *there*. I couldn't abandon her. But clearly the answers were inside.

"Okay," I said. "I believe you. But only if you take me to Mom at this Stricken camp first."

Cael shook his head. "It's too dangerous. You need to be protected inside the gates."

I inwardly groaned. "Cael . . ."

He took a long step toward me until his face was inches from my own. His presence sent a wave of warmth through me, and a sudden peace settled over me. Cael gently lifted a hand and set his palm on my cheek. The touch was light, cool on my skin, and shivers flowed down my back.

"You will go inside the city," he said softly. "You will be welcomed back like the Noble you are. You will discover your true identity in your Cursed life, and then, only then, when you are ready, I'll take you to the Stricken camp myself."

I kept my gaze locked with his, his words flooding through me. I couldn't move. All I could do was nod.

Cael lowered his hand and took my shoulders. He turned me around and faced me toward the towering white fence.

"Step inside. It will all come back."

The feel of Cael's hands calmed me. All the fear and doubt and panic I had felt melted away, and suddenly, I wasn't afraid anymore. Without a word, I crept forward, until Cael's hands slid away. My feet sank into the damp earth, morning light mingling with the fence's white glow. A strange familiarity hit, a pull drawing me forward, like my feet had their own will.

"You won't be alone," Cael said from behind me. "We Stricken will not let any harm come to you. We will be out here. Watching."

The magnetism continued to pull me forward until I stopped in front of the gates, the glow still pulsing. I lifted my fingers and touched the white iron, cool on my fingertips.

"Use your Noble name," Cael said. "It will let you inside."

My heart beat in time with the pulsing light. I shouldn't have known my Noble name, it didn't make sense why it suddenly came to mind, but it was there, flowing off my lips.

"Claera," I whispered.

And I took one last step forward before the gates melted away, and I stepped inside.

7

High Exposure

I blinked, and my surroundings slowly came into focus. The scene before me materialized, and my mouth dropped open.

An entire city stretched across an enormous valley, encased by the white iron gates that extended to the sky, pointing like pitchforks. Small white buildings were interspersed inside the massive space, surrounded by acres of white grass and trees. A dusty white dirt road led up to stone buildings in the center of the area. Each pale building looked like something from a fairytale, with a myriad of levels and walkways. A large domed building sat in the middle, with even more buildings stretched behind it, buildings that extended up along the other side of the gate. Everything was . . .

White.

No color.

Just white.

And I didn't see a soul.

I moved forward a step, taking in more details. Finely groomed paths wove through well-manicured white lawns. Milky trees and flowers lined the paths in full, flawless bloom. The temperature was perfect, the air so still I had no sense of it passing over my skin.

The buildings were all ivory marble, each sculpted beautifully in their own design. Most were supported by columns, with dozens of stairs leading to the entryways. There weren't any doors. At all. Silky curtains hung in their place, thin enough to see through, each embroidered with painstaking detail.

From this vantage point, I could see everything, but as I slowly edged down the hill, the ground leveled out, and I stepped onto a white dusty path. My heart was beating so fast, I thought my chest would explode.

Very slowly, subtle feelings emerged—tickling along the back of my neck—like I really *had* been here before. A shiver ran through me, even though there wasn't a chill in the air. My footsteps were soft as I entered a copse of translucent trees. Their white branches hung over me, shading me from the sun. The path turned a corner and I stopped. I nearly screamed.

"Mother of the Mhystic!" a boy yelled.

"Mother of the Mhystic!" I yelled back. I clasped my hands over my mouth. *How did I know that expression?*

The kid in front of me looked as pale as a ghost. He had red hair and freckled skin. He backed up, as if deciding whether or not to run. I followed suit, taking a step back—I wasn't used to people acknowledging me, let alone speaking to me.

Fear bled from every line of his face, and he swallowed. "D-don't . . . don't hurt me!"

I blinked. "Why would I hurt you?" My brows creased. Then, like a zap to my brain, recognition hit. "Lionel?" I asked. I lowered my hands. *How did I know his name?*

He stumbled back another step, tripping over his feet. "You stay away from me!"

I lifted a hand. "Lionel . . . I . . ." I shook my head. Another wave of familiarity hit. The trees, the town, Lionel. There were other kids here. "Why would I hurt you?" I asked again.

But that was enough. Lionel took off down the path, ivory dust kicking up beneath his heels.

I stood frozen, my mouth gaping. I remembered Lionel. He was the kid everyone made fun of in school . . .

The school.

I looked ahead to where I knew the school sat on the other side of the city. It was tucked up right behind Historic Quarter along the north fence. Hidden from sight were the Noble dorms, classrooms, and the Grand Hall. *How did I know this?*

Without warning, a bombardment of memories surged to my mind and vertigo seized me, whirling me around a few times. I stumbled backward, flashes spotting my vision and pressure building inside my head.

"No . . ." I said. Pain shot into my skull. "No! This can't be possible."

I clenched my teeth tight together and squeezed my eyes shut.

Khalom was my home. The last time I had been here was . . . when I was seven? The sight of the city forced memories to tumble from where they'd been buried in my subconscious. I squatted down and gripped my head.

I was a Noble. I went to school here. Nobles existed to protect the city. Khalom was the link to our two lives. We *did* each have two lives. I remembered. If Khalom didn't exist, then both of our parallel lives would crumble. Our existence was the key to mankind surviving.

I glanced behind me, back to the gate. All those poor people in Desolation had no idea they led another life. And if we Nobles let Khalom be destroyed, then they would cease to exist. We'd all cease to exist. Why did Mr. Tompkins and Robert want me to remember my other life? And why did Cael bring me back to the city now? Why not years ago? Anger rose in my throat, and I tried to swallow it down. He could've been honest with me anytime.

Another set of fresh memories attacked.

I tipped over and landed on my rear, my back hitting a tree. I remembered the night I left. There'd been a fight in my room. A dagger at my throat. Furniture smashed. Two sets of hands fought for me. A set of strong arms carried me from the city. And then . . .

Nothing. Until now.

Someone had tried to kill me. Did my mom know?

Mom.

She was a Noble, too. She had followed me out of the city. *But why?* She was still out in Desolation. And Dad . . . I hadn't known him until Desolation.

Mom must have met him out there.

Too much was happening too fast. My head pounded from the onslaught of memories. It was as if I'd never left. I knew who I was. I remembered every day of my life here. I remembered training as a Noble. *How could I have forgotten any of this?*

But I still didn't know who I was in my Cursed life. I'd gotten flashes from Robert when he'd reached inside my mind, but I couldn't remember anything more.

I needed help. The Mhystic. They ruled the city. They needed to know I was back. I squinted at the white road in front of me. They should be in the Great Hall.

I stood up, brushed off my legs and took off down the path, heading straight into the city. I was finally home, but yet, I wasn't.

I walked through the lower grounds. It was strange to not see any color as I weaved through the paved walkways and sculpted trees.

As I moved between the large buildings that resembled Greek architecture and looked at the curtains in the doorways, I remembered that they didn't believe in doors here.

I didn't see anyone out—perhaps all my peers were still in class. But my stomach trembled at the thought. What would they think when they saw me? Would they remember me? Did they wonder where I went? I wrapped my arms around my middle.

I continued up the path. I took in the foliage around me. The trees were a pearly white and, at the bottom of each trunk, flowers with ivory petals sprouted from colorless grass. I couldn't believe I was here. I came around another bend and slowed my pace, drawing near to four buildings set in a square—the oldest buildings in Khalom. They were Gothic-like in structure, looking more like old cathedrals than a library, study hall, and old house of records. One actually was a church, though it wasn't used for regular worship. Instead, it served as a shrine to Ehlissa, the first leader—the original Mhystic of Khalom. Now there were four of them.

I continued onward, but my steps slowed. What if the Mhystic didn't want me here? Were they the ones who wanted to get rid of me in the first place? Panic took hold and I hurried off the path. I collapsed underneath a massive oak, white leaves dangling from the branches above me. I exhaled, my body trembling.

"Well, what do you know, it's Desolation," a male voice said. "Mind if I call you Dessy?"

I stiffened. The voice wasn't familiar, but something in the air was. I scrambled away from the tree and looked around. I didn't see a soul. He whistled, and I peered upward.

A guy lounged on a tree branch above me, twiddling a leaf between his fingers. Against the colorless leaves, his hair appeared darker, the messy bangs on his forehead a rich brown. His mouth was crooked in a smirk, but his eyes were hard.

"So the rumors are true. Death has returned to Khalom." There was a bitter edge to his voice.

I blinked back.

Death.

I hadn't heard that term in a long time. In fact, I'd forgotten all about Centers. They were our special abilities in Khalom. I put a hand over my heart. I was Death. I was the last of my line.

That's why Lionel had run from me. Death wasn't trusted here in Khalom. It was too powerful of a Center, posing too much of a threat. The last carrier of Death had been my grandma, Laela. Women from my family all looked freakishly alike—he might've even thought I *was* my grandma—or the ghost of her.

The guy in the tree jumped down, barely making a sound. He tossed the leaf from his fingers, and it drifted to the ground. He slowly circled me.

"So, are you enjoying your newfound Noblehood? You ready to hear your name whispered around every corner? Or would you rather be out parading with your shadow friends? Or shadow *friend*?" He lifted a brow.

I stepped back, and he stopped his circling. "Who are you? I haven't seen you before. And . . . you know about Cael?"

His lips flicked upward. "I know he's not any good for you."

He paced in front of me, the air sizzling between us. I would know if this kid had lived here—no one could enter Khalom unless they were a Noble—but I'd never seen his face before.

"Who are you?" I asked again.

"No one."

My forehead pinched together. "Nowen?" I repeated.

"Yeah, Nowen." He paused, facing me, and the sunlight reflected in his eyes. They were two different colors. One blue, one black.

In one swift motion, he reached forward and snatched my chin. He lifted it a notch. "Are you afraid of me, Dessy?"

"No." I blinked. The answer came out too quick, and my heart jolted. "And don't call me Dessy."

He let out a laugh. "Right." He let go of my chin and patted my cheek.

I studied him. He just seemed so familiar, but I couldn't put my finger on why.

Nowen rolled back on his heels and assessed me from head to toe. "You're all right, but you need some work. You don't really look like Death. Not very fearsome, are you? A bit of a disappointment, really."

I tightened my fists and glared. "Listen, Nowen. I'm not sure what sort of weird agenda you have going on here, but I've—"

"Got to find answers? Show them that Death has returned? Prove to everyone that you belong on the Mhystic?" He let out an exaggerated groan. "There are a lot more important things to focus on. One of which"—he lowered his voice—"is getting to know me better." He winked and drew closer once again.

I scooted away until my back hit the tree. He leaned down, his face hovering inches from my own.

Why did I feel like I knew him?

Something moved beyond the gate, a shadow in the dark green foliage of the forest. Nowen's head snapped up and he straightened, eyes narrowed.

"I'll be in touch," he said, and disappeared in a blink.

I stood breathless under the oak, staring at the spot where Nowen had been. My heart kept racing. I peeked through the fence and into the woods, and the green trees rustled. I straightened, squinting into the shadows. *Was it Cael?* My heart flipped at the thought of him. The dark hollows of his eyes washing over me. The way his presence melted my bones. The feel of his voice inside my head.

The trees stilled, and I blinked. No one was there.

"There you are."

I spun around, thinking Nowen was back, but sharp fingernails dug into my upper arm, and I was yanked sideways. I tripped over my feet and a tall figure loomed over me.

"Unbelievable," her regal voice said. "Frolicking around like you're a peasant. I expected better of you, Claera." The woman dragged me down a secluded pathway into an orchard of fruit trees. She crossed her arms. The woman stood like a queen, chin held high, back as straight as if she were sitting on a throne. Her raven hair was slicked into a tight bun, accentuating the severe disapproval written all over her face. "When Aericka told me you were back, I didn't believe it. Yet here you are." She waved a hand in front of her.

Aericka?

Oh, Ricki. Memories of her started rushing back. The school. She'd saved me. She was a Noble here, one of my classmates. And she'd been out in Desolation?

I analyzed the woman's face before I lifted my brows. "Fae?" She was Ricki's grandma. Her features were pinched tight, deep lines around her mouth.

"The High Officials won't be pleased you're here." She pursed her lips. "You should leave. Before they find out."

I blinked. "Leave? Why?"

Fae's lips tightened. She gripped me by the arm again and pulled me into the shadows under a pale tree. The white leaves rustled. "Because as you know, I am one of them, and you aren't trusted. I'll also not lose another grandchild because of you."

My forehead creased.

Footsteps sounded from behind, and Ricki came rushing up the path, her dark curly hair popping against the white scenery. She stopped in front of us, bending over her knees as she caught her breath.

"She's not leaving," Ricki said. "Clara needs to be here."

"No, Aericka," Fae snapped. "We've talked about this. Your duty is to your family. Claera's duty—"

"Should be Clara's choice," Ricki interrupted. "And it's Ricki, remember? I hate my Noble name."

Fae's lips flattened into a thin line. The air around her popped and sizzled, and little yellow sparks snapped in the air around her. The electric currents zapped me, and I jerked back, blinking.

It'd been a long time since I'd seen someone use their Center. I'd seen Ricki use hers back in Desolation, but here, it felt much more real. Each Center—each ability—had a telltale color to it when used. Time and Space was yellow. Earth was green. Body was blue. And Mind was purple.

"Once the other High Officials find out she's here," said Fae, "it'll be too late. We still have time—"

"Clara's grandma would have wanted her here," Ricki interrupted. "She would've—"

"You don't know a *thing* about Laela," Fae said sharply. She glanced at me like I was a discarded toenail clipping. "You're just like her. Thinking you can control everyone around you. Well guess what? You can't. You try and you'll end up in the Dhim with her. Never to be seen again."

Fae spun on her heels and stalked off, the golden sparks crackling behind her.

8
Thin Air

I stared at Ricki, noting the bits of sunlight glinting in her eyes. I didn't know what to feel. It seemed with each passing minute, I discovered more and more people had lied to me. Cael. Mom. Ricki. They'd all known who I was, yet they never said anything. They just let me live out in Desolation like a fool, clueless.

She kept her gaze locked with mine, but I wouldn't blink. I wouldn't be the first to break eye contact. She was the one who had lied to *me*—sitting in that classroom day after day—she could have communicated with me at any time. Ricki finally cleared her throat and glanced away.

"I'm so sorry, Clara," she said. "There were so many times I wanted to tell you who you were back in Desolation, but—"

"How could you not tell me?" I whispered. "All those times *pretending* you were just as brain-dead as everyone else. You lied to me."

Ricki's dark curls hung over her face. She stayed silent, her mouth turning downward.

"I sent a message to the High Officials that you were here," she said, looking at her feet. "I saw that Stricken guy take you away. I followed you. I saw you walk into the city."

"If you had been honest," I continued, "I might've been able to save my mom. Protect her somehow."

"Look, I said I was sorry," Ricki said. She put a hand on her hip. "And I did save you back at the school. Gherald Tompkins and Robert would've done a *lot* worse if I hadn't stepped in."

I flexed my hands, unable to believe she was defending herself, but then I exhaled. She was right. She had saved me, even if Mom was still out there.

"So . . ." I ran a hand through my hair. "So, your Center must be Earth. I remember the flash of green right before the school began to shake."

I hadn't allowed myself to think of Centers yet. I hadn't had time. But it was something I needed to focus on, and fast. Centers were how we protected Khalom. Without them, anyone could take the city. There was Earth. Body. Mind. Time and Space.

And Death.

"Yeah," Ricki replied, and shrugged. "Mini earthquakes are easy. That was nothing."

I nodded. Even though my memories were coming back to me quickly, it was hard to take it all in. I knew my Center was Death, but I was too frazzled to think about what that meant right now.

Laughter traveled from up the path, and I stiffened. Footsteps approached, and I squatted down behind Ricki. I kept my head lowered, praying the newcomers wouldn't see me. I knew I'd have to face my classmates at some point, but I wasn't ready. The students walked by, chatting, until they disappeared up the path and around the corner.

Ricki peered down at me with sympathy. "Hey, let's walk."

She took my elbow and pulled me back to my feet. She guided me in the opposite direction of the kids, cutting through the edge of campus. Silvery white grass stuck up from the ground, each blade separated in perfect precision. I glanced over at Ricki, taking in her small frame. She was almost half my size, but she walked through Khalom boldly, fiercely, like anything or anyone should cross her path only if they dared.

"So . . . how much do you remember?" she asked.

I wasn't sure whether or not to tell her, but I needed to trust somebody.

"It's pretty much all there," I said. "I mean, the faces of my old classmates are beginning to surface. I remember playing with a lot of the kids in school. It's a lot to take in though . . ." I trailed off, praying she wouldn't ask the next question.

"What about—"

"No," I said quickly, and heat shot to my cheeks. "I don't have any memory of my parallel life." I swallowed hard, cursing that she had asked. I was barely starting to remember my life here, and I'd never been connected to my other life.

She paused, digging her small feet into the sidewalk. "What?" she hissed.

The truth stuck out to me like a big piece of garbage.

"How is that possible?" she continued.

I winced, turning my head away. Maybe I shouldn't have told her. It could come back to bite me, but I needed to tell *somebody*.

"You can't let anyone know," she said. "If anyone found out . . ."

"I know." But I didn't say another word. If anyone found out I didn't have my lives connected, they would know I didn't have access to my powers.

And no one could force my memory of my lives on me. It was too dangerous.

If I didn't discover my other life on my own, I could lose my mind completely. Which is why what Robert did was dangerous. We started walking again, a pearly orchard stretching out beside us. A few more marble buildings were interspersed throughout. Most of them were where records were kept.

"Your Center is worthless until you connect with your other life," Ricki said hesitantly. "You won't have any power until you know who you are over there."

"You don't think I know that?" I burst out. I turned on her, and a sudden rush of emotion swelled in my throat. "I've spent the last ten years not knowing who I was. And now that I do, it's like I'm living the same nightmare again. *Not knowing.*" I clenched my eyes shut. Ricki didn't deserve to have me lash out at her. "I'm not a part of your world. Not anymore."

I walked away from Ricki, a heavy feeling settling over me. Dark thoughts filled my mind. I didn't owe this place anything. No one cared that I'd left. Maybe I should just leave. I should go find Mom at the Stricken camp and keep her safe. I didn't belong here, no matter what Cael said. Darkness surged into me and heat rushed up the sides of my face. My pace quickened, my fists clenching in and out. A storm was brewing inside my chest, stronger than it ever had before.

"Clara, wait up!" Ricki jogged up after me. "I'm sorry. I didn't mean to upset you. You're right. This all probably does seem meaningless. But I meant what I told Fae—you belong here."

Heat still pounded behind my eyes, but tears gathered, and I paused. I didn't want to show her any emotion, but I couldn't help it. Maybe a small part of me did trust her. I kept my gaze forward.

"Why?" It was one simple word.

"Because look." She took my hand and drew me forward. Statues were scattered out before me, tucked away in the shrubbery or down the small paths that jutted from the main walkway, their faces and bodies carved in ivory marble. "There's a statue of your grandmother in there. All Nobles who pass into the Dhim are honored here. She would want you to continue her legacy. You're the last carrier of Death. We need you."

I stared out before me, my vision blurring. Was I needed? Death was my Center, yes, but it didn't mean anything when I couldn't use it. I was powerless. I couldn't help protect the city. No one needed me here. Besides, the city wasn't in danger. No one had risen up against Khalom since the Great War.

I shook my head. "I'm sorry, Ricki, but I don't think I can do it. Be a part of . . . all of this."

I moved ahead of her, almost in a sprint. She didn't follow, but I could feel her gaze boring into my back until I disappeared.

I didn't know where I was going, all I knew was that I needed out. Fae was right—I shouldn't be here. Mom was still out in Desolation, which meant she was in danger, and who knew where Dad had disappeared to. What happened to the people in Desolation when the Diviners got to them?

I walked quickly down the white pathways, weaving in and out of the trees. I wasn't welcome here. First, with Lionel and his fear of me, then that Nowen guy. Then Fae, who said the High Officials wouldn't want me here. But what about the Mhystic? Maybe they'd help me. But no, it wasn't safe for me to stay here. Ten years ago, someone had wanted me dead. My murderer could still be inside the city.

The large white fence that surrounded the southeast part of Khalom came into view, and I picked up my pace. My pulse pounded through my whole body, beating in time with the thoughts in my head. I wasn't wanted. I shouldn't be here. I belonged in Desolation now.

I sprinted up to the gates, panting, and gripped the cool iron fence. I didn't know where I'd go when I left the city—probably the Stricken camp. Then I'd come up with a new plan from there. Energy thrummed through my whole body, and heat began to spread into my palms. I closed my eyes, focusing, then said, "Claera."

I took a step forward, ready to pass through, but I rammed straight into the cold metal. My eyes flew open.

What?

"Claera," I said again and tightened my grip on the bars. I tried to step forward once more, but still, the gates were solid in front of me. "What's happening?" I shook the bars. My Noble name should've let me enter or exit.

"I'm not letting you leave," Cael said. He stepped out from the dark green forest and stopped a few feet away from me. Clouds passed over the sun, and bits of light shimmered through him. He cocked his head to the side, watching me. Out of the foliage, more shaded figures came into view. They stood ready and alert, like an army of soldiers.

Cael slowly glided forward, his feet crunching into the earth. "I thought you would try to run." He kept his shaded eyes locked with mine. "But I told you, you need to stay inside the city. For your own protection. I'm more powerful than you, Clara, and I'm not letting you leave."

I slowly lowered my hands. "How do you have the power to keep me inside?"

He didn't answer, only moved closer, his shadow lengthening. "You need to stay inside the city and be welcomed back like the Noble you are. You will go to school and learn everything you've missed. You don't have control over your Center, and I know you haven't connected with your parallel life, which means you're powerless." Cael bent down so his face was right in mine. "You *need* to find that power. You're more important than you know."

I stared back at him.

A swirl of dark wisps circled around his head. Seeing him, being with him again, even though we'd just parted, made my whole body tremble—like I was in withdrawal having been without him even for just a brief period of time.

"Why am I important?" I choked out. I wasn't important. I never had been. I'd always been alone.

"Don't worry about what's happening out here," Cael said. "Your mother is safe. Just focus on you. Can you do that?"

He kept his face near mine, his eyes and lips nothing but shaded features. I wanted to reach up and touch his face, to make sure he was real.

"I'll try," I said, swallowing.

Cael nodded. "Good."

He slowly backed away before he turned. His silhouette darkened until he melted back into the forest, his shadow army following him.

"Wait," I said.

He paused, his shadowy form taking shape again as he tilted his head, listening.

"When will I see you again?" I hated the desperation in my voice.

"We will be out here watching," he said, like he had before.

Then he disappeared.

9

Lurking Fear

My footsteps echoed, bouncing off the high ceiling as I entered the Grand Hall. I peered upward, lost in the vast space, captivated by the detailed paintings and grand chandeliers that covered the expanse above me.

White marble columns stretched from one side of the room to the other, extending upward. Light filtered in through the glassless windows, casting heavy shadows on the floor.

Seven of the twelve High Officials lined up in front of me, looking like angels, with the sunlight streaming down on their white, cascading robes. Fae was among them, peering at me with her chin lifted and her mouth frowning. The High Officials stood behind a wooden altar where a sharp, shiny dagger lay on top.

"Claera!" a heavyset man boomed from the middle of the group. He stepped forward, welcoming me with open arms. "We thought you had left us for good and gone into the Dhim! Please, come here. I am Bhrutus." He smiled through his trimmed black beard, his beefy hands motioning me closer.

A tall, spindly man frowned, his gnarled fingers tightening over his stomach. He had a narrow face with wrinkles that drooped over his eyes. "So you've come back to regain your Noblehood," he addressed me in a nasally voice. "Well, tell us. Have you gained complete knowledge of your other life?"

"Graeg, that's quite personal!" a tall redheaded woman exclaimed. She had deep-set eyes and a strong jawline.

I swallowed, my eyes flicking from High Official to High Official, my gaze settling back on Graeg. His bony fingers tapped on his stomach.

"With what's expected of her, it's not personal at all." Graeg sneered, not taking his eyes off me. "She will have to prove herself capable. *If* she's to stay here."

"I'm not sure she is capable," another High Official said, "with years of Diviners erasing her memory. She will need to be thoroughly evaluated."

Others murmured in agreement.

"I'm not sure she should be here at all. What if she's a plant? What if she's working with the Divining Masters?"

Another woman gasped. "Unheard of!"

"Plausible."

"Perhaps she should be held in the White Wing until we know for sure she is safe."

"That isn't necessary!" the redhead said. "She's a child!"

My head pounded as I looked at each of them. Fae had warned me that they didn't want me here, but Cael had made it clear that I needed to be here.

"The Diviners didn't affect me," I spoke up, and the room froze. My whole body trembled, but I tried to keep my gaze steady. "I have full memory of who I am and—" I paused. They couldn't know I didn't have any memory of my Cursed life. They couldn't know the truth. Not if I wanted to stay here. "I . . . I know who I am in my other life." The lie stuck in my throat. "I need to speak with the Mhystic. Where are they?"

The High Officials murmured to themselves, their voices ricocheting off the walls. I stood with my feet planted, as still as the curtains hanging around the open windows.

There was no breeze—the world as still and perfect as it always was.

"Then it's decided," Bhrutus said, ignoring my comment about the Mhystic. "She'll complete her schooling here. It will be interesting to see how Death will mingle with the rest of us in Khalom." He smiled, and his white teeth flashed behind his beard. "Death, as you know, very well might be the most important of all Centers. You're the only one who can truly protect us from the Divining Masters."

The other High Officials whispered again, and heat spread up the sides of my neck. I didn't want to think about it, but Bhrutus was right.

If the Divining Masters attacked, I was the only one who could truly stop them.

Except for . . .

My eyes flew to the dagger on the altar.

As if Graeg knew what I was thinking, he stepped up to the altar. He reached his hand forward and ran a knotty finger down the blade, a sinister smile twisting his lips.

"This dagger means death," he said, and his voice scratched at my skin. "Yes, it is one thing that can kill here in Khalom." He gently picked it up, turning it over in his hands.

I waited. The entire room watched.

"You may think you're special because you're Death, but you're not. You're not above Khalom's rules." He glared, and the wrinkles around his eyes creased.

I opened my mouth, but my words caught in my throat.

I nodded, swallowing, before I turned my back and headed out of the Grand Hall.

I stood inside my dorm room, which sat on the third floor of a building that faced the classrooms across the courtyard. I hadn't ever stayed in the dorms before. I was too young the last time I was here. I'd lived with Mom on the south end of Khalom. Now, this was where all the kids my age stayed. Training our Centers and honing our powers were the most important things here.

Warm light fell through the window, lace curtains cascading around the glassless frame. The room wasn't much. Two small beds, a desk, and a mirror, though the beds were four-poster with thin white curtains that drifted to the floor.

Fae had cornered me after my meeting with the High Officials and told me Ricki would be my Companion. It was common for Nobles to have a Companion, a Noble you roomed with and went to classes with.

I didn't have anything to unpack. No clothes. No backpack. No personal belongings. I peeked over at Ricki's bed. Nothing was there either. She hadn't been inside yet.

A knock sounded on the wall outside the doorway, and I spun around. A girl poked her head inside, her hair as yellow as sunshine, her smile just as bright.

"Clara! I can't believe you're here!" she exclaimed. "Do you remember me? I'm Deena."

I squinted, the soft features of her face coming back into my memory. "Of course, Daena. We used to have tea parties together."

She squished up her face. "Just call me Deena. Noble names are out. Nicknames are in. And yes, it's so good to see you!" She started forward as if to hug me, but she stopped, a hint of fear flashing through her eyes. She stepped back.

"Anyway, I came to give you your schedule," she said. She shoved a piece of paper in my hands. "You have Mhystic Studies first.

And then I got you into Advanced Celerating. They said the class was full, but I mentioned your name, and they gave you a spot." She paused, and her eyes flicked down to my jeans and T-shirt. "You're not going to wear that to class, are you?"

"What?" I smoothed down my shirt. "Oh. I don't have anything else to wear."

Her eyes widened. "You don't have anything else to wear?" She said it as though that was the worst thing to have ever happened to me.

She spun around and her yellow jumper melted into a miniskirt and blouse, sparkling purple dust particles lingering around her until they dissipated. She giggled and clapped her hands, her blond curls bouncing.

"Your turn!" she squealed. She clapped her hands again and my jeans and T-shirt were replaced by an orange miniskirt and a purple floral top. I peeled the shirt away from my skin, cringing.

Watching Deena use her powers so easily made the pit in my stomach grow. *How* was I supposed to go to my first day of school and not have any powers? I might as well be back living in Desolation. Powerless. Clueless. Being a Noble, I should've been able to wield Death at will. I should've known how to do simple things like Celerate and travel between my two lives. It was embarrassing. If only Dad were here. He'd always known what to say and how to make me feel better. My ribs squeezed tight, and I felt a tight pressure in my chest.

Deena tilted her head toward the empty bed across the room. "Ricki's not back yet. I heard she was your Companion."

My eyes shot to her. "Do you know where she is?"

She frowned. "She must still be down at confinement on the lower campus. I heard they might put her in the White Wing."

"What?" I turned on my heel. "Why would they do that?"

Deena's face twisted grimly. "You don't know? Because of you, of course."

"*Me*?"

"The High Officials found out she was with you in Desolation. She's being charged with conspiracy for your kidnapping. The fact that she's not back yet is a bad sign."

"But she had nothing to do with that!" I exclaimed. "She helped me." *Sort of.*

I looked out the window, down at the white pathways that wove through the courtyard below. If I hurried, maybe I could find her.

"I heard she wanted to leave. You know, to be with her . . . lover."

I spun back around, gawking. "Her"—it was a struggle to get the word out—"*lover*?"

"You don't know?" She paused, excitement in her eyes. "I hear he's a Diviner."

"A . . .?" I burst out laughing. "You think Ricki's in love with a Diviner?" Tears gathered in my eyes, and I wiped them away, still laughing. "Trust me, she wouldn't be in love with a Diviner. No one could. They're awful."

Then I paused. Wait.

Diviners were *people*. I'd forgotten. The Divining Masters turned people into those things.

"You've seen Diviners?" Deena's jaw actually dropped. "Wait until I tell Mhaggie, she's gonna freak!" She whirled, the curtain whooshing behind her.

I stood frozen for a few heartbeats. My mind was a mess of Diviners and Cael and Ricki being questioned at the confinement center. I couldn't let her be punished because of me. She didn't kidnap me. There had been two people who fought for possession of me that night. And the victor had been taller than her, and definitely a guy. I remembered the feeling of his arms around me.

Without another thought, I marched out of my dorm room and raced down the stairs to the courtyard.

School would have to wait.

10
Devil's Right Leg

I tore apart the lower grounds searching for Ricki, but with every turn I took, circling the pathways from one end of Khalom to the other, she was nowhere to be found. The confinement center had been a bust. The High Official on duty said no one had been taken in for questioning. Maybe Deena had gotten her facts wrong.

I raced up the eastern edge once more, toward Historic Quarter, staying alert for any signs of her. I raced underneath white stone archways and shaded trees, making my way back up to the dorms. White roses and other milky flowers dotted the silvery grass. Even though I couldn't feel heat—there was no temperature in Khalom—my limbs burned from exertion.

I knew Ricki and I had just met, but I had to clear her name. She hadn't been part of my kidnapping. Whoever had taken me out of the city had saved me. Fae couldn't send Ricki to the White Wing—she hadn't broken the laws of Khalom. What kind of grandmother would lock up her own granddaughter?

I came around another bend and skidded to a halt.

Nowen leaned against a tree, his arms crossed, one ankle over the other. He smirked as I approached, his eyes twinkling.

"There you are, Dessy," he said. "I was wondering when I'd see you next."

The sense of familiarity that I felt the first time I met him overwhelmed me. I studied him more closely.

"Do I know you?" I blurted out. "I mean from before. I don't remember growing up with you, but I swear we've met."

He shrugged. "Possible. I've been here as long as you. Maybe longer." He winked.

I furrowed my eyebrows.

He pushed off the tree and slowly strolled toward me. He linked his arms behind his back and cocked his head to the side. His lashes were dark against his pale skin.

"I've been watching you," he said. "Waiting for you to do something dangerous. Something *deathly*. But you haven't shown any sign of using your powers. You've been very boring so far." He clicked his tongue. "I wonder why that is."

I held rooted to the sidewalk, watching him approach. Something in the air sizzled between us, but it didn't have a color. Just an invisible energy that sparked from him to me.

He walked as if each step were methodical, and his lips twitched upward again. "You know, I think we'd be a good pair, you and me. You need a friend here, right? You clearly have been avoiding everyone."

I glared at him. "You don't seem to be Mr. Popular yourself. I've never even heard of you."

He let out a chuckle, shaking his head, his dark bangs falling into his eyes. "If only you knew." He paused and tilted his head to the other side. "It will be interesting to see what you can do. I hope you don't keep your secrets from us too long?" He lifted a brow.

Secrets?

Oh, Death.

I swallowed. He wasn't the only one who'd be waiting.

As soon as my classmates saw me, they'd be expecting me to use my powers.

"I'm not a show-off," I said, keeping my gaze locked with his. "And why would I? You know that Death—"

"Is the only Center that can kill?" His lips quirked. "Yeah, I know that." He moved forward again, until our noses were inches apart. He reached down and touched the tip of my pinky.

"I'm glad I have the opportunity to get to know you, Dessy," he whispered. "I've waited a long time for you."

I glanced down at the touch, warmth tingling in my fingertips before I met his gaze again. We stared at each other for a few moments, his one blue eye and one black eye peering down at me, though he wasn't too much taller than me.

"Clara, there you are!"

Nowen's eyes widened, and he took off so fast I barely saw him move. I shook my head, my fingertips still tingling.

Ricki came rushing up the path, her curly hair bouncing.

"I've looked everywhere for you!" she said, out of breath. "Why aren't you in class?"

"Me? I've been looking for you. Where have you been?"

She made a face. "Hiding, proving a point, whatever. Just showing Fae that she can't control my life. Speaking of which," she continued, "she's completely pissed at you. She wanted the High Official meeting to go differently. Man, she wants you out of here."

I rubbed my forehead. I was torn between asking Ricki about whether or not she was taken in for questioning and why her grandmother had it out for me so bad.

Ricki frowned as she looked me over. "But we do need to get to class." Her eyes widened as she glanced over me. "*What* are you wearing? That needs to change. Now."

She took my hand and started to drag me to campus. "I'm not letting you go to your first class looking like that. Come on."

I pulled a white tank top over my head and tightened a new pair of drawstring pants around my waist. The light material hung effortlessly off my body, sliding over my skin like silk. I was lucky Ricki had these.

I stepped out from one of the many curtained alcoves that lined the main hall in the central building at school.

Ricki looked me up and down, her dark hair now braided down her back. "Much better. Now just fake it until you connect your lives."

My lips twisted. Maybe it was a relief to know someone knew my secret and didn't shun me. The other kids wouldn't be so kind. I rubbed my hands up and down my thighs, willing my heart to slow. Death was supposed to be the most fearsome of all the Centers. It was obviously known to . . . kill. But apparently it had other abilities, too. My grandmother Laela once ventured outside the city gates and killed a Divining Master, which helped release his pack of Diviners. A miracle since once Diviners sold their souls to the Masters, it was supposed to be impossible for them to be released. It was also rumored that Death could steal other people's Centers. I shivered at the thought of what I was capable of. But I wasn't my grandmother. What if I never connected my lives and gained my power?

For some reason, the need to be liked blossomed up within me. I shouldn't care, but I suddenly wanted to fit in here. These were my old classmates. I'd once had their respect. Now I was nobody.

A mix of anticipation and fear pulsed through me, but I followed Ricki down the south hall that led to the gymnasium. Large tapestries hung on the tiled hallways, and bright sunlight streamed in through the thin curtains that led to the outside. If only I could transform myself into a bird and escape. People with Mind were able to shape-shift. They were able to levitate objects, read people's thoughts. Pretty much anything using the power of their mind. Or maybe if I were Body, I'd be able to force my way out of Khalom. Was Cael really so powerful that he could keep me in here when I'd have unbeatable strength? Or with Time and Space, I'd be able to reverse time, stop myself from ever being kidnapped. And with Earth, I could open the ground and swallow myself whole, so I'd never have to face my classmates.

But no, I was Death. I was only capable of destruction.

We moved around one last corner, and a long white curtain hung in front of us. We paused, staring at the thin material.

"You ready?" Ricki asked.

I blew out a shaky breath. "Yeah."

Ricki pulled open the curtain and it brushed past my face as I stepped inside. The room was larger than I remembered, with high ceilings and an open floor plan. Everything from a swimming pool to weights was there, even what looked like a gigantic jungle gym. A huge mat lay in front of us. Sharp, angular weapons hung on the far wall.

We walked into the room and stopped at the edge of the mat.

Heads swiveled around, and conversations stopped. About fifty kids sat in separate groups, and I ducked my head, scanning the large space. Whispers broke out, echoing through the room. Ricki gripped my elbow, drawing me close to her side.

"It's okay," she whispered out the side of her mouth. "You were going to have to face this at some point."

Heat spread across my face. A cluster of people off to the left hadn't noticed my entrance. They were grouped in a circle, legs crossed, holding hands. They mumbled under their breaths with their eyes closed. A low hum came from them, carrying through the room.

Flowers sprouted from the floor. As if by invisible hands, the petals were pulled off from the buds and floated through the air into a long chain. Bits of green and yellow sparked in the space around them.

"Time and Space," Ricki whispered. "They like to mingle with the Earth peeps. Both groups are all about nature and healing and the universe and stuff."

"I remember."

We stepped onto the mat, and the thick padding squished under my feet. Immediately, a warmth spread over me and something in the air tugged, a magnetism drawing me in. The pull tickled underneath my skin, and I turned my attention to the right. My eyes locked with a girl at the edge of the group, and purple sparks snapped around her head. In a rush, memories from earlier today flashed through my mind. The Storm. My mom. Stepping into the city. The High Officials. The girl was reading my mind. She flipped through my thoughts like she was rifling through a stack of papers.

"Don't look them in the eyes!" Ricki forced my head away, and the purple sparks diminished. "Those with Mind can read your thoughts. They *can't* know your secret."

I kept my gaze away, but still felt their pull.

"They can also attack your mind, making you feel pain, or they also think it's funny to dive into your parallel life—to try and get little bits of information to mess with you. They once found out this girl Mhaggie—in her other life—got dumped on prom night by her cousin, and it's all anyone talked about for a month."

Ricki and I continued walking, and memories of how Robert dove into my mind surfaced. He'd seen bits of my life. He must've been Mind.

Ricki drew me to a stop just as one kid landed at our feet in a crash. Startled, I looked up, and a muscled boy at the other end of the room grinned. The boy at my feet stood up and laughed, dusting off his hands. "Is that all you've got, Adham?" He loped back over to the muscled boy, and they began to wrestle once more, each flip, dip, and body check adding a new crack in the floor. Blue energy zapped around them, swirling up and over their heads as they fought.

"Stupid Body boys." Ricki rolled her eyes.

Undisturbed by the ruckus were two kids paired off, lips on lips, arms wrapped around each other. Heat rose up my cheeks, but I couldn't look away. I'd never been kissed like that. Or kissed, period. My heart gave a large thump.

"It's disgusting," Ricki said, following my gaze.

"Um . . . yeah. Disgusting." Though I couldn't stop staring.

"Some of the Body crowd likes to see how far they can go before being yanked to the other side. Being physical is a powerful way to travel to your other life."

"And apparently they don't care who's watching." It was strange to see the kids I once knew being so physical with each other. When I'd left, we were still playing hide-and-seek.

I couldn't help but think of Cael and wonder what it would be like if he touched me like that. I continued to stare, my gaze roaming, until I stopped on the guy in the middle.

I gasped. "Holy Mhystic."

"What? What is it?" Ricki asked. She crouched like she was ready to attack.

Nowen sat in the middle of the gym, his dark hair hanging into his face, his heavy-lidded gaze staring straight at me.

"That guy. In the middle of the Body crowd. Do you know him?"

"You expect me to pick out a single person in the middle of that group?" Ricki said dryly. Her shoulders relaxed.

I swallowed. It seemed as if Nowen and I were suddenly the only people in the room. His mouth was twisted like he knew a secret, humor sparkling in his eyes.

An abrupt chill broke through the space, and the atmosphere changed. I yanked my gaze away, though I could still feel Nowen's stare burning into me. The Body crowd disbanded as bodies were torn apart by some invisible force. The Mind group stopped staring down innocent bystanders. The flower chain held aloft by the Earth and Time and Space kids fell to the floor. All of the different colors that snapped in the air vanished.

I peeked behind me. Mr. Tompkins walked in.

What?

He strutted with his hands tucked into his pockets, his muscles stretching through his T-shirt. Thin glasses still framed his face, his sandy hair ruffled on top of his head.

"What is he doing here?" I hissed to Ricki. He was a *Noble*?

"You know the drill." Mr. Tompkins's voice boomed off the walls. "Partner up with someone not of your Center and let's get going."

The room moved at once, bodies shifting around me. A few stares flicked in my direction, but I kept my focus on Mr. Tompkins. I'd spent every day with him in Desolation, and he was a Noble, too? How many people in Desolation had not been telling me the truth?

Mr. Tompkins headed right to me, his arms outstretched.

"Clara!" he said. "Or Claera, I should say."

I backed away, tripping on the mat. Ricki pulled me upright, keeping a firm grip on me.

He continued forward before stopping in front of me. He crossed his arms, and his lean muscles flexed. "I'm sorry about the deception, but I had my orders. Just like Aericka had hers." He winked at her. "Although mine came from higher powers."

Ricki shifted uncomfortably.

"I felt privileged to be one of the few who knew about your existence in Desolation," Mr. Tompkins continued. "And to help protect and watch over you from the Diviners. We must have scared you before. But no matter. Water under the bridge, yes? So happy you've returned home. And *Death*, too."

I shook my head, my mind still catching up. "You're . . . you're a *teacher* here?"

Mr. Tompkins straightened his glasses. "Yes, but call me Gherry. Only first names in Khalom, remember?"

I swallowed, but it felt like my stomach had switched places with my throat. I didn't know what to say.

"We can't trust him," Ricki whispered to me. "I was out there with him. He wants something from you. Why else would he have been out there?"

Mr. Tompkins wrapped his arm around my shoulder, tucking me into his side, leading me deeper into the room. My entire body buzzed, and I itched to get away from him. He swung his hand around, motioning over the gym.

"Now *this* is school," he said. "It's got to be weird after all your time back in Desolation, eh? Look at what we're accomplishing here." A smile stretched over his face, and I followed his gaze. Things had changed. Back when I was here before, we all sat in classes, learning about the day we would have our powers. Now, they were in full force.

Kids were paired up, facing each other off. One fighting pair held spears, and they darted forward, lunging. Yellow and blue sparks zipped in the air between them. One girl was disappearing and reappearing in a new spot around her opponent. Time and Space. The other kid, Body, had muscles that rippled from his skin, but he moved like molasses, stabbing his spear hard into the ground as he tried to catch the Time and Space girl.

Another pair of kids, Deena and someone I didn't remember yet, were having an arm-wrestling match. The two stared each other down, hands linked, muscles straining. The Earth guy was pelting Deena with tiny rocks from behind. Deena slammed up an invisible purple shield and the rocks stopped bouncing off the back of her head. Using Deena's distraction of putting up the shield, the Earth guy surged forward and slammed Deena's arm onto the table, her bone snapping. Deena cried out, but she focused on her arm, streams of purple energy radiating through the air. Her bones mended themselves back together, and the match continued.

To my left, I spotted Lionel squaring off with another kid. I couldn't remember what his Center was. Mind? Earth? It was hard to tell with the green and purple powers clashing in the air around him.

As kids, I'd only read about what we were capable of, but my peers, these kids I'd been little with, were now strong. I swallowed, realizing how behind I really was.

Mr. Tompkins led me over to his desk, where he pulled out a piece of paper from the top drawer. He spread it over the desk before snatching a pen and holding it out to me.

"The High Officials sent over some paperwork for you to sign. Boring school stuff." Excitement lit his eyes as he nodded down to the paper.

My forehead wrinkled. "Paperwork? Why?"

"Who knows. The High Officials take their job too seriously. It's not as if they rule this place like the Mhystic." He lifted the pen higher.

I tentatively took the pen and glanced over the parchment. It was yellow and worn with age, with a burn mark in the bottom right corner. It was a list of names, each written in their own, distinct scrawl. This didn't look like school paperwork. It was just a bunch of signatures. I bit the inside of my cheek. "What is this really? This doesn't look like school stuff."

"Well, it is," he said sharply. His eyes darkened. "Sign it."

I drew my pen away from the parchment, backing up a step. "I-I don't think I want to."

Mr. Tompkins straightened, his green eyes narrowing behind his glasses. Sweat gathered on his forehead. "Sign it, or I'll need to take you to the High Officials myself to tell them you're disobeying me."

I started to reply when a commotion caught my attention. Mr. Tompkins and I turned back to the gym just as the fight between the Body guy and the Time and Space girl intensified. The Time and Space girl vanished, reappeared right behind the Body guy, and stabbed her spear into his back. The Body guy cried out, his face twisting until he disappeared in a blue flash.

The entire room paused, and the Time and Space girl lowered her spear, yellow sparks crackling around her. Silence beat for a few seconds.

"We're not supposed to do that." Ricki stepped up next to me again. "It's against class rules."

I opened my mouth, but I didn't have words.

Mr. Tompkins clapped his hands, and the paper he wanted me to sign vanished. "It's all right, class. He'll be back soon. You all know that when we are mortally injured here, we're only sent to our Cursed life for a time. Khalob will be back."

Mr. Tompkins turned his attention back to me. "Should we see what you can do? You're a gift to us all, Clara." His intensity with getting me to sign the paper had clearly dissipated. "Let's see how your Center compares to the rest of them." His eyes gleamed and he took my shoulders, spinning me to face the room. "To the pool!" he exclaimed.

Pool?

He pushed me forward, and I stumbled, tripping over my feet. Ricki kept pace with me.

"You have to do what he says," she said under her breath. "Whatever he has planned, if you back out now, Mr. Tompkins will *know*."

"He's gonna know my secret if I try and fail."

"You have no choice but to try."

"Try what? What is he going to make me do?"

Ricki clamped her mouth shut, but she spoke through her lips. "You can do this," she said. "You never know what might connect you to your other life and give you your power. Maybe this is the answer—so just try."

I shook my head, my heart speeding. "Ricki . . ."

"Come on." She marched on ahead of me, but I didn't follow. I couldn't do this. I'd gone from being invisible in Desolation to the center of attention in Khalom.

I peeked behind me to the exit, to the white curtain that hung silent, then turned back to the kids gathering at the pool. Maybe Ricki was right. Maybe participating in an activity would jump-start my memory. But the thought of making a fool of myself held me paralyzed.

Cael.

Think of Cael. He said I needed to be in here.

I tentatively moved forward, but my hands shook. I stuffed them underneath my armpits, trying to calm my nerves.

I edged up to the pool, next to a group of kids. Deena stood in front of me across the water, and she smiled and waved. She had changed her clothes again, this time wearing a bright blue dress with yellow flowers. I gave her a nod but couldn't smile. I peeked around the crowd for Nowen, but he was lost in the jumble. Lionel stood in the back, alone.

Two large Body guys shoved their way through the crowd and stopped on either side of me. I took them in, scanning them from head to toe. The one to my left had smooth brown skin and long, blond dreads that reached the middle of his back. I remembered when his hair had been a curly mop on top of his head.

"Adham?"

He nodded but kept his gaze forward. The other guy—who I instantly recognized as the Body guy who had just disappeared in the fight with the Time and Space girl, I guess he was back already —nudged me in the shoulder.

"I'm Khalob," he said. "Remember me?"

He stuck his face in mine, and I leaned back. I recalled his once boyish features, which had now turned chiseled and sharp. His spiky hair was dyed blue, and earrings dangled from both ears.

I pressed my lips together, thinking. "Khalob. Of course I remember. You smashed a peanut butter sandwich into Lionel's face when we were seven."

He barked out a laugh and nudged me again. "I'd forgotten all about that. Loser." He shook his head, remembering.

Mr. Tompkins moved up to the front of the pool and cleared his throat. The class fell silent, and the water slowly rippled beneath us.

"As you know, we have Death among us again." He paused, as if waiting for a reaction.

Every pair of eyes slid to me. I shifted, rolled my shoulders, and ducked my head. I counted out a few seconds, waiting for the attention to subside.

"We haven't had Death in Khalom for a long time. Not since Laela left us," Mr. Tompkins continued.

Eyes slid to me again, and I knew why. My grandmother was famous, and not just because she was Death. She'd been a rebellious soul. She was known for her escapades. She loved to escape from the city and have adventures—the tale about killing a Divining Master and releasing his Diviners being the most famous one. But her last adventure had killed her. She ventured into the Dhim and never returned.

Death had passed through several families in the past thousand years or so, usually down the female line. But Grandma Laela was the last known carrier. Mom should've also been a carrier, but for some reason, Death never emerged as Mom's Center. "Death will be an asset to us," Mr. Tompkins went on. "It will help us with our training. Her strength will push us to develop our Centers even more. A war is coming, and we must be prepared."

"Now." He clapped his hands together. "As you all know, there are two types of death. There is a physical death, and a mental death. A physical death is what can occur in your Cursed life. Your mental death is what can occur here." He stared at me, as if he were speaking only to me. "But I'm not talking about someone sending you to the other side if you were stabbed with a spear, I'm talking about a permanent mental death."

The room went quiet. We had all heard this before, but the reminder was never a pleasant one.

"As Nobles, our bodies and minds are linked," he continued. "So if you are killed in your Cursed life, if you die a physical death over there, then your afterlife takes place in the Dhim, where you will spend the rest of eternity. But what happens to you if you are killed *here*, in Khalom?"

Again, silence. Eyes shifted around.

Mr. Tompkins cocked his head toward Deena. "Come on, Deena, you should know."

She nodded, and she twisted her fingers out in front of her. "If you are killed in Khalom—experiencing a mental death—then you'll cease to exist. You won't have a body in your Cursed life, and you won't have a mind over here. It will be as if you never existed."

A chill settled over the room and seeped into my bones.

And it was all because of me.

Death was the only Center that could kill. And it was the worst kind of death. It would be much better to live out the rest of your days in the Dhim, the dark void that carried the dead. But with my power?

I could erase someone permanently.

"Of course it's not the only thing that can kill," Mr. Tompkins said. "The Mhystic have blessed the dagger in the Great Hall, in case . . ." He paused, and his eyes slid to me. The room's gaze followed, and silence fell again. Their stares seared into me.

Heat radiated in my chest, and I narrowed my eyes. "In case I need to be killed?" I burst out, and my voice echoed through the room. I clamped my lips together tight, and the heat in my chest instantly fled. *Why had I said that?*

Mr. Tompkins's brows shot upward. "I like your bluntness, Clara. But yes, it's true."

The class didn't move, as if they were trapped in a spell. Then, Mr. Tompkins clapped his hands together once more, and the room jerked. "But enough of that! It's time to put the power of Death against the power of Mind." He scanned through the crowd. "Lionel, let's have you step up to the plate."

Lionel's eyes stretched wide, his red brows almost touching his hairline.

"S-Sir?"

"An underwater test," Mr. Tompkins said. "Let's see who can stay on this side the longest, without going over to their parallel life. You drown, you go to your Cursed life. You remain here, you win."

Gasps circulated the room, whispers breaking out. Deena shook her head, stepping forward.

"It's against the rules to willingly send someone to the other side," she said. "Let alone have it be orchestrated by a teacher!"

Mr. Tompkins's lips curved upward. "Things are changing, Deena. Now, more than ever, you need to be trained. The Divining Masters are drawing nearer every day, and we must be prepared." He snapped his fingers. "Adham, Khalob, we need muscle!"

Next to me, Khalob instantly reacted. He let out a chuckle and gripped me by the arm. Adham headed over to Lionel. They dragged the two of us over to the pool; I was too shocked to fight. Adham shoved Lionel in, and he disappeared beneath the water in a splash. He surfaced, gasping, his red hair plastered to his head.

Khalob grinned down at me, his hair extra blue in the fluorescent lights. "Your turn."

"Wait," I said. "This is crazy—"

Khalob shoved me into the pool, and my words were cut off as cold water shot into my lungs. I sputtered as I surfaced and struggled to stay upright.

"Make sure to hold them down securely," Mr. Tompkins said. "Of all the Centers, Mind should give Death the most competition. We'll see how long Lionel lasts."

The air was so heavy, I felt like I was already drowning. Lionel treaded water next to me, his chin quivering.

"Wait," I said, though I wasn't sure to whom. "There's no need for this." Water splashed into my mouth. My classmates moved closer to the edge of the pool, eyes alight with excitement. Some rubbed their hands together, bets being placed.

Mr. Tompkins bent down and patted my shoulder. His face twisted. "Go easy on the kid, all right? We both know he's no match for you." He stood up and motioned to Khalob and Adham. "Get ready. One, two, three!"

The world turned upside down as Khalob shoved me under, holding me securely beneath the surface. I swallowed a lungful of water, and I thrashed against him, trying to swim upright, but his hold was concrete. Adrenaline hit me like a punch to my chest. I struggled, kicked, and thwacked, but no matter how hard I tried to reach the surface, Khalob held me under.

Adham also held Lionel under, except Lionel wasn't struggling. I peered at him through the water, his thin body still. He looked as calm as a summer afternoon, eyes focused inward, body relaxed, ribbons of soft purple energy floating around his head.

He had done this before.

Every muscle in my body snapped like a rubber band. There was no way I could win this. I was going to drown, and I would be sent to the other side. But where would I go? I had no idea who I was over there. And did the other me have any idea of who I was here?

I continued to struggle, but tiny spots clouded my vision. I gulped, and more water filled my mouth. The lights swam above me in dizzying ripples. My vision began to blacken, my arms and legs going still.

Nowen's face came into view over the edge of the pool, wavy through the water. His multicolored eyes stared down at me, his jawbone cut strong along his profile. He lifted a hand and wiggled his fingers, as if saying goodbye.

I opened my mouth to scream, but more water poured inside. Nowen's eyes twinkled, a dark smile curving his lips.

And then I was gone, disappearing from Khalom, traveling between my two lives, to who knew where.

11

Eyes Wide Shut

"Clara! Get your butt out of bed! It's Saturday *and* my favorite day of the year."

I opened my eyes to Daniel hovering over me. His mouth stretched wide from ear to ear, his brown eyes sparkling in excitement. I groaned.

"Come on," Daniel complained. "You and the squad promised you'd be at the car wash this morning. Remember? And you know if you're not there, we'll get at least a dozen guys who won't pay half of what they would and—"

"Okay, okay, I get it," I moaned. I rubbed my forehead. "Fine, I'll be there—but no bikini."

"Ew! Are you trying to make me barf in your face? Don't blame *me* because my friends all seem to think you're hot. But with you being my sister and all, there are certain obligatory sibling rights that I'm entitled to, and I'm sure you wouldn't mind telling the *squad* that swimsuits are a necessary part—"

I threw a pillow in his face.

"Dan, if you want me there, I'll be there—and my squad—regardless of how we're all dressed. Now get out." I tried not to let my smile show. I was happy he was out and about socializing. He'd spent the last year in chemo treatments, battling blood cancer. We were gearing up for another round. It didn't look good.

I fell back into the pillows. Why was I so exhausted? For the past couple days, I'd woken up feeling like I'd run a marathon the night before. Or swum a thousand laps. I could've sworn I'd just been dreaming that I was in a pool. I swung my legs off the bed and staggered into the bathroom before splashing water over my face. I stared at myself in the mirror. I looked caved in, dark circles surrounding my eyes and indenting my cheeks. Why wasn't I sleeping? I fluffed up my short hair, combed out my bangs, and threw on a tank top and a pair of cutoffs before I headed downstairs to breakfast. The scent of fresh coffee and bacon hung thick in the air.

"Hey, Mom, Dad." I yawned and sat on one of the high stools that lined the countertop. Dad hid behind the morning paper and Mom flipped pancakes on the grill. I snatched a piece of bacon off Daniel's plate and nibbled on the end.

"Morning, hon," Mom said, sliding me a glass of orange juice. "Enjoy this meal for what it's worth because you're on your own 'til Monday."

"Oh yeah, I forgot about your antiquing road trip. Sounds fun," I said, laying on the sarcasm.

I took a sip of my juice and gagged on the pulp. "Yuck. If I wanted to chew my orange juice, I'd eat an orange." I reached across the counter and swiped Mom's cup of coffee, burning my tongue as I gulped down a mouthful.

Mom grabbed the cup from me and replaced it with an orange. I started to protest, but then let it slide. They'd be gone for the whole weekend—complete freedom for two days. I sighed and copped another piece of Daniel's bacon.

"Hey! There's like a whole plateful in front of you," Dan complained.

I gave him my biggest grin and chewed, not afraid of letting the food show.

"That's disgusting," he said, but I caught the faint smile that lifted one corner of his mouth.

"You'll remember to take your meds this weekend, Dan?" Mom asked.

Dan grumbled. He hated the drugs, but he also didn't need Mom on his back about it. He was sixteen, not five. I hopped off the stool and circled the counter, taking another swig of Mom's coffee.

"So, what are you guys planning on finding on this antique road trip of yours?" I asked, changing the subject. Daniel threw me a grateful glance. "Some more blue ridge plates to match Grandma Laela's? I can't think of anything more *exciting*."

Dad slammed the paper down, and the room flinched. "Enough of the sarcasm, Clara. You know, I'm starting to be disappointed with who you're becoming. You're getting an attitude, acting entitled. I expected more of you."

Silence filled the room. Dad had never been so fierce with me before.

"You know we don't talk about your grandmother," Dad continued. His usually gentle brown eyes were hard. "So let the topic rest. When we put her in that mental institution—"

"That's enough," Mom said.

Dad clamped his lips together before he turned back to me. "Apologize to your mother. Tell her you're sorry for speaking so irreverently about your grandmother. You know how much she meant to her."

I faced Mom, my mouth open. "I'm—I'm sorry," I said. Dad's outburst still had me in shock. I thought we were past pretending that Grandma Laela didn't exist.

Mom nodded and turned back to the grill, though I could see tears in her eyes. She flipped another pancake. Dad picked up the paper again. "You'll be good this weekend," Dad said as if he hadn't just lectured me. "I expect you and Daniel to behave."

Dan and I slid a glance at each other. What were we going to do? Throw a wild party? We weren't living in a cliché TV show.

Silence beat between us again until I pushed away from the counter. "Welp, I'm out of here. Dan, I'll see you at the car wash?"

Not waiting for his reply, I went out the back door and into the sunshine.

I didn't have a car—my parents didn't believe in that kind of privilege—so I headed on foot to the school parking lot. The warm sun made the day seem bright with possibilities, and I wound my way through my neighborhood, passing clean-cut houses and green lawns with a spring in my step. I kept to the sidewalk, dodging the sprinklers that spouted water onto the walkway.

I couldn't believe Dad this morning. I'd only been joking about Laela. I thought after ten years, the tragic memory of her would've passed. I knew she had disappeared without a trace, and it'd really affected Mom, but I thought some of the pain would've eased by now. She was crazy after all, ranting about other lives and her having superpowers.

The summer heat soaked into my skin, and I relished the warmth. I could live all day outdoors. I waved to a few neighbors as I passed by, my thoughts still swimming. Mom. Dad. Being worried about Dan's cancer. The fact that I wasn't sleeping at night. Our cheerleading competition was coming up and our routine was nearly perfect. More warmth circled me as my mind drifted away.

Out of nowhere, everything went black.

I paused on the sidewalk. I couldn't see. I stretched my eyes wide open and flailed my arms around. Complete darkness. My heart took off.

What?

I staggered around, my arms waving out in front of me.

What was happening?

Then, all at once, a rush of water filled my mouth, gurgling down my throat, filling my lungs. I floundered and my legs left the ground like I was floating. I kicked and opened my mouth, trying to suck in air, but more water spilled inside.

Help!

I tried to shout, but nothing came out. Water continued to flow. Pressure pushed heavy on my chest, collapsing my lungs.

I was going to die.

Right here in the middle of the sidewalk, I was going to drown by some unknown force. I toppled forward, expecting to fall into a pool of water, but my knees met hard cement, and pain shot through my legs.

In a flash, the darkness dissipated, and bright sunlight pierced my vision. I gasped, coughing, air filling my lungs. Gravel bit into my palms as I curled on the ground, panting.

"Are you okay?"

A man rushed over, bending down next to me. His hand touched my back, helping me upright. He had sandy hair and thin wired glasses. His green eyes took me in. Excitement lit his face for a moment before his expression smoothed out.

"I'm . . . I'm fine." I coughed, and my throat seared.

The world continued to right itself. I wasn't drowning. I touched my lips. I wasn't trapped in darkness. The sun continued to shine.

"Here, let me help you up," the guy said. He lifted me to my feet, and the world spun for a minute before it righted itself.

"Can I help you somewhere?" he asked.

His face swam into focus, and I scanned him head to toe. He was good looking for an older guy, probably mid-twenties or so. Lean muscles stretched through his button-up shirt.

I shook my head. "I'm good. Just heading to the school around the corner."

The guy adjusted his glasses, and I swore he held back a smile. "I'll help you there."

I nodded, too frazzled to argue. What had just happened?

We headed down the sidewalk, and I suddenly hoped this guy wasn't a murderer. He'd probably be able to snatch me and take me against my will in the state I was in, but we turned the last corner, and the school parking lot came into view.

My squad was already there, filling up buckets of water, holding posters, ready to draw in our customers. A few cars were already pulling up.

I stopped and turned to the guy. "Well, thanks. Sorry about that. I'm fine now, so you can go."

The guy nodded but didn't move. "Actually, I was on my way over here. I have some friends coming to get their cars washed. I'll just be over here." He pulled out his phone and headed toward the edge of the parking lot, where he had parked under a tree.

I stood watching him, my brows pinching together. Unease prickled along my spine. He chatted on his phone, his eyes sweeping the parking lot until his gaze connected with mine once again.

"Clara!"

I jerked and turned my eyes away. "What?"

Angela Cummings popped in front of me. She wore a bikini top and yellow shorts.

"There you are," she said. "You're on rinse duty." She shoved a hose in my hand and skipped away. My eyes darted back to the guy again. He was still under the tree, but he'd hung up and was just lingering there, arms crossed.

I rolled my shoulders, trying to shove him from my mind. He was just a guy, waiting for his friends at the car wash. He'd happened to run into me and help me. There was nothing sinister about him, right?

The morning passed, and soon cars were lined up down the street. My friends all giggled and joked around, splashing soap on one another, scrubbing down cars, flirting with guys. Dan had arrived and was talking with Angela off to the side. But I stood alone, just holding the hose, still aware of the guy under the tree. He hadn't moved in hours.

It'd been a weird morning. First with Mom and Dad, then with my psychotic drowning incident, then to this guy who bothered me like a sliver under my skin. I peeked over at Dan again. He looked gray, even in the sunlight, sweat lining his face. He shouldn't be out.

"Clara!"

I blinked and slowly turned to the voice. A dark-haired girl came sprinting toward me, pushing people out of her way. Her curly hair was wild around her face, her small features tight with what looked like fear. She couldn't be more than five feet tall. Her eyes slithered from side to side as if someone were after her. She ran right up to me, grabbed my arm, and tried to drag me away.

"What? Who are you?" I asked. I planted my feet securely into the ground and sprayed her with the hose. She shrieked and jumped back, glaring.

"What do you think you're doing?" she yelled. She swiped the water out of her face. She darted forward again and grasped my other arm. I was starting to spray her again when Dan appeared next to me.

"Everything okay?" Dan asked.

The girl looked at Dan like he had just grown a third eye. She then coolly turned her head to me and said, "We have to leave. *Now.*" She gave another futile attempt to pull me. Her face twisted in frustration as she screamed, "They're coming right now! Clara, come on! We have to move!"

I yanked away again. "What are you talking about?"

In a heartbeat, screeching pierced the air as a group of shiny SUVs pulled up, surrounding the remaining sudsy cars. The doors opened in sync, and about a dozen men in sunglasses emerged from the vehicles, stepping into the parking lot. The men glanced around, as if searching for someone.

The girl groaned. "See? I told you! It's not too late. Let's go!"

But I stayed put. The entire car wash stopped. The guy under the tree stepped out from the shadows to greet the men. It was *him*. He'd called them. I looked back at the girl. Maybe she was right. These guys probably *were* trouble. But I continued to stare. I didn't move. The girl grunted in frustration next to me.

Another car door opened and a teenage guy in black holey jeans and a T-shirt stepped forward. A grouping of clouds closed in on the sun, and the abrupt shadows played off the sharp lines of his face. He moved forward, parting through the men, an air of authority about him. His gaze swept slowly through the crowd, stopping when he met the tree guy's eye.

The two guys faced each other, speaking low. The car wash seemed to pick up again, and my friends went back to their games.

"Who are those dudes?" Dan asked.

I stayed fixated on them, unable to look away. "I have no idea."

"I can tell you," the girl said to me. "My name's Ricki. You can trust me. They're here for you. And I'm here to warn you. So listen to me, and let's go!"

The men surrounding the parking lot all wore suits, their eyes hidden behind their sunglasses. They definitely weren't here to use the slip 'n' slide Daniel's friends had set up at the back of the lot.

I turned to Ricki. "Why on earth would I be in danger?"

"Just trust me," she said.

I nearly rolled my eyes. "Well, then, I'm going to go find out why they're here." I spun on my heel and headed over to the group of guys.

"Wait! Clara! No!" She rushed to keep up with me. Dan followed.

Tree Guy and Mr. Holey Jeans Guy both turned as I approached. The clouds covered the sun, and a sudden cool breeze swept in. I stopped, planting myself in front of them. I had no idea what I was going to do—I just wanted to get the dark-haired girl off my back. And the tree guy was still irking me.

The jean guy's eyes lifted, and our gazes caught.

Everything stopped. Familiarity hit me like a smack to the face.

I knew him. I *knew* I knew him.

The guy had dark hair that swooped across his forehead, his right ear framed by multiple piercings that ran up along it. His cheekbones were strikingly unfair, sharp and prominent just like his jawline. His eyes were two different colors—one blue, one black.

I couldn't stop staring.

Surprise lit the guy's face and he smiled, his teeth blindingly white.

"I didn't think you were speaking the truth, Gherry," the guy said. "But look at her. She's right here, flesh and *blood*."

My brows pushed downward. "Do I know you?" I peeked over at Gherry. So that was the tree guy's name.

The cute guy barked out a laugh. Amusement lit his eyes. "I can't believe it. You're right, Gherry. She has no idea." His lips quirked. "I'm Nowen," he said, and offered me his hand.

I stared down at his palm.

Nowen? An odd name.

I didn't take his hand. I just continued to stare. But instead of Nowen drawing it back, he took a step closer to me. He slowly reached his fingers forward and touched the ends of my hair.

"I like it short," he said. "It looks good on you."

I didn't move. I couldn't breathe. I don't know why. I should've jerked back, swatted his hand away, but I stood there, heart pounding.

"Stop!" Ricki said. She dove between us and pushed his arm away. "I don't know who you are, but you—" She turned to Gherry. "I *knew* you were up to no good."

Gherry shrugged and folded his arms. His green eyes narrowed behind his glasses. "None of this is your concern, Aericka. Go back to your grandmother and school and whatever else it is you do."

My head darted to her. "You know him?"

She ignored me. "I'm not letting you take her."

Gherry's face contorted, and he started forward, but Nowen placed a hand on his chest, stopping him.

"No," Nowen said slowly. "The girl is right. Clara, we're not here for you." His mouth curved upward.

I peeked between the three of them. "Then who are you here for?"

Dan, who'd been silent through this exchange, touched my elbow. "I think we should leave," he said.

Nowen snapped his fingers and two men from his entourage stepped forward. One had a bald head and a claw tattoo that ran up the back of his skull. The other had blond hair with frosted tips and sunglasses that looked like they came from the eighties. Both men were stacked with muscles.

"We're here for your brother," Nowen said. "Siv, Dane, now."

Dan's eyes widened. "What?"

It all happened too fast.

Siv and Dane reached forward simultaneously and gripped Dan's upper arms. They yanked him off his feet and started to drag him to one of the SUVs.

"What? Stop!" Dan yelled. "Clara!" He kicked his legs, thrashed side to side, but he was too weak.

I stood frozen for two heartbeats until reality kicked in. I leaped forward. "Dan!"

I tried to shove past Nowen, but he snatched my shoulders, holding me in place.

"Sorry, Dessy," he said. "It's not you I need. But I'm sure we'll run into each other again." He half smiled.

I tried to wrench away, tried to yank back, but he kept me firmly in place until the car doors slammed with Dan inside.

"Dan!" I yelled.

"Don't worry about him," Nowen said. "He'll be fine. I think." His mouth twisted before he patted me on the cheek. "See you soon."

His blue and black eyes took me in for a moment, searching me, almost curious, until he abruptly spun around and headed toward his own vehicle.

The SUVs pulled out of the parking lot, and before I could process exactly what had just happened, my vision started to darken, and stars sparkled in my vision.

Ricki grabbed my arm, steadying me.

"Don't worry," she said. "We can find him. I'll help you find Dan."

I couldn't stop staring at where he had left. This wasn't happening. Dan couldn't have just been *kidnapped*.

"Where are they taking him?" I asked. "What do they want with him? How do you know me?" I had too many questions and not enough answers. It was making me dizzy.

"It's too long of a story," she said. "And you wouldn't believe me if I told you. But just know that I've been searching for you on this side for a long time, and I can't believe I found you. You're in danger."

Was this all a joke? Was she into roleplaying? Were all those guys pretending to be characters because they were obsessive fans of some comic book or TV series?

I rubbed my forehead. "None of this is making sense."

She groaned. "I know—that's the problem. If you could just connect your two lives, all of this would be so much easier."

Anger rose in my chest and I spun on her. "This isn't funny," I said. "Whatever you're doing—whatever you're all doing—this isn't funny. Tell me where Dan is."

"I don't know!" Her voice intensified. "If I knew, I'd tell you. All that we know is that they've been keeping your grandmother Laela captive for quite some time. I thought they wanted you, but clearly not. I don't know what their plan is."

My heart dropped.

Grandma Laela?

"Clara, you have to trust me. I can help you. I'm your Companion. I know that doesn't mean anything to you, but Laela was Companions with my Grandma Fae, and not only just Companions, but Blood Companions. So we have history. You and I are linked. We—"

"Stop." My head was starting to get fuzzy again. She knew about my Grandma Laela? She was mocking her. Somehow, she found out what Laela used to talk about and now Ricki was making fun of her. "Companions" and "other lives" and people "after her." Grandma used to wink at me like she knew a secret that I'd be in on one day. But then she had disappeared, and we never saw her again. And now Ricki was saying these guys who took Daniel had also taken Laela, too?

No.

This was a joke. A prank. She found out about Laela and now she was making fun of my family.

My head felt light, and the stars returned to the fringes of my vision. I tried to blink them away, but every time my eyes closed and reopened the stars doubled in number. I swayed.

"Whoa, Clara, are you okay?" Ricki asked. She gripped my arm, trying to stabilize me, but I knew it was too late. I was going to faint. The ground seemed to tip beneath me, and I fell, the world going black.

12
Lucid Dreaming

Wind whizzed past my face, and my body plummeted.

Darkness.

Nothing but darkness.

I was falling. Traveling. But where?

I'd been to my other life. I didn't know *how* I knew, I just knew. I'd been in the pool, I'd been drowning. And then I was . . . gone.

Until now.

Now I was in this never-ending pit of darkness, traveling fast.

I let the darkness carry me, my body whirling around. I wasn't sure how long I was trapped in the darkness. It could've been days, hours, or minutes. My hands reached out, searching for anything, but I only met air. I'd never heard of such a space. Unless I was in . . .

The Dhim.

The place between our two lives.

Was I in the Dhim?

Panic rose in my throat, and my arms continued to flail. People got lost in here—never to be seen again. It's what happened to my grandmother, Laela. I pushed my legs in a swimming motion. Which way was I going? Back to my life in Khalom? Or my Cursed life? Was

I even moving at all? I struggled for a time. Again—for days, hours, or minutes?

Something in the air began to tug at me, seeming to pull me in one direction. It was like a cord had caught me around the waist and a set of blinds snapped up. Light seared my vision and I blinked.

Ricki hovered over me, a frown between her brows. "There you are," she said. "Are you okay?"

"Ricki?" I coughed, sitting upright. "Where—" I glanced around me. The gym was empty, the swimming pool lapping softly next to me. I shivered, peeling my wet shirt away from my skin.

"You were gone for a few minutes," Ricki said. "You disappeared, which means . . . well . . . do you—?"

I shook my head, the world still coming into focus. "No." I said it short, clipped. I'd only been gone a few *minutes*? Which meant it was longer on the other side. Hours over there were only minutes here.

I staggered to a standing position, my hair and clothes still dripping wet. "What happened?" I asked, though I already knew. Everyone knew I was a fraud. Everyone had seen me lose to Lionel. He'd won, and now I was exposed. I was the loser who didn't have any powers.

Ricki stared at me, slightly pale. She seemed different, like something weighed heavy on her.

"Are you okay?" I asked, shivering.

Ricki let out a small chuckle, but it seemed forced. "Yeah. I just wish you had your lives connected."

"You and me both," I mumbled. "I would've by now if it weren't too dangerous to have someone with Mind do it for me." I thought of Robert before I returned to the topic at hand. "What *really* happened?"

"After you passed out from drowning and disappeared, the room went into an uproar," Ricki said. "A few kids shouted about how you were a fake and how Death hadn't really returned, but then Mr.

Tompkins smoothed it over so fast. He said that you *let* Lionel win because you were afraid of using your Death powers—because we had just talked about how Death could kill, right? That it was *wise* of you to back down. The kids all agreed."

My jaw chattered. "And do you think that? That Death—me—could kill?"

Ricki rolled her eyes. "Please. You're harmless. Look at you." But I swear fear flashed in her eyes.

"Come on." She linked her arm through my elbow. "Let's get you a new set of clothes. You don't want to miss your next class. You're already behind as it is. And we *have* to get your lives connected. Class is our best hope of doing that."

I couldn't shake the darkness that had wrapped itself around me. I still felt as if a part of me was stuck in the Dhim. An icky feeling settled between my shoulders, making me uneasy. I felt like something bad was happening in my other life.

I stood tucked in the corner of the classroom, dozens of stares flicking to me every few seconds. I didn't know why I thought pressing up against the wall would make me invisible. It'd been so long since I'd been around these kids. I'd known them, we had history together, but now they were strangers. I tried to keep my eyes on the marble floor. White desks sat in rows, and kids sat on top of them, chatting in groups.

Several Mind girls stood in front of me, ignoring me. They were giggling, their outfits changing, melting before my eyes, as they experimented with different ensembles. Bright green pants morphed into a pink miniskirt. A deep purple blouse turned to an orange V-neck. Kids loved colors here because Khalom was void of it.

"What about this?" Mhaggie, Deena's best friend, asked. "Do you think he'd like this?" She spun around, and her blue jumper melted into a red silk blouse and skirt, clashing with her red hair and the purple flicks of energy around her.

"Ew, no," Deena answered. "Way too desperate. Maybe something more floral?" Her eyes slid to me before she looked back at her friend.

A loud roar of laughter came from the back of the room. Khalob was doing a dance on top of his desk, his blue spiked hair stiff despite his movement. His eyes caught mine, and he blew me a kiss. I ripped my gaze away and shuddered, forcing myself not to look at him.

My eyes roamed around the room once more, most of the attention off me now. Ricki had left, saying she had somewhere to be, but I wasn't looking for her. I knew who I was searching for.

Nowen.

He'd been the last face I saw before I disappeared inside the pool. But he wasn't here. And if he were, I wasn't sure where he'd fit in. He'd been sitting with the Body crowd earlier, but it didn't seem like his Center was Body. I bit my lips, the vision of his twinkling eyes and smirking face hovering in my memory. I hated to admit it, but he intrigued me in a way that no one else had. I wanted to know what made him tick. And if he was intrigued by me, too.

I shook my head. I shouldn't think of him like that. It was *Cael* who had my heart. Which was ridiculous, considering he was a Stricken and I probably wouldn't see him again. But I couldn't help but wonder what he was doing right now. Was he back at the Stricken camp? Or was he staying true to his word and watching me from outside the gates?

I sighed, remembering the warmth of his voice. It had always slid through me, calming me when I thought the darkness would take over. There was always a lingering darkness that sat dormant in my chest, but the thoughts of Cael kept it at bay. He'd always been my anchor to sanity, but now he was gone. There was a void in my heart and my skin itched, like my body actually needed to be near him.

The room quieted when our teacher walked in. Her high-heeled shoes clopped on the marble floor, and her deep auburn hair was a pile on top of her head. I pushed myself off the wall. It was the High Official who had spoken up for me in the Grand Hall.

She stopped in front of the classroom, her legs long beneath her pencil skirt. She clasped her hands together before she saw me in the corner.

"Claera," she said. "Welcome. I'm Naeomi. Please." She motioned to the desk at the front of the classroom.

The other kids were taking their seats, so I tentatively moved forward before sliding into the ivory wood desk. A skinny kid with blond hair began to sit next to me, but Khalob shoved him aside, planting himself down.

He grinned in my direction, his eyes as blue as his hair. I sealed my lips together and focused on Naeomi. I still hadn't forgiven him for drowning me.

"Welcome to the History of Khalom," Naeomi said. She paced at the front of the classroom, her heels clicking once more. "Today we're going to focus on the days of Ehlissa. If you'll open your books to page twenty."

Naeomi stopped in front of my desk. "I'm so sorry, Claera, but we're out of books. Can you—"

"She can share with me!" Khalob burst out. He scooted his desk over to me, the desk legs screeching on the floor. His cologne smacked me in the face. I tilted my head away, cringing.

Khalob opened the book, leaning in close to me. "Get ready for a snooze-fest. This class is the worst. If you get sleepy, you can lay your head on my shoulder." He lifted his arm and set it close to mine, flexing. He patted his shoulder.

I faced forward, ignoring him. I didn't remember Khalob being this forward with girls back when we were seven.

Naeomi stopped in front of me again. "Claera, it's been a while since you've read our history. Would you mind reading for us? We could all use a refresher."

I straightened in my seat, swallowing. "Me?"

Naeomi gave me a warm smile. "You'll do just fine."

Khalob nudged me. "Do it. You could read in an accent or something. Make it more interesting." He laughed, slapping a hand on his desk. A few other kids broke out in snickers.

Naeomi waited. I glanced down at the page. Read in front of the whole class? I wasn't sure if my nerves could handle that. I already had enough attention on me as was.

But I drew the book closer to me, tracing my fingers along the words. I cleared my throat.

"All of mankind used to live peacefully in Khalom," I said, and my voice squeaked. A few more giggles broke out. I cleared my throat again, heat rushing to my face.

"All of mankind used to live peacefully in Khalom," I tried again, "long before our Cursed life existed. Khalom was where we were created. It was home, until the Great Rebellion. The Divining Masters gathered an army and rose against the Mhystic for control of Khalom. The Mhystic at the time was one person, a young woman named Ehlissa, who held all five Centers. When the battle ensued, Ehlissa, fearing for her life, spread out her powers among the Nobles to protect the gifts. All except Death. That, she kept for herself."

I paused. I'd forgotten Ehlissa had kept Death for herself. Everyone knew she had held all five Centers, but Death had been solely hers.

"She made each Noble sign a contract," I continued, "binding them to Khalom, to hold their Centers sacred, to protect those who weren't Nobles. But it was in vain. Ehlissa lost control of her power and Death killed more people than the Divining Masters did. The Divining Masters overtook the city and the Mhystic's cause was lost. In a desperate burst of will, Ehlissa spread Death across all the land, hoping her people, now gifted with her power, would be strong enough to survive.

"Instead, all of mankind were cast out of Khalom and forced to live in a Cursed world where powers didn't exist.

"The curse brought an end to the battle. Ehlissa governed the city, but the Divining Masters ruled Desolation, where the majority of her people lived. For revenge, the Divining Masters sent their armies out to destroy the memories of all who lived in Desolation, building up their armies to attack again. To this day, they're still determined to overrule the Mhystic."

I paused again, and Naeomi motioned for me to continue, a solemn expression on her face.

I looked back to the book. "Slowly, through time, the people living in the Cursed world have forgotten Khalom and Desolation in its entirety and are now only shadows of their former selves, caught in one of the many layers of thought that happens when they sleep.' They call them dreams, as if Desolation were only a dream.

"Saddened by the loss of her people and ashamed it was her fault, Ehlissa disappeared, having now been gone for a thousand years, never to be seen again."

I shut the book, and silence settled over the room. Though not because anyone was interested. Heads were dropped onto desks, some faces slack with droopy eyelids. One kid was drooling on his desk. I relaxed. People weren't paying that much attention to me after all.

"And you all know that since Ehlissa's departure, the Mhystic is now four separate entities, four individuals who represent each Center. Earth, Mind, Body, and Time and Space," Naeomi said. "They are elected, and members in Khalom give a piece of their Centers to them each year. It's why they're more powerful. Of course Death hasn't been on the Mhystic since Ehlissa herself."

Naeomi continued, but my mind drifted away. An awareness tickled along my back, brushing along my spine, and I knew someone's gaze was on me. I tried to ignore it, tried to focus on Naeomi, but I finally couldn't handle it.

I spun around.

Nowen sat in the back, his lips quirked, his eyes dark with amusement. *When had he gotten here?* I turned back around quickly, my heart beating fast.

"So let's think about the poor people out in Desolation for a moment," Naeomi said, and I tried to shove Nowen from my mind. I'd never had anyone look at me like that. Like he was holding in a secret that only the two of us knew. I could still feel his gaze on my back.

Naeomi linked her hands in front of her. "We Nobles get the privilege of knowing about our two lives, but do you think anyone in Desolation gets glimpses of their Cursed life?"

Deena's hand shot up, but Naeomi ignored her. She focused on me again.

"Claera, you lived out in Desolation for years. Do those poor people have any inkling of their other life?"

The class suddenly took interest, straightening in their seats. The kid drooling on his desk lifted his head. Naeomi cocked her head to the side. No one here knew much about Desolation.

I sat for a moment, thinking. Did they? They were barely coherent because of the daily storms, but they did once have complete memories of their two lives until the Diviners got involved. But did they now?

I thought of Mom. Dad. Angela Cummings's mom.

"No," I said quickly. "The Divining Masters have made sure they don't have any memory of their other life."

Naeomi started pacing again, her lips pinched in a tight line. "Those poor people. What do you think about them on the other side? How much do you think they see of their lives in Desolation?"

We all knew when their bodies slept in their Cursed life, they traveled here to the plane of existence where Khalom and Desolation existed. But I wasn't sure what their "dreams" entailed and how much they saw of their lives in Desolation.

"Whatever they see," I said, "it isn't much. Their minds are so far gone, their glimpses of Desolation are probably a jumble of strange images."

The class remained silent, everyone listening attentively to the conversation.

Naeomi nodded, as if thinking to herself. "I suppose we're lucky then. We Nobles don't realize how lucky we have it."

13
Gateway

The next day, I briefly saw Ricki in the morning. At some point, I'd fallen asleep, which meant I'd been in my other life. All of mankind were either here or there, I just wish I knew where *there* was. By the time I'd peeled my eyes open, Ricki was already up and had rushed out of the room before I could say a word. But I'd shoved it out of my mind because I couldn't focus on her. I needed to concentrate on the tasks at hand.

School.

Death.

Finding my powers.

I swung my legs over my bed and sat for a moment. I shut my eyes and searched my mind, stretched my thoughts and tried to see visions of my other life. Had I just seen anything? Our lives were connected by "dreams" when we slept. But I didn't see anything—just darkness behind my lids. The only clues I had were from when Robert had dived into my mind. My hair was cropped short. I'd been a cheerleader. I had friends.

I groaned and jumped out of bed, refusing to look at myself in the mirror. But Ricki had laid out another pair of fresh clothes on the bed for me. I said a silent thank you and quickly threw on the large red T-shirt and sweatpants. I needed to get to class.

Centers was first, so I wound my way down to the central building on campus and stepped into the main hallways. My footsteps clopped softly until I reached the curtain to the gymnasium. I parted the curtain and stepped inside.

Like before, everyone sat in their cliques, though this time, no one took notice of me. Maybe I was beginning to be accepted here. The Time and Space people meditated with the Earth group off to one side. The Body crowd was paired off, making out in the back corner, and the Mind group, like always, stared people down—except for Lionel. He was Mind and sat on the edge of the mat, alone. He hung his head, a haggard expression on his face. I headed in his direction.

"Hey," I said, lowering myself down next to him. "Nice work yesterday."

Lionel's eyes flicked up to me, and the tips of his ears turned pink. "Not really," he mumbled. His head dipped back down, and he wrung his fingers together.

"No, really," I said, nudging him. "The way you were so calm and composed under that water. I don't think I could ever do that."

"Well, you *let* me win, so I don't know what you're talking about."

I opened my mouth but then closed it. I swallowed down the truth. He couldn't know that he really won. No one could know that I was powerless.

"I remember you from before," I said quietly. "You were smart. Really smart. I'm sorry that—"

"That people only see me as a loser?" he said. He reddened, and his freckles stood out against his skin. "I don't mind. Not really. I've never fit in here."

I fell silent, letting his words hang between us. I didn't fit in here either.

He continued to stare at his hands, and we sat together quietly as I glanced over the large room once more. I knew who I was looking for, but I didn't want to admit it.

I'd first seen Nowen in the Body crowd, and I peered deeper at the clique that had their limbs tangled and lips locked, blue swirling around their heads. Mouths moved over each other, lost in passionate kisses. I forced myself to look away. Heat spread along my cheeks.

I tentatively scanned over the Mind group, and a thick magnetism pushed outward from their direction as they tried to catch the eyes of innocent bystanders. I knew that Centers existed so we would be prepared to defend Khalom at any moment, but I wondered how diving into someone's mind would actually help in a battle.

I forced my gaze away and peeked over at the Earth group.

There.

My heart jolted.

Nowen sat with his long body folded up, eyes closed, meditating. The light cast shadows on his face, accentuating his hollow cheeks and clear-cut bones. His hair was as dark as the shadows under his eyes, jarring against his pale skin. Although he appeared relaxed, his mouth was set tight, tension strumming down him like a taut string. I couldn't help but stare. I'd never been more intrigued by anyone in my life. I wanted to know more about him. I wanted to know what made him tick. I wanted to know . . .

Why he made me feel alive. In a flash, his eyes shot open, and they darted straight to me. I ripped my gaze away. He'd seen me staring at him. Embarrassment swept through me, and I wished I could disappear. Stupid. I was so *stupid*.

"Hey Lionel!" Khalob yelled from across the room. I jerked and peeked over. Khalob had a girl tied around him like a bow, kissing up the side of his neck. "Got yourself a girlfriend?"

Lionel reddened again and his eyes slid to me.

Khalob untangled himself from the girl and sauntered over, his hair extra blue under the fluorescents. "What? No comment?" His mouth crooked upward.

Lionel stayed silent.

Khalob continued to taunt. "I hear Death has even better endurance when it comes to matters of the body. If you catch my meaning." He winked.

An intense energy seemed to come from behind me and I hesitantly turned around. Nowen sat on the ground, his eyebrows pushed downward at Khalob.

People were starting to take interest.

Khalob stopped in front of me, arms crossed. "Why don't you come hang with me?" he asked. "We still haven't hooked up yet. Just because you're Death doesn't mean you have to hang with this loser."

Lionel shrank next to me. I slowly rose to my feet and faced Khalob head on. "You're a bully, Khalob. Turn around and go back to your Body group. Lionel is kinder, cooler, and more brilliant than you'll ever be."

The blue in Khalob's eyes darkened. He moved forward another step. "I know you don't mean that."

I held my ground, lifting my chin. A dark surge of energy suddenly shot into my chest. It swirled and churned inside, burning up my throat.

His smile turned lazy again. "You're missing out," he said. "Body and Death would make a great combination. I'll show you a good time." He reached forward and grabbed my wrist.

Everything stopped.

A shockwave as cold as ice boomed through the room. Pain hit me in a swell so strong, I felt as if my spine had snapped in half. Khalob cried and jerked like he'd been electrocuted. He fell to the floor, twitching, crying out in pain. Black electric currents ran up and down my body, sizzling at my fingertips. Students immediately jumped to their feet, gawking. Shouts rang out and I stood paralyzed, watching Khalob's writhing form.

"Stop!" he yelled. "Make it stop!"

I stared in horror, energy still buzzing through my body. I finally tore my gaze away. Someone needed to help. But only glares were shot in my direction. I glanced back to the Earth group. Nowen was gone.

Khalob continued to cry out. "Get me away from that freak!" He clutched his stomach and curled into the fetal position. "Make it stop!"

I couldn't take it anymore.

I staggered backward, my pulse racing, until I took off, sprinting toward the exit. Mr. Tompkins appeared and gripped me hard on my arm.

"Come on," he said, and dragged me with him. The curtain brushed past my face, and shouts continued to sound from behind. The voices faded as we left the building, racing down the front steps, stopping on the colorless sidewalk.

"Are you *mad*?" Mr. Tompkins growled in my ear. He stuck his face right into mine. "Do you want to get kicked out of Khalom?"

He towed me across campus, farther down the sidewalk. "Clara, you need to keep your powers in check. You know someone doesn't want you here. Or have you forgotten that someone tried to kill you as a child?"

He gripped my shoulders and turned me to face him. We stood right outside the Grand Hall, its white dome tall against the pale sky. A fountain splashed next to us, stone statues spitting water from their mouths.

I froze, my heart pounding. "How . . . how do you know that?"

Mr. Tompkins slowly released his grip.

He ran a hand over his face. "It's obvious," he said. "The people in Khalom have been suspicious of Death since Ehlissa herself. You're a threat to everyone. Did you really think your Grandma Laela just disappeared?" He let out a bitter laugh. "No, someone wanted her gone."

I blinked. *Was it true?* Was Laela's disappearance more than her venturing off into the Dhim to explore? Had someone *harmed* her?

I shook my head. "You think it was me who did that back there? I didn't hurt Khalob."

"Who else?" Mr. Tompkins said, excitement in his eyes. "You've connected your lives, right? I didn't think you had after all that time I spent with you in Desolation. I did that underwater test yesterday just to put students at ease. I didn't want them to be afraid of you. But you *do* have your Death powers."

He waited, eyes intent.

I clamped my mouth shut. What was I supposed to say? Had I been the one who hurt Khalob? I glanced down at my palms. Energy still hummed beneath my skin.

A shadow moved inside the doorway to the Grand Hall, and I turned. Mr. Tompkins stiffened. I stared at the silhouette before my heart lurched.

It couldn't be. I'd know that silhouette anywhere.

"Cael?"

I didn't even think. I left Mr. Tompkins so fast, I didn't even realize I was running. Cael was *here*. Why was he inside the city? Suddenly seeing him was the most important thing in my life.

I hadn't allowed myself to think about it too much—how much I missed him—but the hole was there. Every part of me missed him. His voice. The way he made me feel. The way it felt when I'd seen him for the first time. The way the dark hollows of his eyes had washed over me . . .

"Clara, where are you going?" Mr. Tompkins yelled out.

I ignored him, running until I entered the Grand Hall. I paused in the large foyer, spinning around the marble room, looking around the space.

"Cael?" My voice bounced off the vaulted ceiling. "Cael, please." I glanced around frantically.

I should've been mad at him. He had lied to me for ten years. But he'd also been the only one I could trust. He'd been my only stability for my entire childhood. I'd let myself fall for him. And it seemed like he cared about me, in his own way. He was always there when I needed comfort. He was there when I was alone. He hinted that he cared about me, too, but was it a lie? He had thrust me in here like something he didn't want to deal with anymore. Maybe I was only a job to him. Maybe he'd been ordered to watch over me by some Stricken leader. Either way, I needed to see him. Every part of me ached to be in his presence.

A web of hallways jutted out in every direction, and I looked frantically around, stopping on the far hallway to the left. I squinted. A shadow moved along the wall, traveling fast.

"Cael!"

Why wasn't he answering me? I sprinted into a full run, chasing after the shadow on the wall, its figure always several steps ahead of me. The hallway twisted and turned, and as I ran past portraits of people lining the walls, I felt their eyes on me, judging me.

The hallway began to descend at a deep incline, the air cooling a few degrees. The space narrowed and darkened, with torches starting to line the walls. The flames flickered, casting dancing shadows on the floor.

I didn't call out Cael's name again. I was beginning to think I'd imagined him. Mr. Tompkins hadn't seen anything. But something in the air kept me pushing forward . . . like something in this hallway *wanted* me here. I slowed but continued forward. I'd never been in this secluded section of the Grand Hall before.

The hallway came to an abrupt end, and I paused. A thin, white curtain hung in front of me, the torches illuminating finely stitched swirls and patterns on the translucent material. The bottom of the curtain moved slightly, as if a light breeze wafted inside. I rolled back on my heels, swallowing.

Unease began to spread along my shoulders. Maybe I shouldn't be here. Something beyond the curtain felt . . . eerie. Wrong.

But curiosity drew me forward. And maybe Cael had gone inside.

I gently parted the curtain with one hand and looked inside.

I sucked in a sharp breath.

Before me, a long, white hallway was lined with closed doors. The first doors I'd seen in Khalom.

The doors were made of pale wood, old and worn on the outside, each with a brass knob.

What was this place?

I looked behind me. I'd gone too far. The uneasy feeling in my chest grew. I should turn around, but what was waiting for me? Mr. Tompkins and a lecture? Classmates who thought I was a freak? I faced the hallway of doors once more. Before me was a mystery. The unknown. And maybe Cael. Steeling myself, I tentatively stepped forward.

The moment my foot stepped into the hallway, a cacophony of noise smacked me in the face. I stumbled back, covering my ears.

Loud bangs and screams echoed through the narrow space, scraping at the doors, rattling the doorknobs. The sounds scratched at me from the inside out, making my insides raw. Shadows passed beneath a few doorways, as if people were pacing beyond them. More screams ricocheted. People were *locked* behind these doors. And they wanted out.

It was then I realized where I was.

The White Wing.

It was where they locked the rule breakers of Khalom. It's where they kept the insane. Where they hid people away who needed to be contained. Once you were in here, you hardly ever left.

The screams continued. I couldn't move. It was as if the noise itself gripped me, trapping me.

I tried to see clearly through the chaos, but my vision wavered. A white curtain hung at the other end of the hall, still and silent. I should've gone back the way I came, but in the chaos, all I could think to do was to continue forward. An escape. I forced my feet to move, my heart quickening.

More screams.

More bangs.

More scratches.

Each sound jolted through me, my entire body shaking.

"Help!" someone cried.

"Let us out!"

"I know you're there. I can sense you there."

I wrapped my arms around myself and pushed myself to go faster. I was almost there. Another scream. Like someone was being tortured. Another bang. Another crash.

I reached the end of the hall and threw myself past the curtain.

I paused on the other side and bent over, breathing with my head between my legs until my pulse slowed. The noise was gone. I slowly straightened and peered upward.

A long spiral staircase wound in front of me, circling up to another floor. I glanced around me. I was in a small alcove. I didn't see another exit—it was either back into the White Wing or up the stairs. I cursed myself for thinking Cael was here. I cursed myself for venturing where I shouldn't have. What if something worse was up ahead?

I didn't waste time. The memory of the White Wing was too much. I sprinted upward, taking two steps at a time. Chills stuck to my skin, running up and down my back. Halfway up, I slowed, my hands on the cool, metal banister. I couldn't remember the last time I'd been that afraid. Even the daily storms hadn't scared me that bad.

I continued to wind upward until I stepped into the upper room. The space was small, only a few steps long, with two curtains facing each other on opposite walls. One curtain was white, the other black. The white one shimmered and flowed to the ground, the material light. It had to be the exit. But the black one . . .

It hung motionless, heavy, still as death.

I didn't know what was wrong with me today. Had the White Wing taught me nothing? I shouldn't have continued forward, but something about the dark curtain . . .

As I stared at the thick, black material, an invisible energy pulsed outward, stretching toward me like translucent claws. The energy gripped my chest, creating a warmth that suddenly surged through me. The feeling calmed me, settling my mind, my body, my nerves. It was as if I were nothing but air, existing only for the sole purpose of drawing closer to this black curtain.

I put one foot in front of the other, letting the warmth carry me onward. The closer I approached, the faster my heart beat.

I slowly reached a hand forward, my fingertips brushing the dark curtain. The material was surprisingly silky, smooth to touch, gliding along my skin. My muscles relaxed further, the tension draining from my neck and shoulders. Whatever was behind the curtain, it wasn't bad. In fact, it called to me—*wanted* me to go inside.

I leaned forward, gripping two sides of the curtain, and without another thought, I stuck my head inside.

Vertigo immediately seized me, spinning my vision around a couple of times. The chaos swirled, stirred, screamed—before it let go. Ringing sounded in my ears.

I blinked, trying to focus on one single object, but nothing was there. Complete darkness stretched out before me, nothing but a blank space. I widened my eyes, striving to see anything—but nothing was there. *What was this place?* Though a deep part of me knew. This was the *Dhim*. It had to be. I'd traveled in this dark space before I'd woken up from the pool incident. I kept a firm grip on the curtain beside me. I felt as if were I to let go, I'd tumble inside and be lost in the dark space.

Then I heard it.

Voices.

"So you'll bring her then?" It was a male voice.

"Yeah, I'll figure out a way."

I stopped. I knew that voice.

It was *Ricki*.

"You won't regret this, I promise," the male voice said.

"I know," Ricki said. "Robert, I'd do anything for you. You know that."

Robert?

"You have to bring her outside the gates, don't forget."

"I know. I'll see you soon."

It went silent.

I couldn't take the darkness anymore. I gripped the curtain and threw myself backward, back into the tiny room. I staggered, gripping my head, everything spinning. The world slowly righted itself, and my vision cleared.

Ricki was against me. She wasn't my friend. She wanted to take me outside the gates to Robert. The thought of his greasy hair and crooked nose flashed to mind. She was working with him? Deena had said he was a Diviner. That Ricki'd been in love with him.

I stood still for a long while, trying to process this information. Ricki was lying to me. Just like Mr. Tompkins had lied to me. Just like Cael had lied to me.

Once again, a person I was beginning to trust had abandoned me.

I didn't have anyone.

14
Blood, Love, and Steel

When I emerged from the Grand Hall, Nowen was leaning against a tree in front of me, foot propped up, arms folded. His dark hair stood stark against the white leaves around him, and a smirk stretched over his face. He looked unearthly, mythical, like he didn't belong here. Like he couldn't be just a regular student going to school.

The sight of him made my stomach flutter. I was beginning to look forward to the moments I had with him. Though the revelation with Ricki still hung heavy on my shoulders. I released a frustrated sigh.

"Something wrong, Dessy?" He lifted his brows.

"What are you doing here?" I asked. Even though a part of me wanted to see him, I also couldn't trust him—I couldn't trust anyone.

"I wanted to see you," he said. "You sure were in there a while. What'd you do? Get stuck in the Dhim?"

I stopped, furrowing my eyebrows while concentrating. There's no way he could've known where I'd just been. I shook my head. "Where'd you go, back at the gym? You disappeared, like you always do. One minute you were glaring at Khalob and then—"

Wait. I paused. "Were *you* the one who attacked Khalob?" Maybe it wasn't me after all. Mr. Tompkins thought it was, but it couldn't be. I didn't have any powers.

He scoffed and pushed himself off the tree. His mouth flicked up on one side. "Why would I do that? I have no problem with Khalob. Unless . . ." He slowly sauntered toward me. "You *wanted* me to hurt him? Do you want me to be protective of you? Save you when you're in trouble?"

My heart accelerated. "No." It came out too quick.

He continued forward until he stopped inches from me. A chunk of his hair hung over his forehead, and his blue and black eyes stared down at me. "I would, you know. If you needed me, I'd help you."

I stared back, too afraid to move. Like always, something about him made me feel alive. Little tingles buzzed on my nerve endings, like a part of me was drawn to him—like my subconscious had known him a long time.

"I don't need your help," I said, though I wanted to say the opposite. I wanted someone to help me. I wanted someone to care. I didn't want to be alone.

A trace of a smile teased his lips, and he took a step back. He circled around me, and he linked his hands behind his back. "You really do need to consider that it was you who hurt Khalob. You are Death. Rumor has it that you're seeking revenge for being kicked out of this place for so many years." He paused in front of me again, but this time, he didn't smile. He stared at me intently.

"I would know if I had attacked someone," I said. "And I didn't."

Nowen's eyes narrowed. "Dessy, this is serious." He took my shoulders, and the sudden touch made me freeze. "People think you are about to start a murdering spree. Now, *I* know that's ridiculous." His lips pressed in tighter. "Though, there is something up with you." He studied me. "And I'm trying to figure out what it is."

I didn't have a response to that.

"Walk with me?" he asked. He held out his elbow.

I stared at the offering before shaking my head once more. "No. I don't think—"

He took my hand anyway and linked it through his arm. He headed down the white path in front of us, and I sighed. Maybe it wouldn't be so bad to spend a moment with him.

Clouds partly covered the sky, slivers of white sunshine peeking through. We strolled on the sidewalks that wove through the perfectly manicured lawns, not a crystalized leaf out of place. I peeked over at him. The light played off the deep grooves of his sculpted cheekbones, the sunlight through the leaves casting splotchy shadows on his face.

"It had to have been horrible," Nowen said after a moment. "Living out in Desolation all alone."

I gave him a curious glance. *Did he actually care?*

"In a way, I know what that's like," he continued. "To be alone." His eyes were focused in front of him, his face hard. "I wouldn't wish that on anyone. People should be free, free to live their lives."

I stayed silent, absorbing his words.

We stepped off the path and crossed the grass, stopping under a copse of trees. Nothing surrounded us, just the white shrubbery and the fence a few feet away.

The sight of the fence sent a wave of sickness through me.

Nowen kept his gaze down at his feet. "I know it's probably hard to trust me," he said. "But I guess I just wanted to say that I know what it's like to be trapped in a place you don't want to be." His eyes lifted and he peered out into the dark green forest. "If you ever need to talk about it, I'm here."

I glanced between him and the forest outside the fence. From the way he looked longingly outside the gates, there was a story there. I tilted my head up at him.

"What happened to you?" I asked.

A rustle came from the bushes outside the gates, and Nowen stiffened. His eyes darted over, and he held still, like an animal waiting to be attacked.

"What is it?" I asked, and my heart started pumping faster.

Nowen stayed frozen, his eyes locked in front of him.

"I'm not sure," he mumbled. "Maybe nothing. Or . . ." His eyes widened. His arm abruptly shot out at me, and he pushed me back, stepping in front of me.

One by one, dark figures emerged from the forest, forming a line, the sun shining through their bodies. They stood alert, stiff, as if ready for battle. The figure in the middle stepped away from the group, planting himself in front of them, his hands on a silhouetted sword that hung at his hip.

Adrenaline jolted through me, and I stumbled back a step.

Cael.

Seeing him here was the last thing I expected. *What was he doing?* Was he here to see me? I put a hand over my heart.

Cael seemed to look at me for a moment, the dark hollows of his eyes connecting with mine before he turned his attention to Nowen.

"This is a warning," Cael said. His voice was smooth, silky, and my body instantly reacted. Warmth slid down my spine. His voice had once been my entire life. But I hated that it still had an effect on me.

Nowen's face hardened, lines creasing his mouth. "And what? Come to finish the job you started? You know I would love that. You know your sister would love that."

Sister?

I blinked, glancing between them. "You *know* each other?"

"I'm not here to fight," Cael said, ignoring me.

Nowen laughed, the sound low and menacing. "That's exactly what you're here to do. Why else would you have your little shadow army here?"

The army shifted, poised. Cael held up a hand. "I'm stronger than I was the last time we fought. This time, I will win."

Nowen shrugged, the smirk back on his face. "You win, I win, is there a difference? The end result will be the same."

Nowen turned to me and linked his arm around my shoulders. He drew me close to his side. I didn't move. My thoughts were spinning too fast.

Cael's gaze slowly slid to mine. Our eyes connected again, and something in the air merged between us.

A power? An understanding? Every bit of frustration that had been scratching at my skin melted away. I stayed locked in his presence—I didn't even feel Nowen at my side. It was like we'd never been apart.

I'm still here, he whispered in my mind.

My heart started racing. I couldn't stop staring at him.

Was he saying that he cared?

He was still here.

My thoughts were flipping back and forth too fast.

Nowen's glance jumped between Cael and me, his brows digging together, until amusement lit his eyes. He took a step away from me and barked out a laugh. "Him? *Him?* Seriously? Well, this should be interesting."

Cael and Nowen continued to face each other, standing so alike it was as if Cael was merely Nowen's shadow, cast in the light from the sun.

Nowen widened his stance. "Let's see what you're really made of. You and me, right now. Let's end this."

Cael reached down and unsheathed his shadowy sword. He held it in front of him, taking position. "Agreed."

Tension hung thick in the air between them, the two a perfect mirror of each other.

"Wait, what?" I asked. "What do you mean *end this*?"

Cael's presence still had a grip on me; it was hard to process what was happening.

"Don't worry, Dessy," Nowen said. "I won't let him hurt you anymore." He tensed, and before I could say another word, they charged.

Nowen and Cael rushed toward each other, feet pounding. They hit the gate at the same time. Cael grabbed the bars of the fence and opened his mouth to yell—speak—something, but at the last second, Cael let go and backed away. Nowen bounced off the gate as if it were made of rubber, landing hard on his backside.

"Coward!" Nowen shouted from the ground. "Let me out!"

Cael simply stood there, his chest rising and falling, staring Nowen down, until he turned to me. "Stay away from him, Clara. Don't let him near you. You do, and he will kill you."

15
The Black Rose

Mhystic Studies was located at the back of the old church in Historic Quarter, inside a small, gated area. Our teacher, Bhrutus—the lead High Official—thought it appropriate to have class outside next to Ehlissa's shrine—a statue encased inside a smaller gate, with a large plaque and a swirl of vines that wrapped around the archway that encased her.

Bhrutus hadn't arrived yet, so per usual, my classmates were grouped together, with me alone. This was the first class I'd been to since the Khalob incident. Glares were thrown in my direction, though fear had also creeped into their expressions. Several girls passed by me, but not without scooting as far away from me as they could.

I hadn't seen Ricki since yesterday. I had no idea where she was. Was she still plotting something behind my back? What did Robert want with me? I glanced behind my shoulder, as if someone were watching me now.

More stares came from the Body crowd at the edge of the small gate, and I maneuvered away from them, shaking out my hands. I needed to move. I needed out of here. But where would I go? I stepped away from as many people as I could, but I could still hear their whispers.

"She tried to kill him," one girl whispered.

"She should be kicked out," another one said.

"Look at her, thinking she's better than the rest of us."

"She needs to be stopped."

I paused by Ehlissa's statue, and tucked myself up against her, hiding in her shadow. I breathed in deeply, trying to block out the whispers.

I hadn't allowed myself to think about Cael and Nowen yet. Cael had to be wrong about Nowen. He wasn't a danger to me. It'd been the opposite. He'd opened up to me yesterday. He'd been vulnerable. Though he hadn't responded when Cael accused him. He'd only disappeared, like he always did.

But the words still rang in my mind.

Stay away from him, Clara. Don't let him near you. You do, and he will kill you.

I shook my head. Impossible.

With me hidden, the kids surrounding me began to fool around, pushing and teasing one another, their laughter bouncing off the towering church above us. Off to the side, a Body girl was lifting a stone bench over her head, blue sparks flaring around her with every rep. A few of the Mind kids were practicing their shape-shifting abilities. One kid was trying to shift into a cat, whiskers and a tail sprouting from his body.

But that was as far as his transformation went before, in a shower of purple sparks, he shifted back, cursing. Others had their hands outstretched before them, levitating other classmates off the ground. A Time and Space girl off to the right was using heat from her fingertips to straighten her friend's hair.

They were using their Centers for fun. But could they use them in battle?

I ducked my head and circled around Ehlissa's statue. The clouds above me lumbered along, gray against her porcelain skin. I reached up a hand and gently traced my fingers against the base of the statue, the stone smooth and cool beneath my fingertips. Her face pushed through the stone, her carved features delicate and lovely, but her eyes . . . they looked as if they were screaming in pain. Her gaze seemed to connect with mine, and I could *feel* her fear.

I yanked my gaze away.

Statues didn't have eyes that cried out with pain. *What was wrong with me?*

Two girls who apparently weren't afraid of me passed by. Their eyes slid over me, and they giggled, glancing down at my oversized T-shirt and sweatpants. I peered down, smoothing out the wrinkles and wiping away dirt splotched in several places.

The girls walked away, their clothes morphing into a mirror of my own before they laughed and their clothes changed back into their own colorful ensemble, a trail of purple sparks crackling in the air behind them.

I stared after them, heat rising in my cheeks. So not only was I looked at with disdain and fear, but I was also pitied.

I stepped away, a heaviness swirling in my chest. It gathered like a storm, building, blinding me, turning my vision red. Energy fizzled in my fingertips, buzzing. I suddenly had the urge to *hurt* them. I knew I was capable of it. Death was the only Center that could kill. What would it feel like to eliminate anyone who got in my way?

What? That was a horrible thought. I rubbed the back of my head.

From my peripheral vision, I saw Ricki rush into the courtyard, and I turned. Her eyes scanned the space until they landed on me. She waved at me and started to head in my direction, but I groaned and moved away at a fast pace. I couldn't face her yet, not after I'd heard her and Robert in the Dhim. I ducked around the statue, hiding. I bumped into Deena.

"Oh." I staggered back. "I'm sorry, Deena."

Deena blinked, and an inkling of fear flashed in her eyes. "Clara, hey."

My mouth twisted at the corners. "Are you afraid of me like everyone else?"

Her eyes flicked away, and she ran a hand over her shiny hair. "No, no." She met my gaze again. "Of course not." Though there was hesitancy in her voice.

I took a deep breath. "How is Khalob doing?"

Deena scrunched her nose, seeming to relax. "He's been pretty out of it. He can barely talk and hardly opens his eyes, but he's improving. I hear he's definitely not happy with you."

I nodded. Of course he wouldn't be. He thought I'd tried to kill him.

Deena tilted her head at me. "Something is wrong. Other than the Khalob thing."

I almost laughed. That was an understatement. I'd been trapped in Desolation for years. Mom and Dad were out there. Everyone hated me. I didn't have my lives connected. I was powerless. Nowen was a puzzle. And Cael . . .

"Actually," I said. "Can I ask you something?"

Deena nodded quickly. I wasn't sure if it was out of fear, or if she was excited to share her knowledge. "Anything!"

I took her elbow and drew her up to the fence behind the bushes.

"Do you know anything about a shadow warrior?" I asked. "Have you heard any rumors about one? Maybe one who's famous around here? That lives outside the gates?"

Deena made a face. "I've never heard of a shadow warrior. Why do you ask?"

My mind continued to search. "What about someone who left Khalom? A Noble that went rogue, disappeared, and became a Stricken instead of a Divining Master?"

There was a story between Nowen and Cael, and I had to find out what it was.

Deena cocked her head. "Hmm. I don't know. Any Noble who chooses to become a Stricken and defend the city outside the gates doesn't do it in secret. It's always a big deal when someone makes the decision to give up their Noblehood. You know that people live at least a couple hundred years in Khalom—only the leaders get to live forever—but people who become Stricken choose to give up their long lives. They will only live a normal mortal existence, so I don't think it's possible for someone to give up their Noble name without the city knowing."

Deena paused for a moment before she continued, "But now that I think about it, there is a story about Ehlissa's lost brother. A legend, really, and one that's been passed down for a thousand years."

Ehlissa had a brother?

The thought tickled the back of my brain, and the memory of Nowen's voice resonated inside my head. He said Cael had a sister. I bit my lips. There's *no way* Cael could be this lost brother, could he? Ehlissa couldn't be his sister.

But the idea still had me intrigued.

I gripped Deena's arm. "Tell me."

Her eyes turned serious.

"No one takes the legend seriously. It's rumored that Ehlissa's brother was just as powerful as she, holding all five Centers and, technically, the right to rule over Khalom. If people did take the legend seriously, that would mean Khalom's rightful leader was shirking his responsibilities. And even worse, with all five Centers and the power to destroy Khalom, he would be far more dangerous than any Divining Master. It's said that in Ehlissa's time, *he* wanted the throne, but it was only the female line that was chosen to rule back then. His sole purpose was to lead the Stricken. Together, he and Ehlissa kept balance between the two worlds. One inside the city, and one out. Ehlissa knew it, the people knew it. But he didn't want to leave the city."

"So what happened?" I asked.

"The Great War," she said. "The brother refused to leave and protect the city. But during this time, the Divining Masters started an uprising. It's how they broke through the city—the brother wasn't doing his duty. Of course we know the rest of the story. Ehlissa did everything she could to protect the city, but instead of establishing order, she spread Death across the land, creating Desolation. She disappeared . . . and the brother disappeared, too."

"And no one has seen him since?"

Deena shook her head. "If you choose to believe the legends. There aren't any records to prove he ever existed. For all we know, he could be out there, plotting to take the throne—to take what he believes is his. Or, it could just be a scary story parents tell their Noble kids before bedtime."

"It has to be a story, right? I mean, wouldn't we know if Ehlissa's brother was still out there?"

Deena shrugged. "Anything is possible."

I nodded, mind racing. If this brother did exist, he'd be the most powerful person alive. Once again, I thought of Cael. It couldn't be him. It *couldn't* be. This all had to be a tale.

Bhrutus walked into the courtyard and clapped his hands. Deena jerked and pulled me out from around the bushes.

"Class is starting!" she said.

Bhrutus extended his arms out to the small courtyard. "Welcome, class! Welcome to Mhystic Studies! And fitting to have class today next to the original Mhystic herself—the original holder of all five Centers."

Bhrutus moved over to the statue in the middle of the courtyard. "Without her generous gift, none of us would have our Centers. We owe her everything." He looked at her contemplatively for a moment before he shook his head. "Which is why *studying* the Mhystic is fascinating and important. Ehlissa was the one who appointed our great leaders in the first place."

Bhrutus rubbed his short, black beard. "Before we begin, are there any questions from our last class? Regarding your last assignment or recent studies?"

Deena's hand shot upward of course.

"Yes, Deena?"

"Why is it that we never see the Mhystic? There are four of them. And they *do* rule this place. Aren't they supposed to be the ones advising you High Officials?"

Bhrutus immediately paled before he cleared his throat. He removed a handkerchief from his pocket and patted his forehead. "Oh, they're busy. They're very busy indeed. Any other questions?"

More hands shot up.

"Yes, you, in the back, Mhaggie, is it?" Bhrutus said.

Mhaggie's red hair frizzed out at the sides. "I heard that if you make the Mhystic mad, they'll rip your Centers from you. And that it's the most excruciating thing a person can experience. It's like having your mind peeled apart from the inside out, destroying every inch of you until you cease to exist completely."

Bhrutus let out a hearty laugh. "My dear, that's absurd! The Mhystic would never do that. The Mhystic love us! They are here to guide us and keep Khalom safe. I've spent many hours with the Mhystic, and I assure you they have nothing but love for our city." He broke off and coughed. "Well, no more questions then." He set his hands on his large belly. "Follow me."

But more hands lifted. Bhrutus ignored them and started walking down a small pathway. He led the class away from the statue, turning a corner around the old church and continuing to where a few glass tables stretched out from one end of the courtyard to the other.

On top of the tables were dozens of white roses, like they'd just been plucked, clean and pristine. The kids approached, glancing at one another with questions in their eyes. Apparently Bhrutus had never taught with roses before.

"As part of our training today," Bhrutus said, "it's important to hone and use your Centers for small things. We can't do the larger things if we can't do the smaller things, eh?" He motioned to the tables. "This task goes against the very nature of Khalom, so it will be difficult. Our world is colorless, but today we are going to change that. Each of you will take a rose and, using your Center, find a way to make the rose red—to give it color."

Eyes opened wide and excitement bubbled around me, but my heart sank. This wasn't happening. I was able to escape being ridiculed from the pool incident only because Mr. Tompkins covered for me, but I wouldn't be able to hide behind this. People already hated me after the Khalob situation, what would happen if I failed this task?

"Go, find a rose." Bhrutus waved his hand forward.

My classmates rushed to the tables, shoving one another to find the perfect rose. I sauntered up slowly, my heart pounding with each step.

Bhrutus stepped up next to me. "Go easy on them, Claera. You, more than anyone, should excel at this task. Death is the most powerful Center." He patted me on the back. "So let the other kids at least have the chance to change their roses. Don't end it too quickly."

He stepped away, and I swallowed, continuing forward. If only he knew.

I took a spot behind a rose and stared down at its smooth, white petals. I'd seen red roses out in Desolation, and I'm sure they existed over in our Cursed life so the other kids knew what to do. But I couldn't do this.

Ricki appeared in front of me, taking a place across the table. I forced myself to not look at her, but I could feel her gaze on me. I kept my head lowered, staring at my rose.

"All right!" Bhrutus yelled. "Everyone ready?" He rubbed his hands together. "Get ready . . . set . . . and . . . go!"

At once, kids dipped toward their roses, their faces right up next to the pale flowers. Sparks crackled in the air, yellow, blue, green, and purple light snapping. Several flowers levitated off the table, spinning around in the air. Some kids held their hands right over the flowers, eyes concentrating, mouths whispering strange words.

I couldn't stop staring. I watched each kid work, watched the different colors of Centers explode in the air, even peeked at Ricki whose rose shook violently on the table. My rose remained untouched. What could I do? Nothing. I should just walk away.

But I *didn't* want to be a failure. I didn't want the kids here to think I was pure evil. Maybe if I could make something beautiful, they wouldn't be afraid of me.

I glanced around me. Patches of red started to bloom on several roses, but the petals turned white again after a few seconds. Maybe no one would be able to do it, and I wouldn't be singled out. I just needed to act like I was trying.

I peered intently at my rose, gently lifting it from the table. I twirled the white flower in front of me, analyzing the petals. I could pretend I was trying. No one needed to know.

I closed my eyes and exhaled a shaky breath.

Red.

Think . . . *red*.

I held the rose in front of my face, keeping my eyes closed.

Red.

A rich, beautiful color.

My fingertips tightened on the small flower.

Suddenly, I realized I was trying. I didn't want to pretend.

Red.

Kids growled in frustration around me. Sparks continued to fly around the table. The ground rumbled beneath me.

Focus.

My mind started to drift away. It was just me and the petals. Nothing else existed. No Cael. No Nowen. No Ricki or Robert or Deena or Khalob. No class. No Cursed life. No brother of Ehlissa.

Just the flower and me.

Slowly, a warmth began to tingle in my fingers, stretching up into my palm. It grew hotter, until energy flowed through my veins, every inch of me feeling alert, alive.

My eyes snapped open. Something was happening.

Heat continued to sizzle in my hand, my arm, my chest, my vision. The warmth overtook my body, racing through my veins, until a burst of heat exploded from my fingertips.

Very slowly, a deep red crawled up the petals of the flower. The color bled into the white, taking hold, its texture smooth. Color surged through the small plant, the stem heating up fast. I kept my grip on it, my fingers burning.

Kids around me noticed. They set their roses down onto the table, and I felt every pair of eyes pressing in on me.

I was doing it.

I couldn't believe I was doing it.

After all this time, my powers were with me. They'd just been locked deep inside of me. I'd thought something was wrong with me, that my time in Desolation had done something to me, that the Diviners had hurt me somehow, but no, Death really *was* with me.

An indescribable joy surged through me.

I wasn't a failure.

What would happen next? Would my parallel life suddenly connect? I'd tapped into my Center, which meant I *had* to connect with my other life. But nothing came. I searched through my mind, nothing was there. No, it was coming. My other life was coming. I needed to be patient. Nothing could ruin the triumph of this moment.

The color began to deepen, deepen, then deepen too much. My heart picked up and the stem cooled, the heat fleeing from my body. One by one, each petal began to blacken, the rose started to melt, drooping in my hands, becoming crisp. It shriveled, blackening more, shrinking, until it crumbled, dissolving in my hands.

"No, no, no, no," I whispered. "Stop!"

Whispers erupted around me, and I frantically tried to save the rose from collapsing completely. But the rose disintegrated into ash, the last few pieces slipping through my fingers, falling onto the ground at my feet.

Silence hung.

No one moved. No one breathed.

Not until Bhrutus moved forward.

"Nothing has died here in Khalom since the days of Ehlissa," he said. "I didn't want you to kill anything, Claera. The assignment was to bring color to the rose. I—" He broke off, sweat beading on his brow. "Everyone back to their dorms. We've had enough for today."

I took off first. I couldn't stand there for another second. I sprinted out of the courtyard as fast as I could, desperate to get away from the stares.

I was Death.

But I was still a failure.

I had my Center, but it didn't work right. I didn't have control. Death was known to bring freedom, to defeat the dark, to withstand the Diviners' power, to release them.

But what if I was only destined to kill?

Maybe I had hurt Khalob. I'd killed the rose. What else was I capable of?

I ran up into my room, through the curtain, and threw myself onto my bed. My chest heaved up and down as I stared at the white canopy above me. I squeezed my eyes shut, willing myself to fall asleep. I couldn't be here any longer.

Maybe if I went to my other life, I'd forget all about this one.

I kept my eyes closed for a long time, until my breaths slowed, and I drifted away into sleep.

16

Edge of Time

I slowly sat up from the cement and put a hand to my forehead. Light blinded my eyes as I blinked them open. I'd fainted. One minute, I'd been standing, watching the SUVs peel out of the parking lot, and the next, everything went black.

Wait.

SUVs.

It all came rushing back.

Dan had been *kidnapped.*

The sun beat down; sweat slid down my neck. The dark-haired girl helped me stand, her hands on my back. Her name was Ricki. She told me her name was Ricki. Her mouth was pinched tight, her eyes fixed in a glare.

I still couldn't move. I was probably in shock.

"Dan . . ." I wasn't sure if I said it out loud or not.

"He'll be fine," Ricki said. "I think."

Adrenaline punched me in the chest. I spun on her, clarity sweeping back in. "I need to get to him." If I had been thinking straight, I would've called the cops, but all I could think was to act now.

I glanced around the parking lot. I didn't have a car. I'd have to take one. I brushed past Ricki. The SUVs had turned onto Main Street. I might be able to catch up to them if I hurried.

The kidnappers' names and faces swirled in my head. Dane. Siv. Gherry. And . . .

Nowen.

There was something about Nowen, in particular. Something that ate at me from the inside out. He was so *familiar*.

Ricki hurried up next to me. "Where are you going?"

"I'm going after them," I said, frantically searching for an empty car. My squad still goofed around, soaping up cars, spraying one another with water. Had they not just seen those guys take Dan? Did no one care? Adrenaline pushed me faster. An empty jeep sat up ahead. It was Angela Cummings's. The keys were in the ignition.

I rushed forward, threw open the car door and hopped in the driver's seat.

"Wait!" Ricki said. She slid into the passenger seat as I wrenched the car into gear. I didn't stop her from coming. She clearly knew something about those guys.

I floored it and the jeep screeched out of the parking lot.

Seconds ticked. Wind whooshed into the vehicle, through the open windows. Dan. Dan had been kidnapped. *Where was he?* My hands shook on the steering wheel. Poor, innocent, cancer-ridden Dan. He needed his meds. He needed his cancer treatments. Where were those guys taking him?

I zoomed around car after car, trying to spot one of the SUVs. My eyes darted side to side, in front of me, behind me. I swerved around a car.

Ricki grabbed onto the dashboard. "Clara, calm down. We can get hurt here."

"Here?" I bit out. "As opposed to us not getting hurt somewhere else?" I shook my head.

"We shouldn't be following those guys," Ricki said. "We should be running away from them until we have a plan."

I threw her a dirty look. "I need to go after them. That's the plan. Did you not see them take my brother?"

Ricki groaned. "Clara, if they have your brother, then there's nothing you can do. Trust me, those guys are bad news."

I swerved around another car, honking.

"Can you help me or not?" I asked. "You were pretty adamant about telling me stuff before. You said you'd help me. If you do, then I'll listen to what you have to say. If you won't, then I'll drop you off on the side of the road."

Ricki groaned. "There are a lot more important things at stake than finding your brother," she said. "But yeah. Sure. My family owns a restaurant, Denali's, on the edge of town. Fae, my grandma, will know what to do. Let's go there. She might have an idea where Gherry and the others went."

I nodded and pressed on the accelerator. I needed to focus on something I could control. I took a couple of turns until I said, "So . . . do you know this Nowen guy?" His two different-colored eyes flashed to mind, and my heart thumped. Why did he seem familiar? I'd never seen him before.

"No," Ricki said. She shook her head, and her dark hair swished over her face. "I don't know who that guy is. Which is strange." Her thin brows drew together.

I took a left. "You mentioned my grandma. Why?"

Ricki blew out a breath. "Your grandma was really good friends with my grandma. We think she's alive. And we think these guys have her."

I gave her a droll look. "Seriously? My grandma who's been missing since I was a little girl? All this time, she's been with these weirdos?"

"Maybe," she said. "We're not sure yet. But we're ninety-nine percent sure." Her lips tightened.

"Why?" I asked. "And why take Dan?"

I pulled up to a traffic light and stopped.

Silence hung for a minute, and Ricki twisted her fingers.

"Come on. Talk," I said.

Ricki sighed. "For your blood," she said. "You have . . . a special bloodline. And they want your blood."

I stared at her, mouth open. I wasn't sure whether or not to laugh. If Dan weren't in danger, I probably would have. "You're serious."

"Clara," she said. "I know I must sound crazy. But please, I need you to trust me. I need—"

Ricki broke off, and her eyes widened. Her finger shot up and she pointed at something behind me. "Look out!" she yelled.

I only had a second's warning.

My door flew open, and a pair of strong arms wrapped around me. I was dragged from the car, and a hand covered my mouth. I screamed, but the sound was muffled.

Ricki reacted instantly. Like out of a movie, she exited the vehicle and leaped onto the hood of the car. She dove onto my attacker's back and nailed the assailant in the eye with her elbow. The guy let out a grunt and his hold loosened, letting me go.

"Run!" she yelled again.

I didn't need convincing. I took off down the street in a sprint. I couldn't believe this was happening. Footsteps pounded behind me, and I pushed myself faster. I had no time to think, adrenaline racing through me and keeping me moving forward.

I approached a street corner and rounded it, cutting across the sidewalk. I darted past a parked car and was about to turn another corner when a sharp, biting pain slashed through my leg.

I cried out and fell. Hot concrete met my face, small bits of gravel scraped my skin. It was the last thing I felt before my world went black.

17

Heart of Darkness

I sat up in a rush.

Pain throbbed in the middle of my forehead, and my vision wavered. I put a hand to my head, waiting for the dizziness to subside. My room slowly came into focus. Desk. Chair. Open window. Ricki's empty bed across the way. My pillows squished underneath me as I shifted.

I'd just been somewhere. I could feel it. Unease tickled along my back. Something was wrong.

There'd always been a brick wall between me and my other life, but an echo of what I was feeling over there still lingered in my veins. Maybe the connection to that life was growing stronger. Maybe the barrier was starting to break.

I swung my feet over the foot of my bed, still trying to stabilize. Silence echoed through my room as memories crashed into me at once.

The rose.

Death.

The petals disintegrating, crumbling to the ground.

I groaned and fell back onto the bed.

What did it mean? Had I really used Death? Was it a fluke? I still couldn't remember my other life, which meant I hadn't connected with my Center. Or had I?

I quickly sat up again and sprang out of bed. I paced, the cool floorboards squeaking as I walked back and forth. Maybe I was different. Maybe I didn't need to know who I was on the other side to use my powers here in Khalom. Maybe . . .

I stopped and peered down at my hands.

What if I could use Death right now?

I slowly lifted my eyes to the window. Thin white curtains hung softly, the delicate lace as still as the air around it. The material was white, like the rose. Maybe I could learn to control my powers. I'd tapped into them before, I could again.

Death was known to kill. And Death was known to set Diviners free—which meant that it also restored life. Maybe there was more to my powers than I thought. What if I could restore what was broken? People with Mind were able to read thoughts, and they could also do the opposite: they could block people from their thoughts. What if I could do the opposite, too? Like create life.

I marched over to the curtain, gripped the material, and ripped it down the middle. It hung in shreds, and I was going to mend it. I was going to stitch the material back together. I clenched my fists tight, searching for the dark feeling within me. It was always dark, but warm, and I realized I had always felt it, even back in Desolation.

I narrowed my eyes, mouth set tight. I imagined the material linking together, solidifying once more. I tightened every muscle in my body, every inch of me alive and alert, staring. Within seconds, the dark feeling emerged, and excitement shot through me.

It was there.

It was really there.

But I controlled my excitement, stamped it down, tried to let the feeling gather and grow. I kept my fists tight, and my eyes narrowed.

Mend.

Heal.

The curtain fluttered, and my heart accelerated. I was doing something. I focused harder. The curtain twitched again, the ripped pieces brushing against one another. It moved faster, like a small breeze was pushing each side back and forth. I gritted my teeth hard, my jaw aching.

I was doing it.

Then, the material surged together for only a split second before fire erupted at the tips of the curtain. The orange flame licked upward in a rush, engulfing the entire curtain.

"No!" I yelled. I hurried over, my hands hovering over the fire. "No, no, no."

Smoke billowed outward and I waved my hands, trying to extinguish it.

"What the—? Clara, what is this?" Ricki barged into the room and immediately threw out her hands, a blast of green light shooting toward the curtain. The fire abruptly disappeared, the curtain blackening, until it restored to its original white.

Silence pounded between us.

Ricki's forehead puckered. "What . . . *how* did you do that?"

Instead of answering, I plunked back down onto the bed and covered my face with a pillow.

"I'm mad at you," I said, my voice muffled.

Ricki stayed silent for a few moments. "Why?"

I sat upright quickly, and the bed bounced. "Ricki, *why* are you talking with Robert about me? I know you've been communicating with him. I heard him tell you to bring me outside the gates."

Ricki's lips parted. "How did you . . .?"

"It doesn't matter how!" I slammed my hands onto the bed. "Why are you lying to me?"

More silence.

She stayed absolutely frozen, the color draining from her face, until tears gathered in her eyes. She wrapped her arms around herself and turned away. "I can't handle this anymore. You not knowing. I *need* you to remember who you are."

"Don't change the subject," I said.

"I can't!" She spun back around. "What if you're in danger on the other side?" She slammed her mouth shut.

I slowly straightened. "Why would you think that? Do you know something?"

She sniffed, her face tightening. "You know I can't tell you. It's too dangerous. You could lose your mind if you don't link your lives yourself."

We fell silent.

Finally, I pried once more. "You need to be honest with me about Robert."

She sighed and sat down on the bed next to me. "You're right. I'm sorry."

"Talk to me."

"Robert . . . he's, well, he's in trouble." She sniffed again, wiping away another tear. "And I'm afraid you're the only one who can help him."

"You're serious?" An unexpected surge of anger exploded in my chest once more. I stood up from the bed. "Why would I help him? He tried to invade my mind without asking."

"You don't understand," she said, standing up after me. "He thought he was doing the right thing."

I groaned. "Please don't tell me you're in some sort of twisted, Diviner, power-play relationship with him. I couldn't handle that."

"Ew! Why would you say that?"

"I've heard things. About him being a Diviner. And you being romantically involved with him."

She scowled. "From who? Deena?"

I shrugged, heat on my cheeks.

Ricki stomped like a little girl, and her curly hair bounced. "Robert is a good person!"

"Why are you defending him!"

"We have our differences, and I know what he tried to do to you that day was wrong, but he's more selfless than anyone else I know. And if you knew what he gave up for you—"

She stopped.

My forehead scrunched together. "What'd he give up for me?"

Ricki softened, scrubbing a hand over her face. "His life."

His life?

She nodded. "And I'm not in love with him. He's my *brother*. My older brother. People here knew him by his first name, Bart. He hated the name so he decided to go by Robert. Deena must've heard me talking about Robert at some point with Fae." She swiped a hand over her forehead. "But that doesn't matter. You need to know that you're the reason he sold his soul to a Divining Master."

I gaped. "What? So it's true? Robert is a Diviner?"

Ricki nodded again.

I'd never get the image of those ghost-like beings out of my brain. Deena had reminded me that they shifted between human form and Diviner form.

"You have to help him," she said, and her voice raised in pitch. Tears surfaced again in her eyes. "If you don't, he'll be gone forever. Enslaved forever. Once you become a Diviner, it's your only existence. You don't even exist in the Cursed world. You have to help me save him."

"I still can't believe Robert is a Diviner," I said. We both sat on the bed once again, all the anger from earlier gone.

"Is it that hard to believe?"

I thought of his itchy behavior. His gaunt appearance. Maybe not.

"When did it happen?" I asked.

"Ten years," Ricki mumbled. "Robert's been imprisoned for too long."

Ten years. "The same amount of time I was gone from Khalom."

"Not a coincidence." Ricki twisted her lips.

I lifted my brows.

Ricki sighed. "After you disappeared, Robert never stopped talking about you, even when everyone else forgot. He was convinced that he saw you the night you were kidnapped. He had been wandering along the white gates when he saw a figure carrying you, and the figure stepped through into Desolation. He didn't know for sure it was you until later, of course.

"But Robert had guilt," she continued. "He wouldn't let it go. He felt like he could've saved you—stopped the person from kidnapping you. So he packed up and left Khalom in search of you. It wasn't until later that I heard he'd become a Diviner."

I stilled, every inch of me tensed. I had no idea. Robert had risked his life for me.

"But why did he sell his soul?" I asked. "Why become a Diviner?"

"Clara, how else would he survive out there? He wouldn't have been able to search for you *and* keep his mind without becoming one of them."

Chills spread down my back. There was truth to that.

"So you went out there, too?" I asked.

Ricki leaned forward on the bed, and her dark curls fell over her face. "Fae forced me to. When we learned that Robert had found your location, she sent me out to get him and bring him home, but he wouldn't come back. He *couldn't* come back. He gave up his Noble name. So I stayed. Gherald Tompkins helped protect me.

And I didn't want to leave you alone. When I saw what you were enduring . . ." She glanced away.

"So that's what Fae meant when she said I had already taken one of her grandchildren away from her," I said.

Ricki nodded.

I rubbed my temples. "So now what? How am I supposed to help Robert? I can't stop myself from killing a rose or setting curtains on fire."

Ricki spun to me and took my hands. "Laela did it. She released Diviners. You can, too. So please, let's just go meet with Robert. He wants to speak with you outside the gates."

I pressed my lips together. "Why outside the gates?"

Ricki shrugged. "I don't know. It's more private? He clearly can't come in."

I sat back, my lips tightening more. Something wasn't sitting right. But I had to hear him out. Maybe there was a way I could help him.

"Yeah," I said. "Okay. Tonight. I'll see him."

A smile spread across Ricki's face, and she threw her arms around me. "Oh, thank you, Clara!"

I allowed her to hug me, but I didn't hug her back. I stayed stiff on the bed.

She pulled back and frowned. "I need to return the favor."

My lips tucked inward. "Ricki, there's nothing you can do for me. I'm okay. I'll be fine."

Her frown deepened.

I stood up from the bed and moved over to the window. I peered outside, the tepid air on my face. Down below, students walked through Historic Quarter, wearing their bright colors and smiles.

"We've got to help you connect your two lives," she said. "It's time to start trying. *Really* trying. You haven't heard what the students out there are saying. First the attack with Khalob, and now you destroying the first thing in Khalom since Ehlissa herself? Whispers are starting to circulate. Death is a threat. People might come after you. Not only here, but on the other side, too. If someone finds out you haven't connected your lives, you'll become a target over there. Someone will find you and kill you."

Ricki's words pounded into my being, and I slowly turned from the window. There was fear in her voice, as if she really knew I was in danger on the other side. "What do I do then?"

"You fight back," she said. "Make them afraid of you. Speak up. Show them you're a force. Convince them that you are all powerful. Don't be afraid to use what little powers you have. Your life depends on it."

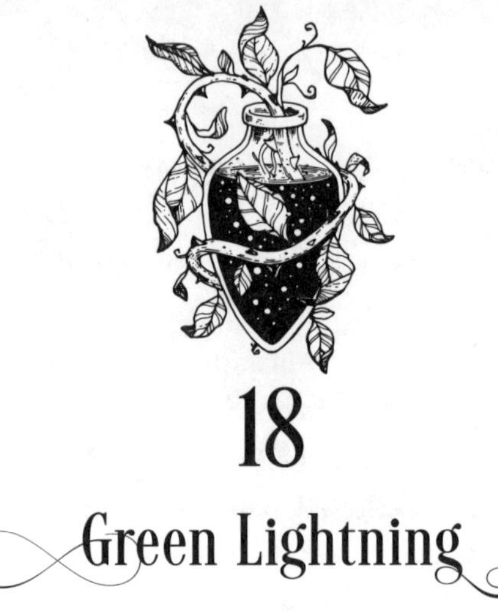

18

Green Lightning

A couple hours later, the class stood at the most northern point of Khalom. Back behind Historic Quarter stretched a long piece of land, the high pearly gates running alongside it. The dark green forest outside stood in stark contrast against the white landscape inside. I peered across the large, pale field. Perfect for a lesson in Celerating. That is, if I could focus on the task at hand.

I sighed, squinting up at the bright sun. Too many thoughts were pulling at me at once.

Connect with my other life.

Save Mom at the Stricken camp.

Keep up my pretense of Death.

Try not to hurt anyone else.

Learn more about Nowen.

Would I ever see Cael again?

I shook my head. I needed to focus.

I stood slightly away from my classmates, waiting for class to start. Their chatter buzzed around my head, floating in my ears, but I forced myself not to listen.

They were probably talking about me.

Graeg, the tall, spindly High Official, glided across the white field, and the class quieted down. He planted himself in front of everyone and linked his gnarled fingers over his stomach. His black robe cascaded to the ground, hiding his bony body.

I hadn't seen him since that day in the Grand Hall—since he'd threatened me with the knife on the altar. His back hunched as he faced us; his tongue darted out as he licked his lips.

"The key to Celerating is knowing you're the one in the driver's seat," Graeg said, his voice gravelly. He looked over each student, one by one. "Like any of your powers, it's the knowledge of this life and the other, combined with your strength of will, that determines how fast you will go."

His eyes stopped on me. "That is if you have your lives properly connected."

I kept still. There was no way he knew.

Graeg smiled slightly before he turned to the rest of the class. "Celerating is important for Nobles to learn because it might be the only way to outrun a pack of Diviners if you are ever attacked." His eyes darkened in humor.

He coughed, and it came out wet and rattly. "Today's assignment is to see who can Celerate the longest distance. The person who Celerates the farthest down the field won't have to stay after class. The rest of you will need to practice for another hour. You should all be able to go from one end of the field to the other in a blink. I'll be watching each of you closely."

His eyes shot to mine again before he faced the class. "Go. Begin."

My classmates dispersed, walking to the edge of the field up by the gate.

Sweat stuck to my skin, even though the sun overhead didn't radiate heat. I edged past Graeg, feeling his eyes boring into my back.

Maybe coming here was a mistake. Yet again, I'd placed myself in a position where I could be exposed. I groaned, forcing myself to keep walking.

Kids down the way had already started to Celerate, their bodies blurring across the field in short bursts. I slowed my pace.

An arm slung around my shoulder, and I flinched. Nowen drew me in close to his side, appearing from nowhere. Even though I should've been used to him appearing whenever he wanted, it still startled me.

"Scared?" he asked, and his mouth crooked up to one side.

I pressed my lips together. "No, why would I be?"

He clicked his tongue. "Dessy, Dessy. I've figured you out. You know as well as I that you can't Celerate. So let me help you."

I stayed silent, my heart pounding.

"You know I could connect them for you," he said softly. "Your lives." He gave me a sly glance.

I shook my head. "I don't know what you're talking about. But even if I did, I wouldn't need your help." But my voice rose at the end.

The kids continued to Celerate up ahead, blurry figures darting back and forth.

Nowen paused and turned me to face him. His hands gripped my shoulders before he lifted one hand and brushed a piece of hair off my face.

"You know you won't be able to do this," he said. "You need my help. Just let me have one peek inside your mind. You know I'm powerful enough to do it."

His one black eye seemed to darken while his blue one lightened. Something about his gaze fascinated me, and I couldn't look away. We stayed frozen on the field together, and I briefly wondered if my classmates were watching.

He lowered his lips to my ear. "It'll only take a second."

I blinked, ducking away. "No. I said no, Nowen. I really don't know what you're talking about."

Nowen's brows furrowed, and his jaw clamped down. "Fine. I'll let you do it the hard way. But you will come crawling to me. You *will* eventually beg me for my help."

He disappeared in a flash, and I wasn't sure if he had Celerated away, or if his Center was Time and Space. I bit the inside of my cheek. *How* could he possibly know my secret?

"Let's go, Clara," Graeg hissed as he walked past me. His fingers were still linked over his stomach, his long black robe brushing the pale ground. His pinpoint eyes danced with knowing humor. "No more stalling."

Heat rose up my cheeks as I stared at his departing form. My feet stayed rooted to the grass for a few moments before I started forward again, setting my chin. I didn't need Nowen. I didn't need Ricki. I didn't need anyone. I only needed myself.

I picked up the pace and joined the students at the edge of the border. I lined up with them, watching kids Celerate forward a few feet, then walk back when they didn't make it very far.

I could do this.

I already knew I could tap into my powers. And I wasn't going to kill or hurt anything this time. Graeg stood off to the side, his eyes on me, waiting. I faced the field again.

Celerate.

I could do this.

I rubbed my hands together, staring at the other end of the field. But the more I stood there, the more students began to notice.

Bodies paused, watching me. Seconds ticked. More eyes slid over to me.

I rubbed my palms on my thighs.

I tried to block out the stares. It was just me and the field. My fingertips buzzed. I wasn't powerless. I just needed to figure this out.

I gritted my teeth together.

Just run.

I forced myself forward, my feet taking off, but I stumbled, barely catching myself. Snickers broke out around me. I glanced around, my cheeks burning, and I dusted off my pants. I swallowed, my pulse in my throat.

I walked back to the lineup and faced the field once more, still ignoring the stares.

I took off again.

I pushed faster this time, breaking into a full run, but I tripped again, this time falling to my knees. More laughter from the crowd of onlookers.

My legs shook as I stood, and I squeezed my eyes shut. I couldn't block out the laughter. It echoed around me, filling my ears. Maybe I couldn't do this.

I started across the field, back to the school.

Ignore them.

I paused.

Cael's voice cut into my mind, and my feet dug into the grassy ground. I wasn't sure if I had really heard him.

"Cael?"

The echo of his voice pounded through my head, pulsing. Not possible. But it had felt so real.

I shook my head, continuing on.

Look to your left.

I paused again and turned my head to look over to the border. A shadow shifted outside the gates, and I stared. Cael stepped outward from the forest.

I sucked in a sharp breath. "Cael."

You can do this. Let me help you.

His voice slid inside my head, and a deep warmth followed, heating my veins. I'd forgotten what it was like to have him inside my head. It flooded through my mind like silk, spreading down my back, relaxing my shoulders.

"But I can't," I whispered.

Celerating is as easy as breathing. Moving as quickly as air. I'm right by your side just outside the gates. I want you to keep up with me.

I peeked over again. He stood just outside the perimeter, his long shadow stretching alongside the trees.

"Keep up with you?"

He nodded slightly. *I'm going to move forward. Stay with me.*

He took a smooth step forward, and his presence shifted in the forefront of my mind.

I gasped, clasping the sides of my head. "How are you doing that?"

Follow me. You want me to stay in your mind? You're going to have to keep up.

"But—"

He moved forward again, and his presence banged in the front part of my skull. I staggered forward a few steps.

More laughter trickled across the field around me, but I ignored it.

Relax, Clara. Just breathe with me, move with me.

The warmth of his voice sailed through me again, and I nodded, closing my eyes. Visions of our life together flashed through my mind. He was there when I was a child. Out in the forest. When I walked through town. When the storms got bad. When Dad disappeared. When Mom . . .

No one had been there for me like he had.

He'd always been my constant.

I missed him. I missed him terribly.

The rise and fall of his chest pushed inside my head, and my own breathing slowed to match his. I felt myself align with him, a heavy power between us.

He moved once more.

I leaped.

Like an invisible cord was tied between us, I was yanked forward. His presence continued to push, breeze forward, and I was carried with him. We breathed together, moved together, sailed together. As if all the molecules in our bodies had merged together.

Although the world sped by around me, my legs barely moved, and I felt no wind on my face. Energy expanded through my chest, and I couldn't help but smile. I let out a small laugh.

The pull between us slackened.

He stopped, and I jolted, skidding to a halt. I caught myself on the fence across the field, face to face with the white railing. I spun around, breathing fast. A hundred yards away, dozens of faces stared back at me.

"Holy crap," I whispered under my breath. I'd gone across the entire field.

Cael stood just outside the gates, tucked inside the shadowy forest. He dipped his head in acknowledgment.

Well done.

19
Silky Natural

Later that day, Ricki had found new clothes for me since I still didn't have the ability to change on my own. I looked like Death as I stepped into the gymnasium. Tight black pants, a black T-shirt, and heavy black boots. I suddenly wondered what I dressed like on the other side.

Thoughts of Cael still resounded in my mind. My heart was light, fluttery, as the echo of his presence sailed through me. Being around him, seeing him, was everything I needed. He was light. He was air. He was life. He was what made me believe everything would be all right.

The usual stares flicked my way as I entered the gym, but I ignored them, lifting my chin. Maybe Ricki was right. Me hurting Khalob and killing that rose could work to my advantage. I needed to be feared for my own safety.

I casually perused the room. Things were as they always were: people separated into groups. Though Khalob still wasn't back. My stomach twisted at the thought of seeing him again. I continued to scan, knowing that I was searching for Nowen. I couldn't help it. He wasn't happy with me before he'd disappeared, and it left me unsettled that there was contention between us. But I saw no sign of his wild hair, handsome face, and smirking eyes.

Mr. Tompkins beat us to the mat. He motioned everyone to come forward, and Ricki and I stopped in front of him with the rest of the class.

"Gather round," Mr. Tompkins said. He adjusted his glasses, and his green eyes swept the space. "Today we're going to talk about Diviners and how they're made."

The class went silent. A chill seemed to settle in the room. Diviners were always a topic of interest—but rarely spoken about in the classroom.

His eyes stopped on me for a moment, his lips tight until he faced the room again.

"As you all know, a Divining Master is a Noble who has rebelled against the Mhystic. They are our enemies—our number-one priority to seek out, find their identities, and destroy. I've witnessed firsthand how destructive their armies are. You don't want to know how horrifying it is to watch the Diviners feed off their victims' memories." His gaze focused inward for a moment.

I swallowed. It was horrifying. People losing their minds day after day, until they disappeared. Mom. Dad. My heart ached.

Mr. Tompkins began to pace in front of the class, his hands linked behind him. I waited, anticipating. He might give me information on how to help Robert.

"It is the Divining Masters' sole purpose to gather as many souls as they can so they can build an army that will help them claim the Mhystic's throne," he continued. "As you know, Khalom is the link to all lives. Our Cursed lives wouldn't exist if Khalom were ever destroyed. And the Mhystic is what holds all the power on this side. They keep order. They keep us safe. They train us to grow. This city is—we Nobles are—the balance both worlds need. But the Divining Masters are biding their time, each building their own individual armies, until they will combine as one unit and attack. When that day comes—"

"When?" Ricki asked, crossing her arms. "Don't you mean if?"

Mr. Tompkins's face hardened. They stared at each other, both sets of eyes narrowed for a few moments. It was almost as if they were communicating without speaking.

"I believe this war is inevitable, Aericka," he said curtly. "The Diviners are growing fast in numbers. It's only a matter of time before they break down the gates and force their way in."

The room stilled, then whispers broke out. Nobles had always felt safe here. These kids had never known anything but peace. Would they really be able to fight Diviners and Divining Masters if it came down to it?

Ricki nudged me, tilting her head. "Stick up to him," she said. "This is a moment you can act like Death. Be authoritative. Don't let those kids be afraid. You know more than anyone it's not hopeless."

"What?" I hissed. I wasn't going to oppose Mr. Tompkins.

"Come on," Ricki urged. "These kids need to know you mean business."

"What? No," I repeated. I shifted my weight.

Ricki shoved me forward, and I stumbled out in front of the group. Mr. Tompkins turned to me, lifting his brows.

"Yes, Clara?"

I shot Ricki a glare. I rubbed my palms on my thighs, every inch of me humming. The class stood waiting. I rolled my shoulders.

"Clara?" Mr. Tompkins asked again.

I exhaled. "It isn't hopeless," I said. I tried to keep my voice steady. "Yeah, Divining Masters are expanding their armies, but we have our own army. We have the Stricken."

Mr. Tompkins's lips flicked upward. "The Stricken? Really? They are useless. They don't have powers. They don't even have identities. They are no match against the Divining Masters."

I shook my head. "No. I've seen them in battle. They're skilled. We don't have anything to be afraid of."

Mr. Tompkins crossed his arms. "You've seen the Stricken fight. Really. I highly doubt that."

"I have," I said. "Of course I have. One of them is my best friend!" My voice escalated.

Silence echoed before snickers broke out. I glanced around at the laughing faces; even Mr. Tompkins smiled.

Heat spread over my cheeks. A surge of darkness flooded into my chest, and I tried to shove it down.

"Anyway," Mr. Tompkins said. "Diviners. Does anyone know how one is made?"

Ricki reached over and squeezed my arm. "You tried."

Deena's hand shot up.

Mr. Tompkins ignored her and focused on me again. "What about you, Clara? You should know since you're the *expert* on Diviners."

More heat swirled inside me. I balled up my fists.

"No?" Mr. Tompkins asked, half smiling. "Well, I'll tell you. Just like Nobles can renounce their Noblehood, people who become Diviners give up their own life. Anyone can sign their life away. Most of them are brain-dead people in Desolation. They sign a contract, and they don't even know they're being recruited."

The class remained silent as they watched Mr. Tompkins and me, eyes bouncing back and forth between us as if waiting for me to object.

When I didn't, Mr. Tompkins clapped his hands and said, "Well, enough of that. Let me show you what we're going to do today." He shot another glance at me, and humor twisted his lips.

"What is his problem?" I whispered to Ricki.

"I don't know," she said. "But he certainly has it out for you all of a sudden."

Mr. Tompkins headed into the middle of the mat, and the class followed. I gave Ricki an uneasy glance, and she shrugged, but we followed, stopping in the middle of the large mat.

"Today, we're going to use our Centers on something not quite as perilous as Diviners, but still a good exercise. We're going to pair up. Both partners will be blindfolded, with one person serving as the caller. The caller will wear the black blindfold and direct their red blindfolded partner through a maze of dangerous objects, all of which could easily maim and hurt you enough to send you to the other side.

"Whoever makes it to the end of the maze first—or whoever makes it to the end of the maze at all—wins. As always, use your Centers. Got it? Pair up and I'll pass out blindfolds."

I stood rooted to the floor as everyone began to shift around me. "Something's off," I said.

Ricki nodded, her gaze narrowed. "You triggered him somehow. Like he's threatened by you." She faced me. "I think he wants to send you to the other side. He wants to make a fool of you. He wants to put you in your place. Which means your threat of Death is working."

I shook my head. "I don't think so. I don't think he's afraid of me at all."

Ricki opened her mouth to respond, but Fae entered the room.

"Oh, crap, I gotta go," Ricki said. She started forward, then paused, glancing between Mr. Tompkins and me. "Er . . . Good luck with this."

"What? Ricki. No. You can't leave me—"

But she took off, disappearing with Fae outside the doorway. I stared after her, heart pounding. She couldn't leave me alone right now. I needed a partner. She needed to help me get through the maze. What if Mr. Tompkins was out to get me?

I slowly turned back to the class. Everyone had paired up, while I stood alone. My eyes darted from person to person, searching for

Lionel. He would pair up with me. And he was strong enough to carry both of us. But no, he stood next to Mhaggie. Maybe Deena. No, she was with Adham.

Mr. Tompkins stood in front of the class, facing the large empty mat. He whispered a few words under his breath, lifted a hand, and flicked his wrist out in front of him. A hint of purple flashed, but the color was dim, barely visible. I'd never seen such a lightly colored Center before. The room before us transformed.

Free-standing steel walls appeared out of thin air, towering above us, jutting side to side, in and out, circling in an endless maze. Mr. Tompkins continued to wave his arm, and knives, javelins, and bows and arrows hung above the maze before he lowered them down into the labyrinth. Giant traps with teeth as large as an alligator's emerged before us, hovering in front of the maze's entrance before the traps entered the maze and disappeared inside. Blindfolds materialized in our hands, some red, some black. I clasped the red handkerchief in my palm. Great. He hadn't forgotten about me.

But I was still alone. I clutched the red blindfold. I needed a caller. Kids continued to shuffle around me, chatter loud in the air. My head began to spin.

"Guess you're with me." Nowen's voice echoed from behind me as he sidled up to my side. A muscle jumped in his cheek as he peered at the maze in front of us.

"You want to be my partner?" I asked wryly. "Daring, considering I'm Death. Aren't you afraid of me?"

His eyes twinkled with amusement, his blue and black eyes sliding to meet mine. "I'd love to see you try and hurt me."

I blinked back at him.

"Of course it's *me* you need to trust." He held up his black handkerchief. "I'll be guiding you through the maze. Since, you know," he lowered his voice, "you don't have your lives connected."

I swallowed. He was right.

"Come on, Dessy. You don't trust me?" His mouth quirked.

He didn't wait for me to respond. He took my shoulders and spun me toward the maze, stepping in close behind me. His breath fell on the side of my neck, his body aligned with mine.

"I won't let anything happen to you. I promise," he whispered.

"Line up!" Mr. Tompkins yelled.

The kids obeyed and gathered in one long line, with me at the end. The maze stood tall and daunting in front of me, with flashes of sharp objects glinting through the dark passageways. My arms shook and I wrapped them around myself. The thought of a weapon stabbing me right in the heart . . .

"Blindfolds on!" Mr. Tompkins's voice boomed.

Nowen snatched the blindfold from my hands and gently placed it around my eyes. His body stayed close to mine. I could feel the rise and fall of his chest. His close proximity made my body become alive, alert. Like every inch of me was aware of his presence. He secured the handkerchief behind my head.

"You'll be fine," he whispered.

But my whole body trembled. Complete blackness pressed in on me. I couldn't see a thing. Nowen gripped the sides of my arms, squaring me forward.

"Just do what I say," he said.

His words slid along my body the same way Cael's did. I shouldn't have compared them, but suddenly, I realized in greater detail that I *liked* Nowen. I'd always felt a connection to him, but now, everything clicked. His voice in my ear calmed me. His body behind me made me melt. Excitement coursed through me any time he was close. But could I trust him?

Cael said I couldn't.

You let him near you, and he will kill you.

So who did I trust? Cael or Nowen?

"And . . . begin!" Mr. Tompkins commanded.

Voices immediately yelled from all directions, the callers guiding their partners where to go. The noise swirled around my head, Nowen still behind me.

"Take four steps forward and two to your left." Nowen's voice rang low and clear through the chaos.

But I couldn't move.

He will kill you.

I shook my head. "Nowen, I think—"

"Four steps forward and two to your left," he repeated, voice stronger.

I swallowed; my hands shook. I couldn't trust Nowen. I couldn't. I hardly knew him. I'd known Cael for years. If I was smart, I'd listen to Cael.

Setting my jaw, I did the opposite. I took eight steps forward and four to my right.

"Stop!" Nowen hissed. "Don't move."

I froze, the tone in his voice searing through me. My body continued to tremble, my knees weak.

"Listen to me," Nowen said. "Take four steps backward, and then two to your left."

Silence pounded between us. Maybe I did need to listen to Nowen. The intensity in his voice couldn't be forged. Maybe Cael was wrong. I tentatively obeyed, sliding my feet back, then inching to the left.

Nothing happened. I released a breath.

Nowen grunted. "Good. Now take another step to your left and then one foot forward."

I tried not to hesitate, deciding I needed to trust him. I did what he said.

"Please don't do that again," Nowen whispered. "I'm not out to get you, Dessy. When will you learn that I'm on your side? Now, three more steps forward."

"How can I?" I said. "I really don't know anything about you. Other than you roaming around this place like you have complete freedom. And Cael not trusting you."

"Don't talk about him," he said harshly. "Another step forward, then three to your right."

I moved through the darkness, my feet continuing to hit smooth ground. But distant sounds jarred me. Fizzles of Time and Space snapped on the air. The ground rumbled a few times, and I knew it was Earth. Screams ricocheted, and crashes and bangs echoed. I cringed, trying to shut it out.

I wanted to ask more about Cael, but I let it drop. Nowen clearly wasn't going to talk about him. Once again, I wondered what went down between Nowen and Cael. How did they know each other? And why were they enemies?

We continued forward, and with each step, the tension slowly drained from my shoulders. We were doing it. Nowen directed me, and I followed. Step by step. Command by command, his voice taking me through the maze with ease. I was like a puppet, with invisible strings strung between us.

It was easy, between Nowen and me. He clearly wasn't trying to hurt me. My mind continued to drift away, and I imagined his lips on mine.

Would he ever kiss me? Did he want to? Sometimes, when he looked at me, I thought I saw something more in his eyes. Like maybe he liked *me*.

I took a few more steps, distracted by my thoughts until Nowen yelled, "Duck!"

Adrenaline shot through me, and I dove to the floor, heart thumping. A whoosh zipped by my head and I froze, made worse by everything being black behind my blindfold.

"It's fine now," Nowen said. "It's fine. You can stand up."

I slowly rose, but my whole body shook.

"It was a steel arrow," he said. "I'm sorry about that. I-I was having too much fun watching you."

His words jolted me, and my skin tingled. *Was he flirting with me?*

I nodded, ignoring his statement, though I felt numb. I wasn't sure if I could continue. I tried to focus on something else.

"Why don't I remember you?" I asked, and he gently gave me another command. "From when I was here before? Ten years ago? I don't remember you."

I felt his smile spread along my back. "I don't know. I was here. Maybe the Diviners had more of an effect on you than you realize."

I shook my head. "No way. There's no way I'd forget you."

I stopped.

Heat brushed my cheeks. *Was I flirting now?* "I mean—"

He chuckled. "I like hearing that I've made an impact on you."

I took another step without Nowen's direction. It was instinct. I'd forgotten he was leading me.

"No!" Nowen yelled.

A thud hit me from behind, and I flew forward, tumbling to the ground. I coughed, the air escaping out of my lungs. My blindfold went flying, and Nowen let out a huge grunt as he landed on top of me. His face came into focus as I blinked, his dark hair hanging over his different-colored eyes. He laughed, his chest heaving on my own. I was hyper aware of how his body felt on mine.

His lips slid up into his usual smirk. "That was a close one." His smile deepened.

In a rush, the maze melted away. The weapons and traps disappeared in front of my eyes, and students stood in various places around the gym where the maze had been. They were far behind, not nearly to the location where I was.

I scrambled out from under Nowen, and we both stood. Across the gym, Mr. Tompkins's brows lifted before they pushed downward.

"Impressive, Clara," he said, confusion lining his forehead. "Not only were you the first to the end, but you did it without a caller. How you did that is beyond me. The power of Death . . .?" It came out in a question.

Without a caller?

I glanced around me. The students slowly clapped, a mixture of surprise and wonderment on their faces.

What did he mean without a caller?

I spun to Nowen, opening my mouth to speak, but Nowen had vanished.

What?

"Everyone, to your dorms," Mr. Tompkins said. "Take the rest of the class off. You deserve it."

I stood there for a long while, feet rooted to the floor, until everyone had left. Then I slowly made my way back to my room and fell asleep.

20
Thin as Ice

Hands gripped my shoulders, and the world slowly came into focus. Bright sun pounded down, and a guy's silhouette lingered over me. The guy spun me onto my stomach, keeping me pinned. My face pressed into the warm sidewalk.

Ricki's scream ricocheted in the distance and I struggled, fighting off my assailant's hold, kicking, thrashing. Little rocks dug into my cheek. Everything came rushing back. I'd been in the car with Ricki. We'd been attacked. I'd tried to run, but I'd been . . . tasered. My leg still burned.

A truck rumbled to my left and pulled up next to me. My attacker yanked me to my feet and shoved me toward the truck. I stumbled, tripping, knowing I had to get away. If I got in that vehicle, it was over. I staggered forward a couple of more steps until I went for it. I darted to the left, sprinting as fast as I could, but the guy easily snatched me again and forced me toward the vehicle.

"Inside," he said. I peeked over at him. It was Siv, the guy with the large claw tattoo that climbed up the back of his bald head.

The truck door slid open and Siv pushed me forward. I hit the truck's floor hard on my tailbone, and pain shot into my back. Ricki screamed again, but her voice was cut off as the truck door slammed closed.

Panic hit, and I scrambled around. The truck was large—and *cold*. Stainless steel doors and a high ceiling surrounded me, along with stacks of coolers everywhere. My breath blew out in white puffs, and I shivered. *A refrigerator truck?* The vehicle rumbled as we took off.

Dan.

He had to be in here. I quickly scanned the area.

"Dan?"

The vehicle bumped, and I tumbled backward, ramming into a stack of coolers. The coolers toppled over, and I groaned, rubbing my shoulder. When I straightened, a pair of bloodshot eyes came into view and I yelped, scrambling back.

An old woman with tangled gray hair crawled over to me, her eyes wide and curious.

"Crap," I said, setting a hand on my heart. "You scared the crap out of me. Who are you? And . . . what are we doing in here?"

She stared at me, her lips clamped together tight, wrinkles around the corners. She cocked her head to the side, as if analyzing me.

My forehead tightened. "Do you talk?" It came out sharply, but I wasn't sure if it was because I was scared or exhausted. Probably both.

She stayed silent.

"Great," I said. I staggered to my feet, brushing off my legs. The burn still ached. "What are these coolers anyway?" The truck bumped once more, and I stumbled.

I wandered around, taking in the stacks. The lids were all closed, but I bent down next to one and ran a hand along the top. As I touched it, a sinking feeling settled in my stomach. Something was off. Something was wrong.

I peered at the old woman, then back to the cooler. I knew I shouldn't have opened it, but I peeled open the lid and froze.

Pouches of blood filled the space, packed on ice. I stared at the red liquid swishing inside the plastic bags and gawked.

What?

I slammed the lid shut. My heart jolted, and I whirled back to the old lady. I had to be in a horror film. There was no other explanation.

"What's going on?" I asked. "Please tell me."

She shook her head, her bony arms wrapping around herself. She was in a loose gray dress that looked like it hadn't been washed for a month. Her mouth stayed closed.

The vehicle came to a sudden stop, and I lurched, slipping onto my backside. The vehicle shut off, and footsteps clopped outside. A door at the back of the truck opened, and sunlight streamed inside. I squinted, shielding my eyes.

Nowen stepped inside the cool space, earrings glinting along his ears, his hair swooshed off to the side. He still wore his ripped jeans and black T-shirt. Siv followed in behind him. Nowen's different-colored eyes stared me down, and I wasn't sure which was more menacing—the blue one or the black one. Nowen folded his arms, tilting his head at me. He watched me, guarded, but tension lined the edge of his jaw, like there was an emotional war going on inside of him. Then he relaxed, a slow smile lifting one side of his mouth.

"Hello again, Dessy."

I pushed my brows together. "My name isn't Dessy. You have me mistaken for someone else. Same with my brother, Dan. Where is he?" The words came out like I was in a Bond film. This wasn't happening right now. Things like this didn't happen.

Nowen's eyes slid to the old woman. "I see you've had a little reunion here. Sorry Laela isn't more coherent for you, but she's been through some . . . trauma." His lips twitched.

I paused, my heart picking up again.

Laela?

No.

Not possible.

But behind the mass of gray hair was a face framed with the same delicate features that ran in our family.

Large almond-shaped eyes mirrored my own as she dazedly stared at me. Was this for real?

Was my grandma *alive*?

"Grandma?"

Nowen stepped forward and lowered himself to my level. Taking my chin in his hand, he said, "Don't worry, I'll take care of you, Dessy. This must be all so frightening for you. I didn't want to get you involved over here, I really didn't, but I need to now." His gaze flicked down to my arms.

His face was close, too close. It was odd—I felt a mixture of fear and comfort at being in his proximity. I shut my eyes, trying to breathe steadily. This was all a mistake. He'd realize who I was soon enough, and he'd let me go.

"Dessy?"

I wrenched my eyes open. Nowen's face was right up next to mine, his eyes worried.

My pulse thumped in my ears, pounding through my whole being. I couldn't take this anymore. Dan. Nowen. The visions. The blood. My grandmother.

"Please just let me go," I said. "I'm not Dessy and I can't help you. And *please* tell me where Dan is."

Nowen's face softened and he patted my cheek. "Don't worry. I'll take good care of you." He spun to his bodyguard. "Siv, get a sample and spin the blood. We need to know if Clara's blood will work since her brother's failed."

"My . . . what?" I asked. My voice squeaked. "Blood?"

Nowen stood up, tilting his head again. Shadows lined underneath his jaw. "You really are a wonder, Dessy. And I like your hair. It's shorter here."

I stared at him, speechless, watching him until he left the truck and slammed the door closed behind him.

I stared where Nowen had just left.

He'd left me alone with Siv and my grandmother, Laela. I couldn't reflect on *how* she was here and *what* she was doing here. I'd have to process that later. But for now, I needed to find a way out of here.

Nowen had said something about blood and spinning it. What kind of operation did they have going on here?

Siv's head was shiny in the truck light, and he stalked forward, a pointy needle in his hand. I staggered to my feet, edging back a few steps. I bumped into a cooler and caught myself.

"It's best not to fight Nowen," Siv said, his voice raspy. "He always gets what he wants. She wasn't able to escape him." His eyes darted to Laela.

"Where's Dan?" I asked. "And what did Nowen mean by his blood failed?"

Siv smiled. "Oh, he has other uses now."

I shook my head, a knot forming in my throat. This wasn't real. This wasn't happening. My body was on full alert, and I inched to the side, trying to circle toward the door. Siv followed, keeping himself in front of me.

"Just let us go," I said, and my voice trembled. "I promise I won't tell anyone about this."

Siv chuckled, taking another step forward. I maneuvered to the side again.

"I just need a bit of your blood. It needs to be tested. See if the Death that runs in your veins will work. We need another generation. Hers is too weak now." He winked at Laela.

Death?

I shot Laela a look. "What is he talking about?"

She only shook her head, her scraggly hair poofing out at the sides. I inwardly groaned. What had they done to her?

I was taking another step to the side, slowly creeping, when Siv leaped forward. I tried to dodge, but he was too fast. I shoved against him, trying to push him back.

"Run!" I yelled to Laela. "The door's free—get out of here!"

Siv wrapped a hand around my throat, shoving me back against the wall. I choked, gasping, my eyes wide. I tried to suck in a breath, but nothing came. I pushed against him, hitting him, kicking him. But nothing phased him.

Black spots danced in my vision; I felt lightheaded. My throat burned horribly, and I desperately tried to gasp for air, but my windpipe was sealed off tight.

"Just hold still," Siv said. "I only need a little blood."

My vision continued to darken. Ringing sounded in my ears, and my body went limp. This was it. I was going to die by a man with a claw tattoo trying to take my blood. I could've never predicted this.

A sharp pain pierced my arm, but I hardly felt it, my vision continuing to blacken. He was taking blood. Siv was taking my blood.

Then Siv released his grip, and he cried out, staggering away from me. I heaved, curling forward, my throat burning as I sucked in a lungful. I coughed, sputtered, and collapsed onto my hands and knees. I breathed in shaky breaths, my body humming. My vision cleared, but pain still throbbed in my throat.

Siv cried out in pain, and I squinted upward. A needle was stabbed right into his eye, and his hands hovered over it, clearly not knowing what to do. He continued to cry out, floundering around, shoving aside coolers, blood leaking down his face.

"Come on," Laela's voice said, scratchy. She thrust a hand toward me, and I stared at her arms. Bruises ran up and down her skin, dozens of tiny wounds where needles had been stuck in her.

But I couldn't move. Pain radiated everywhere, and my head was too fuzzy to process my surroundings.

"I said come on," Laela said. She hefted me to a standing position and guided me to the door. I limped, my feet dragging, but she pushed open the door, and fresh air flowed over my face. Sunlight streamed down; little spots still floated in my vision.

We jumped out of the truck, and Laela yanked me forward, pulling me down a sidewalk.

"Where—where are we going?" I choked out.

"Later," she said. "Just follow me."

We raced down the sidewalk as fast as we could, turning corner after corner. Pain seared my lungs. My vision started to blacken again. In an instant, it was as if all the adrenaline had drained out of my body. I slowed to a walk, my chest rising and falling rapidly.

"I think I'm going to pass out," I said.

I curled over, trying to steady my breaths, but nausea hit, and I fell onto my hands and knees. Darkness overtook me.

21
Ghost in the Shelf

My eyes snapped open.

I'd just been somewhere. Again.

Residual adrenaline pumped through my body, throbbing in my veins. Things were getting worse over there. I felt like I'd been running. My legs ached as if I'd been sprinting at full speed. I put a hand to my chest, willing my heart to slow. I *hated* not knowing my other life. What if Ricki was right and I really *was* in danger?

I quickly peeked out the window. The sun had descended, and tiny stars were starting to twinkle in the sky. Crap. Robert and Ricki. I was supposed to meet them at the gates. I jumped out of bed and went out the dorm building and into the night air.

I hurried down the walkways of Khalom, the white world around me almost glowing in the dark. I wove toward the eastern border. The stars grew brighter overhead as darkness completely swallowed the sky. I slowed my pace, almost there.

Hopefully I wasn't too late.

I was just about to turn one more corner when I heard him.

"Nice work today, Dessy."

I spun around, my eyes wide in the dark, but I couldn't see him.

A rustle sounded from above, and I squinted upward. He was in a tree. A soft thump hit the ground, and his shadow unfolded before me.

Moonlight shone down, highlighting his silhouette. For a moment, I thought he was Cael.

"With the maze." His voice cut through the night air. "We make a great team."

I watched as he sauntered forward. Just the sight of him sent a thrill through me. I was . . . *happy* to see him? Anticipation buzzed in my body as he stopped in front of me, cocking his head to the side.

"What happened?" I asked. "Why did you disappear? Everyone thinks *I* did that course on my own."

He shrugged, clicking his tongue. "That doesn't matter. But what does matter is that I know your secret."

Not this again.

"Nowen, I really don't know what you're—"

He held up a hand. "No use pretending."

He chuckled, the sound low in the dark, and nudged me in the shoulder. "I've been watching you, Dessy. Don't think I haven't."

I swallowed, but my tongue stuck to the roof of my mouth. I didn't know what to say.

"You're trying to make people think you have your lives connected, but you don't. Though I do wonder how you have pulled it off so far." He clicked his tongue again. "The rose. That day in the pool. Attacking Khalob. I almost believed you had your powers. But I know that isn't true." He lifted his brows.

I slowly backed away, but Nowen followed. Humor sparkled in his eyes as my back hit the white fence.

"You're wrong," I finally said. "I do have my lives connected."

"Oh, Dessy, Dessy." He chuckled again. "What if I told you I've seen you on the other side? And you have *no idea* who you are over there?"

My fingers gripped the cool iron posts behind me. "You can't. You're lying."

He tsked. "I'm not out to get you, Dessy. Let me help you. I can help you connect your two lives. Think how powerful you'll be when you have Death with you full force. I can do this for you. I can give you this gift."

Nowen lowered his gaze to my level. I tried to keep my eyes averted, but a magnetism pulled in the air between us. I knew that feeling. It was the power of Mind. I allowed my gaze to connect with his. The second our eyes locked, a warmth surged into my chest, spreading through my veins, traveling up and down my limbs. His single black eye was as dark as a starless night sky. Melting, beautiful. I was trapped in his gaze, and he knew it. But I didn't fight it. I wanted to have that connection with him. I *wanted* him to help me find my other life. I believed with every fiber of my being that he could do it for me.

His gaze continued to pierce into mine, and every muscle in my body slackened, like all the tension I'd been carrying since I came here drifted away. It was just Nowen and me. I wished I could be closer to him. I wasn't close enough.

"That's it," he said. "Let me help find you."

His voice cut through the comforting haze, but my body stayed swimming in the warmth. He took my face in his hands, and then, like it'd been with Robert, images flashed through my head.

I was holding a hose, washing cars. The image changed. I was driving a car, angry, zooming through traffic. The image changed again. I was running, tripping, falling. Someone hovered over me.

"Stop!"

I slammed my eyelids shut.

It was too dangerous.

"Stay out of my mind," I said. The world slowly righted itself, and my consciousness reconnected with my body.

Nowen made a noise at the back of his throat, and I reopened my eyes.

He pushed away, pacing before me, running a hand through his wild hair. "You're making a mistake, Dessy. You're not going to be able to keep up this charade forever. And I'm not always going to be able to help you like I did in the maze." He paused, his gaze piercing me again. "But fine. Your decision." He kicked a rock and headed down the moonlit path. "I'll see you in class tomorrow."

I watched him depart, his body slowly fading into the dark. My entire body hummed, too much energy snapping beneath my skin. Had Nowen almost connected my lives? Robert had tried to do it. But I'd stopped both of them. Was that a mistake? I should've let him continue. But it was too much of a risk. I could lose my mind completely. I stood against the gate, feeling like I was a piece of glass with a million cracks in it.

Any more pressure and I would shatter.

The bushes rustled behind me, and I whirled around, adrenaline still pounding through me. Robert's face appeared on the other side of the fence, his greasy hair hanging around his face.

"Crap! You scared me!" I placed a hand over my racing heart, backing up a step. I thought Nowen was back. "Robert, hey."

Ricki rushed up the path and joined me, panting. "Sorry I'm late." Her frame was small against the towering fence. "Were you just"—she glanced around—"talking with someone? I thought I heard a voice that wasn't Robert's."

I swallowed, my throat thick. "What? Oh. No. Just . . . reconnecting with Robert here."

He peered at me darkly through the fence, his face unmoving. But my gaze skated to where Nowen had been. I didn't know why I didn't want to tell Ricki about Nowen. She might've been able to give me advice.

But something about him felt . . . secret.

"Well, I'm glad you've met on better terms," Ricki said, and I snapped back to the present. "Clara, this is my brother Robert. Robert, this is Clara."

Robert stayed motionless, the darkness hollowing out his eyes.

Ricki cleared her throat. "Well, we're here," she said. "Robert, you said you needed to speak with us at the gates."

Robert's eyes slowly slid to her. "We can't speak unless Clara steps outside."

Ricki shot me a glance, but I didn't budge. Whatever he had to say he could say through the gates.

Robert's eyes slithered back to me. "It won't work," he said as if reading my mind. "I can't go into Khalom. I'm not a Noble—not anymore. You need to come out here to help me. To release me from this prison."

"How?" I whispered. "I don't know how—"

"You're Death," he answered. "You know as well as I that you're capable. You have to try. After all that I did for you, the least you could do is step outside of the gates and *try*."

Unspoken words hung in the air between us as we both fell quiet. Moonlight reflected off the sweat on his nose.

My lips tightened. I didn't even think I could leave. Cael hadn't allowed me to.

And I'd only tapped into bits and pieces of my Center. I was nowhere near trying to release a Diviner from his Master.

Robert shifted his weight, rolling his shoulders, like he had an itch. His eyes darted to the sides of him.

Ricki's brow furrowed. "Robert, are you okay?"

"I'm fine," he snapped, his head shooting to her. "I told you to bring her, so now come out so we can talk." He peeked behind him, back into the forest. He scratched at his jaw, then dragged his nails along his arms and legs.

"I think we should go," I whispered.

Ricki shook her head quickly. "No, we have to help him." She turned to her brother. "Robert, just tell us what Clara can do. *Please.*"

They stared each other down, silence stretching for a long moment. A sudden gust of wind blew in, and Robert's long hair brushed over his face, the trees bending back and forth behind him. The wind picked up, and his body began to flicker. His skin turned a light shade of gray, almost transparent, his eyes and mouth blackening into holes, then his color was restored.

"Robert?" Ricki edged back.

The wind intensified, dark clouds rolling in overhead. Something howled in the distance.

I froze.

I knew that sound.

The Storm.

The Diviners.

I marched up to Robert and gripped the fence. "*What* did you do?" I stuck my nose up close to his. "Why are there Diviners coming?"

He didn't flinch, lips sealed tight not saying a word.

"Robert!" I shook the bars. I spun to Ricki. "We need to leave. Now."

"No! We need to help Robert!" she cried. More wind rushed in.

I gripped the gate harder. "You were trying to trick me. Why do you want me outside the gates? So you could set the Diviners on me?"

More sweat beaded on Robert's brow. "No."

His eyes were intent, mouth set, but behind him, the familiar dark cloud curled out from the forest, crawling around the trees, engulfing where Robert stood. I kept a firm grip on the gate, though everything outside was a swirl of black chaos. As I peered closer, it was easy to distinguish the individual Diviners. Their ghostly forms swirled in and out of one another, churning like a tornado.

Ricki screamed, clasping a hand over her mouth. "Robert!"

"He's one of them," I said. "He won't be hurt."

Robert's form flickered until he began to morph fully into one of those things. His body darkened, his presence thinned out, eyes and mouth became three black holes. His mouth opened in a silent scream, and he floated up into the air before being sucked backward into the Storm.

"Robert!" Ricki cried.

My gaze shot to where he had been—to his ghostly form joining the other Diviners—and my eyes narrowed. Robert was right—I did have the power to release him. I just needed to figure out how. Laela had done it. So could I.

Wind continued to surge outside the gates as the Diviners whirled around. I kept my gaze fixed on Robert's being, not breaking eye contact.

Focus. I wasn't sure what exactly I was focusing on, I just knew that it was in my blood to release him. Somehow, I'd hurt Khalob. Somehow, I killed the rose. Somehow, I set the curtains on fire. So somehow, I could release Robert.

I called on the darkness that lay dormant within me. It was always there, hovering beneath the surface, and I willed it to come forward. I allowed the warmth to gather in my chest, to build, until I knew I could use it.

The Diviners howled in the air, and Ricki screamed something behind me, but I couldn't hear. I kept all my attention on Robert's ghostly form, swirling through the chaos.

Very slowly, the gate around my hands became hot, and heat began to sear into my palms. I broke my focus, and my eyes darted down. The white fence began to darken, transforming into a deep black. The iron grew hotter, so hot I cried out and tried to pull my hands back, but they were stuck.

"Clara! What's going on?" Ricki's voice cut through the chaos.

But I couldn't speak. Pain radiated from my hands up through my arms, nearly blinding me. I tried to let go once more, but it was as if my hands had been seared to the iron.

"Help!" I yelled. More pain. More heat. "Help!" I yelled again.

Ricki rushed up next to me and gripped my wrists, trying to yank my hands from the gate, but it was no use. I tried to find Robert again, but he was lost in the mix, the howls growing louder.

The pain was too much. I sagged against the fence. It was as if my bones were melting, melding into the gate. But then, the pain started to lighten. My fingers loosened, and chunks of the gate crumbled around me. Like the rose, the iron bars were disintegrating, black particles flying out into the air.

What?

I looked down at my palms, then up at the gate.

Had I done this?

The gate completely collapsed, and in a whoosh, the Diviners rushed in. They engulfed Ricki and me, and she cried out, scrambling toward me. She swatted her hands over her face, trying to fight them off. I was paralyzed as the ghost-like beings darted to and fro, the white trees around us whipping side to side. I was too numb to think. I could only stare at my hands.

But the Diviners didn't linger long. They shot down the path toward Historic Quarter. I sat shaking, my jaw chattering.

"Ricki . . ." I swallowed. "We need to stop them. The Nobles here can't face them." But I still couldn't move.

Ricki had curled over, her hands wrapped around her stomach, her body crouched. She shook her head. "That was . . . terrible. I . . . how do the poor people in Desolation live with that every day?"

I wobbled to a standing position, and I reached a hand down to her. "Did you never see them in Desolation?"

She stayed curled up. "No. I mean, yes, but no. Not like that. Not with Robert as one of them."

I helped her stand, and I turned her to face me. "We have to think of the kids here. They're in danger. We have to go *now.*"

Ricki nodded. "O-okay."

We took off up the path north, and I ran as fast as I could. Moonlight lit the sidewalks, the wind pushing us along. I'd never seen wind in Khalom. The people here couldn't face Diviners. They'd never even *seen* a Diviner before. My mind was racing faster than my feet. I couldn't let them hurt anyone. This was my fault. I needed to stop them.

Ricki ran with me, and my eyes shot around, searching. We curved up the pathway, the Grand Hall in sight.

Then I heard it.

The screams.

"Come on!" I pushed faster.

We came around the last bend to the Grand Hall and I stopped dead. The dark cloud of Diviners churned round and round, completely immersing several of my classmates. The kids screamed, trying to run, but the Diviners kept swooping in, stopping them. Deena cried out in the fray, trying to swat them away. Adham stood next to her, punching them, using his Body strength, but the Diviners were unphased, zipping around.

Mhaggie stood frozen in the middle of the chaos, her red hair swirling around her head. Her entire body shook, her face open and blank.

No.

The Diviners attacked her from every angle, entering her mouth and her ears. Her jaw hung open.

"Mhaggie!" I yelled.

Deena caught my gaze and screamed. "Clara! Help!"

My heart took off. I frantically glanced around. I needed a weapon. The Stricken were able to defeat the Diviners with their swords. I needed something sharp. My eyes shot to the nearest tree.

"Ricki, come on!" I sprinted over and started to break off a branch.

Ricki followed, panting. "What are you doing?"

"Get a branch," I ground out. "If you stab them, they disappear. I saw the Stricken do it with swords. Help me."

Together, we pushed down, bending the branch until it snapped. I grabbed the pointy piece of wood and threw myself headfirst into the chaos. Ricki started on her own branch.

I darted my arm in and out, upward and downward, the sharp edge of my stick connecting with Diviners. They howled as I pierced them, then they vanished in tiny particles.

Ricki followed in after me, also using her weapon, and together we fought, circling around, jabbing, fighting. Several kids had escaped the chaos, but they stood watching.

"Help!" I yelled. "Get a weapon. Help!"

They stayed paralyzed.

I shook my head and continued to fight. Visions of Cael and how he moved like oil flashed to mind. I'd never forget the way he fought, gliding around the enemy. I tried to mimic his movements, taking down as many Diviners as I could.

But there were too many of them. It was as if they were duplicating. Mhaggie still stood incoherent in the middle of the madness. Deena had escaped and watched with horror.

My arm ached, and my lungs burned, but I continued to fight. Why weren't the others helping? We could defeat them together. But the other kids just stared as Ricki and I struggled.

And then, the Diviners swirled upward. They hovered above us for a moment before they quickly dispersed and sped up a path around the Grand Hall.

I stood blinking, my chest heaving as I tried to catch my breath.

"What—" I cut off.

"What just happened?" Ricki asked.

I dropped my stick, and it clattered on the sidewalk. Ricki stood a few feet away, panting. Her eyes widened.

"Clara!" She dropped her branch and rushed over. I turned, brows creased, then stopped.

Mhaggie lay on the ground, her limbs splayed, her eyes looking blankly up at the dark sky. Moonlight caught in her red hair, her body slack, her chest still.

She wasn't breathing.

Deena screamed, covering her mouth. She backed away, shaking her head.

My classmates went into an uproar.

"It was *you*!" they cried.

"You brought them in. You're Death."

"Only Death would do this!"

More shouts erupted.

The kids began gathering into a group, a mob, coming straight at me.

I couldn't move. I could barely see past the pounding heartbeat in my eyes. *Me? They thought I did this?*

But I had. I'd let the Diviners in.

More shouts rang around me. The world spun. Mhaggie's body was still lifeless on the ground.

The mob started to close in on me, shouts echoing, faces twisted in anger. I staggered backward several steps, my heart hammering. Ricki backed up next to me, and she clasped my hand. The shouts heightened, and Adham rubbed his hands together. Deena clenched her fists, purple sparks snapping around her head. The kids sprinted forward, and I waited for the onslaught, but a hand shot out of the darkness and yanked me sideways, Ricki stumbling after me.

Fae yanked us around the corner of the Grand Hall and pulled us inside a small alcove. She flicked her wrist and yellow sparks shimmered out in front of us, like we were trapped inside an invisible bubble. She stood in the shadows, her lips pursed in disappointment, but her eyes glistened with worry. Kids stopped in front of us, glancing around, but they didn't see us. They continued onward, running up the path until the shouting diminished.

"You and you. With me. In the library," Fae said before disappearing through the curtain behind her. The invisible bubble dissipated, bits of yellow streaks drifting to the floor. Ricki and I glanced at each other. Fear was written all over her face, but she moved forward, and I slowly followed behind.

22
Doom

Fae slapped down a large leather book onto the table where we were sitting. Ricki and I glanced at each other, eyebrows raised, though she still looked shaken. She couldn't maintain eye contact with me for long.

The library ceiling towered stories above us, supported by marble columns that encircled the large space. Each wall was filled with books and lined with sliding ladders stretching up to the tallest stacks. Books towered from the top of the ceiling to the floor, every shape, size, and color lining the wooden shelves. The white drapes that usually covered the glassless windows were pulled back, the stars in the night sky winking through.

"We don't have much time," Fae said. "When those kids can't find you, they'll go to their parents, who will go to the High Officials, and then everyone will be searching for you." She pinched the bridge of her nose and started pacing. "But there's so much more for us to focus on."

She paused and faced me. "You need to know more about the history of Khalom. It will help us." Her sharp nail pointed down at the book in front of me. "We have scribes here whose job is to write every detail of our history. In fact, that Diviner attack has probably already made it into the books. Everything from the days of Ehlissa to the present is written and documented here in this library."

Ricki gave me another look and I shivered.

"You know Clara didn't do this, right?" Though Ricki didn't sound convincing. It was almost like a question.

"Of course I do," Fae said stiffly. "Not on purpose, anyway." She raised a single brow. Her nail tapped on the book. "This is why we're here."

"Please don't tell me you expect us to read that. If everyone in the city is really after Clara, we don't have time," Ricki said.

Fae ignored her. "This is installment nine thousand eight hundred and seventeen of our history." She drew her finger over the golden number embossed on the cover. Her mouth tightened. "I brought you here because history is repeating itself and you should be aware."

"What do you mean?" I asked. "How?"

Fae's shoulders sagged, and her mouth relaxed. "I owe you an apology, Clara. I wanted you gone, but I shouldn't have tried to push you away. I see now that you're essential to Khalom's safety."

I titled my head in question, brows creased.

But I already knew.

A war was coming.

Death was the only thing that could stop it.

I shook my head. "I can't help you."

Fae's thin brows slanted inward. "I should've been kinder to you. You are Laela's granddaughter after all. And with Laela having been my best friend . . ." She trailed off, her eyes turning wistful for a moment. "Did Ricki tell you that we were Blood Companions? I once saved Laela from a Diviner attack, in the early days, before she developed her strength to defeat them. We are forever linked—or were. When one becomes a Blood Companion with another, when one saves the life of another Noble, you give them a piece of your Center. You're linked whether you want to be or not.

"But Laela was a careless soul," Fae continued, and sighed. "She was always escaping from the city to embark on adventures. She was always getting into trouble. And I always cleaned up her messes. Being her Blood Companion is how I was able to find her when she ran off. But, one time I couldn't save her."

Fae dropped her eyes. "She was determined she could travel between both worlds without using her Center. She was a daredevil—she wanted to experiment. And so, she was lost in the Dhim, having traveled incorrectly between both worlds. When one gets lost, they're torn apart. You lose your mind. You lose your soul." She fell silent again. "I never got over it," she whispered. "The guilt and anger I have . . . that I could've stopped her . . . that combined with losing Robert . . ." She peered up at me again. "I do owe you an apology, Clara. None of this is your fault."

I lowered my eyes. "No. You have every reason to be angry at me. I'm the reason Robert left. If it weren't for me, he'd still be here."

Fae turned back to the book, blinking away a few tears. Her pointy nail dragged along the spine.

"Ricki's told me that you haven't connected your lives, which is why it doesn't make sense that you're able to use your power here. It only shows what you're truly capable of. But it's not enough." She drew her hand away from the book. "There is a war coming, Clara. The Diviners have already entered the city. Their leaders will be following. And once that happens, it will be another Great Rebellion."

Fae shook her head. "I need to tell you something." She stepped away from the table and began to pace in front of us once more. "I'm going to tell you a secret, but you can't reveal this to anyone." She paused, eyeing us. "The Mhystic have disappeared. No one knows but the High Officials. We haven't seen them for months. We've been doing our best to run Khalom, to keep peace, but without the Mhystic, we have no chance against the Divining Masters."

"*What*?" Ricki asked. "Where have they gone?"

"We don't know," Fae said. "But we need to find them, which is why I'm setting you to the task."

Ricki stood up from her chair. "You know we can't do that." She gave Fae a knowing look. "We have enough on our plate. With helping Clara here and everything on the other side—" She broke off and glanced at me.

I shot her a curious look.

Ricki cleared her throat. "We have more important things to do than finding the Mhystic."

Fae stared her granddaughter down before she turned to me once more. "If Khalom isn't protected, then everything else will be moot." She motioned to the book again. "This book is the history of Mind in Khalom. There might be something in here to help you find them."

She drew her hand back. "But I'm afraid that the Mhystic won't be strong enough alone. They need to be whole—to be five strong—instead of four. Death needs to join them. Which is why we must find them—you especially, Clara."

We were all quiet for a few moments. I stood up from my seat and wandered over to the bookcase. I traced my fingers along the polished books, clean and pristine like the rest of the city. Moonlight streamed down into the open windows.

"Yes," I said. "We can try."

"Good," Fae said with finality. "Now, go. Before they find you."

Ricki and I nodded. The safety of Khalom was on our shoulders. We'd have to work together. I snatched up the book, and we quickly left the library and headed through the back hallways of the Grand Hall before going outside.

23 Night Fever

We ended up back in our shared bedroom. Finding the Mhystic was a priority now. And this book could be the key.

Ricki lit a candle where she sat on our bedroom floor. The flame flicked and flickered in the dim room. I lowered myself in front of her, crossing my legs. Wind stirred the white lacy curtains, and moonlight tumbled down onto the floor, casting strange shadows. A breeze still circulated throughout Khalom, the lingering residual of the Diviner attack.

Ricki set the heavy book down in front of us and turned a few pages. Each page had a different scrawl, different historians in Khalom documenting events through the years.

"I think I found something that could work," she said. "It's a Mind spell. I know you haven't connected fully with your Center, and none of us are Mind, but maybe with the combination of whatever power we have, it might be enough to help us find the Mhystic."

I stared down at the book with her. Doubt twisted in my gut, but I knew I had no choice but to go along with it. My spirits were starting to drop. I'd never have control over my Center. Each time I tapped into it, something went horribly wrong. What if using a Mind spell only made things worse? I thought of Mhaggie's lifeless gaze. I didn't even know if she had survived the attack. Was her mind gone forever?

And what about Khalob?

Maybe he was worse than I thought.

I peeked over at Ricki, who silently read the words on the page, eyes intent. I still wasn't sure how I felt about her. She'd really been my only friend, other than Cael. And Nowen . . . was he my friend? But Ricki's motives were all for Robert. Did she really have my best interests at heart?

She drew the book closer to the candlelight, clearing her throat before chanting.

Around the fire, with blood shared,

Two Nobles linked, with hands paired,

Softly singing the Journey Together,

Eyes unbreaking, or the Nether forever,

She paused, lifting her head.

"That's it?" I asked. "We just need to hold hands and chant 'the Journey Together'?"

Ricki's mouth quirked. "Almost. There is the blood part."

"The—" I hiccupped.

She removed a rock from her pocket and set it down in front of her. Its edges were jagged, cut sharply in many angles. "This should do it." Ricki lifted a hand and held it over the rock.

The rock began to rattle, shaking side to side, until it slowly rose off the floor. Green sparks ignited in the air, snapping around her fingers. She twisted her wrist, and the rock spun around, floating in front of her.

"This might hurt," she said. She flicked her wrist, and the rock came sailing toward me, diving down toward my hands. The rock sliced my finger, and little drops of blood beaded on my skin.

"Ow!" I said, clutching my hand. "Seriously?"

She wiggled her fingers, and the rock sailed back to her, allowing it to cut her finger open, too. The rock clattered to the floor, and she quickly reached over and clasped my hands.

"Around the fire with blood shared," she said.

I glared, unable to hide my expression. I was okay with a lot of things, but not with anything involving blood. It creeped me out.

Ricki met my gaze head on. "Now repeat the phrase with me," she said.

I exhaled, following suit. "Okay." Our eyes locked.

The Journey Together.

The Journey Together.

We continued to chant.

The Journey Together.

The Journey Together.

Very slowly, warmth grew in the pit of my belly. Like it had a few times before, a strange tingling sensation swept through me. It continued to spread outward through my limbs, my fingers and toes prickling with energy.

I let the warmth overcome me.

The Journey Together.

Ricki kept her gaze on me. It was happening again. There was always a warmth that built up into me before something happened. But I wasn't sure if it was good or bad.

"Think of the Mhystic," Ricki said. "Mind has the power to see images, to search people's minds. We need to get a glimpse of where they are."

I felt disconnected, like I was floating somewhere over my right shoulder. Darkness began to cloud my vision, sights and sounds blurring around me. Then the horror began. Screams suddenly screeched inside my mind, bright flashes in my vision. Pain seared in my skull, and I let go of Ricki's hands, grabbing my head.

"Clara!" Ricki yelled.

My whole body went numb, and I started to shake violently. My teeth chattered.

I felt myself slipping away in all directions, my mind being ripped apart from myself. Screams cut into my mind.

The shaking continued. Cold was seeping into my veins, my body freezing, my limbs stiff. The warmth had left.

"Clara!" Ricki screamed again. "I'm so sorry! I didn't—"

Pain sliced into me, peeling away my skin, stripping my mind apart bit by bit. The anguish seeped into every pore, and I opened my mouth, not sure if I was screaming or it was someone else.

"Stop!"

I jolted awake, and the pain immediately dissipated. It was like I'd been thrown back into myself. Warmth surged into me in a rush, and the shaking stopped.

Nowen stood in the doorway, his hand outstretched, the echo of his voice still ripping through the room. He stared down at me, intensity in his gaze. His dark hair fell over his forehead, and his chest heaved.

He'd saved me.

I didn't know *how*, but he'd saved me.

"Clara!" Ricki threw her arms around me. "I'm so sorry. I thought I knew what I was doing, but I clearly don't."

I kept my focus on Nowen. The moonlight highlighted his face, deepening his defined cheekbones. I don't know how long we stared at each other.

Finally, Nowen spoke, "You owe me one now, Clara."

Ricki didn't notice him. She buried her head into my shoulder, tears starting to soak my shirt.

"Owe you what? How did you do that?" My voice came out in a whisper.

"How did I do what?" Ricki lifted her head, wiping her nose.

"Not you," I said. "Him." I pointed to the doorway.

Ricki sniffed, her forehead creasing together. "Who?" She glanced around. "Clara, no one is there."

Nowen stood there, smirking, lifting his brows.

"You can't . . ." I swallowed. "Ricki, you can't see him?"

The line between her brows deepened. "Clara, no one is here."

My heart started racing. She couldn't see him. In fact, now that I thought about it, I didn't think anyone had ever seen him. I'd never seen anyone talk to him. No one had seen him that day in the maze. He always appeared and disappeared whenever he wanted to.

He was invisible.

He gave me a wink and backed up into the corner, crossing his arms, waiting. Ricki still didn't see him.

"You should rest," Ricki said. "You're hallucinating. I'm going to go get Fae, see if she can help."

I nodded, but my mind was adrift, my reality crumbling around me. A voice in my head. An invisible friend. I really was losing my mind. I peered back at him, and he still hovered in the corner, smirking. Ricki walked right past him as she left.

I resisted the urge to tuck my knees to my chest and rock back and forth.

The Mind spell.

Finding the Mhystic.

The screams. The pain. Nowen invisible in the corner. He'd saved me. And now he said I *owed him.*

He continued to stare, but I couldn't face him now. I gripped my knees tight. I didn't belong here anymore. I didn't have anyone. Mom and Dad were gone. I hadn't heard from Cael since Celerating. And a mob of kids were after me.

I remembered what it was like to leave the city the first time. I'd been afraid, yes, but I'd also felt protected. Whoever carried me from the city had saved me. Now, I was terrified. I didn't know where to run. If I was forced to leave the city, I don't know what I'd do. But if my classmates found me, they'd torture me. They'd hurt me. And could I trust Nowen?

I looked over at him again.

His lips twitched upward, and he pushed off the wall from the corner.

"I'm tired, Nowen," I said. "And I'm not in the mood for games." I stood up, rolled my shoulders, and sat down on my bed.

Nowen took another step forward, lifting a brow. "All right. No games."

I stared at him through the dark.

"I like you, Dessy." He lowered himself down on the bed next to me. "You're entertaining. You're passionate. You're smart." He reached a hand over and linked his pinky finger through mine. "And you're brave."

I allowed the touch, but *how* was he able to touch me? If he was invisible, shouldn't he have been a ghost or something? But he felt too warm to be dead.

"We aren't so different," he said. "We're both outcasts. Both misunderstood." He kept his gaze fixed on our linked hands. "Maybe we're meant to be together." He lifted his eyes, and the difference between the two different colors became apparent in the dark. The black eye absorbed the darkness, while the blue one caught what little light there was and glistened with it.

"Why are your eyes like that?" I asked.

He looked away quickly. "That isn't something I talk about."

I sighed, removing my hand from his. "Then will you tell me why no one can see you?"

His mouth tucked inward. "That isn't something I like to talk about either."

I bit down hard on my tongue. "Then what *do* you want to talk about? Why are you here?"

He smiled once again. "I missed you."

I shook my head. "Nowen, stop. You're a tease, and I can't handle that right now. I need to leave before my classmates find me here."

His gaze connected with mine again, and his eyes lit up. He began to play with the ends of my hair. "I thought I liked it short, but I think I like it better long. Or maybe I just like you," he repeated.

I stiffened at his touch. But once again, I allowed it. Nowen had always had an effect on me. Small tingles rushed down my body, making me feel alive, alert.

"I think you like me, too," he said softly.

I kept my eyes lowered. Silence hung between us.

He was right.

But did I want him to know that? Knowing him, he'd use it against me. Thoughts of Cael rushed in, and I tried to shove them to the back of my brain. Cael wasn't here. Nowen was. My heart picked up speed as he continued to play with my hair. Warmth swam in my chest, and I relished in the feeling. It was . . .

Dark.

I liked dark. It resonated deep within me. It stirred the small storm that always seemed to be brewing inside. It came alive, giving me power.

But it didn't give me comfort. Not in the way Cael made me feel. He always eased the tension in my body, always calmed my soul.

But then the image of the Body crowd kissing surged to mind. I lifted my eyes to Nowen and stared at his lips. My stomach fluttered, and I couldn't help but wonder. What would his lips feel like on mine? Did he want to kiss me? Like I did him?

Nowen seemed to read my mind. A half smile curved his lips, and he took my face in his hands.

No.

I blinked and shook off the touch. What was I thinking?

Nowen had lied to me like everyone else. He'd been invisible this whole time, and he clearly had his own agenda. I scooted away.

"I need to go," I said.

Nowen leaned closer to me and touched my chin, turning my face to him.

"Then I want to redeem my favor," he said.

My brows pushed together. "Your what?"

"My favor." He shrugged. "You owe me a favor, don't you remember?"

I stared at him, his fingers still on my face.

I shut my eyes. "Nowen. I like you, I do. But, like everyone else, you're not honest with me. Can you please give me a reason to trust you?"

He lowered his hand, and I peeked an eye open.

"Fine," he said.

I lifted my brows. I didn't think he'd agree so readily.

"I can't help being invisible," he said. "It's not my choice." There was darkness in his tone.

"What do you mean?"

He gave a one-shoulder shrug, his eyes flicking away. "Your lovely Cael took my name and *locked* me in here. I can't help what happened to me. I can't help what I am."

His gaze slid back to mine.

I pursed my lips. "You're lying. Cael wouldn't do that."

He chuckled. "Believe what you want, Dessy, but I assure you I'm telling you the truth. Why do you think I go by Nowen?" he said bitterly. "Cael took my Noble name, so I'd be trapped in here for good. Only people with Noble names can pass in and out of the gates."

No one.

Nowen.

He didn't have a name?

And Cael *took* it?

"But . . . I know Cael," I said. "He would never do anything so cruel."

"Pffft," he said. "You're so oblivious." His gaze ran down me in cold waves. "But you know what? I'll tell you everything you want to know about Cael," he said. "For a price. But if I tell you, you won't ever look at your shadow boy the same way again."

His words took a moment to process before my eyes widened. He knew more about Cael. Cael, who I'd always wanted to know. Cael, who had meant so much to me but never opened up to me. I'd spent years asking questions, but Cael never gave me answers.

"I'll do it," I said without thinking. "Whatever the price. Tell me."

Nowen drew even closer to me, locking me in his gaze. "Are you sure?"

"Yes," I breathed. I was sure. I'd never been so sure.

He released a small laugh. "All right then, you're going to let me look in your eyes for a whole minute. Then I'll tell you everything you want to know about your shadow boy."

"Wait, what?" I choked on my spit, coughing. "No, never mind."

Nowen sat back. "Fine. Your call. But you'll never get this opportunity again. No one else knows Cael's story. Not even the history books."

My mind started spinning, my thoughts racing back and forth. I believed him. I could see honesty in his face. And they clearly knew each other, based off the encounter at the border.

"Okay," I said, before I could change my mind. "Do it."

A slow smile swept over Nowen's face.

In an instant, he gripped me by the shoulders, and I had no choice but to look into his eyes. He held me firm, and his vast, dark depths seized me, spinning around me like the night sky. I dove headfirst into the abyss, drowning. Warmth immediately surged through me, capturing me, paralyzing me. My body was rooted to the bed, every inch of me on fire. Nowen held me completely under his power—I couldn't move if I wanted to.

Nowen's voice drifted far away, fading, as I swam through the dark. Another rush of warmth spread through my body, though this was different from when Robert and Ricki had dived into my mind—more powerful. I liked it. Wanted it. Welcomed it.

The warmth grew, swelling, burning. I seemed to be traveling forward, and I moved my arms and legs like I was swimming, until I smacked headfirst into something solid. I floated backward, but instinct told me I needed to push forward once more. I righted myself in the strange, floating darkness, and thrust myself forward again. But like before, I rammed into a wall of sorts.

A bit of light twinkled in the dark up ahead, flickering. It was far away, but I strained to focus on it. I didn't know where I was. Was I in my own mind? Was I in Nowen's? Was I in . . . the Dhim? But it didn't matter, as the light began to grow stronger. It pulsed, stretching through the darkness. I tried to move forward again, but once more, I hit an invisible barrier.

"I'll help, Dessy." Nowen's voice rang through the dark.

His presence shifted behind me, and his face appeared next to mine. He flashed me a smile, then reached down and took my hand. I wanted to ask him where we were, but the light ahead consumed all my thoughts.

"Together," he said. "We'll push through the barrier together."

It shouldn't have made sense, but somehow it did. I instinctively knew what to do.

We shoved our weight forward at once, still keeping our hands linked, our heads and minds pushing against the invisible force. The light grew. Was it traveling toward us? Or were we traveling toward the light?

Together Nowen and I pushed, kicking through the dark. We threw our weight forward, and we let go of our hands, pounding and beating our fists against the force.

And then, a dam of light burst, pouring into my mind.

My heart stopped.

Light flooded in.

Everything rushed into me at once.

I remembered.

Everything.

It was like I had been living without a pair of lungs my whole life and I had just taken my first breath. I was Clara Banks, from Denver. Everything came to mind—my parents, friends, my younger brother, Dan. The tightness in my chest loosened and energy stretched out past my fingertips.

Death was there inside of me. It swirled around like a ball of fire in my chest, burning me from the inside out.

My Center.

It was with me full force.

It gathered underneath the layers of my skin, traveling through the pathways of my veins, as if it had been there the whole time.

Without warning, I was lurched backward, a hard tug throwing me back into the dark. My head spun around, and my vision blurred. I traveled backward at a fast speed, until my feet hit hard ground. Nowen's grip on me tightened, and my vision came into focus.

I was back in my dorm room, standing, Nowen smiling down at me.

"Feel different?" he asked.

"I . . ." I put a hand to my forehead. It was all there. Everything. I knew who I was over on the other side. "I can't believe it!" I threw my arms around him and pulled him into a tight hug. His hands pressed into my back, drawing me closer.

"See? That wasn't so bad," he said close to my ear.

I started to draw back, but he didn't let me go far.

"Now, about that favor," he said.

I paused. "What? I just gave you your favor. You wanted to look into my eyes."

He gave a small smile. "No, that was the price I wanted to give you information on Cael. You still owe me my favor."

I swallowed. He was right. How could I have been so stupid?

"What do you want then?" I asked, though I could barely speak.

"A kiss."

His eyes met mine, searching, waiting. I couldn't look away. I gave the briefest of nods. The silence between us pulsed. Anticipation buzzed through every part of me.

Then, he dipped his head forward and his hands cupped my face. His lips gently pressed against mine, drawing me closer to him.

I reacted instantly.

My hands reached up and gripped the back of his hair, and I pulled him closer. I'd always wanted to feel this. To be loved. To not be alone. To be wanted. To be *seen*.

I gave in to the kiss, letting him take control of it. I matched his movements, enjoying every second. So this is what it felt like.

Finally, he smiled, and I felt his teeth against mine. "Your debt is paid."

He lifted his head. It was over too soon. Want still traveled through me. Could he see it on my face? I glanced away, wrapping my arms around myself.

Nowen shifted so he was in front of me again. "What are you thinking?"

I raised my eyes back to him, and the moment I did, more memories rushed to mind. I saw Nowen standing in front of me with piercings running up his ear. We were at a car wash. He took off in a black SUV.

Then we were in a refrigerator? Coolers of blood.

I gasped.

He *knew* me over there. He knew me and he wasn't good.

He was the bad guy.

I shook my head, backing away, heart pounding.

Nowen's head cocked to the side. "I asked you what you were thinking."

I continued to edge away. I peeked back to the door. "I need to go."

A line formed between Nowen's brow before realization dawned on his face. His expression twisted and he leaped forward. I tried to dodge, but I wasn't fast enough. He gripped my wrist, holding me secure.

"What is your deal?" I asked, trying to yank away. "You kidnapped Dan! And why are you trying to take my blood over there?"

He stared me down, moonlight tracing the outline of his sharp cheekbones. For the first time, the darkness I'd felt from time to time rushed into me like a wave. But it was stronger, more potent within me. All the anger and hurt and frustration that I had felt over the past several years gathered in a tight ball in my chest, ready to burst.

Nowen slowly released his grip and crossed his arms, smiling. "Feeling a bit of power? I can see it all over your face."

The dark feeling began to grow, expanding outward. It traveled down my arms and into my fingertips, buzzing.

"You can't hurt me," Nowen said plainly.

I gritted my teeth, glaring. I didn't believe him. My anger increased, more heat gathering in my veins. I flexed my hands, then closed my fists. I *could* hurt him. I knew it with every fiber of my being. I began to lift my hands—to do what, I didn't know—but I instinctively knew that was how I released my power.

Nowen chuckled, not moving an inch.

In a flash, I threw up my hands, but a hand shot in my peripheral, gripping my arm, stopping me. I spun around, heat in my gaze, ready to attack whoever was thwarting me.

Cael stood before me, long and dark, the moonlight shining through his silhouette.

"Don't," he said.

I stumbled back, and Cael lowered his hand. "Cael . . . what . . .?"

Nowen's face lightened a shade. For the first time, I saw fear in his eyes.

Cael's head slid back and forth between us. How long had Cael been in here? Had he seen Nowen and me kiss?

The fear fled from Nowen's face as he put up his mask once more. He leaned against the bedpost, crossing one ankle over the other. "So you came in through the gates after all. I didn't think you had the guts."

"I had no choice," said Cael, and his dark gaze returned to me. "I felt Death return to Khalom. Now that Death has returned fully, I won't let you take it from her. I won't let you kill her."

I froze. "What?"

Nowen sneered, barking out a laugh. "I don't want to kill her. I want to rule next to her. As do you."

Cael remained still. "A change of heart then?"

"*You're* the one who threw it all away," Nowen spat. "We could have ruled over Khalom. Death was our only threat. No one was more powerful than us. Now we're both nearly Centerless. Powerless. Because of *you*."

"It wasn't our right," Cael said. "Wasn't our throne to take."

"Oh, so it always belonged to Ehlissa?" He tsked. "She was the fool. She gave up her gifts, and for what? To fail? But we, we almost had it all." He threw up his hands. "And now look at us. You out there holding nothing but a name, no longer a Noble. And me, locked in here, invisible to everyone, with no name. Let's finish what we started, regain our power, and be who we were destined to be. A true leader."

I glanced between them. Too many words too fast. I couldn't keep up.

Nowen straightened off the bedpost and faced Cael directly.

They stood so alike, it was as if Cael were merely a shadow of Nowen.

Cael faced me again, the moonlight continuing to shine through him. "I am sorry you had to find out this way, Clara. But it was me who came to attack you in your room that night. I was there to harm you . . . to . . . to take your Center from you. But I couldn't do it. So I took you out of the city that night to protect you."

I shook my head. "What? That doesn't make any sense. You would never harm me. And . . ." I thought of the arms that had carried me out of Khalom. *That had been Cael?* "But there was someone else there," I continued. "There were two people fighting in my room that night."

Cael nodded solemnly. "When I came into your room, I had every intention to take your Center from you, but someone else was there with the dagger—though I couldn't make out who it was in the dark. It was then that I knew you needed to leave the city, that you weren't safe."

"So you *did* save me," I said.

"Oh, he's not the hero, trust me," Nowen said. "He was there to take your Center. Which is worse than dying, in my opinion. He would've taken your Noblehood, your purpose, your entire identity."

"And how would you know?" I barked out at him.

Nowen smiled, a hint of satisfaction gleaming behind it. "Because I was there, too, Dessy. *Both* of us. Well, him really, but also me." His smile deepened.

"What?"

Nowen continued, "Do you really not know? Can't you see our resemblance? Cael is me. I'm Cael. *We* tried to take your Center from you that night. But the coward ripped himself from me that night—separating us into two different beings—in order to save you from your imminent murder. I wanted your attacker to kill you. Cael didn't. So he gave it all up to save you. It's too bad. Your death would've solved everything." He shook his head at the memory, what looked like regret flashing in his eyes. "But yes, Cael and I used to be one person—heir to the throne and a mighty force—but *he* suddenly had to grow a conscience. He took you and my name with him, leaving me—his other half—locked in here. Without a name, I couldn't leave." His gaze narrowed.

My heart was pounding its way up my throat. This couldn't be true. Nowen and Cael had been the same person? And they'd been ripped apart, like . . . good and evil? And why did they want my Center?

Nowen lifted his palms up, as if in surrender. "I don't want to harm Clara anymore," he said to Cael. "I see more of a benefit of ruling with her than against her. Let us join forces again and take control of this kingdom—with Clara by our side. I'm not meant to be locked up, and you're not meant to be a shadow of yourself."

Nowen's words spun around my head a few times. I couldn't decide what to focus on. Then it clicked.

"You're the one Deena was talking to me about the other day. You're Ehlissa's brother! You hold all five Centers. You wanted the throne for yourself, but your duty was to rule the Stricken. And you disappeared . . ."

Nowen's mouth flicked upward. "*Did* hold five Centers. We lost most of our power when Cael ripped himself away from me. The throne was always ours to take. It shouldn't have belonged to our sister."

Cael was silent. Energy strummed down his shadowy form, so tight I thought he would explode into a hundred tiny pieces. He slowly turned to me. "I'm so sorry, Clara. I didn't mean to betray you by keeping this knowledge from you. I used to be power hungry." He glared at Nowen before returning to me. "I was threatened by you. I wanted to rule Khalom, and your power could have prevented that. We've tried to destroy all the carriers of Death through the years, but every time we thought we'd succeeded, another carrier of Death would emerge. It's jumped from family to family, until it landed on yours. Your grandmother evaded us for a long time, until we thought she was dead, which is why we attacked you."

His voice cracked as he continued, "I'll do my best to make it up to you. But for now, there's something I need to do." Cael unsheathed a shadowy sword from his hip, the silhouetted weapon looking just as dangerous as if it were steel.

Nowen's eyes narrowed, the hollows in his cheeks casting heavy shadows. "So that's it then? You've made your choice?"

Cael raised his blade.

Nowen growled and crouched down. "All right. A duel. We'll see who the stronger half is. If I win, I take Clara and we rule Khalom. If you win, well, that won't happen." Nowen lifted a hand out in front of him, and from thin air, a sword materialized in his fingers. It glinted silver in the moonlight. "I've been waiting for this moment for a long time."

I couldn't look away. Nowen couldn't fight Cael. Cael couldn't fight Nowen. They were two halves of the same person. But who was stronger? Could one of them really overpower the other?

"Guys, please stop," I said. But my throat swelled up tight.

"I should've finished this a long time ago," Cael said softly, matching Nowen's stance.

Nowen smiled, his teeth gleaming in the dark.

In a heartbeat, the two charged.

Nowen lunged at Cael, his weapon darting straight for his heart. Cael grabbed the blade with one bare hand, unflinching, and ripped the weapon from Nowen's grasp. He righted the sword and plunged it into Nowen's stomach. The sword ran right through him, sticking out from his back.

Nowen laughed, then pulled the blade from his torso. He smiled, holding the sword up again.

His eyes slid to me. "Wounds don't send me to the other side. I have complete control here. Though Cael, on the other hand, is barely human. He won't survive this fight if I win."

I shook my head. Not possible.

Cael attacked once more, grabbing another shadowy sword from his hip before slicing it down. But Nowen dodged, attacking from beneath. They met blow for blow, their smooth, catlike movements snaking around each other. Cael took each strike with astounding strength, never allowing Nowen's blade near his torso. Nowen wasn't so careful. He had no reservations about the weapon getting too close. They moved so alike, it was astonishing I hadn't seen their resemblance before. They had the exact same figure.

Around the room they danced, every clash of the sword clanging inside my brain. In an odd way, the fight was beautiful, almost like Nowen was practicing alone in his bedroom, Cael as his shadow, the moon their spotlight.

I couldn't look away. Adrenaline pumped through my body, but I couldn't move. I should've protested, but I knew I couldn't do anything to stop this. This was a war that had been stewing for a long time. I still couldn't wrap my mind around the fact that *they were the same person*.

No wonder I felt a connection to Nowen. But how were they so different? Even though my first instinct was to root for Cael, there was a small part of me that didn't want to see Nowen get hurt.

But he'd betrayed me. He wanted my blood on the other side. And I didn't know for what.

I'd never find out Nowen's plan if Cael destroyed him. But if Cael got hurt . . .

I'd never be okay again.

Time seemed to stop. Nowen took an unexpected lunge to the left and jabbed his sword forward, right toward Cael's heart.

The sword slid easily into his body, slicing right through him.

I screamed.

Cael staggered backward, dropping his own sword, and it clanked to the ground. He collapsed, hissing, and fell flat on the floor.

Ringing sounded in my ears, and I distantly heard screams. They were probably mine. I rushed over, collapsing on my knees next to Cael. My hands hovered over his chest, shaking.

My head darted up to Nowen. "What did you do? *What* did you do?"

Nowen's hair hung in wet strands, his cheeks dappled from exertion. The moonlight outlined his frame, giving him an unearthly glow. "I suppose I just killed the weak part of me. Good riddance."

My hands continued to shake. "Cael, what can I do?" My teeth were chattering. Did I pull out the sword? Could the Stricken die? Nowen said he could. Cael reached up and placed a hand on my arm. "Run," he croaked out. "Run. Get far away. I warned you that Nowen would kill you. He'll take my name back and be free. You can't trust him. Run."

My whole body was trembling now. Nowen's presence loomed over me like a monster. Cael's words repeated over and over again in my head. I couldn't speak.

Cael's body began to flicker, his shadow brightening into human form, pale skin flashing before it dimmed again. I stared, wide-eyed. His body continued to flicker in and out, and for a quick moment, his frame revealed a body identical to Nowen's, except Cael's eyes were both blue, like the bottom of a flame.

The sight kick-started my heart, and clarity swept through my head.

"Don't!" I said. "Cael, *don't* you dare! Don't you dare leave me alone. I was alone for ten years with no one. I thought I was crazy, except you made me sane. You were the only reason I survived out there. I couldn't have done it without you. Day after day, all alone with those brain-dead people . . . If you hadn't existed? Cael, I couldn't bear it if you left right now. Please. I couldn't bear it if you left me ever again!"

His blue eyes stared up at mine, sorrow lining the face that looked exactly like Nowen's. It was so strange to actually *see his face.* To see the lightness of his eyes. To see the softness of his features.

"I tried to make my betrayal up to you," he said. "I'm sorry I failed. But it isn't too late to stop him. Death is with you now. Use it."

He looked gently at me for a few seconds, then his body sagged, and he went limp. I didn't move. Couldn't move.

No.

Then, like chalk being rinsed off a sidewalk, Cael's form began to wash away, disappearing until he'd faded away completely. I stared at the empty floor, still trembling.

Nowen stared at where Cael had just been, horror on his face. He should've been horrified. He'd just killed the best part of himself. Now both of his eyes were black—as black as the night sky outside the window. Cael was no longer a part of him. He was gone.

I jerked around at the sound of the curtain over my doorway being ripped off. I still couldn't move. Khalob and a few other kids barged in. I blinked, then blinked again.

Khalob?

He was okay.

But he wasn't. Murder was on his face, jaw tight, eyes narrowed. His hair was that bright blue.

"Get her," he said.

Adham and a Body girl marched toward me and hefted me to a standing position before I could say a word. Their fingers gripped around my arm, digging into my skin. Deena stood behind them, her features pinched tight.

Khalob's eyes lit up, and his mouth curved in an evil smile. "You're going to regret hurting me like you did. We're going to make sure it *never* happens again." He spun to Deena. "Show us the way."

She nodded, her hands clenched into fists, but there was a hint of fear in her eyes. She wouldn't look at me. She kept her gaze away.

"Let's go," she said.

The Body kids yanked me backward, dragging me to the door. My eyes shot to Nowen, but he stood transfixed, staring at the place where Cael had been.

"Nowen!" I yelled. But he didn't move, just continued to stare. I didn't know why I was asking for his help—he'd just killed Cael—but at least Nowen didn't want to hurt me.

The kids continued to pull me backward, Khalob laughing, the kids shouting, Nowen silent.

I tried one more time. "Nowen!"

He flinched, like he'd been startled. He slowly lifted his gaze, and his two black eyes met mine. He could've moved to save me, he could've done something, but he didn't. He only watched as the kids pulled me from the room.

And suddenly I didn't care. Cael was gone.

They pulled me from the dorm into the courtyard. My classmates roared and cheered, chanting how Khalom would be safe again. I knew I should've fought, tried to get away, tried to talk myself out of this, but I was numb. Cael was gone. Cael was *gone*. The night air brushed past my face as we traveled up campus, the kids dancing and celebrating around me.

I wanted to ask where they were taking me, but my mind still didn't work.

Cael.

Cael was gone.

Deena walked next to me, her eyes intent in front of her. Wind blew in and ruffled her hair. Clearly the Diviners still had an effect on the city. My arms ached where the Body kids kept their tight grip, and my head pounded, but I barely felt the pain as my classmates dragged me down the pathways. The pain in my heart was much more intense.

We entered the Grand Hall, and the marble hallways sped by. I stumbled, tripping over my legs. We turned corner after corner, until a hallway descended downward. Torches lined the walls, their flames flickering, laughter bouncing in the small space.

My mind slowly cleared.

I knew this place.

No.

"It's in here," I heard Deena say.

A few of the kids quieted down, but Khalob continued to laugh.

"Come on!" he said.

I struggled against their grip, trying to dig my feet into the floor as the curtain to the White Wing appeared. It hung menacingly before me. I knew what was beyond it. The curtain brushed past my face as strong hands pushed me down the white hallway full of wooden doors.

The screams began. Like before, a cacophony of noise hit. Shouts. Scratching at the doors. The knocks. The bangs.

The kids around me freaked out, their eyes widening. Several took off, rushing back out the way we came. But the Body kids stayed, along with Deena and Khalob.

"This way," Khalob said, and I was dragged forward once more.

No.

I shook my head. I couldn't find my voice.

This wasn't happening.

Deena stopped in front of a door, took one look at me, then turned back. "In here," she said, and her fingers wrapped around the brass doorknob.

Adrenaline hit like a punch to the gut. "What? No!"

Khalob grabbed me and shoved me forward. I pushed against him, elbowing him in the side, but he clasped my shoulders and forced me in front of the door.

"You deserve this," he said. "Death shouldn't exist. You've proven that you can't be trusted. And you should've never come back."

Deena swung the door open, and a scorching light hit my eyes. I blinked, and a wave of heat smacked into me.

"Have fun, princess," Khalob said and shoved me inside.

24

Cuts Like a Knife

When I woke, I was lying flat on the sidewalk.

Sunlight seared my vision, and I squinted, slowly sitting up. My head spun. Bits of gravel stuck in the skin of my palms, and I brushed it off.

Laela came into view above me, her gray hair wild. She held out a hand, motioning me to take it.

Was I seeing things?

No, she was real. *My grandma* was right in front of me. I scrambled to my feet without taking her hand, but my thoughts were still fuzzy. I stared blankly at her, a strange sensation humming through me. Something was different, though I didn't know what. I set a hand to my forehead. It was almost like déjà vu, but the feeling was stronger, like I'd just been somewhere, but I hadn't been. I'd been here this whole time. The feeling reminded me of when I'd wake in the middle of the night, and the dream I'd been having would feel *real*. What an absurd thought.

But then it hit.

Sights, sounds, and visions came flooding into me. They smacked into me like a ton of bricks, and I staggered backward, the breath knocked from my lungs. I was paralyzed. But it wasn't like when I felt like I was drowning earlier today; this was different. It wasn't a vision. It was like my mind peeled itself apart, allowing thoughts and memories to surge inward.

Khalom.

How did I know that name?

Death.

My Center.

What?

My brain seized up. I was suddenly caught in a wheel of memories that wouldn't stop spinning around me. I clutched my hair. A strange past forced its way to the forefront of my mind. Claera. Clara. Two worlds.

Was this real?

Reality struck me like a blow to the stomach. I had two lives, two different lives with two sets of memories. Who was I? Was I Clara Banks, popular cheerleader from Denver? Or was I Claera, the Noble from Khalom, who spent ten years living out in Desolation with no one but an invisible friend to keep me—

"Cael," I said. "The last time I saw him, Nowen had—"

Nowen.

He'd run Cael through with a sword.

"No, no, no. Cael." I dropped back to my knees. This was Nowen's fault. Nowen was behind everything.

My head snapped up. Laela was still here.

"We need to get to Khalom, but wait, how are you here?" I asked. "Where have you been?"

Laela stayed silent, just stared at me with her bloodshot eyes.

I shook my head. She wasn't going to talk. I needed help. Was Siv still after us? Last time I'd seen him, Laela had stuck a needle in his eye. And Nowen . . . I couldn't believe his deception. Maybe Ricki and Fae could help.

"We need to go," I said. "Nowen could come back any minute. And you—" I peeked down at Laela's bruised arms. "You need to tell me what those guys want with our blood."

This all didn't make sense. My grandma was *alive*. And she'd been with Nowen all these years? Nowen and his crew had kidnapped her. They held her hostage, to take her blood? Is that what all those coolers held in the refrigerator truck? Her *blood*?

My head was still swimming. Memories of Khalom were still colliding with my memories here. I didn't know how I hadn't had my lives connected before. I felt whole. Complete. My two selves merging felt as easy as waking up from a dream.

I shook my head. I couldn't think about that now. We needed to move.

I reached out and grabbed Laela by the arm. "We can't be out in the open like this. Come on."

I tried to pick up the pace, but the world was whirling around me. We continued onward, the hot summer sun beating down on us. Sprinklers watered lawns, kids ran around, playing outside. It felt strange that this day was normal for other people.

Laela dug her feet into the sidewalk and stopped. "Not this way," she croaked. "To the restaurant."

I paused with her. "What?"

"To the restaurant," she repeated. "Not your home. Not safe."

My brows pinched together. "What restaurant?"

"Denali's," she said. "Where Fae is."

Her eyes connected with mine, and the intensity there convinced me.

"O-okay," I said. "To the restaurant." I'd had the same thought. Ricki and Fae were the only ones who could help us.

Laela led me through town, and I still marveled at the fact that she was right next to me. Alive and well, if a bit off. I had faint memories of her from when I was a little girl but, like everyone else,

I believed she was dead. We kept to the edge of the sidewalks as we headed into town, tucked in the shadows against buildings. Mom and Dad were going to freak when they saw her.

Wait.

Mom and Dad.

My parents didn't know who they were. Mom gave up her Nobility to find me in Desolation. And Dad had disappeared in Desolation. Which meant they had no idea who they were here in this Cursed life.

But they were here now. They'd raised me here. And they had no idea who I was. They'd think I was as crazy as Laela if I started spouting off about another life and Nobility.

Mom and Dad hovered in my thoughts until we reached the end of town. The streets were empty, save for a few people smoking outside amid the trash littering the sidewalks. We turned down a small alley, passing a trash bin that released an awful stench into the air. Goosebumps broke out on my arms.

"You say there's a restaurant down here?" I wrapped my arms around myself. Maybe I was too quick to trust her.

Laela nodded, and her gray hair wobbled up and down. "This way."

We took one more corner before I saw it.

Denali's.

It was definitely a hole in the wall. But there were a few other shops surrounding it, with buzzing OPEN signs in the windows.

Laela pushed open the door and a bell jingled when we walked in. Small circular tables scattered the space, each with a white tablecloth on top. Flower centerpieces adorned the middle, silverware placed neatly alongside empty cups and menus at each setting. A dim light flickered overhead.

Ricki was standing at the bar speaking with Fae. Like always, Fae's dark hair was slicked back into a tight bun, and Ricki's hair curled outward in all directions like she hadn't brushed it for days. They paused their conversation and turned.

"Clara!" Ricki exclaimed. "You're okay." She rushed over and threw her arms around me in a hug. "Those guys took you. I didn't know what to do. And I couldn't find you on the other side—"

"Aericka, that's enough," Fae said.

Ricki drew back. "Sorry. I know I'm not supposed to say anything."

"No, it's okay," I said, reassuring her. "I know who I am."

The room paused.

"You do?" Ricki whispered.

Fae lifted her brows before giving me a regal nod. "It's about time." Her eyes lingered on me for a moment before she turned to Laela. A combination of shock, relief, and anger crossed over Fae's face. "So it *is* true."

"Hello, old friend," Laela croaked.

The corners around Fae's mouth creased. "I don't understand how—"

Laela waved a hand. "No need for words. Now get us something to drink. We've been in the sun for hours." She marched forward and planted herself at one of the tables, slapping her hands on top.

Ricki and I gave each other a glance. Moisture gathered in her eyes. I couldn't imagine the frustration she must've gone through, living both lives and me not knowing who I was.

"Thank you," I whispered to her.

She nodded back.

I turned back to the room, as thoughts and ideas were still flooding into my mind.

Faces. Names. Friends.

Ricki and Fae were connected to Laela. And Laela was connected to Nowen.

And Nowen was connected to . . .

My heart thumped, and I sprang forward. I rushed over to Laela, parking myself on a chair across from her. "Where's Dan?" I asked. "What do you know? Tell me!"

Laela shook her head slightly. "Too many questions too fast. Don't you have anything nice to say to your grandmother?"

Fae continued to stare at Laela, all the color in her cheeks gone. Her mouth had finally closed, but her throat bobbed as she swallowed. "We only had suspicions that you were alive, a part of me knew it because of our connection, but deep down I thought it impossible. Why didn't you find us before?"

Laela's bloodshot eyes darted to her before they landed on me again. "No time for a reunion. We need to get Dan and stop Nowen's little blood operation before it's too late."

I nodded quickly. "Maybe we can enlist the help of the police."

I pulled out my cell phone and was dialing when a slow heat began to radiate in my hand. It burned in my palm, and I pulled the phone away from my face. The phone case reddened and became scalding hot.

What?

Pain shot into my hand, and I dropped the phone. It clattered to the ground and the screen cracked.

I jumped to my feet. "What the—"

Fae stepped out from behind the counter. "You can't call anyone."

My jaw dropped open. "*How* can you use your Center here? Centers don't exist here in the Cursed world."

Fae pulled out a small vial from her pocket and held it up. She shook it, and red liquid swirled inside.

"It's a bottle of Laela's blood," Fae said. "Gherald Tompkins has figured out a way to use Death's blood to amplify our Centers. That's how my power here just worked."

My eyes darted from Fae to Laela to Ricki. "Seriously?"

"We had suspicions about Gherry and that he was involved with something bad over here," Ricki added. "We thought he was the one heading the blood operation up, but—"

"It's Nowen," I said. "Mr. Tompkins is working for Nowen."

"Who is this guy?" Ricki asked. "How do I not know who this Nowen guy is? We know everyone in Khalom."

"Nowen is . . ." How did I describe him? Ehlissa's brother? The power-hungry half of Cael? A guy I had kissed? I settled on, "He's bad news."

Ricki tightened her lips.

"So what does Nowen want with the blood?" I asked. My gaze shot over to Laela.

Laela stayed quiet.

Fae continued, "Whoever he is, the blood is a big problem." She held up the small vial again. "When consumed, Death's blood makes it so we can use our Centers on this side."

"That shouldn't be possible."

"It is," Fae said. "But currently, only for us Nobles. Death's blood taps into our Noble blood, which activates our abilities. However"—her eyes narrowed—"the blood operation has gotten worse. We have reason to believe that this Nowen wants to give the blood to non-Nobles."

"What? Why?" I asked.

"We've been following their movements. They've been testing it on non-Nobles."

My mind was racing. *What was Nowen doing over here?* Then a memory surfaced from Nowen back in the refrigerator truck. "Nowen needed another generation," I blurted out. "That's why he took Dan. Laela's blood was too weak. But Dan's blood didn't work, which is why he wanted mine."

Fae nodded. "Then it's confirmed. He's trying to create a concoction that gives non-Nobles powers."

"But why?" I asked once more.

Laela coughed, and the sound scraped the inside of my ears. My head spun over to her.

"You must know why," I said. "They've been taking your blood this whole time."

She placed a hand on her chest, her coughs easing. "My blood was no longer working. Yes, they need their concoction to be stronger. They thought a male line would give them the extra power they needed, but Daniel clearly doesn't have Noble blood."

"It's because Dan is my stepbrother," I blurted out. "My dad was married before. Dan is from another marriage. Dan isn't Noble."

Laela grunted. "Of course. That makes sense."

Fear for Dan rolled through me again. "Tell me more about this concoction. What can this blood do exactly?"

"Aericka, show her," Fae said. She tossed the small vial to Ricki.

Ricki caught it and her brows shot up to her hairline. "Really?" Excitement lit her eyes. "Fae is pretty stingy with the blood," she said to me. "We don't have very much."

Ricki unscrewed the lid, and poured out a couple drops of Laela's blood onto her wrist. It pearled on her skin, and she rubbed it around, smearing it over her arm. "It just needs to absorb."

I waited, mouth parted, slightly horrified. She was absorbing blood into her skin. Laela's blood.

Death's blood.

Ricki stared down at her wrist, until her mouth curved upward. "It's starting." She rubbed her hands together. "What do you want me to do?"

Fae motioned me to speak.

"Um . . . I'm not sure," I said, pulling at my ear. "Can you . . . disappear?"

Ricki rolled her eyes. "Easy." She vanished in a heartbeat, green smoke swirling into the air where she had been. Poof. Just like that.

A second later, Ricki appeared next to my left shoulder. "Lame," she said. "Choose something else. I've only got about thirty seconds left. Make it something good."

This was unreal. Even though I was used to powers in Khalom, being here, a part of me still felt like Clara Banks, where powers didn't exist.

"Can you fly around the room?" I asked.

Ricki groaned. "Seriously, Clara? That's all you can come up with?" Ricki slowly rose off the ground, her feet hovering a few inches from the floor.

She started floating forward, then Fae gripped her sleeve and pulled her down. "Clara gets the idea." Her eyes locked with mine. "Like we said before, the blood has only been used with Nobles. But now, if they get your blood, all non-Nobles here could have power. Can you imagine the uproar? People would do anything to get their hands on it. It would be the end of the Cursed world as we know it."

"I just don't understand why," I said. "Why is Nowen doing this?"

"We can focus on the why later," Fae said. "For now, we need to find you on the other side. Where have you been?"

I stopped. Where was I in Khalom? My heart rate picked up as I searched my mind. I didn't know. *Why* didn't I know?

My thoughts spun as I thought back. Cael's death was the first thing that came to mind. Cael and Nowen had fought. And then . . .

Khalob.

Deena.

My heart thumped harder. "I'm in the White Wing," I blurted out.

"What?" Ricki gasped. "How?"

I rubbed the sides of my head. "Khalob and Deena threw me in there."

Ricki groaned. "Are you serious? Clara, this is bad!"

I screwed up one side of my face. "Maybe not. It doesn't matter what's happening over there. I need to focus here and now. I need to get to Dan."

Fae shook her head. "No, Aericka is right. This is bad. The White Wing is a prison, meant to drive a person mad. It's meant to incapacitate you completely. Each prison attacks you differently. For example, if you were Time and Space, you'd be lost in a world of open space. You'd be floating in the middle of nowhere, forever, going mad. Consumed in nothingness."

She eyed me, a slim brow raised, and continued, "If you were Earth, you might be trapped in a dark cave with no sunlight, perhaps buried deep in the earth. No food. No water. All alone."

Her footsteps clopped on the floor as she paced. "And if you were Death . . ."

Her body went still, and her voice lowered. "It's possible you're being stabbed to death over and over again. Or trapped, drowning in an ocean. Or locked in a room with no chance of escape. You would be in a dying state forever."

I swallowed, my heart heavy in my chest. Maybe this was bad. "Can't one of you release me?"

Fae made a noise with her throat. "If only it were that easy. Only someone with the same Center as you can open the door. So one must hold Death to open Death's door." Her eyes slid to Laela. "And your grandmother hasn't been seen in Khalom for years. For all we know, she's lost the ability to travel."

We turned to Laela. She just looked back at us.

I sagged, rubbing the back of my neck. "Great. So I'm stuck. What are we going to do?"

"You're going to find Dan," Fae said. "I'll keep an eye on Laela." Her mouth pressed tight. "Take the blood. Ricki, go to the Sandman. It has to be where they are." She faced me again. "And then we'll find a way to get you out of the White Wing."

25
Crimson Chrysalis

Ricki drove Fae's sedan, and the road passed fast beneath us. I sat bouncing my leg and twisting my hands in my lap. It was so strange to see the world through my new eyes. Everything seemed . . . so much brighter. Clearer. The trees. The sunshine overhead. The mountains in the rearview mirror. For the first time in my existence, I saw the world through both of my lives.

And I felt alive.

Powerful.

Even now, as Ricki drove, Death hummed through my veins, a quiet buzzing, ready to be called upon at any moment. I'd never used Death to its full capacity, I'd only accidentally used it, but I had a new determination to use it for good.

In Khalom, all I'd been focusing on was connecting my lives. But now, I knew that wasn't enough. Mom's and Dad's lives were at stake. They didn't know who they were—just like all those poor people in Desolation. The Mhystic were missing, which meant Khalom didn't have any powerful leaders to protect it. If the Divining Masters took over the city, Khalom could crumble, which meant our lives here would crumble, too.

And with Cael gone . . .

Who knew what Nowen would do.

Nowen.

Just the thought of him made my insides scream. I couldn't believe I'd *kissed* him. And I'd wanted to. It'd been amazing. And now, all I felt was disgust.

I wanted to close my eyes, to try and shut out the memory of him, but all I could see was Cael's blue eyes looking up at me before he vanished.

"You okay?" Ricki asked.

I jumped, then turned to her. "What? Oh, yes. Fine."

Wind blew in from the open windows, tangling her hair. She scrunched her nose. "Really? I'm sure this is a lot to take in. Knowing both lives so suddenly. It's got to be a shock."

"I guess it is strange," I said quietly. "I mean . . . I know I'm Claera, but I also have full knowledge of Clara. But I guess it's like, I've put on a pair of glasses I didn't know I needed. It's jarring, but it's also so much better." Energy thrummed in my palms as I said that, as if my Center heard me.

"They're both *you*, Clara. Just let it *all* be a part of you. We each have many facets to who we are and our personalities. It's what makes us unique and special. But with our parallel lives, it gets to a point where you just make it one big life."

She fell quiet as she drove. Her face turned inward, as if she were deep in thought.

"And what about you?" I asked.

She gave me a sidelong glance. "Me? Oh, well, I'm not okay. I'm not sure *when* I'll be okay. Not with Robert still as a Diviner. I won't rest until he's free." She clenched her jaw.

I nodded before I said, "Tell me about him."

The car rumbled beneath us for a minute. Ricki's grip on the steering wheel slackened.

"Well, he's the only one who sees me for who I am," she said. "When Robert looks at me, he really *looks* at me, you know? When I lost him in Desolation, I was so *angry* with . . ." She paused, and her eyes skated to me.

"Me," I said.

She nodded. "You were the reason he gave up his soul. His Noble name. It's kind of why when I found you out in Desolation, I didn't do anything. I just let you sit out there. Day after day." Moisture gathered in her eyes as she stared at the road in front of her.

I sat with my back pressed up against my seat, my heart hammering. I had no idea she felt this way. Of course, it made sense.

"But now," Ricki continued, and a couple of tears escaped from her eyes. "I know it wasn't your fault. Robert made a choice. And he was trying to be the hero. It just backfired."

She fell silent. I knew the love of a brother, too. I felt it for Dan. I'd also venture out into the unknown for him—I'd do anything to save him. Only, Ricki had chosen to be my friend despite her anger. She could have still blamed me, but she didn't.

"I'm sorry," I whispered. I didn't know what else to say.

Ricki turned another corner and slowly pulled off to the side of the road. She cut the ignition and faced me. She took my hands and squeezed them tight.

"You and I are forever Companions, Clara. We may not be Blood Companions like Fae and Laela are, but I still feel bonded to you. I'm the one who should be asking for your forgiveness. I found you out in Desolation. I saw that your parents had lost their minds. And I still didn't bring you home. I'm the one who's sorry."

I nodded, staring down at our linked hands. I'd never had a friend like this before. She was right. We were Companions. Friends. And indebted to each other.

"I'm going to release Robert," I said softly. "I promise. I'm going to release him."

More tears escaped from Ricki's eyes, and she pulled back, wiping them away. "And we're going to find your brother, too."

We traveled to the other side of town, taking a few side streets until we pulled up and parked next to an alleyway. Old lamp posts lined the road, and though this had clearly once been a historic part of town, it had now been renovated, with new shops, bistros and cafes, clothing stores, and ice cream shops. It was a happening place at night.

The Sandman sat at the end of the street in a Victorian building with the club located underground. I'd heard of the Sandman. My friends had spoken about it at school, though I'd never been here.

"Why does Fae think Nowen and the others are here?" I asked. We exited the vehicle and our doors slammed. Ricki stepped up next to me and we peered down the street.

"We've been following Gherry for a while. The only places he goes are here and his day job at the hospital. He's a phlebotomist. So he clearly works with blood and is familiar with it."

"Nowen said something about spinning it," I said. "They must have some sort of formula."

Ricki nodded. "We suspected as much."

"I can't believe all this was going down and I had no idea," I said. "It's still so strange to have my lives connected." A flash of darkness zipped into my chest, and I flexed my hands. I itched to use my power on Nowen. He'd killed Cael and kidnapped Dan. He needed to be stopped, punished, dead.

I bit hard on the inside of my cheek. "Let's go."

Ricki and I jogged across the street and sidled up to the old Victorian home that had been remodeled into the club. We didn't go through the front doors but crept along the side of the building where a back stairwell led down. We snuck down the stairs and faced a plain steel door. I knew it would be locked, but I rattled the knob anyway.

"How are we going to get in?" I asked.

"With this." Ricki pulled out the vial of blood.

I eyed it with disgust. "I really don't want to use that."

"You don't have to," Ricki said. "I will."

Like before, she poured out a couple of drops onto her wrist and rubbed the bloody concoction into her skin. We waited several seconds, cars rumbling in the distance, laughter trickling from the street above.

"Okay," Ricki said. "I can feel it working." She wrapped her fingers around the knob and pushed. The door immediately swung open in a swoosh, but Ricki underestimated her strength, and the doorknob broke off. "Whoops." She held up the broken metal, then set it down by her feet.

I gaped but didn't say anything. This blood *was* powerful. And Nowen wanted to give it to the masses?

What was his game?

Before us, a hallway stretched long and dark. Several doors lined the space, and as we stepped inside, voices drifted toward us, spilling out into the hall.

My heart took off.

Dan.

Dan was probably inside. It took everything in me not to call out his name.

I motioned Ricki to follow, and we slunk forward toward the voices, our feet silent. Energy hummed through every part of me, making me feel like I was on fire.

At the end of the hall, we stopped. A door was slightly ajar, and the voices inside heightened, echoing out.

I peeked through the crack in the door.

Inside, Nowen was pacing in the middle of the room, rubbing the back of his neck. His hair hung down on his forehead, the lines of his face pulled extra tight. Several men sat around him, on couches and chairs that were strewn all over the room. Tension hung thick in the air, everyone watching Nowen.

My body reacted at the sight of him. So strange to see him here on this side—and for people to actually *see* him. And now I watched as he stepped into his own as the leader of an underground blood operation.

"I still don't know how you let her slip through your hands," Nowen growled, throwing a glare at Siv. He had an eye patch covering the eye Laela had injured. "How hard is it to keep tabs on a teenage girl and her old grandmother?"

Mr. Tompkins sat off to the side, his eyes narrowed behind his glasses. "They *are* both Death. They're pretty powerful."

Nowen whirled on him. "Shut up. I didn't ask your opinion." He continued to pace.

My eyes frantically scanned the space. Dan. *Where was Dan?* My eyes darted from person to person.

Then my heart stopped. There.

Dan sat at the edge of the room, hunched over. His skin was a sickly gray, and sweat shone on his forehead. His eyes looked like two bruises. I hadn't seen him look this sick in a long time. He needed his meds.

"Dan!" I started forward.

"Shh," Ricki said, yanking me back. "We need more information first."

My heart was beating triple time. He was here. He was alive. But Ricki was right—we needed more information. I forced my feet to stay put.

Nowen continued to pace, the room remaining silent, until he paused. "We must continue forward as if on schedule. Siv, you were able to get some of Clara's blood, and from the preliminary tests, it will work." He shot a look at Dan. "Your sister's was powerful enough." He faced the room again. "We'll call it *Deaeth*. We'll be able to distribute the drug for now, but we'll need more blood soon to continue our operation."

"Why is he doing this?" I whispered.

Ricki waved me away, shushing me.

"Now to do a final test." Nowen slowly faced Dan, lifting his brows. "Maybe you won't be useless after all." He clicked his tongue.

I gripped Ricki's arm. "What's happening?"

Nowen snapped his fingers. "Siv. Dane. Give Dan some of Deaeth. Since he's not Noble, we'll see how it works on a mundane person."

Siv and Dane immediately strode across the room. They yanked Dan up from his chair and dragged him over to the couch. They shoved him down, and Dan cried out. Nowen tossed them a little pouch, and Dane ripped it open, sprinkling a light pink powder onto his finger. He set his finger underneath Dan's nose, waiting for him to breathe it in.

"No!" Dan yelled. He kicked and thrashed, trying to shove the guys off him. Mr. Tompkins sat back, not doing a thing. Nowen's eyes lit with excitement.

Siv reached down and covered Dan's mouth, stopping his air flow. Dane kept the powder right underneath Dan's nose.

"Stop!" Dan yelled, but his voice was muffled underneath Siv's palm.

I stared in horror, my heart racing at an impossible speed.

"They've turned the blood into a powder," Ricki said. "That way people will buy it. They'll think it's a real drug."

I couldn't take it any longer. "I'm sorry, Ricki, but I'm going in." I burst into the room before she could stop me.

The room paused, all heads turning to me.

Even Dan's eyes connected with mine. Nowen rocked back on his heels, his mouth sliding upward.

"You're just in time," Nowen said, amusement in his eyes. The look used to make me melt, but now all I felt was anger.

"Let him go," I said. My heart pounded furiously, my body on fire.

Dan still struggled on the couch. His face was a bright purple, his eyes bulging.

"I said let him go!" I screamed. I sprinted forward, running to Dan, but Nowen caught me by the arm. Ricki rushed in after me, stopping just inside the doorway. Nowen's eyes snapped to her before they returned to me.

"It's okay," Nowen said. "I'm helping him. I would never hurt someone who mattered to you, Dessy."

I shook my head, trying to yank out of his grip. Dan's efforts to hold his breath were slackening, and tears leaked from his eyes.

"Please, Nowen." I turned to him. "If you've ever cared about me at all, let him go."

"Oh, Dessy." Nowen lifted a hand and touched the bottom of my chin. "I'm doing this *for* you."

Dan's lungs gave out. He inhaled frantically, breathing in the powdered blood. Siv and Dane immediately released him, and Dan lay back on the couch, panting. He coughed several times, curling over.

"Dan!"

Nowen finally let me go and I rushed over to him. I set a hand on his back. "Are you all right?"

Nowen stayed put, crossing his arms.

Dan nodded, slowly sitting up. "I think so."

I patted his face, then touched his arms, just to make sure he was there. Ricki still hovered in the doorway, the vial of blood clasped in her hands.

I kept my focus on Dan, all my panic and fear slowly calming, my nerves stitching themselves back together. Maybe Nowen's Deaeth didn't work. Dan seemed perfectly fine.

Other than his cancer. I took in his sickly face again.

But then, very slowly, the color started returning to his face. His gray pallor washed away, replaced by a healthy pink. The bruises that lined his jaw disappeared. His back straightened, and light came into his eyes. He glanced down at his arms, rubbing them.

"I . . ." he started.

"What is it?" I asked.

"Deaeth is working," Nowen said, lips quirked. "He's being healed. When we're on Deaeth, we become strong. Unbelievably strong."

"What?" I slowly rose to my feet. "Why—why are you doing this?"

Nowen's shoulders softened. "Because you know more than anyone, Dessy, how awful it is to be trapped. As do I. I'm not all that bad. I want to give the people here in this Cursed world a taste of what Nobles have. Is it not fair that Nobles get to have power? That they get to have lives when the rest of the people in Desolation have nothing? Nothing there or here? They deserve to have freedom."

I stared at him. *He was doing this to help people?*

"But I can't do this without you, Dessy," he continued. "Your grandmother's blood isn't powerful enough. I didn't want to get you involved, but I have to. I need your blood to make this work. It's why I needed your lives connected. Death needs to be with you full force."

I opened my mouth, but I didn't have words. He'd been manipulating me this whole time. Had he ever felt anything for me? What about our kiss? And getting the people here in this Cursed world hooked on Deaeth was wrong. Once they started taking it, they wouldn't be able to stop.

Nowen smoothly took a step toward me. "What do you say, Dessy? Will you help me?"

My mind was screaming. I needed to get Dan out of here. I eyed the door behind me. It was the only exit.

"Help him," Dan said. "Please. Look at me." He rose from the couch and touched my shoulder.

I spun to him. "What?"

"Clara, the way I feel right now . . . if you . . ." Tears pooled in his eyes. "Please. I never want to feel sick again. Give Nowen your blood. Let me keep living like this."

I was paralyzed. My mind was being pulled in too many different directions. I couldn't speak.

"And you *can* continue to have it," Nowen said, eyes soft. "As long as you have this." He pulled out another pouch from his black jeans and tossed it to Dan. "Will you help us spread the word? We're debuting Deaeth tonight here at the club. Will you help?"

Dan caught the pouch and grasped it in his hand. He stared at it for a minute before he nodded. "I'm in."

Nowen gripped his hand and shook it.

I blinked, the exchange finally processing. "No! Dan!"

I was reaching for the pouch in Dan's hand when Nowen snapped his fingers again. Siv and Dane were on me in two steps. They gripped me by the upper arms and started to drag me out the doorway.

"What? No!" I yelled. "Dan!"

But he stayed put, standing next to Nowen. Siv and Dane carried me toward the door.

Ricki leaped into action.

She must've taken some of the blood again, because one minute she was standing by the door, and the next, she was on Dane's back, choking him. She punched him right in the face, and he cried out. Ricki jumped off him and hit him again. He flew backward twenty feet and crashed into the wall. Siv shoved me to the ground and faced Ricki, cracking his knuckles before he charged toward her.

Ricki's eyes widened, and she quickly whirled to me. "Clara, the blood!" She tossed me the vial, but it fell short and hit the floor. The glass broke in shards, the red blood splattering everywhere.

"No!" I yelled.

Siv had Ricki in a headlock, and she struggled, elbowing him in the stomach. The blood must've been wearing off. I frantically glanced from Ricki, to Dan, to Nowen, to Mr. Tompkins, who still lounged in a chair like he was watching a movie.

I needed to get Ricki and we needed to get out. But I couldn't leave Dan. He stood next to Nowen's side, not helping.

"Dan!" I shouted. "Come on!"

But he shook his head.

I scrambled to my feet and started toward Ricki and Siv. Dane appeared from behind me. I briefly saw his face before he smacked me in the head, and everything went dark.

26
Burnt Offerings

Searing heat parched my skin and intense light blinded me.

I licked my lips—cracked and dry.

I felt as if I were burning inside and out. The heat pounded down, an unforgiving sun above me. I'd tried to walk earlier, find some way out of this strange world I was in, but exhaustion hit, and I'd collapsed. I didn't know how long I'd been lying down.

Sand stuck to my sweaty yet dry skin, in my fingernails, in my mouth. My throat burned with thirst, the sun beating down unrelentingly.

I was in a desert—that much was clear—but it seemed to be unending, the sand stretching beyond the horizon. I didn't know how I wasn't dead yet.

But then I knew.

I couldn't die a physical death here—I wasn't in my Cursed life.

I was in the White Wing.

I didn't know the White Wing was torture like this. I thought it would just be a prison cell, but then Fae's words echoed in my mind.

It's a prison, meant to drive a person mad. It's meant to incapacitate you completely—consume you in a world that affects your Center.

I was Death. This was my own personal torture.

It was hard to focus on what was happening in my Cursed life. I had my lives linked, so I was able to remember what was happening over there when I returned to consciousness here, though the torture in the White Wing muddled my brain.

I'd just been inside the backroom of the club. They'd forced Dan to take Deaeth, and he'd liked it. Nowen was there. And Mr. Tompkins. Ricki was fighting Siv, and then, I was knocked out.

And now I was here.

I must have only been here for seconds. I could be yanked back there at any moment—which I prayed for. Nothing over there could be worse than being in this heat.

My skin continued to burn. I swallowed, sand in my throat, thirst burning. I licked my lips, but they stung. They were so dry. How much longer could I last? Was I trapped in this torment forever?

I closed my eyes, the sun hot and red through my lids. I waited for darkness to take me again. I couldn't handle being here for another second.

27
Tidal Wave

I woke in a plain white room. At first, I thought I was in Khalom again, but the pain in my head told me otherwise. I hissed as I touched the back of my skull, my vision wavering. I tried to focus on single objects.

White walls. White desk in the corner. White sofas and chairs placed intermittently. I slowly sat up. I was on one of the white sofas. White rug. White light.

"You're awake."

I jerked, snapping my head up. Across the room, Nowen leaned against the far wall, his dark hair and clothes making him look like a spot of black ink on a white canvas.

"I've been bored waiting for you to awaken. Where have you been?" He lifted his brows.

I knew he meant where was I on the other side, but I didn't want to tell him I was locked in the White Wing. Somehow, he'd use it to his advantage.

"I was worried about you." He frowned. "When Khalob and those kids dragged you off, I didn't know what happened to you." He tilted his head, analyzing me.

"You mean right after you *killed* Cael?" The words stung, jabbing right into my heart. I hadn't allowed myself to process it fully yet. Cael couldn't be gone. But he was.

Silence settled for a moment. Nowen continued to stare at me, an unreadable expression on his face. He cocked his head to the other side.

"I want to kiss you again," he said.

"You *what*?" His words screamed through me. I allowed them to settle in my chest before heat boiled in my veins. "You know that'll never happen again."

Nowen sighed and pushed himself off the wall. "I know. Especially with me taking your blood from you without your will." He nodded to my arms.

What?

I peered down. A fresh Band-Aid had been placed at the crook of my elbow. I gently touched it before looking back at him. "Are you serious?" I jumped up from the couch, and my head spun. I swayed, catching myself on the couch. "You took blood from me?"

Nowen frowned again. "Only when I need to, Dessy. Though it's not as potent when you're on the other side. I need you here. Mentally and physically. The Death that runs through your veins is priceless."

My gaze briefly flicked to the door, and Nowen caught my gaze. Before I could move, he threw a hand outward, and metal appeared out of nowhere. It melted over the door, the doorknob losing shape, becoming one large clump of metal until it all disappeared, sealing me in.

"We don't want to take any chances," Nowen said.

"Why?" My voice shook.

Nowen slowly glided forward, tucking his hands in his pockets. The light above made him look sickly. His eyes and cheekbones were two black holes. "I told you. People here deserve to know what it's like to be a Noble. I lived so long trapped powerless on the other side. I'm going to give them freedom. You of all people should know they deserve it."

My heart sped up the closer he approached.

"But why?" I asked again. "You killed Cael. Don't you have your freedom now?" I raised my brow. "Unless you don't?"

He stopped a breath away from me, taking me in with his two black eyes. The blue was gone. Cael was no longer there. He lifted a hand as if to touch my face, and I stayed unmoving, waiting, but he paused. His eyes searched mine for a moment before he lowered his hand.

"It'll be all right, Dessy," he said. "You'll see in the long run, this is what is best."

And in a blink, he disappeared from right in front of me, like he always had in Khalom, leaving me alone in the empty white room.

I paced for what felt like hours. Or days—it was hard to tell. Minutes ticked by slowly, my feet wearing out the white flooring beneath me. I couldn't stop wringing my hands.

I couldn't slow my racing mind.

I understood Nowen's reasoning. I understood wanting to give the people here freedom. I'd seen firsthand the horror that people experienced in Desolation day after day. But to give people the ability to have Centers here with Deaeth? It could completely destroy the balance between our two worlds. I agreed we needed to help people, yes, but this wasn't the answer. We needed to stop the Divining Masters. We needed to stop the Diviners. If we gave people their lives back in Desolation, they could live full, connected lives. They could find happiness with their families. Power isn't what brings happiness.

And I still couldn't process that he was Ehlissa's brother. Cael. And Nowen. What had they been like when they were one?

More pacing. My mind wouldn't stop.

Nowen appeared from time to time, probably to make sure I was there. I didn't sleep, which meant I didn't travel to the White Wing—though I knew I was still being tortured in my other life.

I just needed to find a way out.

But as much as I tried to free myself from the sealed door or to scream and pound on the walls, I was locked in. I kept hoping that Ricki or Fae or Dan would come to the rescue, but they probably didn't even know where I was.

Finally, Nowen appeared once more.

"We need more blood," he said.

I'd collapsed on the couch, my legs aching from all the pacing. I eyed the phlebotomist kit in his hands, mouth tight. He set the kit down next to us on the couch and started fiddling with the supplies.

I twisted my mouth. "You know, if you cared about me at all, you wouldn't do this."

He paused, his hands still.

I bit my lip. "This isn't you, Nowen. All of this. What are you trying to prove?"

A muscle ticked in his cheek. Energy rolled off him in waves. I knew he wanted to answer, I knew he wanted to defend himself, but instead, he turned back to the kit.

"You'll see, Dessy," is all he murmured.

I sat back, watching him in silence. My only angle was to try and talk him out of it, and I had repeatedly failed. I eyed the sealed door. I needed another way out. My pulse spiked as Nowen prepped more of the supplies.

"Our big debut is in a few hours," Nowen said. "We only have so much time to make more Deaeth. Word will spread. It will be a huge success."

My gaze darted from him to the door to the needles in his kit. My pulse raced faster. All I had was my words.

"I cared about you, Nowen," I said. "Not just Cael, but *you*. In fact, there was a time I wasn't sure who I cared about more. And I know you felt the same about me. I have to believe I was more than just blood to you. So," I paused and swallowed, "so if you care about me at all, show me and let me go."

His jaw tightened, and for a moment, I saw indecision on his face, but he dipped back down, prepping the kit, mouth tight.

Silence stretched between us for several moments. Then he paused and lifted his head.

"Don't you want to do this for Dan?" he asked. "You should see him. He's healthy. He's never been happier."

I kept my body still. He knew how to play the game, too. Nowen knew Dan was everything to me.

"We can figure this out," I said. "A way to keep Dan healthy. A way that you don't take my blood. A way that we can save those poor people in Khalom."

Nowen shook his head. "There's nothing you can say that will change my mind, Dessy."

He scooted closer to me and picked up my arm, setting it in his lap. I didn't even try to fight. I couldn't outrun him. I couldn't beat him in a physical match. My mind was still jumping from thought to thought, trying to find a way to solve this.

Nowen took out a cleansing wipe and gently cleaned the crook of my elbow. Shivers erupted along my skin. I needed to come up with a plan to get out of here.

He reached into the kit and pulled out a needle. My heart rate accelerated.

Think, Clara.

Think.

I was powerful. I was Death.

There had to be something I could do. But Death couldn't be used over here in the Cursed world, could it? Nowen lifted the needle to my arm. My mind was screaming.

Think.

I needed to do something.

We're coming for you, Clara. Just hold on.

I froze. My head shot over to Nowen. "What did you say?"

Nowen's brows pushed together, the needle pausing at my arm. "What do you mean?"

We're coming.

There it was again.

I knew that voice. I would *never* forget that voice. That voice was my life. My heart. Everything that was important to me.

But he couldn't be real. Cael was dead. *How* was I hearing his voice?

Nowen must've read my face. He dropped the needle and gripped my shoulders. "What's happening? Something is happening."

I turned my mind inward, willing myself to hear his voice again. I prayed that I wasn't imagining it. Maybe he was real. He *had* to be real.

We're coming, Clara. Only one more moment.

It was real. I knew it was. I could feel an energy building in my bones.

I leveled my gaze with Nowen's. "Sorry, Nowen. But it's time for me to go."

His eyes widened, and desperation briefly flashed over his face. His grip on my shoulders tightened.

"No," he said. "What's happening?"

We're here! Come to our voices!

A deep warmth began to travel through my body. It started in my core, building, growing, stretching down my limbs. My eyelids drifted closed, heavy, like they weighed a hundred pounds.

A light roaring sounded in my ears.

My mouth lifted in a smile. "Goodbye Nowen."

"No, don't leave!" He shook my shoulders. "I need your full Death power here. If you're on the other side, your blood isn't as strong!"

But his voice became distant, the world darkened, and my mind slipped away completely.

Wind brushed past my face, and I knew I was traveling—fully alive and alert. I had felt this before when I'd traveled with Nowen in the Dhim. It only lasted a few seconds.

Then, heat blasted down at me, and I opened my eyes to bright light searing my vision. My fingers dug into the scalding sand beneath me, and an immediate burning surged into my throat.

"Cael?" I croaked. "Cael?"

"Clara!" Ricki's voice echoed from a distance. "Over here!"

I squinted all around me, peering into the endless desert. My eyes locked on a small light—a different kind of light from the bright sun overhead. Ricki's silhouette came into view, dark in the doorway full of light.

"Clara, come on." She reached out a hand. I rolled over, struggling onto my hands and knees, but I was too weak to stand. Every part of me shook with exhaustion.

Ricki's hand reached farther, and then the ground warped. The sand rolled, and the ground tipped, and my body slid rapidly downward to where Ricki stood. The earth rumbled and sand flew everywhere. The earth gave one last lurch, and I tumbled into the hallway where Ricki stood.

She slammed the door shut. Fresh air immediately sank into my skin, revitalizing like a cool liquid flowing through my veins. I lay in the white hallway, my skin slowly stitching itself back together.

"How . . ." I croaked, coolness still seeping into my skin. "How long have I been in there?"

Ricki's fingers wrapped around my hand, and she pulled me to a standing position. I swayed, and she stabilized me.

"Too long," she said. "You very well could've died mentally in there. I'm surprised you still have your sanity."

Did I? I had heard Cael's voice. I'd probably imagined it. My heart dropped into my stomach. I was stupid for thinking he was alive. But I was here. I was free. I was away from Nowen. I knew my body was still over there, but he said my blood wasn't as powerful when I was here.

"You're okay," I said. "Last I saw you, you were fighting Siv."

She nodded. "I got away."

I stared at the door I'd just fallen through. "How?" I asked. "Only someone with Death can open Death's door. How did you . . .?"

Ricki took my shoulders, stabilizing me once more. A smile lit her face. She spun me around to face the end of the hallway.

"I didn't," she said. "But he did."

Cael stood tall and perfect at the end of the hall, in his full physical form, flesh and blood. He stared at me with two blue eyes, piercingly cold like a deep ocean. He looked so like Nowen, with his sharp cheekbones and dark hair, except his was cropped short against his head.

"Cael," I whispered. I nearly passed out.

He nodded. "Let's go. We've already been here too long."

28
Rock Wars

I couldn't breathe. Not next to him. He was the most beautiful thing I had ever seen. I'd wished for so many years to *see* him—be with him. And now he was real. Alive. Well. I didn't even care how it happened, all that mattered was that it did happen.

My mind wouldn't stop spinning as we left the Grand Hall. I couldn't believe Cael was right next to me. Cool night air washed over me, and I glanced at the goosebumps on my arms. It was cold. Khalom wasn't supposed to fluctuate in temperature. I rubbed my arms.

Cael glanced down at my arms. "The city's protection is down." His soft voice was loud in the quiet. "The Diviners are coming in and out of the city at will now, scouting out the city's defenses. The Divining Masters haven't infiltrated yet; they're gathering information before they attack. Most of the students and High Officials here are hiding. Come on, we need to get to the border."

I couldn't stop staring at him. The moonlight traced his features, severe like Nowen's, but there was a light in his eyes, a determination Nowen didn't have. I had so much to ask him. How was he here? How was he in his physical form?

Why was he helping me? And where were we going?

But instead of asking, I followed him and Ricki through Historic Quarter, weaving through the white pathways. The milky trees gently swayed in the light breeze that carried on the air. We were nothing but shadows in the moonlight, slipping through Khalom. Cael's body stayed tense as he led us, as if ready for a sign of threat at any moment.

My heart was beating so fast, I thought it would explode. But we continued quietly down through Khalom, my body alive and alert, my nerve endings on fire. We approached the gate, and it glowed menacingly in the dark, its posts shooting up into the night sky.

Cael paused at the border, the green forest dark on the other side of the fence. He turned, and his blue eyes connected with mine. They wrapped me up and held me, like I would never suffer again.

"We're not safe here anymore," Cael said. "We need to regroup. We need an army to protect Khalom."

An army?

I shook my head. "We shouldn't leave Khalom. The Divining Masters. If we lose the city to them, it's all over."

"The Divining Masters already tried to snatch you up, Clara. You're not safe," Ricki said.

My brows slanted inward. "What do you mean snatch me up? You mean Nowen?"

Ricki shook her head. "No, Nowen isn't a Divining Master. Mr. Tompkins is."

My eyes opened wider.

"Here, look." She pulled out a parchment from her back pocket. "Remember in class when Mr. Tompkins tried to get you to sign this? He told you it was school paperwork, but it isn't. I knew something was off, so I stole it."

I reached out and took the piece of paper from her. I analyzed the writings.

It was the same paper. I recognized the names, remembered the burn mark on the bottom of the paper.

I glanced up at her. “Why are you showing me this?”

Ricki pointed. “Look closer.”

I scanned the names that were listed. Each name was signed in a different scrawl, then I stopped in my tracks.

“No,” I whispered. Adrenaline hurdled into my chest. “Robert’s name is on this list.”

Ricki’s chin quivered, and I could tell she was fighting back tears. “This is Mr. Tompkins’s Diviner list. He was trying to get you to sign your Noblehood away. He was trying to make you one of his Diviners.”

The adrenaline spread outward, pounding in my veins. “But . . . Mr. Tompkins is with Nowen on the other side. What is he doing?”

“Gherald is the one we need to be worried about,” Cael said. “He’s more of a threat than Nowen. After Nowen killed me—when I thought he killed me—I reappeared here in Khalom. But Nowen isn’t here. He’s trapped over in the Cursed world, as I am trapped here.”

“Another reason why he wants power over there,” I said. “He’s still trapped.”

Cael nodded.

“But Gherald Tompkins has access to the blood over there and his Diviners here. He plans on taking over Khalom and the Cursed world. He wants to rule it all. He’s keeping Nowen in his pocket until he can strike him down.”

A softness immediately sprang to my chest for Nowen, though it shouldn’t have. But once again, he was confined. Yes, he was making the wrong choices—but his intentions weren’t evil—not like Mr. Tompkins. Nowen was trying to give people in the Cursed world some semblance of freedom. He was trying to give himself freedom. Mr. Tompkins was trying to take it away.

I faced Cael head on. "So what do we do?"

"We go to the Stricken camp," he said. "We gather our army. We make sure the Divining Masters don't overtake the city."

I still couldn't believe Cael was here. That he was *talking* to me. And that I could *see* his physical form. But I kept my emotions under control and nodded.

He turned toward the gate, and I started forward when Ricki grabbed my arm. "I can't go with you," she said. "Not yet. I need to make sure Fae is okay. She's still with Laela on the other side. Laela's not able to travel on her own. Nowen or Gherry might try to find them for her blood. Fae could be in danger because of it."

I paused, processing her words. She was right. Fae and Laela could be in danger. But I didn't want Ricki to be alone. She'd done so much for me, and I didn't want to leave her now.

But I didn't have an alternate solution, so I said, "Okay. Yes. Go."

She reached out and squeezed my hand. "I'll see you soon." She peeked up at Cael. "Take care of her."

A question hung in Cael's eyes for a moment, then he blinked and his face relaxed. "Always."

Ricki gave me one last look before she took off into the night, back up the path, leaving me and Cael alone.

29

Vein of Gold

We stepped through the gate, and the white bars dissolved and, after we'd walked through, reappeared as we immersed ourselves fully into the shaded forest. I followed Cael as we walked, our footsteps crunching softly. The trees were tall and dark in the sky, little stars peeking through the treetops.

"We need to walk and not Celerate," Cael said. "The Diviners can sense when Noble powers are used." His voice carried out into the forest. "It might take us some time."

I nodded silently, though my mind was still doing jumping jacks. He said after Nowen stabbed him, he immediately came to Khalom. It must've been because of who he was. He was one of the original holders of all five Centers, Ehlissa's powerful brother. And Nowen was a part of him—maybe it was impossible for a piece of him to kill himself.

We traveled for a time, the forest thick around us. The last time we'd been in these woods together, he'd been nothing more than a silhouette. Now, he was skin and muscle. Flesh and blood. He looked just like Nowen, yet nothing like him. Where Nowen was pale, Cael was tan. Where Nowen had a slight cock to his head and a slanted stance, Cael stood tall and commanding. Where Nowen made me feel alive, Cael had captured my heart and soul.

Silence hung between us as we walked, but every part of me ached to speak with him. He'd hinted in the past of caring for me, but I didn't know what that meant. There was an undeniable connection between us. He *had* to feel it. There had to be more between us than just him being my protector. But why would an almighty being care about me? Really care about *me*?

We traveled all night, nearly silent for the entire walk until morning light began to peek through the trees. We'd barely said a word to each other—just Cael giving me directions and telling me where to watch out for branches or dangerous roots on the ground.

Always the protector.

Finally, after several more minutes, I couldn't take it anymore.

"Did you kiss me that day in the forest?" I blurted out. "When I asked you to?"

Cael stopped in front of me. His back was stiff, unmoving.

"Why do you ask?"

"Because I need to know." I hated that I sounded desperate, but suddenly, it was as if I had no filter. "You know I care about you, Cael. More than care about you. I need to know if you feel the same. I can't—I can't go on not knowing."

He slowly turned his head so I could see one side of his face. The morning light cast heavy shadows on his cheeks.

"I don't . . ." He paused for a moment. "I don't express myself very well, Clara. I never have. And . . ." He heaved out a sigh. "I've never been able to forgive myself for what I did to you. For trying to take Death from you."

"But you didn't," I said. "And you weren't the one who tried to kill me. That was someone else."

He kept his profile to me. "I might as well have—taking your Center from you is unforgivable. And for what? So I could rule?"

He shook his head. "I was jealous of Ehlissa. I wanted her fame and power. I always resented that she was chosen as the leader of Khalom when I was just as powerful. I didn't want to rule only the Stricken. I wanted it all. So, I waited, patiently, for the right time to take the throne. A thousand years passed, and you were born, the very last carrier of Death. You were the only threat that could have stopped me from ruling Khalom. You were the only other entity who could kill me."

He turned and faced me fully. "You want to know if I care about you? Clara." He took a single step forward and the leaves crunched beneath him. "I care about you more than you'll ever know. You gave me a reason to live day after day—to keep living every day when the guilt ate me alive. You gave me a reason to not go into the Dhim and be swallowed up in the dead like my sister. She wasn't strong enough to face her decisions. But I . . ." His eyes lowered to the forest floor. "You gave me the strength to live. To face my wrongdoings and take responsibility for my actions. To try and right my wrongs.

"At first, I stayed in Desolation with you because of the guilt. I swore to protect you at all costs. But then . . . it became more than that. I stayed because I *had* to. I couldn't leave you. I didn't want to." His eyes lifted. "You have no idea how many times I wanted to show myself to you. Be with you."

Silence pounded between us, and I swallowed.

"I kissed you that day," he finished.

Cael's words were what I'd waited so long to hear. They flooded into me and began to seal up all the little wounds that had cut me through the years. His words flowed through my veins, warming me from the inside out. They played over in my mind, calming all the hurt and anger I had swirling around.

It had always been him and me. From the beginning.

"Cael—" I started forward, but he held up a hand, motioning me to stop. My feet dug into the earth.

"Don't," he said. "I expressed what I felt, but that doesn't mean we can be together. I know you care for Nowen, and I can't be with you knowing that. He is the worst part of me, and I can't have anything to do with what reminds me of who I used to be."

I started forward again, then paused. I wanted to say he was wrong. That I didn't care about Nowen, but I knew that was a lie, as much as I hated it.

"I care about you more," was all I said.

Cael nodded before turning back around. "We need to keep moving."

I could barely walk. My legs shook so bad it was a struggle to keep moving them forward. Tears gathered in my eyes several times, but each time they came, I blinked them away. I needed to be strong. Cael and I didn't matter right now. Nowen didn't matter. What mattered was getting to the Stricken camp, recruiting an army, and stopping Mr. Tompkins and the other Divining Masters.

But with each step, my heart hurt more. It was worse knowing how Cael felt. I thought it would make me feel better, but it didn't. Of course I cared about him more than Nowen, but Nowen was a part of him, too.

Maybe I just loved all of him.

We stopped at the top of a large hill, and the morning light illuminated a deep valley below us. I moved slightly ahead of Cael, peering below, my eyes stretched wide. It was a campsite. Tents were scattered on the dusty ground with dozens of fires smoking over the valley. There weren't any trees—just a red dirt landscape. People bustled around their tents, throwing wood on the fires; a few children ran around.

Then I stopped and looked closer.

They weren't normal people. They were silhouettes—they were Stricken, just like Cael had once been.

The Stricken camp.

I turned to Cael, and my mind immediately went to Mom.

"Is she here?" I asked. "Where is she?" My breath hitched. The last time I'd seen her over here, her brain had been badly damaged by the Diviners.

"I'll take you to her," he said. "But there's someone I want you to see first."

My brows pinched together, but I followed him down the hill. Little rocks rolled down the mountain, and dust kicked up from beneath my heels. The trees slowly dispersed until they were gone entirely, replaced by large boulders that scattered the area.

"Is everyone here a Stricken?" I asked.

Cael nodded. "In a way. A Stricken, by definition, is a Noble who chooses to give up their identity to become a warrior to protect the city. Just like a Diviner signs away their Noble name in a contract, the Stricken also give up their Noble name and their physical appearance. They give up their Centers and vow to be with the Stricken for the rest of their existence. However, it used to be just Nobles who became Stricken, but now, people in Desolation who are coherent enough to make the choice can also choose to take the Stricken vow."

I kept my eyes locked on the valley at the shadow people tending to their morning chores, at the kids playing by their mothers' feet.

"Why are there children?" I asked.

Cael frowned. "It's safer for them to take the vow and be with the group then to be on their own out in Desolation. You of all people know it's not safe for them there. They're not old enough to fight, but they are one of us."

"Us?" I asked, eyeing him. His tanned skin shimmered in the morning sun. "But you aren't really a Stricken, are you?"

Cael's blue eyes slid to mine. "When I ripped myself away from Nowen that night, I lost my physical appearance. But the Stricken knew who I was. They knew I was always destined to lead them."

I nodded, falling silent, but I snuck another peek at him. His hair was cropped close to his head, his jaw cut sharp. Cael moved forward once more, and I followed after him down the hill.

We maneuvered around large boulders and tents, watching shadow people attending to their business. Several heads turned in my direction, and I could feel their dark gazes on me. I kept my head forward, not wanting to stare, but I wanted to know their stories. Why had they chosen to become a Stricken? Were they once Noble? Or did they escape the throes of the Diviners out in Desolation?

We wove through the dirt pathways around the tents to the other end of the valley, where a large tent was tucked up into the mountainside. Cael opened the canvas flap and motioned me inside. I squinted, trying to see through the darkness.

"You'll just have to go inside, Clara," he said.

My name on his lips was only one word, but it was enough to make me crack. I peeked over at him before stepping inside.

Inside, candles lit the entire area, flickering on the canvas walls. Dozens of bodies—physical bodies—lay on pallets that lined the floor, silent, not breathing. A heaviness hung in the air, the flames highlighting their exteriors. It was like I was in a morgue.

I shuffled back a step. "Are these all—" I couldn't finish. "Are they *dead?*"

"They're fresh attacks," Cael said. "We're waiting to see if they survive or not. Some make it, some don't. We come and retrieve people in Desolation when they're nearing their end, trying to give them a chance. They then have the choice to become Stricken or find their own way."

Retrieve?

Realization dawned and I put a hand over my heart.

"This is where the people in Desolation disappear to. Like Angela Cummings's mom. Like . . ."

Every part of me froze. My lungs had turned to ice.

"Dad," I whispered.

The tent flap opened, and daylight spilled inside. A silhouetted man entered, broad shoulders, slim hips, a ruffle of hair on top of his head.

My heart stopped.

I stared for a few seconds before the tears hit.

"Dad!"

I rushed forward and threw my arms around him. He wrapped me up tight, holding me.

We hadn't been separated in the Cursed world long, but I hadn't seen him on this side for many years. And he didn't know who he was over there.

"Whoa, Clara. It's okay." He pulled back, keeping his hands on my shoulders. I took in every inch of him. A silhouette from head to toe, but I still recognized the shaded line of his features. Even though his eyes were two black pits, I still remembered the twinkle in his eye from our time here.

"Dad, what happened?" I asked. "I don't understand . . . all of it. We were together out in Desolation. But then you disappeared. And you in the Cursed world . . ."

"It's a lot, I know," Dad said. "We'll talk." His hands dropped from my shoulders, and he faced Cael. "Can I have leave? I know we have training this afternoon, but—"

Cael lifted a hand. "Of course. You never need to ask again." His sharp eyes connected with mine for a moment, intense, before they skated away. "I'll see you tonight."

Cael strode out of the tent, leaving Dad and me alone with the sleeping people in recovery. Candlelight flickered throughout the room and my gaze wandered around at the still bodies. How many of them would choose to become a Stricken? How many would choose to venture back into Desolation and most likely be lost for good?

Dad set a hand on my shoulder once more. "Come," he said. "I've waited a long time to see you again, Clara. Let's walk."

I nodded numbly, allowing Dad to pull me from the tent.

Outside, the sunlight was bright, warming the whole valley. Smoke billowed up into the air between tents grouped together. Shadow people were busy at work or lounging by the fires.

"I'm sure you have a lot of questions," Dad said. His tone was as it always had been. Warm, kind. We brushed shoulders as we headed down a dusty path.

"None of this happened the way your mother wanted, Clara. But the wheels were put into motion long before you were born." He sighed. "Your mother believed that Death was a death sentence. Everyone with Death had either died or disappeared. It's why she refused to use the Center itself. And when you were taken from Khalom, she decided it was a gift. That you could live outside the city and have a full life.

"And that's when she met me," he continued. "We fell in love. And then she couldn't leave. We were a happy family." The dark hollows of his eyes slid over to me.

"But in the end," he went on, "fate took control. The Diviner attacks became worse over the years. Cael found me after the Diviner attacks became too much for me, and I chose to become a Stricken, regaining my memory of who I am on this side."

"But you and Mom on the other side—"

"We don't know what's going on over there. When the Diviners muddle your mind here, you lose that connection. Like I said, we knew the risks, and all that mattered was keeping you safe."

We passed a shadow family on my left and their stares seared right into me. "And Mom?" I asked.

He shook his head. "She hasn't woken yet. I hope she will become a Stricken like me, but . . . I don't know what she'll choose."

We paused at what seemed to be the middle of camp.

A large fire leaped into the air, dominating the other fires. Several shadow people sat on logs surrounding it, their feet kicked out, arms crossed. The fire's warmth brushed my face; little chills ran up and down my back.

Chatter stopped as we approached, the Stricken watching me.

"Everyone relax," Dad said, leading me over to the far side of the fire. "She's with Cael."

At the mention of Cael, they relaxed, turning back to their conversations.

"Wow," I said. "The Stricken really respect Cael here, don't they?"

"He's saved all of us," Dad said. "This camp didn't exist until he organized it. Most of us were lost, aimlessly wandering after losing our minds, but Cael found us and gave us a home. We've been able to regain who we are . . . for the most part."

"I remember when it got bad for you," I said. "Back at home. The Storms . . . I mean, the Diviners . . . I don't know how you survived that." I plunked down onto the log below me. "When can I see Mom?"

Dad softened, sitting next to me. "Soon."

We fell quiet. The fire snapped as the flames licked upward. The shadow people whispered softly across the way.

"But that isn't what I want to talk to you about," Dad said.

I straightened. "What could be more important than Mom?"

Dad leaned in, his head close to my ear.

"You shouldn't be here," he whispered. "I know Cael wants you here, but you shouldn't be here."

My brows creased, and I leaned back. "What?"

"I don't think we have a chance of defeating the Divining Masters. They're already hovering outside the gates of Khalom. We

Stricken have blocked them out for now, but the Divining Masters are closing in. They're constantly rebuilding their armies. We can't establish peace on this side unless we get the Mhystic involved."

"But the Mhystic have disappeared. No one knows where they are."

"I'm sure they're in hiding," Dad said. "Biding their time. They know a big war is coming, and they're not at their full strength without you. They need Death. The Centers need to be five strong."

The flames crackled between us again.

Dad sat back, folding his arms. "There's a reason Ehlissa's power went to you, Clare-Bear. You need to leave camp. Go find them. Don't let Cael know. He'll try and stop you, but you don't need protection. You're Death. You're the only one who can stop this. If you don't, the Diviners will take over and we'll all lose our minds—for good this time. Even the Stricken aren't immune to the Diviners. But you are. It's one of your abilities as Death. How do you think you survived all that time out there?"

I looked over at him, my eyes widening. *What could I do to stop this*? He said himself how dangerous it was. And I had just gotten here.

And now he wanted me gone?

"What if I don't want to?" I asked.

Dad's shaded face screwed up tight, and he started to talk again, but I didn't hear. All I heard was that he wanted to send me away. Could I leave him? Mom? Cael?

Shouting erupted down the way, echoing across the field, and the Stricken by the fire sprang to their feet, grabbing their swords. Dad stiffened next to me, also reaching for his sword.

"Stay here," Dad said. "Something's happening."

The Stricken took off away from the fire, but Cael came into view, motioning for them to stop.

"It's fine," he said.

A few other Stricken came forward, dragging a young man into the center of camp. His red hair was tousled, and he had scrapes and burns on his face and arms. His arms and feet were limp, his body crouched over.

I blinked, and I scrambled to my feet.

"Lionel?" I asked. My mouth fell open.

Lionel barely lifted his head; one of his eyes was swollen. Dried blood covered his lips, and his clothes were torn and singed. I couldn't remember the last time I'd seen him. In class?

Lionel slowly lifted his eyes, and his mouth opened and closed, like he was trying to find his voice.

"A warning," he said, and coughed. "From the Masters. From Gherry Tompkins."

Then he collapsed.

30
Cold Fever

"The Diviners are taking over Khalom."

A shadow woman helped Lionel sip some water and he coughed, sputtering. Blood still stained his mouth. Cael had taken us to the far end of the valley, inside his tent. Lionel sat on a thin pallet with a torn blanket around his shoulders. Dirt hung in clumps from his red hair, and he leveled his gaze with mine.

I stared back, still unable to believe he was here. "Mr. Tompkins attacked you?"

He coughed again. "Not just him, the other Divining Masters, too. Their armies have breached Khalom. They're setting up camp inside the city. And Gherry is leading them. He says the Stricken camp is next. They're coming here to attack and weaken the Stricken army."

Silence fell; Dad and Cael exchanged looks from either side of me.

Cael crossed his arms, and his sword dangled at his hip.

"They want to hold a ceremony. Make all the people in Khalom swear their allegiance to them." Lionel's voice shook. "And they want Death on their side. They want Clara beside them."

All eyes swung to me.

"She's not going," Cael growled. "We must prepare our training regiments and plan for battle."

He spun on his heel and left the tent, the shadow woman following, leaving the three of us alone.

Lionel couldn't keep his eyes off Dad. "Are you a Stricken? A real Stricken?" Dad nodded and Lionel's eyes brightened despite the heavy conversation. "I've never seen a Stricken before."

"Come on, we can watch them train," I said. I led Lionel out of the tent, my stomach churning as I imagined Khalom overtaken with Diviners.

I leaned against a large boulder, a ways off from camp, where an open dusty field stretched for about a mile. Dozens of shadow soldiers were lined up, Cael pacing in front of them. The line of his jaw was tense, and his eyes were hard. Again, I marveled at how much he looked like Nowen, yet they were completely different. Cael's walk was clipped and purposeful, even his pacing was deliberate. Nowen moved languidly, spontaneously. He was calculated, sure, but you'd never know the wheels were always turning from the constant smirk on his lips and the way his body seemed to lean casually against any surface.

Cael started speaking, his words flowing in another language, but I was able to pick up bits and pieces. I'd learned a bit of the old language before I'd been taken out of the city all those years ago.

"Pair off," Cael said. "Use the technique we've worked on. Number one rule, don't let a Diviner attack you from above. Keep your sword raised at all times."

At Cael's command, the shadow army immediately attacked one another, darting back and forth, lunging in pairs, dust whirling around their feet. Cael continued to throw out commands and I stayed locked in my place, the shade of the boulder cooling me against the sun. The warriors' swords clanked, echoing over the large field. The hot afternoon light reflected through their dim exteriors.

It had been a difficult few hours.

Dad had taken me to Mom.

The thought of her crushed me. I couldn't get the encounter out of my head. I replayed it in my mind.

Mom had lain on a single pallet in Dad's tent, her body still full of color but her face void of any coherency. Her eyes had stared up at the ceiling, blank, her mouth slightly parted.

I hadn't moved for what felt like hours. I had my memories of her on the other side, full of life and love, making pancakes on the grill, taking me shopping for prom dresses, but there was no sign of her here. She had given up her sanity for me, given up the connection to her other life. She had no memory of what a good mother she was to me—in Khalom/Desolation or in our Cursed Life.

I'd slowly approached, and my hand lingered over her for a long time. I wanted to brush the hair out of her face, I wanted to comfort her, but she was gone.

"I don't know when she'll wake or *if* she'll wake," Dad had said behind me. "Sometimes the wounded here never regain their sanity."

I'd turned, moisture building in my eyes. "I can't believe you don't remember her on the other side."

The line of Dad's dark mouth turned down. "Are we happy?" he asked.

"Yes," I said quickly. "Very happy."

I'd turned my attention back to Mom. I couldn't handle the thought of her never having a life here. All the people in Desolation. With the Diviners out there, this was their fate. The Divining

Masters wouldn't stop until they had control over Khalom and all the people out in Desolation, including the Stricken. I stared at her for a long time. Her wispy blond hair, her pink lips and almond eyes.

I'd blinked away the memory of Mom and spun to Dad. "I think I need to go back to Khalom," I said. "I won't be able to help here. I need to go back to the city and stop things before they get worse."

Dad's eyes flashed with worry. But after a moment, he reached out and squeezed my hand. "You can leave tonight during the Stricken ceremony. It will be the perfect time to escape."

The day's events washed away, and I turned back to Cael, watching him train his army. Tonight it was. I would leave at dark.

Night fell, and I approached the center of camp with Dad. We lowered ourselves onto a log by the fire, and it spit and spat, smoke twisting up into the air. Lionel sat across the way, his head in his hands. I hadn't said much to him. I'd been too busy with Dad and Mom. But my heart did ache for him. He'd been kind to me at school, and I didn't know what the future held for him.

Cael lingered on the other side of the fire, his feet planted on the ground, his eyes scanning the area, as if danger could jump out at any moment. He stood with his weight on the balls of his feet, his hands clutching his sword. Shadows from the fire played over his face, and I couldn't help but stare. I would never get over the feeling of seeing him in his full form.

An eerie feeling hung over camp, a solemnness in the soldiers around me. More Stricken gathered, and soft chatter buzzed around me. My gaze roamed over them until I peeked up at the sky.

Bright stars dotted the dark canvas, each clear and distinct. It was like a telescope had been placed over my eyes or like I had put on a pair of high-def glasses. I'd never seen the stars so defined before.

“Beautiful, isn’t it?” Dad said. “I still get taken aback by it. When you get out and away from the city and from where the Diviners have left their mark, the sight is really something.”

“Yeah.” I didn’t say anything else.

The soft murmurs created a low hum through camp and the firelight flickered through the people around me. I peeked over at Cael again. His mouth was set tight, his gaze still sweeping the area. Cael stepped forward, lifting a hand, and silence immediately fell through the camp.

“It’s starting,” Dad whispered. “Stay for a few minutes. Then you can leave. I want you to see the Stricken vow.”

“Stricken vow?” I asked.

Dad nodded. “It’s a cleansing ceremony of sorts. The people who wish to join the Stricken army need to be cleansed. It’s how all people become Stricken—Nobles and regular people.”

A log was thrown on the fire and the flames exploded upward, better illuminating the group.

“Tonight is a significant night,” Cael said, and his voice echoed out into the crisp night air. “We have new members of our family to welcome and celebrate.” He swept an arm out to the side, and several people pushed through the crowd. I covered my mouth. They must’ve just woken up in camp. They were full of color, full of life, though a somber feeling still hung in the air.

The people gathered in front of the fire, lining up with Cael in the middle. The Stricken around me acted as if everything were normal. They clearly had seen this many times. Cael nodded and, very quietly, a deep drum began to throb. It resonated low, vibrating through me. More drums joined, the heavy beat surrounding us from all angles.

“What’s going on?” I whispered.

“Just watch,” Dad said.

I looked around camp. Everyone stood still, unmoving, calm.

But Lionel was enraptured, his eyes wide, his mouth slightly parted. "They're each going to answer the same questions now," Dad said quietly.

I looked back to Cael and the line of new Stricken, staring past the dancing flames, Cael's eyes focused intently on the fire.

A small woman stepped out of the line and stopped in front of Cael. She had a thin frame and her brown hair was braided over her head. A power ran through her, nearly visible in the air.

Cael offered her his hand and she took it, moving closer to the fire. The drums continued to beat.

"Do you accept the responsibilities as one of the Stricken and promise to stand by your brethren?" Cael asked.

The woman stayed stiff but nodded her head. "I do."

The flames crackled.

"And do you understand that you must give up the remainder of your life for the good of the group and never leave the Strickens' side?" Cael asked.

"I do."

"It's what keeps the army strong," Dad whispered in my ear. "They need to promise that this is their new life—now and for always."

"But... forever?" I asked. "What if they don't like being warriors? Can't they go back?"

"What other life do they have?" Dad said. "There's nothing for them in Desolation. Better to fight than not do anything at all."

Dad's words repeated in my head. Once again, a determination to help the people in Desolation surged. If the Diviners were destroyed, everyone could have a better life. They could connect their lives and find happiness. Mom and Dad would remember each other on the other side. All these people deserved freedom.

Another man, with curly blond hair, stepped forward and answered the same questions.

Each time he said "I do," my body grew tighter and tighter.

Another person stepped forward. And then another. The flames licked higher.

As soon as everyone had accepted their vows, Cael stepped forward once more. "Is there anyone else?" he asked. "Another soul who wishes to take their vows this night?"

The fire snapped.

His eyes swept over the camp. He nodded sharply and turned back to the new recruits. "Then it is time to finish this."

"Wait!" A voice came from the crowd.

Everyone paused. Lionel stood up from his seat, his face extra pale in the dark.

"I wish to be a Stricken."

"Lionel!" I hissed. I jumped to my feet. "*What* are you doing?"

Cael lifted a hand. "Are you sure?" he addressed Lionel. "Once you join our ranks, you can never turn back. You'll give up your Noble name."

"It's what I want," Lionel said, though his voice trembled. The flames flicked again, as red as his hair.

"Then it is a great honor," Cael said, holding out his hand.

Lionel moved forward, quiet in the dark. Everyone watched. I stayed standing, nervous energy thrumming through me. He couldn't do this. He'd be giving up his Noblehood.

"Lionel, please—"

"Clara, don't," Dad said and tugged me down. I plunked down next to him, unable to look away. "It's his choice."

Cael spoke, and Lionel answered, but I could barely hear the words. Lionel had never shown any inkling of wanting to be a warrior. And he wasn't the warrior type. He was too fragile. He was just . . . Lionel.

Cael said something else, but it echoed far in my mind. He motioned his hand forward once more, and the new recruits began to circle the fire. They took hands, and the drums beat faster. Everyone in the crowd hummed along with the drums, a kind of half chant. The haunting melody weaved around, twisting into my being.

Lionel and the others began to circle the fire, walking clockwise, the chanting growing louder. The sound pressed into me, and I covered my ears, unable to take it. Cael didn't move, he only stared intently at the group, his expression tight.

I bounced my legs. Lionel couldn't do this. He couldn't sign his life away. But what else did he have? I needed to leave, but I couldn't move. The people circling as the flames danced was hypnotizing. It was almost sensual, the way the flames brushed and curved around the circling bodies.

They started to draw closer to the fire.

My heart pounded faster. "What's happening?"

But Dad didn't answer.

They walked closer to the flames.

I gripped Dad's arm. "They're getting too close. Lionel is getting too close—"

Dad placed a hand on mine, loosening my grip. "It's fine. This is the most important part."

One by one, the new recruits stepped into the fire, including Lionel. I sprang to my feet, mouth open, ready to yell, but it was too late. Lionel was completely immersed in the flames. His body started to become translucent, the color from his skin and hair washing away. The other new Stricken followed suit, their bodies transforming from solid beings into silhouettes. The flames shifted through their new forms.

The drumming finished abruptly, and silence echoed around us. The flames died down and the new Stricken stepped away from the fire.

"It's finished," Dad said and rose next to me. "You need to go. There will be a celebration now."

"But . . ." I looked back to Lionel. *Now?* Would he be okay? My gaze slid to Cael again. Warmth emanated from his face as he shook hands with the people surrounding him. I suddenly felt out of place. Like I didn't belong here. This was Cael's place, his home. He was needed here, wanted here, loved here. I needed to let him go.

I left Dad and squeezed through the shadow bodies to make my way over to Lionel. I couldn't say goodbye to Cael, but I could say goodbye to Lionel.

I stopped in front of him, and it was easy to know it was him from his lanky frame and tousled hair.

"Hey," I said.

He rolled his shoulders as if his skin itched. "Hey," he answered. I started to speak again, but Lionel kept talking, as if answering an unspoken question. "I never fit in at school. Maybe this is where I've belonged this whole time. And I always wanted to fight for something. I don't know, something just came over me now and I . . . knew."

Conversations buzzed all around us, celebrations in order. I stared at Lionel's silhouetted face. Maybe Lionel would have a place here. I wished I knew my place, where I belonged.

"I'm—I'm glad," I said. "I'm proud of you."

His body relaxed a tad. "Really?"

I nodded. "Really."

I lingered with him for a moment, trying to gather my strength. Every part of me ached to say goodbye to Cael, but I knew I couldn't. He would never let me leave. I reached out and took Lionel's hand. "Good luck."

I turned and headed away from Lionel, away from the fire, out into the cold night. I maneuvered my way through the crowd of shadow bodies, my heart pounding harder with each step. I couldn't believe I was leaving. I was leaving without saying goodbye. I wanted to take one last look at Cael but knew I shouldn't.

I'd almost made it out of the crowd when loud cries echoed in the distance.

Everyone froze—including me. Looks were exchanged, and soldiers quickly reached for their swords.

More cries sounded. My mind immediately went to the Diviners. *Were they here?* Had Mr. Tompkins brought his army here? Had they found the Stricken camp?

Cael marched in front of the group, holding a finger to his lips. He unsheathed his own sword, motioning his soldiers to quietly follow.

I stayed rooted to the dusty ground.

Lionel followed the warriors, though he didn't have a weapon. I peeked back to the forest on the mountain. It was my way out. I needed to leave, but I stayed put.

More shouts echoed in the distance, and they intensified, growing louder. Cael and his army stayed crouched, silent, waiting for an attack. Then, in a burst, a group exploded into camp. I cringed, waiting for the onslaught of Diviners, but they were Stricken, carrying a couple dozen kids, one girl in particular flailing her arms, her body strung over a warrior guy's shoulder, her blond hair yellow in the moonlight.

"*Deena*?"

"Let me down!" she screamed, banging her fists on his back.

I blinked. What was Deena doing here? Adham and Khalob flew into camp after her, pinned by four shadow warriors. More and more of my classmates appeared in the camp, carried by Stricken. Deena was still throwing punches, purple snaps sparkling in the air.

I sprang into action.

"Stop!" I yelled, sprinting forward. "I know them!"

Cael stalked up next to me, sheathing his sword.

The Stricken hesitated for a moment, still holding the kids, before they relented with a nod from Cael, letting them go. Khalob's gaze immediately darted to mine, and he screwed up his face, his hair a dark blue in the moonlight. Deena caught my gaze, and she bounded over to me, throwing her arms around me in a hug.

"There you are! We came to find you. I'm so glad you're here!"

My teeth ground together, and I pushed her back. "You locked me in the White Wing."

Color dotted Deena's cheeks. "Yeah . . . sorry about that. In hindsight, I realize that was a mistake. We're really sorry. Aren't we Khalob?"

A mistake?

I looked at Khalob again. He was still glaring, though a hint of fear flickered in his eyes. My mouth tightened.

"What are you doing here?" I asked.

Deena bounced on the heels of her feet. "We came to help you, of course. We're Nobles. You need our power. You don't think"—she peeked around her and scrunched her nose—"that you can defeat the Masters on your own. We followed Lionel here. So . . . you're welcome." Her teeth flashed in a smile.

"Just ignore her." Ricki pushed her way through the crowd, planting herself in front of me. She crossed her arms. "Though yeah, it seems like you could use our help."

My heart stopped. I didn't think I'd see Ricki this soon—or at all. She gave me a half smile.

I couldn't help it. I rushed forward and pulled her into a tight hug. "You're here."

"Of course we are," she said. "And we're ready to train. We're ready to help."

I peered past her shoulder and up to the mountain behind her. The forest was waiting. Mr. Tompkins was waiting. I couldn't stay here, could I?

Cael appeared to my left, and his arm touched mine. My skin tingled at the touch.

"We're glad you're here," he said to the group. "We can use your help."

As I watched their faces, I knew I couldn't leave Ricki and the others. And I wasn't ready to leave Cael.

I guess I wasn't leaving now. Not yet.

31
Cold Fusion

My classmates were gathered in a group, hovering next to the mountainside, just outside of camp. I stood in the back of the pack, waiting. A few trees surrounded us next to large boulders, the ground dusty at our feet.

Ricki was late.

It was our first training session, and she was late.

Cael had instructed her to be our leader, to help us train, though I still couldn't handle the thought of any of these kids battling Diviners. The Stricken, trained warriors, could barely hold them off. My classmates had never fought anything other than one another in class, and now they were supposed to jump in and take back our city? Of course that's why our Centers existed. They had been practicing using their powers since their first day of school. But using our Centers in a real life-or-death battle was different from sparring with one another in class.

Seconds ticked by, and the group grew restless. Sweat ran down their faces, and most of them fanned themselves. Khalom's temperature was always perfect—they weren't used to this heat. Cael's voice boomed from the valley, and the shadow warriors moved in perfect unison, practicing their form. Lionel kept up with the movements, staying right with them.

"I'm going to get burned," Deena finally said. "My skin isn't used to this sun." She groaned, wiping the sweat off her neck.

Khalob darted glances my way every minute or so, his face fixed into a permanent frown. I tried to ignore him. I wasn't sure how I was supposed to feel. Sorry that I attacked him? Or mad because he threw me into the White Wing?

Finally, Ricki jogged up to the group, panting.

"Sorry I'm late," she said. "I needed to get someone."

"Who?" I asked.

A smile lifted on Ricki's lips, and she turned to the mountainside. "Robert, come on out, don't be nervous."

Behind a boulder, Robert slowly emerged. His greasy hair hung around his narrow face, his eyes two dark beads. Several of the kids gasped, edging back a step. He moved forward, stopping next to Ricki, but he shifted awkwardly, keeping his head lowered.

"I've brought Robert here to help you train," Ricki said. "He's our best chance. He's a Diviner, and he'll help us defeat them."

More gasps circulated. My classmates gave each other wary glances.

Ricki took Robert by the arm and positioned him in front of the group. He shot his sister a dark glance, but she gave him a warm smile and encouraged him forward.

Robert straightened and planted his feet, facing the group. He narrowed his eyes. The wind seemed to pick up, and the clouds passed over the sun. The hairs prickled on the back of my neck.

"I am a Diviner," Robert said, and the group stilled. Another breeze swept in. "So listen up. We are the most powerful in packs. We build off the airstreams we produce in flight and use it to our advantage. It's all about unhinging the mind to a certain point of madness. The Storm helps create that. Once an individual lets the chaos overtake their mind, it's easy to reach in and take a few memories."

Robert slowly started to walk through the group, making eye contact with each of my classmates. They shuffled out of his way, allowing him a path.

"Because we're most powerful in packs, the key to defeating Diviners is to separate us."

Robert stopped and peered down at the ground. His eyes scanned the area. He bent down and picked up a rock. He tossed the rock up in the air and turned it over in his hands a few times. Silence settled over the group, and looks were exchanged. Then he turned to me and grinned. He wound up his arm and chucked the rock right toward me. Pain exploded behind my eyes as it smacked me in the face.

"Holy Mhystic!" I yelled. "Ouch!"

Robert chuckled, then found another rock on the ground. He spun on Ricki so fast, I barely saw him. He threw the rock with even more force, but Ricki's hands shot upward. The rock paused in midair, floating out in front of her. She grinned back at her brother, then flicked her wrist. The rock sailed back toward him in a trail of green streaks, and he dodged before it hit the ground.

More looks were exchanged.

"See?" Robert said. "We all have our strengths. But imagine what it would be like if we combined them as one."

Pain still throbbed in my head, and I rubbed it, glaring.

"That's a great speech," Deena said dryly. "But how are we supposed to practice? Throwing rocks at one another isn't going to do much good."

Robert's eyes darkened as he looked over at the Stricken. "We're going to practice on them," he said. "The only way to strengthen your Centers is to use them. In real battle. But first, I want to see what you can do."

The kids all nodded, though doubt was plastered on their faces. I sidled up next to Ricki.

"I can't believe Robert is here," I said. "How?"

"He can be here until his Divining Master calls on him." Ricki looked directly at me, worry filling her face. "Until Gherry calls on him."

A deep anger built as I thought about all my time with him. He'd been with me day after day in Desolation, probably creating his army while he kept a close watch on me. Then he pretended to be my teacher, tried to gain my trust, when all along he'd wanted to control me. He'd even tried to get me to sign away my Noble name for him. I clenched my hands into fists, then released the tension, rubbing them on my thighs.

Ricki's forehead furrowed. "Something's up with you. Are you okay? Last night . . . it was like you were disappointed we were here."

I shook my head, though she was right. I needed to leave. I shouldn't be here training with my classmates.

"It's good. I'm fine," I said. "Come on, let's see what everyone can do."

For the next couple of hours, Robert watched the group, pacing in and out of the kids, instructing them. Khalob and Adham practiced using their strength together, picking up large boulders and seeing how high and how far they could throw them. Deena and another Mind girl stood next to each other, holding hands, staring Khalob and Adham down, trying to control their movements and stop the boulders with their minds. Ricki helped an Earth girl levitate and throw objects and create small earthquakes that made a lot of us lose our balance. A Time and Space boy disappeared and reappeared, popping in and out of the kids, trying to distract them. Another Time and Space kid conjured fireballs from his hands and sent them sailing through the air.

It was impressive.

And Robert did well guiding the kids—like he was a born leader.

But it wasn't battle.

I had no idea how they would fare against real Diviners.

Time passed and, as I watched, my fingertips tingled, my Center like a current underneath my skin. It itched to be used, threatened to burst out of my fingers at any moment. But I kept it clamped down. I hadn't tried to use my full power yet. There hadn't been an opportunity to, and I was too afraid. But it was there, growing.

Finally, Robert regrouped the kids, and we all huddled together.

"It's time," he said. He glanced up at the descending sun, then over to where the Stricken were finishing up. They had moved to the top of a hill and would be traveling downward soon. "You know what to do."

Robert instructed us where to hide, around various boulders that lined the pathway back to camp. The rocks and earth were a deep red, almost orange as the sun slowly lowered in the sky. I was tucked up against a large boulder with Robert and Ricki. Behind a different boulder, Deena hid with the two Body boys.

The last sounds of training diminished, and the Stricken headed down the hill back toward camp. Their bodies were dark shadows against the sunset, low chatter among them, their swords at their hips.

They moved smoothly, and I spotted Cael at the back, his toned muscles flexing as he grasped his sword. Fatigue lined his eyes in a way I had never seen before. His gaze seemed as if it were turned inward, like he was living in another time and place.

"Steady," Robert whispered.

They had almost reached us.

We waited two more heartbeats, then Robert yelled, "Now!"

My classmates attacked at once.

Chaos exploded, flashes of blue, green, yellow, and purple in the air.

Deena, Khalob, and Adham darted out from across the way. Another group appeared. And then another. I sprang out, keeping up with the group. We sprinted at the shadow army at full speed. The soldiers paused, clearly confused.

Cael stopped in the back, and his eyebrows raised. Then his eyes lit, and humor teased his lips.

"This should be interesting," I heard him say.

In a rush, a surge of wind hit, strong, like a hurricane. Robert held his hands out, his presence wavering in and out between his dark ghostly hue and his human form. The wind hit me from the side, and I staggered, peering through the madness.

Deena faced a woman soldier, focused on her shadowy sword. Deena concentrated, and the weapon slipped from the Stricken woman's fingers and floated in the air between them. The Stricken reached for it, trying to retrieve it, but Deena only grinned and floated the sword away. Khalob and Adham worked together, punching down into the earth, and it shook, making a few of the Stricken topple over. The Time and Space kids zoomed quickly around camp, evading each attack that came their way.

Death awoke within me, and I tried to shove it away. I couldn't join and fight. It was too dangerous. I didn't know what I was capable of. I could *kill* someone.

But a couple of soldiers appeared in front of me and pointed their swords straight at me. I blinked, then edged back, though Death woke once more, as if it had a mind of its own. The Stricken glanced at each other, nodded, then charged. I stood frozen. But Cael appeared from nowhere, stepping in front of them, blocking me. They stumbled back.

"She's mine," Cael said.

The soldiers paused, lowered their swords, and bowed, before going after one of my other classmates.

Cael slowly turned to me, unsheathing his own sword. He lifted an eyebrow, stalking toward me.

I took a step back, my heart beginning to speed up. "You're . . . not serious?" *He wanted to fight me?*

A small smile lit Cael's face. "Oh, I'm serious." He raised his sword.

I'd never seen that expression on his face before. It was playful, smirking. It reminded me of Nowen.

I shook my head, inching back farther. "I can't fight you. I don't know what I'm capable of."

Cael continued to glide forward, his eyes alight with humor. "I think it's time to find out."

"Stay back," I said. "I'm strong. I can feel it."

Cael chuckled. "You were never that coordinated. I remember once you tried to jump rope as a little girl and you ended up in a tangled mess." His mouth stretched wide at the memory. "Go ahead and try."

Heat ran up the sides of my neck, and embarrassment swept through me. "Okay," I said, narrowing my eyes. "Let's do this."

I rubbed my hands together, the buzz of Death sizzling in my fingertips. But this time, I allowed it to build. I didn't try to shove it away. I had hurt people and made mistakes in the past, yes, but Cael was powerful. I was sure I couldn't hurt him.

Cael moved closer, and I lifted my hands out in front of me, taking another step back. More heat gathered in my chest, as if my Center knew I was about to be attacked.

He leaped forward.

I threw out my hands, and heat shot from my fingertips. In a black blast, Cael flew off his feet, sailing in the air. He hit the ground hard and slid until he rammed into a large rock. Cael's mouth quirked upward and he jumped to his feet, holding up his sword again.

"Not bad," he said. "But can you do this?"

Cael lifted his sword and plunged it deep into the earth. A spiderweb of fire shot out from the blade of his sword and exploded outward, flames licking up into the sky. Several of the Stricken and my classmates turned to watch. Cael lifted his sword once more. Smoke drifted into the air from the spot in the ground where the weapon had been.

I set my chin, keeping eye contact with him. He strolled forward, a lazy grin—Nowen's lazy grin—playing at his lips.

I didn't know what I was capable of, but I knew I could do more. I rubbed my palms together again, and little black sparks of heat sizzled on my skin. He kept moving forward, but instead of holding my ground, I met his stride and came right at him.

I lifted my hands, more heat building, but rather than throwing them outward, I touched my temples and closed my eyes. I didn't have a plan, I just instinctively knew what to do—like Death was the one guiding *me*.

Red seared my vision, cutting through my mind like a hot knife, and a loud boom ricocheted over the valley. My eyes flew open, and streams of orange fire covered the whole field.

Cael lifted his brows. "I've never seen that before."

The Stricken and my classmates had completely stopped fighting and were watching us, weapons hanging limp at their sides. But Cael and I stared at each other like we were the only people who existed.

Cael sauntered forward, his sword dragging on the ground, his smile easy, relaxed, in a way I had never seen on him. Humor danced in his eyes.

I shifted my stance, unsure what he would do next. My mind should've been reeling that I was actually *using my Death powers*, but

Cael's stare had me so wrapped up in the present moment, it was hard to think of anything else.

Then he stopped and cocked his head to the side. "Can you do this?"

He disappeared in a blink, leaving the landscape empty before me. My heart stopped and I frantically glanced around. His sudden disappearance jarred me. Seconds ticked by. Then he appeared next to me and grabbed me around the waist, spinning me.

He let out a laugh, and it echoed over the field. I'd never heard him laugh before. Not in Desolation, not outside the gates, and not here. The sound made my heart beat faster, and I filed it away in my memory to savor it always.

Cael paused, his arms still around my waist. He held me close, his blue eyes searching. His chest rose and fell, and every inch of me tingled. I'd never been this close to him before. Even when he was in my mind, he didn't feel *this* close.

Unspoken communication hovered between us. He'd admitted that he cared for me, but that we couldn't be together, not with Nowen in the picture. But in this moment, all the walls were down. I could see it in his eyes.

"Cael—" I started.

But that was enough. My voice shook him out of his reverie. He backed away, running a hand over his short hair. My brow puckered.

"I'm sorry," he said. "I can't."

"Why?" I took another step toward him.

"I told you. You still care about Nowen, and that reminds me of the worst part of me. I will live the rest of my existence trying to make up for my wrongs. I ruined your life. Your parents' lives. If I hadn't been so selfish—"

"Stop," I said. "Cael." I took another step forward. "You didn't ruin my life. You *gave* it to me. Someone tried to kill me that night. I don't care if you tried to take my Center. I would've been killed if you hadn't taken me out of the city. And you know it wasn't just that. Day after day . . . you saved me each day that I survived out there. Just by being with me."

Cael's gaze softened, and he moved forward until we were inches apart again. Except, this time, Cael didn't run. He stayed fixed, a new energy running up and down his body.

Something shifted in his gaze, and I knew that he wanted to kiss me.

I'd dreamed about kissing Cael since I was old enough to develop feelings for him. It's what I had begged him for that day in the forest. I stared at his lips. I couldn't help it. He had to know I wanted it.

"Clara," he said, and a flash of doubt crossed his face.

"Cael, please," I said.

The desperation in my voice must've been enough. In a heartbeat, one of his hands slid into my hair while the other wrapped around my waist, drawing me up against him. I didn't even care about the stares around us.

His mouth was on mine in an instant, and I immediately pulled him closer, dragging my hands to the sides of his face. He kissed me. Then kissed me again. His lips formed perfectly to my own, and my Center shifted inside of me, awakening. I could feel his power mingling with mine.

Nowen's kiss had been different, more relaxed. Cael's kiss was urgent, like it would never happen again.

Cael started to pull away, but I pulled him back, holding him secure. I wasn't ready for the moment to be gone. If this all ended badly, if we didn't beat the Diviners and find the Mhystic and restore order, we might lose our minds forever. I kept my hands on his face, waiting, staring, willing this moment to last.

Finally, Cael took my hands and lowered them from his face. Darkness had descended over the sky.

“It’s time,” he said. “We’ll train more tomorrow.” But sadness hung off the end of his words.

Cael turned and headed back to camp, followed by the rest of the Stricken and my classmates. I stood in the field for a long while, well into the night.

32
Death Proof

"That's good, you guys!" Ricki yelled. "Keep going!"

Her voice echoed across the small valley, clouds moving fast over the sky. Robert stood a distance away, his eyes dark between the strands of his hair. The wind seemed to come from him, dirt swirling around his ankles and up into the sky.

I hovered next to a large boulder that shielded me from the sun. My classmates were in full training with the Stricken, and Cael stood on the other side of the field, calling out commands to his men.

Adham stomped into the ground, and the earth cracked open; several Stricken soldiers fell inside, but they climbed back out, continuing on. An Earth girl had sprouted large vines from the earth, and their green tendrils entangled several Stricken, keeping them pinned. But Lionel knew how to break her concentration, and the vines shriveled away, until she could try again.

My eyes skated over to Cael every few seconds. I couldn't stop looking at him—couldn't stop looking at how the sun played on his hair, and the way his sharp blue eyes watched his army. I replayed our kiss over and over again. I didn't understand why we couldn't just be together. I could live here at the Stricken camp. We could fight Diviners. I'd be with Mom and Dad—sort of. I'd have my classmates.

But it didn't fix anything. Were we supposed to always live our lives fighting? And what about the city?

I rolled my shoulders, sneaking a peek up at Cael again. Our eyes caught, and he stared at me intently for a moment. Then he gave me a nod and returned to his command. I sighed, warmth swirling in my chest. I really could be with him here forever.

Footsteps sounded to my left and I slowly turned, expecting Dad or Ricki. Instead, Mom stood before me, a shadowed sword in her hand. She was flesh and blood, like she had always been, her hair perfectly combed, her eyes wide. And she looked at me with coherency.

"Mom?" I asked. "How . . . What are you doing here? You're awake!"

"Yes, Clara. I'm here," she said. Her eyes softened.

I shook my head. "I can't believe you're okay. You—" I cut off as Mom drew closer. I watched her approach. She looked completely normal on the outside, but something felt off. *Why was she carrying a sword?*

"Mom, are you okay?"

Lines creased around her eyes as she gave a tired smile. "Yes, Clara. I'm okay. Everything is okay, as long as you are protected." She continued to inch closer.

I stayed put, my brows digging together.

"I will protect you," Mom said. "You'll be safer on the other side. You let us fight this battle on this side."

My eyebrows tugged together. "Mom?"

"You can't travel by your own will yet," she said. "I can see it in your eyes. It's Death's greatest weakness when your Center isn't aligned. Your grandmother lost the ability to travel to her other life, too." She stepped closer. "If I send you to the other side, you'll be safe. You won't be able to return until it's safe. I'm going to keep you safe, Clara."

She took two more steps away from the boulders behind her and right in front of me. I didn't have time to react.

Mom threw herself on me, bringing the shadowy blade up over her head. I stared, wide-eyed, as the blade plunged into my chest.

Pain exploded, and I gasped for air. I fell to my knees, hitting the soft earth. I opened and closed my mouth, but I couldn't find my voice. Too much pain.

Mom hovered over me, her wispy blond hair curved around her face, until my vision faded, and I knew I was being thrown back into my other life.

33

Pitch Black

My eyes snapped open.

The room slowly came into focus. White walls. White table, desk, chairs, sofas. Nowen leaned against the wall in the far corner, watching me. Earrings framed one ear; a chunk of his hair hung over his forehead. Black clothes, as always.

"There you are," he said. "I've been waiting hours." He chewed on his lip.

I set a hand to my forehead and slowly sat up. Pain radiated along my skull, and the backs of my eyes hurt. Mom. Mom had . . . stabbed me.

She had sent me here.

"It's been quite entertaining watching you sleep," he said. "Though it is maddening not knowing what's going on over there. Care to share updates?" He didn't move from where he stood against the wall, arms crossed.

I squinted over at him, my vision still righting itself. I frowned. "Nothing you need to concern yourself with. Unless you care about the destruction of Khalom, the Divining Masters taking over the city, the Stricken gathering an army, and—"

Nowen barked out a laugh, cutting me off. "The Stricken? What good will they do?" He kept his arms crossed. "They don't have a leader."

My brow furrowed. "What do you mean? Of course they—"

I paused. Nowen didn't know. Nowen didn't know that Cael was alive. I felt the blood drain from my face, and I quickly turned away, hoping to hide my expression. Nowen couldn't know. He couldn't find out.

He'd just try and kill Cael all over again.

Nowen's eyes tightened, and he slowly unfolded his arms. "What happened?" he asked.

I kept my gaze away, though my heart started pounding furiously. He pushed off the wall, and his gaze seared right through me.

"I asked you a question, Dessy. Something happened, what was it?" He lunged forward and gripped my arms, pulling me to a standing position. I kept my gaze away, but he forced me to look at him. His dark eyes locked with mine, searching for the answer I didn't want to give.

"No," he whispered. He released his grip and staggered back a step. He swiped a hand over his face. "Impossible."

I clenched my eyes shut. I'd always been an open book.

Nowen whirled on me. "How?"

I shook my head. "I don't know how."

His brows slanted together. "You've spent time together." It was a statement, not a question.

My heart took off as I envisioned the kiss we'd shared. Heat brushed my cheeks, and Nowen's face turned murderous.

"Dammit, Dessy!"

He reached forward once more and snatched my arm. "You're clearly not able to travel by yourself yet, which means you're mine, for now. Come on, you're back just in time. It's time for Deaeth's debut."

Nowen was clearly on Deaeth, because he unlocked the door with a wave of his hand. He led me out into the hallway, and I recognized it as the Sandman's. Music pulsed down the hall, the bassline vibrating to my bones. I stumbled after Nowen as he dragged me down the hall, the music growing louder.

It was strange to be here. My mind still felt as if it were back at the Stricken camp. Worry pummeled through me. I'd left everyone back there, which meant I hadn't returned to Khalom. Gherry Tompkins and his Diviners would attack the camp and everyone inside. I'd left them exposed. I should've immediately gone back to the city.

Nowen tugged again and set a hand on the door at the end of the hall. He turned to me before he pushed it open.

"You're going to forget about your life over there," he said. "You won't want to leave when you see the good I'm doing here. There's nothing you can do for those poor people out in Desolation, Clara, but these same people can live here and now. We can give them freedom in their Cursed Life."

He pushed open the door and we stepped inside.

The party was in full swing. Techno music spun in the air, bodies danced, and neon lights flashed. Strobe lights pulsed. The atmosphere was electric, and my adrenaline surged like I had a thousand mgs of caffeine running through my veins. Nowen pulled me through the crowd, keeping a firm grip on me. Bodies brushed past my shoulders, and a mixture of sweat and perfume hung in the air.

We struggled through the crowd, like we were swimming, and my gaze shot in every direction. I was alone here. Mom and Dad were clueless and out of town, Ricki was on the other side. I didn't have Cael or my classmates. I didn't know where Fae and Laela were. And Dan . . .

Dan.

He was a few people away from me, dancing with Angela Cummings. Sweat stuck to his skin, but not in a sickly way. He looked healthy, dancing back and forth, a large grin on his face.

"Dan!" I cried, but my voice was swallowed up.

Nowen tugged me farther into the club, until we stopped in the middle of the room. He lifted a hand, and the lights abruptly shut off. The music cut off. The dancing stopped. The crowd groaned in complaint. A blue spotlight cascaded down on the middle of the floor, right where Nowen and I stood. The deep blue light lit up Nowen's face, hollowing out his cheeks. His mouth curved upward as he leaned in and whispered in my ear.

"I'm glad you can share this moment with me. You are the star of the show after all." His eyes flicked down to my arms before he straightened and extended his arms out to the sides of him.

"Welcome to Deaeth's debut," Nowen said, and his voice boomed through the room. His mouth crooked upward as he linked his hands behind his back and began to pace under the spotlight. I stood frozen, my heart thrumming.

"Why are we here?" Nowen asked, his voice echoing. "Are we here to suffer? To live powerless like a piece of driftwood floating in the sea?" He lifted his head and scanned the crowd. "No. We're here so we can live. So we can experience pleasure." Nowen's eyes slithered over to mine, and a dark smile lit his face. "Life is to enjoy, not endure. Deaeth lets us live like we deserve." He kept his eyes locked with mine. "Deaeth is beautiful. It's seductive. It's everything you wish it to be."

Someone whistled from the audience, and another person cried out, "Yeah!"

Nowen's mouth twitched as he circled the dance floor once more. "I'm giving you all a gift tonight. Your first taste of Deaeth. Free of charge."

Cheers sounded from the crowd, and Siv, Dane, and other men started handing out packets of Deaeth. People passed the pouches around, and my heartbeat sped faster.

No.

My mind was still catching up. I still felt as if I were on the other side, that I was living a nightmare right now, but this was real. Giving people this kind of power was reckless. Nobles could barely be trusted with Centers. If normal people could do whatever their hearts desired, it could create absolute chaos in this Cursed world. And think of the addiction . . . people would do whatever it took to get their hands on Deaeth, which meant that I would be a walking blood host for the rest of my life.

Dan and Angela had their pouches and they ripped them open, pink powder puffing up into the air.

"Dan! Don't! Stop!" But I could barely hear myself.

The crowd buzzed with excitement, and the music came to life again. The spotlight on Nowen shut off, and bodies closed in on me as they started to dance.

Deaeth's effects were starting to take root. Looks of ecstasy and delight filled the room. People started hovering off the ground. Boys were growing muscles and girls were holding handfuls of cash. Some people vanished from thin air, and others started making out with strangers.

More Deaeth puffed up into the air as more pouches were torn open.

This was wrong. So wrong. All of it.

Nowen still stood in the middle of the floor, even though his spotlight was gone. I zeroed in on him, clenching my fists. But he didn't seem to notice me. His eyes were lifted to the strobe lights above him, his palms open in front of him. I strode forward anyway. Somehow, I would make him stop this. He had to see what a horrible idea this was.

I marched up to him and gripped his arm, yelling in his ear. “Nowen, please. We need to—” I broke off.

The world went dark.

Once again, like the drowning incident on the sidewalk, I was thrown into a vision.

I blinked, the black slowly fading away until a scene unfolded before me. My classmates came into view, marching alongside the Stricken. Wind whipped fiercely around them, and a dark cloud swirled above them. They shifted their stances, swords and hands lifted, clearly ready for an attack.

I’d know that cloud anywhere. It wasn’t a cloud.

Robert stood beneath it, his hands lifted, whispering words, his long hair flying all around him. Ricki stood behind him, worry plastered over her face. The wind intensified, and Robert’s body started to flicker between his human form and Diviner form. Robert secured his stance, digging his feet into the ground, but his body started to fade again, until he became wraithlike, transparent, his eyes and mouth stretching into black chasms. His body lifted off the ground, and he swirled up into the gathering Storm.

“No!” Ricki screamed.

In a flash, the Storm burst outward, and the Diviners separated. The ghostly figures darted in all directions, shooting down toward the Stricken and my classmates, immersing them. I was paralyzed. I knew I was still back in the club, that this vision was just a strange phenomenon that I was able to see, but it still felt as if I were really there. The Stricken sprang into action. They separated, lining up in different groups, a tactic Cael had taught them.

Cael.

Where was Cael?

I squinted past the clashing swords, at the Stricken jabbing their weapons upward, at the Diviners who vanished into mini clouds of dust when they were hit, but I couldn’t see him.

Where was he?

Powers started to emerge from my classmates. Khalob and Adham were grouped together, grasping at Diviners and ripping them apart with their bare hands in showers of blue sparks. Deena stood in the middle of the battle, staring each Diviner down who threatened to get near her. Purple sparks crackled in the air around her. The moment a Diviner tried to get close, the thing whooshed backward, clearly unable to touch her.

The ground shook, cracks opened in the earth, balls of fire were tossed. The Stricken used their swords. The Diviners continued to zip up and down, moving much too fast for some of my classmates to properly stop them.

Ricki hovered off to the side, her eyes wide, her lips moving like she was praying. She kept her gaze fixed on the Diviners, probably trying to keep track of Robert and make sure he wasn't killed.

My eyes shot from person to person.

Cael.

Where was Cael?

I squinted through the chaos, through the shadow warriors and the zooming Diviners. I didn't know how long I'd be in this vision. I needed to find him before I was pulled out of it.

There.

The world seemed to pause as Cael came into view. He moved swiftly, furiously, dodging around Diviners and stabbing them one after another. It looked like a dance, the way he moved around the ghostly beings. His jaw was clenched, his striking eyes narrowed. Sweat ran down the sides of his face, but his strength was continuous.

A group of Diviners parted, and I squinted through the opening. Dad came into view, fighting with the same strength that Cael had. He darted back and forth, stabbing Diviner after Diviner, dust particles flying around him. His shaded form moved with ease, as if he were able to predict the Diviners' movements.

Behind him, Lionel also fought, his thin frame struggling to hold his sword upright. His arms shook as he hefted his sword. He tried to strike a few Diviners down, but he missed by a long shot. Several Diviners seemed to notice because they turned their attention to him. Lionel let his sword fall to the ground and he stood panting, chest heaving, his shaded form ready to collapse. A group of Diviners traveled quickly toward him, but he didn't see. He just stood there, unaware.

Dad noticed. He whirled toward Lionel and shouted for him to look out.

Lionel glanced up, but before he could move, a Diviner wrapped its ghostly form around his neck. Lionel gasped, choking, trying to swat it away. He fumbled around, and more Diviners swept in toward him. He cried out, continuing to flail.

Dad immediately took off toward him, his sword at the ready. He thrust himself into the swirl of Diviners, his weapon everywhere, piercing Diviner after Diviner. The Diviners around Lionel dispersed, including the one around his neck, and Lionel collapsed to the ground, coughing. Dad crouched down next to him, setting a hand on his back. He spoke to Lionel quietly, and Lionel nodded his head, as if thanking him.

I almost looked away, back to find Cael or Ricki, when Diviners started to regroup above Dad's head.

My body tensed, and fear shot through me.

Dad.

"Dad!" I yelled, though I knew he couldn't hear.

The Diviners above him churned together, gathering, swirling. He still didn't notice. He was making sure Lionel was okay.

"Dad!" I tried again, though I knew it was useless.

The Diviners shot down in a blink, speeding toward Dad, their eyes and mouths stretched open. Dad scrambled to lift his sword, but a Diviner descended too quickly. Its mouth widened, its jaw unhinging as it chomped down over Dad's head. Dad's body slackened then tipped over sideways, falling lifeless to the ground.

I screamed. "Dad! No!"

Fingernails bit my arms, and my body shook back and forth. Someone was shaking me. I continued to cry out.

"Dad!"

But the battle scene dissipated, and I was thrown back into myself. The Sandman came back, the pulsing music, the flashing lights, Nowen's face in front of mine.

"Come on, Dessy," he said. "Let's get you out of here."

34
The Gift

Fresh air hit my face as Nowen pushed me into an alley outside the back of the club.

Moonlight peeked through wispy clouds overhead, and a streetlamp buzzed to my left, flickering down the silent street. Sounds of nightlife and traffic were muted from the main road.

Siv and Dane left with us, and Siv glared down at me behind his eye patch. But I hardly noticed.

Dad.

Dad was gone.

I thought back to my class with Mr. Tompkins. *If you die in Khalom, you die a mental death.* A mental death was much worse than a physical death. It meant you didn't exist. Is that what just happened with Dad?

Nowen drew me down the street and pressed me up against the nearest building. The bricks were cool on my back.

"What did you see?" Nowen asked. His dark eyes took me in, and it was hard to focus on his face. It blurred in and out.

"It's him, isn't it?" he said before I could answer.

"Who?" I blinked, trying to catch up.

Nowen threw up his hands and paced away from me. "Cael, of course. You were with him again, weren't you?" He continued to pace, dragging his fingers through his hair. It stuck up in all directions. "I can see it on your face. You always get that look when you . . . think of him."

He paused abruptly and spun on me, attacking me with a glare. "What does he have that I don't?"

I stared back at him, my heart in my throat.

"The good looks?" Nowen joked, but it fell flat. He began to pace again, the moonlight casting shadows on his face. Siv and Dane hovered a few feet away. A myriad of thoughts crossed over Nowen's face.

Reality was still coming back to me.

"Who's the better kisser?" he asked sharply, voice terse.

The question took me aback. "Excuse me?"

"Who's the better kisser?" Nowen pressed again. "I know you kissed him."

I stayed flat against the brick building, my palms digging into the grout. I still couldn't keep up. My mind was caught between here and there, and I couldn't think straight.

"Nowen, please," I said. "We don't need to talk about this now. My dad. Can we—"

"No!" He whirled on me, attacking me with his dark depths. "No, Clara. No."

I froze. He *never* called me Clara.

"I've been in the back seat my entire life," Nowen said. "Even when I was part of Cael, he was always the stronger one. He was the one who had the power to rip himself away from me. And then, I was the one locked inside Khalom while he had freedom to roam. Now, I'm, yet again, the one locked in a world that's powerless, while he is free. So just *once*," he bit out, "I want to be the winner. The one who is more important. The one who has the freedom."

His words beat through me, his emotion cutting to my core, but I narrowed my eyes. "You have your blood operation. Isn't that what you want?"

"You think I care about that?" Nowen exploded. He gripped the ends of his hair and pulled. "I thought I wanted it, but I don't. I'm not giving those people freedom." He waved violently at the club. "I'm giving them false hope that they will ever have a happy life. Just like me. I will *never* have a happy life."

He froze. A cloud covered the moon, casting his face in shadow and deepening the dark circles under his eyes, cheeks, and jaw. The look cut me deep, like all of this was *my* fault. Like I was the reason they'd been ripped apart in the first place.

"So what do you want then?" I asked quietly.

Nowen kept his gaze glued to me. He slowly glided forward. "I want to know who is the better kisser." He stopped in front of me, waiting.

Energy pushed and pulled between us, prickling my skin. I felt trapped in his presence, like I had many times before. But I realized I *wanted* to be caught in his presence.

Cael was right.

I did care about Nowen. More than I'd realized.

And Cael was right to not want to be with me. I would always care for Nowen. And that connection would always haunt him.

I opened my mouth to speak, to say something, to reassure him that I cared about him, that he did mean something to me, but a bright orange light appeared in my peripheral vision. It looked like a ball of fire, zooming toward us at an impossible speed. Nowen turned, and his eyes widened.

"Look out!" Nowen grabbed me and threw himself on top of me, covering me from the blast.

The brick building next to us exploded, pieces of the wall spraying everywhere. Rubble covered Dane, and he collapsed onto the ground, buried. Panic ignited in Siv's one eye, and he took one look at us before taking off down the street.

"This isn't good," Nowen said, his body still on top of mine. "We need to go. *Now*." He lifted me to a standing position, but the minute we were on our feet, another blast came at us. This time, it hit the Sandman, windows shattering, chunks of cement flying. The building rocked, and screams sounded from the inside.

Dan was in there.

"Dan!"

I started forward, back to the building, but Nowen held me secure. Fire erupted inside the building, its orange flames licking out from the windows.

"He'll get out," Nowen said. "Everyone's on Deaeth. They'll be able to escape." He tugged me down the street. Smoke billowed around us, and I waved my hands over my face, coughing. We only got a few feet down the road when another ball of fire sailed toward us. It hit the ground at our feet, exploding upward, gravel showering us.

"What's going on?" I yelled.

"I don't know!" Nowen answered. "But it's someone powerful."

People started to rush from the building.

Another blast hit, rattling my bones.

"We need Deaeth." Nowen frantically patted his pockets. "We won't be able to escape without it."

I shook my head. "I won't take it. It's wrong!"

"We need to Celerate out of here! *Where* is it?"

His pockets were clearly empty.

More people rushed from the building, and Dan appeared, his eyes wide, glancing around. His gaze caught mine, and he ran toward me.

"Clara!"

"Dan!"

He sprinted up to me and yanked me into a hug. "I'm so glad you're okay." His head snapped over to Nowen. "What's going on?"

But Nowen didn't have time to answer.

A whoosh of wind blasted us from down the street, and the three of us staggered. A white fog began to curl toward us, so thick it covered the entire street. It churned along the gravel, more orange blasts shooting out from it.

"This is bad," I said, though none of us moved. We stood watching the fog approach.

Then he came into view.

Through the thick fog, Mr. Tompkins emerged, his green eyes glaring. He flexed his hands in and out as he walked, the muscles rippling in his forearms and biceps.

He strolled forward, the white fog a roiling carpet at his feet, the buildings around us on fire.

"Gherald, what are you doing?" Nowen asked, calmly, coolly.

Mr. Tompkins's mouth curved up in a tight smile. The streetlamps next to him flickered and buzzed out.

"Taking Clara for my own, of course." He continued to glide forward.

Nowen held his ground, his lips twisting upward.

"It took a while to find her, did it not? I aligned myself with you to locate her. I got closer to her on the other side to try and track her down here."

"You tried to turn me into a Diviner!" I said.

Mr. Tompkins twisted his face, his eyes shooting to mine. "A desperate attempt to control you, I know. I knew Nowen was closing in on you, and the moment he started to take your blood for his drug, your power would be drained. I needed you strong. I needed you by my side."

"But how do you even know who you are? You gave up your Nobility to become a Divining Master. You left the city."

"It's the blood," he said, mouth lifting. "Taking Deaeth kept my Nobility intact. It gave me the ability to travel in and out of the city. I didn't lose my Centers over on the other side—though it was a tad weaker. But here, with Deaeth, I am at my full power." Satisfaction gleamed in his gaze.

This was too much. I shut my eyes for a moment before I opened them.

"Why does everyone want to use me?"

"In order to control Khalom, you need to control Death," Mr. Tompkins answered. "You're our greatest threat. Now that the Divining Masters have taken over the city, it's time for me to be the sole Master. I don't want to share. And you are the only one who can make that happen. By killing the other Masters."

"I'm not going to kill for you," I said. "You—" Moisture sprang to my eyes. "You set your Diviners on the Stricken camp. You *killed* my dad!" I threw out my arms, and heat immediately shot to my fingers. Black sparks zapped the air around me, and Mr. Tompkins's eyes stretched open.

"Are you on Deaeth?" His gaze darted to Nowen. "You gave it to her?"

Nowen looked just as shocked as Mr. Tompkins did. "Impossible."

I didn't know how, but I had Death with me—without any help. I narrowed my gaze at Gherry, inching forward.

"I'm *not* going to let you take Khalom. I'm *not* going to let you use me to kill anyone. I'm *not* going to let you hurt anyone else." I rubbed my palms together, more heat building.

Mr. Tompkins's face contorted. "Then we'll see who's stronger."

"He's on Deaeth," Nowen whispered to me. "It's the only way he has power here. It will wear out soon."

Mr. Tompkins threw his hands out to the sides of him. Orange fire shot out from his fingertips, shattering a few more windows.

"Let's take out your help first." Gherry flung his hands toward us this time, and another blast struck right where Nowen stood.

Nowen flew backward into the air and hit the ground hard, skidding on the pavement. His back rammed against the nearest building, and he hissed, sagging against the brick exterior, flames leaping out of the window above him.

"Nowen!" I yelled. I started to rush after him, but another blast shook the pavement in front of me, and I fell to my knees, scraping my skin. Pain stung, and I winced, but I forced myself to stand again. Dan stood paralyzed. I spun on Mr. Tompkins.

"Stop," I said. "This is between you and me."

Mr. Tompkins grinned, and he flicked a wrist toward Dan. A blast hit him in the chest, and his eyes bugged wide as he landed onto his backside.

"Dan!" I called out.

"Who to kill first?" Mr. Tompkins said. "Nowen? Or your brother?" His hand flew out to Nowen again, and a burst of light flew from his fingers. Nowen cried out as he smacked the ground, his head flopping to the side. Blood ran down the sides of his face.

"Stop it!" I yelled. "Don't hurt him!"

Amusement twinkled in Mr. Tompkins's eyes. "You actually care? After everything that he's done?" He started to turn to Dan again.

"Just take me," I said. "Let's go. Just leave Nowen and Dan alone."

Mr. Tompkins tsked and he let out a laugh. "But this is too much fun."

He shot his hands out once more, and this time an explosion rocked the window above Nowen, black smoke soaring up into the air.

"Nowen!" I screamed, starting to rush toward him, but then I paused. Heat ignited in my core, so intense that my feet rooted to the ground. The feeling consumed me, and I whipped around to

Mr. Tompkins, my hands clenched into fists. I wouldn't let him get away with this. He was a Divining Master. He would never stop until he had ultimate power.

Red pounded behind my eyes as I stared him down. More heat billowed up within me, and I let it flood through me, traveling through my veins, filling my whole body. Every part of me buzzed. I'd felt this feeling many times before, but never this powerful. Death was with me and wanted to be used.

Heat radiated from me, burning through every one of my pores. The energy flowing through me increased, growing by the second.

Something changed in Mr. Tompkins's face. He paused, fear flickering over his features. He edged back a step.

The warmth in me reached an all-time high as it hummed through me, itching to burst outward. I slowly stalked toward him.

"You know that Death can kill," I said. "You taught me that, that day in class. You said that Death had the ability to erase something from this side and the other."

He inched back another step.

"I want to see if that's true," I said. "Should we find out?" I flexed my fingers, and tiny black sparks crackled in the air.

Mr. Tompkins stumbled over his feet, tripping. His eyes widened. "Claera," he said. "I was only having fun. You're right. Let's just go. I'll leave Nowen and Dan alone."

But I glided closer as he continued to back away. More energy built up within me.

"No," I said. "I'm *sick* of being weak. I'm *sick* of not living to my full potential. I'm *sick* of not really being me."

I tossed out my hands and the earth shook. A black blast exploded from my fingertips, shooting right toward Mr. Tompkins. All the heat, all the anger released out of me in one big whoosh, and I stumbled back, setting a hand on my heart.

The blast hit Mr. Tompkins in the center of his chest.

His face whitened, and his eyes connected with mine. It was only a second, but it felt like an eternity that we stared at each other. I'd known him in Desolation. He'd been my teacher in Khalom. He was the source of so many lies and destruction. I had every right to destroy him, but as my power blasted toward him, regret flooded through me and I rushed forward, trying to stop it.

"No!" I ran forward.

But Mr. Tompkins's face slackened, and his eyes went white. He fell backward, stiff as a board, slipping through the fog before his body shattered into a thousand tiny pieces. The particles were as black as the rose I'd disintegrated, floating through the air until they rested on the ground. The white fog parted, slowly disappearing, and I stood silent on the street, a single streetlamp bearing witness to what I'd just done.

35

Bon Voyage

Dan staggered to his feet, setting a hand on his head. Sirens echoed in the distance, growing louder. I hurried over to him and placed my hands on his face. "Are you okay?"

"I'm fine," he said. "Just shaken."

I took him in for a moment, color still in his cheeks, no apparent bruising in his skin. I turned to Nowen. He lay on the ground, blood oozing from his head, his eyes closed.

"Nowen!"

I sprinted over, clearing away the smoke that hovered around him. He groaned, his eyelids fluttering, and I helped him sit up, propped against the building. Blood ran down the sides of his face, and he gave me a lazy smile.

"Nice work with Gherry," he said. His eyes started to close again. His body tipped, and I gripped his shoulders, holding him upright.

"Nowen. You need help. We can get you to a hospital." *Did Ehlissa's almighty brother need a hospital?* Yes, he didn't have his Nobility here.

He was Centerless.

He groaned again and shook his head.

"It's too late," he said. "I can feel him, Dessy. I'm dying, which means Cael wins. It's strange. I almost feel . . . relief." His head bobbed to the side, and I helped him lie on the ground. His eyelids fluttered again.

"You're not dying, Nowen," I said. "You're an almighty being. You're Ehlissa's brother. You have a long life ahead of you." But I wasn't so sure.

His head rocked back and forth, disagreeing. "You can't feel it. My body will die, and Cael will take over. My time here is done." He cracked an eye open, and humor teased his lips, despite his apparent pain. "It's been fun, Dessy. I'm glad I got to know you. You really did make me a better person." His head lulled again.

Dan hovered over us, a statue, clearly unsure what to do. My head snapped up to him. "Are you still on Deaeth? I need you to go find help. Go find Fae, go find Grandma Laela. They'll know what to do!"

Dan paled in the moonlight. "How—" he started.

"Just think it," I said. "Will yourself to transport. It'll work. Now go!"

Dan nodded quickly, doubt clear on his face, but he shut his eyes. Nowen moaned, his body starting to twitch.

"Go!" I said again.

Dan scrunched his face, bit his lips and, in a blink, he disappeared. Hope ignited in my chest, and I turned back to Nowen.

"It's going to be fine," I said. I placed my hands on his face. "We're getting help."

Nowen kept his eyes closed, but his lips quirked upward. "I appreciate you trying, Clara."

I paused, every part of me freezing. He called me *Clara*. Again. This was twice in one night now.

I gripped Nowen's shoulders and shook him. "Nowen, stay with me!"

But Nowen's body slackened, all expression leaving his face.

"Nowen!"

His breaths slowed, his chest barely rising and falling. More blood pooled behind his head. My hands started to shake, until my whole body was trembling.

"No, no, no," I whispered. This wasn't real. This wasn't happening. I hated all the time I had wasted with him. In my head, it had always been about Cael, but I realized now I cared just as much for Nowen. I'd always known there was a connection between us, I just didn't know how much it had taken root in me, so much so that I was crumbling right in front of him.

"Nowen!" I patted his cheeks. "Please wake up." His eyes stayed closed, and his skin started to lighten, becoming transparent.

I drew my hands back.

His breaths came out in rasps, his breathing shallow. He looked thinner than he ever had.

"Help!" I yelled, but the streets were empty. Fire engulfed the buildings around me, the sirens grew louder.

Nowen's skin began to sink in on itself, his facial bones collapsing inward. More blood spilled around him.

"Nowen!" I barely heard my voice. It sounded distant, far away, almost like an echo.

I set a hand on his chest. My jaw chattered. The sirens grew louder. Nowen's body continued to lighten, shrink, all the color washing away, like he was disappearing.

I opened my mouth, wanting to cry out one more time, but I didn't.

I didn't have time to.

Light flashed, and a ball of energy soared from Nowen's chest, striking me square in my own. I fell backward, smacking the ground hard. Heat radiated in my core where the blast had hit. I dug my fingers into the gravel, tiny rocks embedding under my fingernails.

I lay panting for a moment, heat burning through me in fiery waves. I struggled upright, fumbling to my hands and knees, crawling back over to Nowen, but he was gone.

No.

I stared at the empty space, scrambling around.

"No, no, no." I patted the empty ground.

He really was gone.

36

Flame Out

I sat on the empty street for as long as I could, but soon firetrucks and ambulances and news reporters arrived. I needed to move, but I wasn't sure where. I could go back to the restaurant to find Fae and Laela, but Ricki and the others might still be fighting at the Stricken camp.

I should go to them, but I didn't want to face Cael. Had Nowen merged back into him or was Nowen gone completely? I shook out my hands. Regardless, I couldn't see him.

There was only one place to go.

And I needed to go alone.

And it meant I needed to travel. I hadn't been able to travel on my own yet, but somehow, I knew things were different. Somehow, I knew I could if I tried this time.

Something had changed.

Something had shifted. It was almost as if a new power buzzed inside of me. And it wasn't Death, it was more. And it happened right before Nowen died. Something had happened when that light from Nowen had blasted into my body.

Nowen.

I forced the thought of him away. I couldn't be weak. I needed to be strong. If I thought of him now, I would break. I only had one last purpose—and it had always been my purpose.

The people in Desolation.

Death existed for a reason. And it wasn't just to kill. Grandma Laela had been able to release Diviners from a Divining Master once upon a time; I could do the same. I could join the Mhystic and help restore order to people in Desolation so they weren't living day after day in Diviner attacks.

They could have a life, free from the Cursed world. They could even link their lives and live a full happy life.

I just needed to find the Mhystic.

Mr. Tompkins was gone. I could find the other Divining Masters and destroy them, too. I just hoped Cael and my classmates were okay.

I shuddered and let my eyes close. I focused inward, tapping into the powers that were still alert within me. I knelt in the middle of the street where Nowen had disappeared, my hands in my lap.

I was alone.

But I wasn't alone. Death was with me.

Very slowly, I felt myself drift away. Warmth lifted me off the pavement, and a rush of power surged through me before wind attacked my face. Everything went black, a tether at my waist. It was as natural as stepping into the next room. I don't know why I hadn't been able to travel before.

My feet landed hard on the ground, jarring my knees, and my head spun around a couple of times before I blinked. I staggered to the side, leaves crunching beneath my feet. Tepid air brushed my skin, so still I knew I was close to the city. Trees surrounded me, shooting up into the dark sky, stars barely visible through the gray wisps of clouds above me.

I moved through the forest, weaving my way in the dark. My footsteps seemed loud in the quiet, crunching softly on the ground. Memories and thoughts threatened to overwhelm me, but I stamped them down. I couldn't allow myself to feel anything. I needed to focus.

The white buildings of Khalom came into view up ahead, almost glowing in the dark. I crept up to the gate and peeked inside.

The streets were quiet. Too quiet. I expected chaos. I expected Diviners to be swirling in the sky. I expected Divining Masters to be running around every corner, shouting at their victory of taking Khalom. But it was just . . .

Empty.

I furrowed my brows and wrapped my fingers around the gate. No energy hummed within the barricade, and I stepped through without using my Noble name. My mind was doing somersaults.

I slowly made my way toward Historic Quarter. The trees were still alabaster sentries lining the paths around me, the moonlight glowing on the white leaves. I kept to the sidewalks, heading upward.

Thoughts of Nowen and Cael slipped through my barriers, but I shoved the thoughts away. If I allowed myself to feel fully, I'd be paralyzed. All I needed to focus on was finding the Mhystic. They had to be here.

With each step, my heart beat faster and faster. My stomach tightened. Unease spread along the back of my shoulders. Small gusts of wind occasionally drifted my way, and with each breeze, I'd freeze and glance around, expecting Diviners, but none came.

I itched to turn back, but I forced my feet forward, heading through the dark pathways up to the top of campus. Silence echoed around me, and I tried to absorb it, as if it would be the last time I experienced the quiet ever again.

I took one last corner, and the Grand Hall appeared above me. It stretched long into the dark sky, the moon peeking up behind it. Large white columns adorned the outside of the building, and a white curtain hung silently in front, the doorway inside.

I circled around the fountain in front before I headed up the stairs. I walked slowly, tentatively, my eyes darting side to side. The unease spread, but I continued onward until I brushed past the white curtain.

Inside, my footsteps echoed on the marble floor, the ceiling towering high above me. I peeked over to the left, to the hallway that led to the White Wing, but I traveled to the right, to the main hall.

It felt strange that I had been a student here. That I'd had a life here. Everything felt foreign, even memories that I'd made a few days ago felt like a distant memory. I moved through the hallways, feeling like a red leaf on a barren tree, out of place, until I stepped into the main hall.

The room stretched long and silent before me. The detailed paintings still lined the ceiling, white marble columns on either side of me. A slight breeze came in through the glassless windows, chilling my skin.

Diviners had been here recently.

My eyes swept the space, stopping on the dagger that lay on the altar. Moonlight sparkled in the reflection of the sharp blade. I stared at it for a few heartbeats, then I turned away.

My feet shuffled around, and I waited, my heart pounding. What did I expect? The Mhystic to just surface? I continued to circle. I had no choice but to search.

"Hello?" I asked, but no one emerged. It was just me and my voice bouncing off the ceiling. "Please, you have to be here somewhere."

More silence.

I waited a few more heartbeats, then the curtain parted on the far end of the room. Graeg entered, his black flowy robes dragging on the ground. His bony fingers were linked across his stomach, the wrinkles by his eyes tightening.

"You're back," he said, his voice echoing. "And I was hoping we had gotten rid of you for good."

I sighed, too tired for his antics. "I'm not here to see you, Graeg; I'm here to see the Mhystic."

He snorted, and the sound came out gargled. "Get in line."

So he hadn't seen them either. "Where could they be?"

Instead of answering, Graeg strolled over to the altar and peered at the dagger before running a finger down the blade. "This dagger is infused with *Death*, did you know that? Some say Ehlissa didn't run away and leave her people. They say she used it to kill herself. You know the story, that she couldn't bear to lead her people to destruction. So she used this blade upon herself. And that's how Death is embedded into it." He peered at me beneath his tangled brows.

A heaviness hung in the air, and I only thought of Cael. Had he known? Did his sister really kill herself?

Footsteps came from down the hall, and Bhrutus and Naeomi stepped inside. They paused when they saw me before looking back to Graeg.

"What's going on here?" Naeomi asked.

Bhrutus rubbed a hand over his beard, eyeing us.

"Claera wants to see the Mhystic," Graeg said, his lips curling upward in humor. "I've tried to tell her she's out of luck."

Bhrutus's large frame softened, and his eyes rested on mine. "Oh, dear, Claera. You really shouldn't bother yourself with such things. They'll come. You'll see. We just need to wait."

"Like you have been for months?" I asked, my voice rising. "You haven't been doing anything. Any of you." My eyes narrowed at each of them. "You haven't protected the city. Look at this place!" My arms flew upward.

A sudden gust of wind whooshed in through the open windows, fluttering the curtains. Chills erupted along my skin, and I looked between the three High Officials.

Did I do that?

"There's no need to lose your temper, Claera," a scraggly voice said to my left.

The entire room turned.

Laela hovered in the doorway, her gray hair wild around her head. Her eyes were clear as they connected with mine, a sinister smile on her lips.

I set a hand on my heart. "Grandma?"

"*Don't* call me that, stupid child." She yanked someone in after her, and Ricki came into view. Laela gripped her by her curly hair, dragging her forward.

"Ricki!" I took a step forward and paused. I looked between them. "What is going on?"

Fae followed in after Ricki and Laela, her mouth tight, fear etched around her eyes. Our gazes met before she shook her head and looked away. Bhrutus, Naeomi, and Graeg took in the scene and slowly backed away.

"What's happening?"

Laela jerked Ricki forward and she collapsed to her knees, hands on the floor, crying out. Laela kept a hand on Ricki's head, pinning her down. She kept her gaze on me, clarity still in her eyes.

"Surprised to see me?" Laela smiled. "It's been a while since I've been in here." She glanced around the space.

My heart was beating triple time. What was she doing? I glanced down at her hold on Ricki.

"What's going on?" I asked again. "Grandma—"

Laela's face contorted. "I said *don't* call me grandma!" She threw out her hands and streaks of black flew from her fingertips. They shot toward me, and a blast of power hit, throwing me off my feet.

The impact struck me like a punch to my chest, and I landed hard on the ground, pain slicing through me.

I lay still for a few seconds, groaning, before sitting up. “What is wrong with you?” I staggered to my feet.

Laela squared her shoulders, her lids lowering. “You. You are what’s wrong with me. You existing.” She took a step forward, dragging Ricki with her. Ricki cried out.

“Everyone thinks I ventured into the Dhim,” she continued. “But no. You see, *I* was the one who tried to kill you that night. Only I should be Death. You were the only threat to my power. You think the Mhystic should rule Khalom? The High Officials? The Divining Masters? No, Claera. It’s been Death’s spot from the beginning, since Ehlissa herself, and I am the first in line.”

She paused, still keeping a tight grip on Ricki’s hair. “When I tried to kill you that night, that brother of Ehlissa’s stopped me. He took away Death’s ability to travel, which affected you, I believe.” She lifted a brow. “I had to bide my time in the Cursed world, willingly giving Nowen my blood for his little operation, only because I thought I could use it to my advantage, which I did. But then you discovered how to use your power, which released both of us. So now I’m here.” She smiled.

I glanced down at my hands. I had found Death. But I also felt something else stirring within me. And somehow, I knew it had to do with Nowen. Bhrutus and the others had completely hidden themselves behind the pillars at the back of the room. Fae stood frozen, energy strumming through her. I slowly got to my feet and faced Laela head on.

“So that’s your plan?” I asked. “Take Khalom for yourself? Like every other evil person here?”

Laela’s face twisted and she yanked Ricki up to a standing position. She wrapped a hand around her throat and Ricki gagged, her eyes wide. Fae let out a whimper from the corner.

"You know only the leaders of Khalom get to enjoy eternal life. And the Mhystic don't deserve that gift. I do! And who was clever enough to get rid of them? Me."

I swallowed, adrenaline pumping through my whole body. "Laela, what did you do with the Mhystic?"

Her mouth twitched, and her grip on Ricki squeezed tighter. "I locked them away where they would never bother me again."

I stood paralyzed. Ricki gagged. The Mhystic were gone? Laela had locked them away? That's why they weren't here.

Laela chuckled. "My best adventure yet."

"How? You've been stuck—"

"In the Cursed world? Yes. For the past few months, I've used Deaeth to briefly travel here to lock the Mhystic away one by one. You don't actually think Nowen and his men could keep me captive?"

She was using Nowen. Using him and his blood operation to travel. Her grip tightened on Ricki, who let out a cry.

"Stop!" I said. "Let her go. Please." I started forward, but Laela threw up a hand, and black sizzled at her fingertips, threatening to attack again. I stopped in my tracks.

Laela cocked her head to the side. "You can't stop me, Claera. Which is why I have your dear friend here." She yanked Ricki's head back again. Tears streamed down Ricki's face, her eyes wide with fear.

My heart pounded. Every inch of me was humming.

"You don't need to use her," I said. "I'm right here. It's just you and me."

"You're right." Laela's lips slowly curved upward. She released her fingers, and Ricki heaved, falling to her knees.

Laela took a step toward me. Her gray hair matched her drab dress, her feet bare on the floor.

Fae rushed over to Ricki and dropped down next to her. She set a hand on her back, helping her breathe.

Laela kept her gaze fixed on me. "So how do you want to do this?"

"You and me," I said, voice trembling. "Death to Death."

She cocked her head to the other side, thoughts flashing across her face. Then she smiled. "As you wish." Her loud cackle erupted through the hall, and she threw her hands out in front of her.

I didn't have time to blink.

A black light shot out from her fingers, sailing straight at me. The blast struck me right in the middle, and pain washed over me in a swell, like hundreds of tiny blades piercing my skin.

I gripped my chest, staggering back. I gaped. I didn't think she'd actually attack me.

She must've read my thoughts on my face. "You're my competition," she said smoothly, gliding toward me once again. "There can only be one Death. And that is me."

I pushed out a painful breath, regaining my balance. "And you think you can kill me? You're Death and I'm Death. You can't kill me."

Humor sparked in her eyes. "A Center can always overcome another Center, silly child." She threw out her arms again and my lungs froze as I was hit again. My throat tightened, and I gagged. It was as if my lungs were being crushed.

I hit the ground, and slid several feet, my back against the floor. I held still for a few heartbeats. She wasn't going to stop. I would *have* to fight her back.

Her footsteps clopped softly toward me, and her presence drew closer. I lay unmoving on the floor, gathering myself.

Focus, Clara.

Just breathe.

I was strong. I could do this.

I curled my fingers on the cool marble floor.

My Center.

Find my Center.

Energy began to build within me, but instead of a dark heat surging inside of me, it felt light—like wind brushing against my face. I didn't know what it was—it felt different from Death, but it still felt powerful.

I slammed my hands onto the floor, green sparks emitting from my hands, and in an instant, the entire building rocked. A pillar tumbled onto its side, crashing to the floor. Pieces of the ceiling fell, cracking the marble floor on impact. A huge chunk fell toward Laela, but she spun out of the way. I scrambled to a sitting position, peering down at my hands.

That wasn't Death.

That was Earth.

My eyes shot to Ricki. *Had she done that?* No, her head was buried in Fae's chest. She wasn't paying attention.

Laela's eyes widened before her lips pursed. "Seems you might be more of a problem after all."

I still stared at my hands. That *couldn't* have been me. There was no way. I didn't have any other Centers.

But the moment with Nowen rushed to mind—the light that had blasted from his chest into me. *Had he transferred some of his Centers to me somehow?* I thought he didn't have them. But Death did have the ability to steal other Centers.

What else could I do?

My eyes skipped around the room, past Bhrutus and the others, past the altar, before stopping on the windows. My mind buzzed, and a pressure began to tingle in the back of my mind. I focused on the air flowing in and out. A deep energy started to gather in my mind, until I felt heat push out from my eyes, yellow snaps of energy sparkling around me.

In a whoosh, a whirlwind erupted into the room, spinning toward Laela. The mini storm hit Laela in full force, and her gray hair spun around her head. She tripped over her feet, and the tornado tossed her onto the floor. She glared up at me, her hair still swirling around her.

Time and Space

I'd just used Time and Space.

Laela pushed herself to her feet. "I don't know how it's possible you're tapping into different Centers, but now you really need to die."

She tossed out her hands, and another stream of black light shot out from her fingertips.

My own hands lifted, as if to block, but instead, purple sparks shot from my hands, flying toward Laela. She immediately gripped her head, screaming out in pain. She staggered around, pulling at her hair, continuing to yell.

Mind.

I was attacking her with my mind.

Laela's black blast disintegrated into thin air before me, little sparks tumbling to the ground.

Laela's eyes went wild, and she charged toward me, her wrinkled face contorted, her steps long. She attacked again, throwing out her arms, but this time, her power hit before I could stop it. A stream of black air shot toward me, wrapping around my throat. My air was cut off, and my eyes widened, little black spots immediately filling my vision.

My hands flew to my throat, and I gagged, trying to rip the power away, but I was grasping at air. Panic hit, and my eyes shot to Fae and Ricki, then to Bhrutus, Naeomi, and Graeg. Everyone watched as I choked, mouths open, not doing a thing to stop it. I continued to struggle, my throat squeezing in tight. My chest heaved, but still, no air would come.

Laela laughed, and the sound echoed in my ears. Distant, even though she approached.

"There is no one to help you, Clara. No one is more powerful than me. The Mhystic are gone. Now *you* will be gone." She raised her hands up again.

My mind was screaming.

More spots danced in my vision. My body started to tingle and grow numb. I didn't have too much longer until I passed out—or died, I didn't know which.

I scrambled, thinking of every possible solution. I couldn't take Laela down myself. No one was helping me. I felt my Centers slipping away. My thoughts flashed to Cael, and I wished his army was here to fight for me.

My vision continued to fade. Suddenly a swish of wind blew through the room. It tossed up Laela's hair, her wild eyes still on me. Another surge of wind swept in, and with it a wisp of black sparks. My eyes flew to the window. A dark cloud roiled outside, churning inward, curling rapidly toward the Grand Hall. My heart jolted, my throat burning.

A figure stepped to my left, and at first, I thought it was Cael, but it wasn't.

It was Robert.

He stood with his body taut, his hands in fists. He glared at Laela through the greasy strands of his hair, his eyes dark. His eyes connected with mine, and he gave me a slight nod.

Then the room erupted.

Diviners invaded the room, flooding the entire hall. Their thin, ghost-like forms swirled up and down, forming their infamous dark cloud. Laela's grip on me loosened. Her eyes shot around, confusion on her face.

I crumpled over, gasping for breath. Air filled my lungs, and my throat throbbed. My breaths came out raspy, but I was able to stand upright and regain my footing. These were Mr. Tompkins's Diviners, but it was as if Robert was controlling them.

The Diviners whirled around Laela's head, and she swatted them away. Bhrutus and the others ran to hide, ducking as the Diviners zoomed in their direction. Wind surged violently, and more dark fog filled the space. I stood with my feet planted, my own hair whirling around my head.

I wasn't afraid of them. They were here to help.

Death built within me, filling my chest, burning hot. I kept my gaze fixed on Laela, a black swirl of Diviners over her head. They darted down, dove around, and continued to attack her. She flicked her wrists as each one approached, black blasts flying at them. Some Diviners dodged midflight, while others disintegrated into dust. But more always came.

Additional strength began to weave through my being, little bits of warmth stitching themselves together, solidifying my power.

Laela caught sight of me again, and she screwed up her face tight. She marched toward me once more, charging through the cloud of Diviners. Heat emanated from her eyes, and it seared into me, the chaotic wind blowing around us.

"You will never win this, you know," she said, her voice threatening through the madness. "I am too powerful for you. Even if you do think you have other Centers."

The Diviners continued to shoot down toward Laela, but she only swatted them away. I held my ground, heat continuing to build beneath my skin. It pulsed through my body, and I clenched and unclenched my fists, waiting.

"Let's end this," Laela said.

Pressure built up in my ears, and ringing sounded as the Diviners continued to swirl. Too much wind. Too much chaos. Too much noise. I couldn't handle it.

I threw out my arms and yelled, "Stop!"

The Diviners paused. They all hovered in the air, floating. Ricki's eyes widened. Fae took a step forward.

Silence echoed through the room.

"I release them," I said. "I release them."

The air shifted, energy pushing and pulling through the air. Laela's eyes opened wide as she took them in.

The Diviners' ghostly bodies started to lighten and solidify. They slowly descended to the ground, their eyes and mouths becoming solid, skin reforming back together. Arms and legs appeared, and feet landed on the floor. Heads, hair, hands, and skin appeared. People began to materialize all over the room. Men, women, and children. They peered down at their hands in wonder.

Even Robert started to change. The darkness in his eyes eased, his hair becoming sleek. His gaze darted to me, and wonderment washed over his face.

Death really did have the power to restore life. I wasn't only meant for destruction. There was some good to my power.

"I don't need them," I said, turning back to Laela. "It's you and me. Which apparently has always been the case."

From the beginning, she was my enemy. She'd tried to kill me. She'd tried to take over Khalom. She'd gotten rid of the Mhystic. She'd lied to all of us. And she was the greatest threat of all.

I wouldn't blink. We kept our gazes connected, understanding between us. Only one of us would live. Only one of us would walk away tonight.

I don't know how I got to this point—I didn't expect to be battling my grandmother for my life—but here I was. I'd never wanted to use Death to kill. Yes, I'd killed Mr. Tompkins, but I'd instantly regretted it. If I killed again, would that make me a true murderer?

It's not what I wanted.

But I had no choice.

Laela would destroy us all.

We stared each other down, until our hands lifted in sync.

Energy exploded from my fingertips.

Her black attack met mine. Sparks ignited as our power merged in the air between us. Pressure gathered, growing, energy flowing from her fingertips into mine. We both kept our arms outstretched, power radiating between us, around us. More heat built up inside of me. I remembered how good it felt when my full power was released on Mr. Tompkins. Would I have to do the same thing now?

I didn't want to be a murderer.

I didn't want to be Death.

Laela took a step forward, the former Diviners scattered over the room. Her power pushed me, and I stumbled back a step. She smiled, and I was pushed back more. The pressure from her fingers began to break down my barrier and my arms shook. I gritted my teeth, struggling to hold on. I knew if I lowered my hands, her blast would kill me.

Laela raised her arms high, keeping the energy linked between us. She continued to edge forward, and I continued to stumble back. I wouldn't be able to hold on much longer. My entire body shook, quaking, my arms starting to lower.

The entire room watched us. Ricki. Fae. Robert. Bhrutus and the others. All the Diviners who had been released. But they couldn't help. This was on me.

Laela's lips peeled up into a smile and she winked. Then she threw out her hands one last time. Bright light hit me, almost blinding me.

"No!" Ricki screamed.

Something hit me head on. I wasn't sure if it was Laela's power or someone who pushed me out of the way. My head hit the marble floor and my mind drifted away, sights and sounds muted around me.

Screams.

Footsteps.

The world spun.

More screams. More footsteps.

My vision blackened, and a set of voices drifted through my mind.

Don't give up, Clara. I'm here.

No, I'm here, another voice said.

Don't listen to him, focus on my voice, Clara. You're using Death, so you've reached us. We're in the Dhim. We're here, waiting.

I wanted to tell her that, the other voice said. *Why do you always get to take the reins?*

My head cleared a tad, and I tried to work my voice. "Cael?"

Of course you would say his *name first.*

I blinked. "Nowen?"

A laugh. *Yes, Dessy, we're both here.*

I knew I was in the Grand Hall, but I felt removed from myself. My body continued to sail away. Were these voices real?

And we've been in here for too long. Geez, Dessy. When are you going to come and get us out?

Was I dreaming?

I tried to work my voice, to say something else, but all sights and sounds came rushing back to me. My eyes snapped open.

Fae screamed. The horror in her voice stabbed me in the gut, and I frantically searched around, until my eyes landed on Ricki, who lay motionless on the marble floor, her dark hair splayed over the white marble.

I quickly sat up and my head shot to Laela. "What have you done?"

Laela gave me a satisfied smile. Her face wavered in my vision, shock and horror still pounding through me. I looked back over to Ricki. Her chest was still, her face lifeless on the floor.

No.

She'd taken the impact of Laela's last blast. She'd pushed me out of the way. I couldn't move. I only stared at Ricki's still form.

Defeat washed through me, and I went numb. She'd been the first real friend I'd ever had. Yes, Cael had always been there, but Ricki was different. She was my Companion. A friend that I would never find in anyone else.

It didn't matter how hard I tried, death always seemed to win. It would always hover around me. I couldn't fight anymore. Laela had won. Even if I tried to fight, I couldn't. I didn't have the strength. My shoulders sagged, and every ounce of energy I had gave way.

Laela's laugh echoed through the hall, and my vision blurred, too many sights and sounds clashing together.

"It's a shame you had to exist, Clara," Laela said to me, another laugh slipping out. "If you had been anything but Death, you might've had a happy life." I slowly turned back to her, and she raised her hands one last time.

This was it. There was no Ricki to save me this time. And I didn't even want to hide. I waited, watching, heart pounding, accepting the inevitable. Would it hurt to experience a mental death? What would it feel like to cease to exist? Nothing, I suppose.

Laela drew her arms back, but before she flicked her wrists, her eyes bulged. Her mouth opened and closed like a fish, and her hands clasped her throat. A stream of red blood flowed out from her neck, and she staggered side to side, swaying on her feet. Fae stepped out from behind her, holding the dagger.

Laela clawed at her neck, blood flowing through her fingers. Fae watched her for several seconds before the dagger clattered to the floor. Laela's eyes widened at her oldest friend, fear and shock on her face. She tried to speak, but nothing came out. Something passed in her gaze. Sorrow? Anger? Regret? Fear? Humor?

She collapsed onto the ground, lying next to Ricki, both unmoving.

The Diviner people stood around the edges of the room, but Bhrutus and the others slowly came closer.

Graeg stopped in front of Laela's lifeless body before bending down and picking up the dagger. "I've been waiting for someone to use this." Satisfaction settled on his features.

Fae dropped to Ricki's side, her hands hovering over her. Every part of her shook. A cry escaped her throat, and she clasped a hand over her mouth.

Naeomi gently placed a hand on her shoulder. "It will be all right."

I shook my head, scooting back a few inches. Ricki. Laela. Fae. Cael. Nowen. Dad. Mom. Mr. Tompkins. Daniel. Too much death. Too much heartache. And I still hadn't helped anyone. I'd only caused more destruction.

I pushed myself to stand, and the world spun before it righted itself. I stumbled back a few steps, moving toward the exit. No one noticed. They all stayed fixed on the two bodies on the floor. I inched back farther. My heart pumped fast. I needed out. I couldn't be here any longer.

I finally took off in a run, sprinting out of the room, leaving the scene behind me.

37
Loose Ends

I knew where I was going.

It was the only hope I had left. It was the only thought I had left. It was my only chance to do one last good thing.

I'd failed Ricki. I'd failed Fae. I'd failed Mom and Dad. I'd failed Cael and Nowen. I'd even failed Laela and Mr. Tompkins.

The memory of hearing Cael and Nowen's voices still echoed in my mind, but I knew it wasn't real. They weren't still out there. I couldn't get my hopes up. I could only do one more thing to set things right. And *then* I would leave. I wouldn't stay in Khalom any longer.

I raced down the hall, my footsteps against the marble floor loud in my ears. Night sky still hovered outside the glassless windows as I tore into the foyer. Spinning around, I spotted the long hallway to the left and I sprinted toward it.

With each step, dread pounded into me. But I knew this was where they were. The Mhystic were in here.

The White Wing.

I wound my way downward, the flames on the walls casting eerie shapes in front of me. I wasn't sure which was pounding faster—my feet or my heart. Ricki's lifeless body flashed in my mind over and over again.

I could do one last good thing.

One last good thing.

I couldn't let my life be for nothing.

I skidded to a halt when I faced the entrance to the White Wing. The thin, translucent curtain hung before me. Adrenaline pumped through my entire body, making my vision white. Every part of me shook as I drew my fingers forward, parting the curtain.

The hallway of doors stretched long and white, sounds immediately bombarding my ears. But I stepped forward anyway, keeping my head high. I wouldn't let the sounds paralyze me. I knew what was beyond these doors, and it was nothing to be afraid of.

Doorknobs rattled.

Screams echoed.

Scratching grated.

Shadows paced.

I wasn't afraid. I slowly inched forward, noise attacking me from all angles. But I continued on, Fae's words resonating in my mind.

It's a prison, meant to drive a person mad. It's meant to incapacitate you completely—consume you in a world that affects your Center.

Laela had known what she was doing.

I approached the first door and planted my feet outside of it. I slowly lifted a hand to the knob and wrapped my fingers around it. It was cool to touch, sending chills up my arm.

You have to hold the Center to open the door.

I prayed I did. Nowen had given me power right before he died.

I turned the knob and the door swung open.

It worked.

Inside, pitch black greeted me, a gust of wind whooshing into my face. As I stared, I began to notice stars dotted the space, a universe full of color stretching out before me. Swirls of gas and dust scattered over the dark sky, going on for an eternity. The colors churned in and out of one another in the bottomless sky. I felt that if I were to fall forward, I would never stop falling. I wasn't sure how long I stared, but long enough that a hand shot out of the darkness and clasped my arm.

I jerked back, swallowing a scream.

"It's about time," a warm voice said.

A guy with short brown hair and a strong jawline stepped through the doorway, sparkles in his eyes. "Time and Space," he said. "Or Era. Nice to meet you." The door slammed shut behind him, and he gave me a small bow. "I've been locked in there for what's felt like an eternity. I knew you'd come though. Thank you, Claera."

He shook my hand, and golden sparks snapped in the air around our touch.

His gaze swept down the long hallway. "Am I the first? Have you released anyone else?"

I blinked, rubbing my hand on my leg. "Y-yes. You're the first."

Era flashed me a dazzling smile. "Well, I'm grateful. Let's release the others, shall we?" He motioned to the other doors.

I coughed. "Right."

Era wasn't what I expected. I imagined the Mhystic to be . . . scary? Old? Snobby? Era was down to earth. Young. Kind.

He followed me as I made my way to the next door. He moved up next to me, and his shoulder brushed my own. He nodded at me to open it.

I slowly reached a hand forward and turned.

A jungle, lush and green, greeted me, with bright vines that grew up and around tall trees. Flowers filled the area, with plants and dirt, rocks and hills. The heavy scent of rain filled my nose.

"This is Earth," Era said. "Or Avani. We've been dating." His lips twisted wryly. "But she's got commitment issues."

A yelp sounded from the jungle, and a woman swung forward on a vine, speeding our way. She leaped into the hallways and Era shut the door closed behind her.

"Finally!" Avani said. She dusted off her hands. Her wild blond hair framed her face. "Took forever." She eyed Era and gave him a slow smile. "I've missed you." She planted a kiss on his cheek.

Era's mouth flicked up before his eyes slid to mine. "Let's continue onward, shall we?"

Avani gave me a look of appreciation as she linked her arm through Era's elbow. I nodded, then moved forward, facing the next door. I swung it open.

Mind's prison was a plain, white room, though an assortment of objects floated in the air. A chair hovered above the ground, spinning, until it morphed into a lion. The lion roared, and I staggered back, my hand gripping the doorframe.

"It's okay," Era said. "He's in here somewhere."

A floating candlestick shimmered before it changed into a steak sizzling on a plate. The aroma tickled my nose, and I stretched my eyes wide.

"Incredible," I said. "None of my classmates with Mind could ever do something this amazing in school."

"I should hope not," a new voice said. "Then those classmates of yours would take my spot on the Mhystic." A disorderly man with glasses emerged, white hair on top of his head. He smoothly stepped into the hallway, a wide smile on his face. "I didn't *mind* staying in here," he said. "I just paced and thought about my life. See what I did there?"

The man chuckled at his own joke. Even though his hair was void of color, he didn't look old, his skin was smooth and flawless. His shirt was halfway tucked out of his slacks, his glasses crooked on his face. He closed his own door. "I'm Cato." He nodded his head toward the last door. "Shall we?"

I blinked at him, then peeked over at Era and Avani. The Mhystic had been here this whole time. And were treating me like old friends.

When I opened Body's door, a guy was rock climbing on a cliff face, a violent ocean below. He had muscles that rippled from his skin, and he free-soloed the climb, no rope, undeterred by the jagged rocks in the waves beneath him.

His fingers dug into the rock, more muscles flexing, when Avani whistled, "Hey Kwan! Over here!"

Kwan slipped, but he secured himself back on the rock. He turned his head toward us, and a smile burst from his face. He quickly finished the climb, topping out. He jogged over to us, panting.

"Hey, guys." Kwan shook his head, and the brown curls on top of his head bristled. "I thought I'd never leave this place." The mountain disappeared behind him as he shut the door. "I thought I could beat this door down, or scream my way out, but I was wrong. It's good to see you guys."

He clapped his buddies on the back. "And *you* must be my savior." He grinned and pulled me into a bear hug, spinning me around. I yelped at the sudden contact, and he set me back on my feet. "It's nice to meet you."

We all fell silent as we exchanged looks. Era, Avani, Cato, and Kwan studied me carefully, but there wasn't any awkwardness in the air.

It was comfortable. We shared space for a moment before I shifted on my feet.

"I-I have to go," I said. "I can't stay here."

Reality rushed back. I had done my duty here. I'd found the Mhystic; now I could leave. There wasn't anything here for me. Not anymore. For a moment, I had forgotten about Ricki and her lifeless body.

But it was only a reminder of the danger that I posed.

Cato lifted his brows, straightening his glasses. "Why ever not?" He peered at me closely, and a zap went through my head, as if he were trying to read my mind. I yanked my gaze away.

"I shouldn't be here," I said. "My last goal was to release you guys. I'm so glad you're here. But now I need to go."

Era's lips pursed. "And why is that?" His eyes were blue, and they reminded me of Cael.

Why were they asking so many questions?

"Because I've failed everyone," I whispered. "All I've wanted from the beginning, since I was back in Desolation, was to be loved. To not be invisible. To have a name. To be important. To have a family. And when I thought I had all those things, I lost it. I'm Death. I'm cursed. I don't want to hurt anyone else."

Era unfolded his arm from Avani's, and he took me by the shoulders. He dipped his head close to mine.

"You are loved. You are one of us. And you have more good in you than you can imagine. What is it that you want?"

I stared back, captured by his blue depths. "So much," I said, and a part of me broke. The admission sent a wave of longing through me, and tears gathered in my eyes. "I want so much. I want to be with my family. I want the people in Desolation to be able to truly live. I want the rest of the Divining Masters tracked down and stopped. I want all the Diviners to be free from the Divining Masters. I want Ricki to be okay. And I want . . ."

I stopped, and my heart pounded fast.

"Go on," Era urged.

"And I want Cael and Nowen to be here. With me."

Era squeezed my shoulders once before he straightened. He faced the other Mhystic.

"We've been gone a long time," he said. "I don't know what faces us out in Khalom, but there's nothing that we can't handle." He turned and peered down at me once more. "Sometimes we don't get what we want. Sometimes we dream, and things don't turn out as we desire. But we keep trying, and when we don't stop, sometimes miracles happen."

He lifted his brows, as if challenging me to disagree with him.

"I don't believe that things will ever align for me," I said. "There aren't any miracles left for me. There never were."

Cato cleared his throat, and we all turned. He put a hand to his temple and closed his eyes, concentrating. A myriad of thoughts flashed across his face as purple sparks sizzled in the air around him. "I'm catching up on everything," he said. "I can see everything. The city gates are down. Diviners are in and out of the city. A lot of the Divining Masters have fled because Gherald Tompkins was killed. Students are gone. But . . ." He peeked his eyes open and looked at me.

"Cael and Nowen are still here."

Everything paused. The world skidded to a halt. My heart beat at an impossible speed.

"Not possible." It came out in a whisper.

"Where are they?" Avani asked.

Cato's eyes narrowed. "I think she already knows."

I took off so fast, I almost felt bad for ditching the Mhystic, but I couldn't stand there any longer.

Cato was right.

I *did* know where they were.

I sprinted up the stairs at the end of the hallway, my hand gripping the metal banister, circling the steps two at a time. I finally reached the top of the stairs, my heart racing, my mind on high alert.

Was Cato right?

I spun, facing the edge of the small room where the motionless black curtain hung like death. I slowly stepped toward it, my footsteps soft, my heartbeat loud. I stared at the black veil, knowing what was beyond it.

The Dhim.

I tried to control the shaking in my limbs, but it was impossible. I continued onward, flexing my fingers in and out, inching closer.

I stopped, facing the black curtain, doubt flickering through my mind for a short moment before I lifted my hand and parted the curtain. I gripped the material and stuck my head inside.

Unlike before, the world didn't turn upside down, no pain shot to my forehead, and my head didn't whirl around. Death buzzed inside my veins, and when I stuck my head inside, being inside the Dhim was as simple as peeking into the next room. It was like Death righted me.

I blinked into the darkness.

"Hello?" I called. "Cael? Nowen? Are you there?" My voice echoed out into the long stretch of quiet, only silence answering back.

Darkness swirled in front of me, churning and curling, a never-ending chasm. I squinted, straining to see anything, but there was nothing there. I kept my grip firm. They *had* to be in here. Cato had seen it. He was Mind. He wouldn't lie to me.

I narrowed my gaze, remembering their voices. They'd spoken to me. Which meant they were both in here. I don't know how Cael got in here, but he must still be linked to Nowen. I continued to search, my eyes straining in the dark.

There.

My heart skipped a beat.

Two forms struggled out in front of me, swimming through the dark space. Their arms were linked around each other, hands around each other's throats, legs kicking. They twirled around, as if there was no gravity, turning round and round, floating.

I blinked, straining to see more.

Another form came into view.

There were *three* of them. Not two. I gripped the curtain tighter, sticking my head in deeper.

Shouts erupted through the dark. The three fighting forms traveled closer. The light from the hallway where I stood highlighted one face. Then another. Then another.

Cael.

Nowen.

Laela.

What? Laela?

The three were entangled in a fight, Cael and Nowen struggling to keep Laela off. They pulled at her hair, one sneaking in a punch while the other held her.

"Good one, Cael!" Nowen yelled.

Cael smiled, his teeth flashing in the dark. "Only because of your help, other me."

Muscles strained. Sweat glistened. Laela fought back, sending a blast at Nowen, who tumbled back, clutching his stomach. Cael retaliated. Laela jerked Cael to the side, and he grunted. But the two attacked once more, smiles on their faces.

"What's going on?" I shouted. I couldn't process everything. Laela was in the Dhim? And Cael and Nowen *really* were here.

All three heads turned toward me.

Cael's lips parted and Nowen's eyes widened. Laela's face twisted, her eyes flashing.

Cael and Nowen nudged each other.

"Clara!"

"Dessy!"

Laela sprang forward again and yanked Cael's arm back into a twisted position.

"I'm Death," Laela yelled. "I rule here in the Dhim. Which means I can torture them forever!" She threw out a blast to Nowen, and he dodged, grinning.

"Or we get to torture *you*, forever," he said.

I couldn't let them stay in there, battling Laela in an endless fight—to be doomed to an eternity of this.

Laela laughed as Cael charged her once again. Cael smacked into her and flipped her over his back. Nowen attacked her from the other side, climbing on top of her. He held an elbow across her windpipe. Then he went flying. Laela pushed back, her Center uninhibited by the Dhim. The boys continued to fight back, Centerless, but strong when united together.

"Stop!" I yelled. "Just stop!"

But they only smiled and continued. I gritted my teeth together. Were they going to make me go inside? I squeezed my eyes shut. I'd never traveled willingly into the Dhim before. If I stepped in now, would I be able to get out?

Cael, Nowen, and Laela kept at it. Somehow, I knew that if I were to walk away and close the curtain, I would never see any of them again. They would be lost in the Dhim forever. I groaned, hating what I was about to do. But if I made one more thing right, I might be able to live with myself.

I released my grip from the curtain and allowed myself to fall forward. The darkness consumed me, welcomed me, carried me along. I hovered in the air, buoyed up, and the curtain closed behind me.

Cael looked over. "Clara, no!"

The light diminished, and the vast dark space stretched out before me. The fighting forms were barely visible up ahead.

I pushed my arms forward, then back, kicking. Cael took another punch to the gut, trying to shove Laela off. "Clara, go back!"

Nowen paused, catching sight of me.

"Dessy, are you insane? Get back!"

But it was too late. I looked back, and the curtain was sealed off. Nothing but a complete stretch of dark.

Nowen pushed away from the fight and started sailing toward me, swimming through the space. Cael held Laela by the hair as she swatted at him.

Nowen sped toward me, his face pale in the dark, excitement in his eyes. But he hit me hard, unable to stop his momentum, ramming into me. I took his hands, steadying him.

"What are you doing here?" he hissed. "Do you know how dangerous this is?"

I opened my mouth, waiting for a hundred words to gush out, but they didn't. Nowen was right in front of me. He was alive. He was here. My eyes shot to Cael. He had Laela in a headlock.

"Get her out of here!" Cael yelled.

"You think I know the way out?" Nowen called back. He rolled his eyes and whispered to me, "Cael. Am I right?"

I blinked at him. I hadn't thought this through.

All I could think of was to get to them, but I didn't have a plan. And seeing them both, after thinking I had lost them, was messing with my mind.

"I said get her out!" Cael yelled again.

Nowen shook his head. "You heard him, Dessy, let's at least try and find a way out of this place." He reached down and touched my hand.

The moment our skin touched, the world seemed to pause. An orange glow radiated between our fingers, building, growing, lighting up the dark. Cael noticed and turned his head. Even Laela stopped struggling. Nowen peered down at our touch, and his eyebrows lifted.

"Are you doing this on purpose, Dessy?"

The glow expanded, illuminating from my hand to Nowen's, until it sank into his skin. He lifted his palm and analyzed it, his forehead puckered.

"If I didn't know any better, Dessy, I'd think—"

The light burst outward and raced toward Cael. It hit him hard in the chest, and he flew back a few feet. Laela's glare darted between us. Nowen stared down at his still-glowing palm.

A sudden emptiness cut into me, like a part of me was missing. The familiar buzz of Death still ran in my veins, but the power I'd recently received was gone. The empty space made me feel caved in, carved out, like I wasn't whole. I hadn't realized the power I had until it was gone.

Laela's head snapped from Cael to Nowen. Light emanated from Cael's chest and Nowen's hands. They both slowly turned and faced her, their orange glows pulsing in the dark.

Laela's eyes opened wide, and she scrambled back through the dark.

"Not possible," she said. "How?"

Cael and Nowen gave each other a sly glance, an unspoken conversation flowing between them before they charged her at once.

Laela flailed, struggling to swim away, but Cael and Nowen were faster. They gripped her at the same time, pressing their hands right into her face. She cried out, trying to shove them off her, but they were too strong. The glow coming from their bodies shot into her, and light exploded.

Her body seemed to catch on fire, the orange glow igniting at the ends of her hair down to her fingertips. The light appeared to eat her, push her downward through the darkness. She screamed as light burst out from her eyes and mouth, and she continued to fall, traveling deep below us.

Beneath us hundreds—no thousands—of wispy gray bodies twirled below. They swam around one another, writhing, a sea of dead caught in the Dhim. Laela descended quickly toward them, and the dead reacted immediately. They swallowed her in an instant, piling on her, some grasping at her hair, her wrists, her ankles, dragging her down. She continued to scream, the sound piercing the dark, until it became muffled. The dead enveloped her completely until the light dimmed and she was gone.

I stared down into the black.

It was over so quickly.

She was gone.

I stayed frozen for several heartbeats. I didn't try and move. I only stared. I didn't know how she had survived the dagger in the Grand Hall, but it was probably because she was Death. But now? She was gone. Eternally.

I vaguely felt myself moving. I hadn't intentionally drifted away, but somehow, I had floated away from where Cael and Nowen were. I allowed myself to float. To think. To ponder.

I was tired.

It had all been so much. From the start of my existence to this moment.

I was *tired.*

I didn't want to fight anymore. I just allowed myself to lie back and be carried by the darkness. Let silence settle in my brain.

Maybe this place wasn't that bad.

A heaviness started to numb my mind, and I gave in to the feeling. There wasn't noise here. There wasn't chaos. There wasn't hurt. There was no pain. Maybe this was where I belonged.

Living was too hard. Living meant pain. Living meant experiencing emotions. Here, floating in the dark, I didn't have to think about those things. I could spend an eternity here, not having to worry about others or living up to their expectations. I could just be me, lifeless, painless. Just existing. Floating.

I continued to allow myself to be carried away, to let the feeling of numbness overtake me. Every so often I would see a gray body drifting by my side, their presence only a wisp of what it once was. Gray and translucent, a sliver in the dark. Is that what my fate was if I stayed here long enough? If I allowed the dark to overtake me?

But I didn't care. Becoming a wisp of what I was would be better than feeling hurt. Feeling pain. Feeling like a failure. Hurting others.

But then something changed in the air. It was a slight shift, but enough to bring me up a level of consciousness. I lifted my head, listening.

There was a power that emanated behind me, like something was drawing me to it. My head cleared a little, and I righted myself, moving my arms and legs in a swimming motion to keep myself upright. But still, the energy dragged me toward it, and my heart began to pick up.

Maybe this was a mistake.

What was I doing here? What was I thinking? I didn't want to become one of those gray wisps of people. That was no life. Wasn't it better to feel pain and know what it was to love? Cael and Nowen were still out there, even if neither of them ever loved me back. Even if Dad and Ricki were gone, even if Dan fell sick to his cancer again, wasn't it better that I still lived? It was a gift to be alive. A gift to know these people even if for a short time.

And I wasn't ready to give it up yet.

"Stop!" I called out, though I wasn't sure to whom. I frantically swam in the opposite direction of the pull, but its strength intensified. Soon, I was being dragged backward at full speed, caught in an invisible current.

Then it stopped.

My body hovered and everything was silent, my heart thrumming through my whole being.

I spun around, squinting through the dark. Maybe Nowen and Cael were still searching for me. I continued to look, my eyes wide in the dark. Several gray wispy bodies floated past me. I cringed, trying to swim away, when another group floated by. More bodies came, closing in on me, and I tried to push them away.

Bodies with gray, slack faces.

Protruding eyes.

More bodies.

More dead faces.

Leering.

Looming.

My heart pumped faster.

I desperately pushed away, a cry trapping in my throat. The bodies floated closer until suddenly they scattered.

A face came into view, floating ahead of me, pale in the dark. I'd seen this face many times before. The statue in the courtyard. In all the history books.

"Ehlissa?" I gasped.

Ehlissa stared at me, face expressionless except for the pain that radiated from her gaze. Her eyes bulged in silent agony, piercing right into me, screaming at me to run.

What was she doing in here?

Was this where she had been hiding this whole time?

But she wasn't whole. She'd clearly lost her mind.

"Ehlissa?" I asked. "Can you see me?"

But her face remained blank, just the agony flowing from her eyes. It didn't make sense. She'd had everything. She'd had power. The ruler of Khalom. But one mistake, spreading out her power, had been her downfall. She'd only been trying to do the right thing, and it had blown up in her face.

Like me.

We were so alike. Or were we?

Ehlissa had run. That was the reason for her pain. It wasn't because she'd abandoned her people or that she'd created a Cursed world that shouldn't have existed. It was because she *chose* not to live.

I blinked, suddenly realizing where I was. I was alone. In the Dhim. Surrounded by the dead. I had just about chosen the same fate as Ehlissa—running away from life to hide myself from hurt. I would stay here until I became only a sliver of myself. Consumed in the dead for eternity. But choosing this would only cause more pain.

I scrambled backward, trying to swim away. More gray bodies closed in, circling Ehlissa. She reached out and cradled one by the face, laying her head on it. Her eyes stayed wide, pain extending out into the eternal darkness.

Adrenaline kick-started my heart.

"Help!" I screamed. I swirled around, not knowing up from down. "Help!" I tried again. But everything looked the same.

I was going to be lost in here forever. There was no way out. The darkness stretched on all sides, nothing but a black canvas with no stars. My heart was racing, and I kicked my arms and legs out, but I had no idea if I was traveling back the way I'd come or farther into the Dhim.

But I *wouldn't* stop. I continued on, continued to search, until I was sure my heart would give out. How long could I stay in here? When would I crack?

Time passed. I continued to swim. More time. I kept pushing. Every part of me ached, and the backs of my eyes hurt from squinting so hard. But my body was giving out. My spirit was breaking.

Then I heard it.

"Clara?" It was soft, familiar, and came from up ahead.

I slowly turned toward the sound, Death coming alive in my veins. Like it *knew* something.

"Clara?" The voice came again. "Clara?"

That voice. How did I know that voice?

"Clara, where are you? Follow my voice!"

Ricki.

Impossible.

"Ricki!" I called out.

"Clara, over here!"

A crack of light cut through the darkness, spilling inside the deep black chasm where I floated. Ricki peeked her head through the curtain, searching, before her eyes landed on me.

"There you are!"

"Ricki!" I kicked. I pushed my arms out. A sudden burst of energy rushed through me. I propelled myself toward her, locked on the light. If the curtain closed, I'd be lost in here again.

Nowen and Cael also poked their heads through.

"Clara."

"Dessy!"

They pushed the curtain aside and both reached down for me at the same time. Their hands connected with my arms, and they hefted me up, pulling me out of the Dhim. The curtain closed behind me, and I blinked at the sudden brightness.

Nowen's face was as it always was: mouth quirked, eyes humorous. Cael's was more severe, but his eyes were soft. I took them in. Inhaled. Exhaled. Relished their presence. I could've stared at them all day, except I turned to Ricki.

"How are you here?" My voice caught at the end. She was dead. I'd seen her die because of me. I'd heard Fae's cries.

"The act of saving you made me your Blood Companion," she said. "Just like it did with Laela and Fae." She took my hand and squeezed.

I glanced down at the touch. "You sacrificed your life for mine. You saved me." Of course. My gaze skated to Cael and Nowen. "You all saved me."

Ricki squeezed my hand again. "Come on. The Mhystic have gathered everyone in Khalom. They're waiting for you."

38
Silhouette

Brightly colored ribbons hung from the ceiling in the Grand Hall, with sparkling tinsel wrapping up and down the pillars that lined the room. Candlelight gave the room a soft glow, and stars sprinkled in the night sky outside.

I stood in front of the crowd, Era, Avani, Cato, and Kwan beside me. I shifted under everyone's stares but was still grateful to be standing here. I'd almost been lost in the Dhim. I'd almost had the same fate as Ehlissa. Now, I had no idea what was going on. Why had the Mhystic gathered everyone?

I scanned my classmates' faces. But they weren't the only ones here. The Stricken had also been let inside the city. They had marched here, ready to fight Divining Masters, but the Masters had fled. I spotted Lionel off to the side, his shaded head sweeping the room as if looking for danger. But the city had been sealed off. Cato had made sure of that.

Cael and Nowen hovered next to each other in the back, Nowen with his arms crossed, that smirk on his face, and Cael with his feet planted, hands behind his back. They both stared at me, and it was a struggle not to stare back. I didn't know what to do about them.

Different pieces of myself loved them in different ways. Cael was my heart, but Nowen made me feel alive. How was I supposed to choose between them? Or maybe I didn't need to. They might have other plans that didn't involve me. They each had all five Centers, and they had every possibility in the world to explore.

The High Officials lined the room, standing in their long white robes, faces beaming now that the Mhystic had returned. A string quartet played in the corner, soft music floating through the room. People were still entering the Grand Hall, and I spotted Deena and Khalob in the back. Khalob—surprisingly—shot a small smile my way.

I took in all the people who had once been Diviners, their faces full of life and wonder. Robert and Ricki stood with them. If I had released them, I could release the rest of the Diviners. I just had to hunt down the Divining Masters.

Mom had also returned. She hovered off to the side next to some of the Stricken. They'd probably been comforting her after Dad's death. Ricki had told me briefly that her memories were slowly coming back.

If only Dad were here.

Bhrutus stepped forward and clapped his hands. The music in the corner stopped, and silence echoed in the hall.

"It is a time for rejoicing," he said, his voice booming. "A time for us to dedicate ourselves to the Mhystic. We will each give a piece of our Centers to the Mhystic to keep them strong. To make sure they will always lead us."

The audience murmured in agreement. It was the way it was done. It was how we supported the Mhystic and let them guide us.

Era lifted his hand, and the room silenced.

"Times are going to change," Era said, and his kind voice hovered over the room. The other members of the Mhystic all nodded beside him. Looks were exchanged through the hall. "Khalom isn't strong enough with the Mhystic as its rulers. We need better protection. Ehlissa's brother has returned to us. The holder of all five Centers. We want the true leader of Khalom to step forward and take his rightful place on the throne."

Cael and Nowen stiffened in the back of the room. Shock flitted across both of their faces, and their eyes slid to each other. They hadn't been expecting this.

Nowen shook his head, the color draining from his face. But he didn't move. Didn't speak. It was Cael who stepped forward. His piercing blue eyes swept the space, his hand on his sword at the hip. The room turned, waiting, watching.

Cael cleared his throat. "Nowen will take the place of the Mhystic. I would trust no one else to lead Khalom. He is Ehlissa's brother through and through. He holds all five Centers. He will keep Khalom safe and create a more peaceful land in Desolation." Cael's eyes connected with mine. "And I will choose to remain a Stricken and protect the gates."

Whispers erupted through the hall, but faces were full of relief and gratitude. Era and the others extended their arms toward Nowen, welcoming him up to the front of the hall. Nowen swallowed, his face pale, and he turned to Cael.

"Why?" he asked.

Cael wrapped his arms around Nowen and pulled him into a hug, holding him close. "Because I know you. Your heart is good. And you deserve freedom. And peace. And love." Cael's eyes cut to me for a brief moment, and my heart thumped.

He pulled out of the hug and clapped Nowen on the back. "To the Mhystic!"

"To the Mhystic!" the crowd cheered.

Music began playing again and the room breathed at once. Avani linked her arm through Era's, smiling up at him. Era nodded his head when our eyes met, satisfaction on his features.

People began dancing, moving together, hands linked, laughter tinkling. Lionel, in his shaded form, stepped up to Deena and gave her a small bow. Deena blushed and slid her hand into his. The two swept away, whirling together in a type of ballroom dance, weaving in and out of the other couples.

Nowen was immersed in the crowd, being congratulated, surrounded by smiles and words of excitement. A light I had never seen before lit his face, and my heart cracked a tad. It was all he'd ever wanted. He wanted to be seen. He wanted to be loved. He wanted to have freedom. And now he had it, all because of Cael.

Cael.

My eyes shot to the back of the room. He was gone. I looked around frantically, but he wasn't anywhere in the crowd. The curtain fluttered at the back of the room.

There.

I took off, pushing my way through the crowd, shoulders bumping into me. Panic seized my chest, my lungs tight. I drove myself to run faster.

I rushed outside, and I stopped on the white sidewalk.

Energy thrummed inside of me, a swirl of Death surging into my veins. I flexed my fingers, telling myself to calm down. My eyes shot around the courtyard. He wasn't here.

I immediately sprinted down the path out of Historic Quarter, the white flowers and trees glowing in the dark around me. The moon was fat and round overhead, sparkling on the translucent leaves. I wove down campus in a full run.

"Cael!" I called out, and my throat burned. "Cael!"

I rounded corner after corner, more panic building. What if I never saw him again? Was he gone for good? I couldn't handle that. Tears stung the backs of my eyes.

I came around one last bend at the edge of the city and skidded to a stop. The towering white fence stood before me, tall and bright in the dark. Shadows shifted outside the gate, and I moved forward a step.

"Cael, please."

The trees rustled, and Cael emerged from the forest, stepping into the moonlight. The light illuminated his face, tracing the sharp lines of his cheekbones.

My stomach flipped at the sight of him. "What are you doing out there?"

"I'm leaving," he said quietly.

Silence fell as I processed his words.

"Why?" It was all I could ask.

Hurt jabbed like a spear to my chest. This wasn't happening. He couldn't just leave.

Not after everything.

"I need to be with the Stricken," he said. "It's where I belong. Nowen will be a great ruler. I want you to stay with him. He will need you."

I shook my head, his words heavy in the air. "No. I-I don't understand." *I thought he cared about me.*

"Clara."

The single word struck me, and I flinched. The deep sound of his voice only reminded me of how it used to feel inside my head. Warm, comforting.

"Order is being established here, but the city still needs to be protected. The Stricken still need a leader. And that leader is me. You know that's true."

Did I?

I did, but I didn't want to admit it. How did I think this was going to end? I couldn't be with both Cael and Nowen. But it had always been Cael and me. And he was right. The Stricken needed him. Khalom and Desolation needed both him and Nowen.

I needed to say goodbye.

Without words, I stepped up to the gate, and whispered, "Claera." I walked through the barrier and stopped in front of him, until we were only inches apart.

Cael didn't move, the dark green trees behind him. I searched his face, searched the emotion in his eyes. He cared about me, I knew that, I knew from the way he'd kissed me, but his true love was protecting those who needed it. Just like he'd protected me.

We stayed standing together in silence for a few moments, and I set a gentle hand on his chest, his heartbeat thrumming underneath my fingertips. Something caught my attention behind him, and my brows shot upward.

"Impossible." I took a few steps away and bent down, picking up an old, leather book.

It was my journal. I gripped the cool leather and dusted off the dirt on top. I turned it over in my hands, every word I'd written inside still memorized. It held every emotion I'd ever had toward him.

Leaves crackled behind me, and I turned. Cael stepped closer and stared down at the journal. "Can I have it?" he asked, voice thick.

My fingers dug into the leather. "Why?"

"Because I'll need it when I need comfort. I never want to forget you, Clara."

I let his words wash over me before I extended the book out toward him.

His mouth curved upward in a half smile. "Thank you." His fingers brushed mine as he took the book.

Cael turned and slowly made his way back into the forest. My feet stayed rooted to the earth, my entire body humming. I tried to memorize every line of him in case it was the last time I saw him. I wouldn't blink. I couldn't.

Then Cael paused and turned his face, the moonlight highlighting his profile.

Shadows sank into his cheeks and darkened the harsh line of his jaw.

"I'll always be with you," he said, placing a hand over his heart. "Know that I'm out there, and I'll always be here for you."

He moved forward once again and disappeared into the forest.

I stood waiting for a long time, staring into the shadows, until his words finally solidified in my head.

He would be.

He would always be with me.

Acknowledgments

To that little girl who believed that magic was real. To that little girl who was always creating stories in her head. To that little girl who believed all things were possible. So much thanks to my mom and dad, who gave me that magic.

To boo, who helps me keep that magic alive. To my original Inkies, who helped me develop this story: Wendy Higgins, Leigh Fallon, John Macdonald, Evie J., Jeyn Roberts, Sharon M. Johnston, Nyrae Dawn, Jen Conroy, Ryan Greenspan, Russell Dillingham, Cara Ruegg, and Laura Toeniskoetter. For Cortney Pearson, Jason Matthews, Kory Gott, Lisa Cresswell, Anne Pfeffer, Jolene Perry, Ryan Dalton, Lani Woodland, Jerry Bennett, Kristi McManus, Brynn Ahlstrom, Tiana Smith, Elizabeth Briggs, Tammy Theriault, Evelyn Skye, and my other dear friends who have helped me along the way. For Mandy Davis, who never stopped cheering me on.

To my first agent, Karen Grencik, who saw potential with my writing. To my agent, Marisa Corvisiero, for helping my dreams come true. So much thanks to my team at CamCat: Kayla Webb, Elana Gibson, Helga Schier, and Sue Arroyo for your brilliance.

To Aaron, forever and always. To my four sweet kids, who let mommy write. And to everyone out there with a story in their heart . . . don’t be afraid to share it with the world.

About the Author

Morgan Shamy is an ex-ballerina turned YA writer.

She has been immersed in the arts since the young age of four. She's performed alongside a professional ballet company for over seven years and has danced on prestigious stages like soloing at Carnegie Hall in New York City. She has taught hundreds of girls in her fifteen years of teaching, with some of her students receiving full-ride scholarships to schools like School of American Ballet, the Harid Conservatory, Kirov Academy of Ballet, and Pacific Northwest Ballet, to name a few. Morgan is also an accomplished concert pianist. She was the first girl in Utah to receive the 75 pt. Gold Cup in the Utah Federation of Music in the piano solo/concerto competition.

Morgan discovered writing when her three-year-old son was diagnosed with cancer. It was through that experience she discovered the need to share art and magic with children through words on the page.

Morgan currently lives with her X-Games gold-medalist husband and four children in Salt Lake City, Utah.

If you enjoyed
Morgan Shamy's *The Stricken*,
please consider leaving a review
to help our authors.

And check out another great
read from CamCat:
H. J. Reynolds's *Without a Shadow*.

1
Two A Dozen

It was just a game at the start. Adlai learned the rules from her father; they would go out into the blazing sun, when the day was at its hottest with shadows burning black holes in the sand, and he would say, "Pick one, little drizzle," and she would slip her hand out from his to search the crowd.

Even back then the marketplace had the best crowds, and not just of people, but of things. Metallic ornaments winking a thousand suns at every turn; gems dripped on stringed necklaces; long luscious silks slipping like water through her hands . . . There was the smell, too. Aromatic herbs smoking in pots, and the stench rising out from the herds of exotic beasts that were either caged or flying from chains high above the tents, their claws swiping at careless passersby.

When she looked at the people in the market and the baubles all around her, Adlai felt like the luckiest girl in the world. All she had to do was turn to her father and say, "There, over there," and he would play the game.

The Shadow Game, he called it. You could only teach your shadow one trick. So, while she distracted the vendor, her father would come near—not quite by the stall of her choice, but near. It was always difficult for her not to look back—he'd tell her off if she did—but she loved seeing it happen.

His shadow would move, it would shimmer like a haze and become longer as it reached for something—all the while, his body stayed stock still—and when it passed over the item, then his shadow became faint. Fainter and fainter until his shadow would be gone altogether—along with what she'd wanted.

That was when they would leave the crowd, get back home, and her father would present her with whatever small thing had caught her eye. Sometimes he'd give Adlai an extra surprise. A little trinket or silk scarf. Always, he picked something golden—the color of her hair, he'd say.

There were no curtains in the attic room, just a collection of bright, colorful scarves draped haphazardly across the single window that glared down above Adlai's bed. Cold sunlight slithered in through the rainbow of fabric. A few of the scarves were starting to fade; reds turned to browns, blues to deathly gray. She would have to change those out. There was nothing more depressing than waking up to rags fluttering their last.

Her roommate, Penna, was already up and dressed. Her dark figure was quietly making her bed, and Adlai turned away with a sigh.

Getting up was never easy. Adlai wanted nothing more than to sink back into her dream. It hadn't felt like one. Her father had been right there in front of her, his shadow snaking over a stall as he played the Shadow Game one more time.

She pulled out the drawer of her bedside table and looked down at the heap of trinkets inside. Some were worthless. A dented tin matchbox, earrings with a cluster of fake pearls, an aged book on a royal family that had long since died out.

Others, though, she thought might fetch a decent price if she tried to sell them. Her fingers brushed over a bangle that had a large fiery topaz embedded in the gold. Everything in her drawer shone golden. Her father had picked each one for her, seemingly not based on its value but based on something else she couldn't quite understand as she stared down at the odd collection.

They shone. The worthless trinkets gleamed as much as the truly expensive ones, and perhaps that's all it ever was: pretty, shiny things to distract a child who asked too many questions and who didn't know how to listen.

She was about to close the drawer when she saw the bee pendant. She remembered him giving her that one. It was of a golden little honeybee with the tip of the wings grabbing onto the thin chain on either side of it. Adlai hadn't worn the pendant for a while, but it winked at her as she sat up and the memory that came with it was a sweet one. Bittersweet, as it was one of the last things he'd given her. On impulse, she reached out and fastened it around her neck.

"Did I wake you?" Penna's soft voice called over. Adlai shook her head. Now she was up, she wondered how it was possible she'd been deeply asleep only moments ago. A baby was crying on the floor directly below them and if she strained her ears further, she could pick up a thousand other noises. Much like a dripping tap, once heard they were impossible to unhear.

Living in an orphanage with twenty other kids of varying ages wasn't the best environment for peaceful sleep. But Penna and Adlai were fortunate enough to be stuffed up in the attic, where the sounds were somewhat muffled and there were no little feet storming over their beds to demand breakfast. That was the benefit, Adlai supposed, of being too old for any family to want to adopt you: they got to be tidied away.

Penna took the tidying away a little too literally and kept her side of the room as undisturbed as possible. There were no personal items, despite having lived at the orphanage longer than Adlai. Her clothes were folded and hidden away in the chest of drawers, and on top of that single piece of furniture she kept only what was needed: a comb, a small mirror, some lotion, and a soap bar that smelled of lemon. If she left tomorrow, there wouldn't be a hair or thumbprint to say she had lived there.

Adlai's side, on the other hand, would take a few trips up and down to sort through. She headed over to a pile of clothes to dress. Unless she could bring herself to wake before the sun, which she wasn't likely to, she knew the washroom wouldn't be free again until nightfall. She pulled on white trousers with a shine fabric and a wrap top the color of an atomic sun. It was bright and garish enough. Adlai had plans to play the Shadow Game herself today, and wearing something attention grabbing had always been her father's advice. It was the folk that covered themselves up in hoods and tried to melt in the background that garnered the suspicious looks in the desert market.

Sliding her sandals on, she let Penna climb down the ladder first. A mistake, as her friend was wearing a long, green dress with fine stitching she was careful to protect as she climbed down the rungs. Adlai's stomach was growling by the time Penna finally dropped to the floor and the ladder shook, ready for her. She slunk down it, realizing at the same time that the crying she'd heard had finally stopped. A door opened and Mother Henson, cradling a sleeping newborn, looked over at them.

"Well, at last. While you two have been dozing, I've had the whole morning full of things to do. Couldn't count them to tell you," she said in that offhand way that told Adlai nothing had been done. Especially as she followed it up with, "I'm going to need some extra help today."

Adlai rolled her eyes to that, but Henson pretended not to notice. Every day she needed help for something or other, and it was always for jobs she was supposed to do. With one year left before Penna and Adlai were considered adults, their files had long been collecting dust.

"What do you need?" Penna asked. Adlai wanted to hit her for so easily offering.

Mother Henson smiled. It looked odd on her, more so as she must have been at the mirror moments before the baby started fussing and had makeup on only one eye. It looked like a dark, dusty bruise while her other eye shrank in comparison.

"You're a good girl, Penna, dear. I'll just need the meals cooked and some of the rooms cleaned. Gilly has a potential match so her area will need tidying up the most. And if you could get her presentable too—you know she's always running wild with the boys." The baby whimpered slightly, and she rocked him closer to her chest. "Perhaps you can make some honey cakes? The family will love that."

Penna had work in the afternoon and all those tasks would take most of the morning without any help. She side-eyed Adlai, hopeful, but Adlai shook her head. She was done scrubbing floors and cooking for an army of ingrates. Mother Henson might have given her a roof over her head, but that was all she did these days.

"Leave it to us," Penna said brightly. Adlai sighed and wondered why Penna still bothered to stay on Mother Henson's good side. As soon as the baby started to whimper, Henson forgot they were even there.

It was only the helpless, screaming babies who could stir the mother in Mother Henson. Once a child started talking and walking, the mistress of the orphanage could easily forget the same child still needed food and attention. Adlai at least had been old enough when she'd been forced through the doors to know not to look for love from such a woman, but some of the younger ones learned the lesson harder.

"You know you don't have to always help," Adlai said as they walked down to the kitchen. There were three other kids inside picking at corn muffins that looked like the runt of a baker's litter.

"I don't mind." Penna's eyes swept over the open cupboards and started putting things back in their places. Her busy hands stopped on a roll of mangoes. "What I do mind is good fruit going to waste. If I were to make a big fruity mash, do you think there'd be enough to satisfy the greediest little monkeys?"

Adlai sighed, knowing Penna wasn't really talking to her and that she'd be distracted making breakfasts for a good while. She took some fruit for herself and headed to their usual spot out on the balcony.

Outside, the air was warm but not the sticky, sweating kind it would turn to later in the day. She jumped up to sit on the banister ledge and swung her legs over the dust path below. People were starting to head to their work or make those early morning purchases, as much a part of a routine as getting dressed. The same sight as always.

She looked farther ahead. The Arbil pyramid shone golden in the distance, creating a three-sided sun with the morning light glinting off its massive walls. They were ancient walls, older than the city gates, but the gold brick made it look brand new. Like the trinkets from her father, the pyramid was the city's treasure: a place of birth, healing, and death. Adlai took a bite of her pear; it was overly sweet but cooler than a glass of water. She was onto the second one when Penna arrived. Her dress had wet stains on the front and one of the kids must have pulled at her headscarf as the top of her tight curls were showing underneath.

"You know it's Henson's job to cook the meals and prepare the kids for their appointments. She's *paid* to look after us," Adlai said.

There was a small, crooked table and two creaking chairs on the balcony. Penna sat down on one and stared dreamily out to the same horizon Adlai overlooked. "Mother has her hands full with the little one. It used to be fun." She turned to Adlai. "Remember that game we'd play? *Tell Me How*? We could play that again this morning."

Adlai laughed. Penna had round dark eyes that were hard to say no to and one of those genuine smiles that a child might make when presented with a treat. The problem in this was that the treat was a stupid game she'd invented to pretend they weren't cleaning up sick or peeling away their life in buckets of potatoes.

Penna had been her best friend these last seven years. Her only friend. But while Adlai wanted to flip the page to when they could get out of this place, she sometimes thought Pen wanted to freeze time and stick her feet into the foundations.

"I'm not staying here all morning," Adlai said, already regretting it.

The bath water had warmed to a level that, while it wasn't exactly hot, was at least pleasant to run her hand through. Adlai was sweating from hauling several buckets up and down the stairs and could do with sinking into a clean bath herself, but the water wasn't for her.

Not that Gilly was grateful for their effort. Adlai turned over the empty bucket and sat on it as she watched Penna fight off the girl's muddy clothing.

"I washed yesterday!" Gilly argued. Adlai didn't believe her. Some of the kids might splash water on their face and rub soap through their hair, but not many of the kids bothered filling a bath. Gilly looked, and smelled, as though she had been many days without even this cursory wash.

"Come on," Penna said gently, "you want to look your best for your appointment, don't you?"

Gilly snorted but let Pen pull off the last of her underclothes. Naked, the girl looked even more wild. Her dark hair ran long down her back in a tangled mess, and she had an assortment of cuts and bruises, some healing, others fresh from a recent fight. They could hide most of them in nice clothing, but Adlai didn't like her chances.

There were more boys than girls at the orphanage. There always were because when people wanted a child, what they really meant was a son. Mother Henson turned girls away like they were rotten food she didn't want dumped in her kitchen, only occasionally adding one or two to her collection for the rare couple who actually wanted a daughter over a son. Gilly, wild and unruly, was unlikely to be the girl the couple were coming for.

"We still have cooking to do," Adlai said, "so unless you want to help out with that, get in the tub and let's make this quick."

Gilly scowled at Adlai.

"Ignore her," Penna said. "She's in a mood. You can go back to playing later. But right now, you have to be clean."

Gilly scowled again and made sure the water splashed over Adlai as she climbed into the tub. At least she was in though.

An assortment of bottles and soap bars lined the shelf over by the small, glazed window. Penna took a few items from there and handed Adlai nail files as she poured in oils that smelled of jasmine and smoke. Gilly wrinkled her nose but didn't complain. That came when Penna dipped the girl's head back and started work untangling her hair.

"Owww!"

"Why don't we play the game?" Penna said. "Tell me how . . ." she looked over at Adlai as she dug the comb through a particularly large knot, "you learned to swim?"

"I don't need to swim today, do I?" the girl asked, confused.

"No," Penna answered, smiling. The knot loosened and more water splashed over the edge of the tub and gathered by Adlai's feet.

Adlai reached for one of the girl's hands and began picking the dirt from her nails. "How I learned to swim?" she repeated, thinking for a moment. It had been a while since they played this game. "I never had to learn to swim. My mother was a mermaid, you know, so I was born with a fishtail. Before I could talk, I could swim." She looked down at Gilly's confused—yes, definitely confused—expression. "I know what you're thinking. But where's your fishtail now? Well, fishtail scales are worth a lot of money, and when I was very young, three or four years old, I was kidnapped for them. They peeled off my scales like I was a vegetable for a summer stew."

Gilly yanked her hand away. She had the look of someone who'd long ago stopped listening to fairy tales, probably right around the day her parents didn't come home. Had Adlai once been this child? The girl's features seemed to be screwed up permanently in anger, her frown as deep as claws.

"Don't worry," Adlai said, grabbing Gilly's other, equally dirty hand. "My father saved me. I wouldn't have legs at all if he hadn't brought me quick to the desert market. Everything is sold there, you know. Including a magic potion to grow limbs. He had to use his blood for it and that's why I have his knobbly knees, and I have to shave every day or else I break out in man hair. Though," she lowered her voice to a conspiratorial whisper, "sometimes I still get the odd scale . . ."

The tooth of the comb became stuck in another big knot, but both Pen and Gilly ignored it. "What color were your scales?" Penna asked.

Adlai thought for a minute. Her eyes drifted over every color in the room—the blue tiled floor, the white tub, the cracked, gray walls. She discarded them each in turn. "They were colorless. They picked up all the colors in the light, like glass does."

She could tell Penna liked this idea. Her pretty, dark face was all entranced and even Gilly loosened her frown, staring wide-eyed between them. They were adults in her eyes, albeit adults talking nonsense about mermaids, but for a moment all three forgot what they were doing in the room. Playing the game could sometimes make Adlai forget this was an orphanage, or that Pen hadn't always been family to her. The thought tugged at something she wished it hadn't.

"Have you ever seen a mermaid?" Penna asked. She pulled the comb loose and smiled down at Gilly. "They look so beautiful in the picture books, don't they?"

Adlai finished cleaning out the last nail and dropped Gilly's hand. She stood up and came away from the tub. "How many mermaids you expect to come across in the desert, Pen? It's not like orphans, where we're two a dozen."

Penna shook her head. "But there are other places. Oceans and mountains out there. Places with snow even. Do you think they really exist?"

"Mermaids, or other places?"

"I don't know. Both, I guess."

Adlai didn't answer her. The truth was she wanted it all to be real. If she could leave Libra and travel the kingdom, she thought she might see things just as impossible as her shadow that could steal. She stared down at Gilly. "What do you think?"

"I think this game's stupid, and I don't see why all this fuss has to be made every time one of us has an appointment. I don't want to be adopted. I'm going to move into the attic when you two leave."

Adlai shook her head. "Then you're even more stupid than if you'd believed I was half-mermaid. Don't you get it? You have a chance at a family today. Take it."

2

Nothing But Dreams

The waiting room was the only part of the orphanage that had a homey feel about it. There were two plump sofas with feathery cushions, a bookcase with little ornaments—mostly of cartoonish animals, and a feature wall of drawings that the younger kids added to periodically. Even the tiled floor was of a happy, bright orange.

This was where the adoption appointments took place. Adlai and Penna were busy setting the stage for Gilly's potential new family, while Mother Henson had taken the girl to her office to run through the script of what to say and do, as well as what not to say and do. That was important too. Adlai had messed up each and every one of her appointments through some perceived slip. Once, she'd stolen the watch off a woman who'd made her open her mouth to check her teeth. Another time she'd spilled the tea a man had demanded she serve. She had never been able to be the girl the couple wanted. She doubted Gilly would either.

"How is it you were never adopted, Pen?"

Penna, at least, was the exact kind of girl any couple would be proud to call their daughter. She was pretty, kind, and talented at all those things girls were supposed to be; she cooked, she cleaned, she liked being around kids. If anyone was going to be adopted, Penna was the model child.

"Oh, I was close once," she said with a fake kind of breeze to her voice. "Everything was going well and then they asked me if I liked to read . . ."

Adlai frowned. "But you do like to read."

"Because you taught me. Before then I used to pretend the stories in my head were what all those jumbled letters on the page were saying." She smiled and took a small, well-worn book off the shelf. The cover's title was written in a playful, childish script and read, *Fantastical Fables of Glories Gone—Heartfelt Heroes and Irredeemable Ignobles.*

"I was eight," she continued. "They thought I was a little old to still be inventing stories about dragons and princesses. Mother actually apologized for presenting such a simple-minded child to them." She put the book down. "After that she had me helping out with the cooking and I didn't get any more appointments."

"You mean she saw you'd do her work for her." Adlai dropped the cloth she'd been wiping the end table with. She was starting to wonder if the same thing hadn't happened with her. Weren't they always the ones doing Mother Henson's work for her? "Maybe we didn't screw up as bad as we thought, Pen. Maybe this whole show with Gilly is just to groom her into our replacements."

Penna shook her head. "You don't really think Mother would play with our futures like that?"

"I think Mother doesn't see us as having any futures."

Penna started to defend Mother Henson, as she always did, but Adlai wasn't listening. She came over to the book and flipped through the pages. Some of the stories were as familiar as if she'd written them herself: smoke dragons living up in the clouds and causing droughts, firebloods who died and were reborn again, and of course the shadow wielders. She'd read the tale of Menko and the Shadow Wielder a thousand times as a kid. Menko was the hero, sworn to save a princess whose land had been ravaged by disease. The tale showed three gallant princes, each using knowledge from their lands to try to solve the crisis. The Capri prince grew better crops to feed the people, the Libran prince brought superior medicines to cure the people, and the Piscean prince built an array of fresh water spots to cleanse the people. But the crops died, the medicine failed and the water grew dirty, and the princes died with the people. Only Menko could see what others had failed to: for the princess was a shadow wielder. To keep her youth and beauty, she'd been sending her shadow out across her land and stealing from her people. Not riches, she had plenty of those. Her shadow could steal the rosy complexion of a young maid, or the strength of the strongest man. If not for Menko, who plunged a sun dagger through her shadow as it tried to steal wisdom from his brow, she would have lived forever.

There were other tales that showed shadow wielders at work. Some were just petty tricksters, but most played the part of villain. It used to make her laugh to read of these great powers they supposedly had. Other times she was glad her shadow had only learned to steal. She knew the stories were made up for children, after all every legend had a sprinkling of truth among the dung, but even so, she wouldn't want a shadow that could do half of what she'd read the legendary shadow wielders capable of doing.

The door to the waiting room opened and Mother Henson came swooping in with an almost unrecognizable Gilly at her heels. The girl's wet hair was braided back and she wore a light, frilly dress with long sleeves that covered up the scraps and bruises. Gilly plucked at the frills and shot both Penna and Adlai a look, daring either of them to laugh.

"You look lovely," Penna said, and no doubt meant it.

"How she looks will hardly matter if everything else is out of place," Mother Henson said, brushing her finger over the table Adlai hadn't finished wiping. "What have you two been doing all of this time? Where are the honey cakes? They should be by the sofa for the guests."

"Would you like us to pick fresh flowers too?" Adlai said. "Or hand sew a welcome flag?"

Mother Henson eyed Adlai with her usual coolness.

"I shouldn't be surprised to hear you making jokes." A thin smile played on her reddened lips. "All your appointments were a complete disaster, weren't they?"

Adlai shrugged. "Or you decided me and Pen were more useful here. Doing your work for you."

The coolness left Mother Henson's eyes. For a moment she looked at Adlai the way she did when a small child was being led through the doors for the first time.

"You think I turned people away from adopting you?" Henson said softly. "Simple child. I wouldn't ruin your few chances in life. Yours might not be the saddest story to come my way but I still felt for you when you arrived. A father walking out on their child is a sad thing."

"My father didn't walk out on me." Adlai gripped the book so tightly her nails punched through the leather.

Henson arched her brow. "Of course not. Mystery night intruders, wasn't it? Strange they didn't take you too."

It wasn't the first time Mother Henson had mocked Adlai's version of what happened the night her father went missing—the authorities hadn't believed her either. There had been no blood, no sign of a fight, no items stolen. And no body. Her father had simply vanished. Only Penna had listened to her, and probably she was just being nice. Like how she was now, coming over to Adlai and resting a hand on her arm to calm her.

"Don't you have anything else to do?" Adlai said, her voice steady. "I know how busy you are."

But Mother Henson didn't leave. She came closer. Close enough that Adlai could smell that sickly rose perfume sticking to the air like hot vapor. She looked down at the book Adlai was still holding.

"It always surprises me how many children come to my home with dreams fogging up their heads. They have nothing but dreams, even after life has already been so cruel with them." She turned to Gilly. "Let these two be a lesson to you, child. Almost full grown and living like rats in my attic. If you have any sense, you'll take this adoption seriously. There are so few chances for girls like you."

She looked down at Adlai and Penna, her gaze lingering on Adlai as her voice became soft as a whisper. "You think I ask too much, but the minute you turn eighteen, you'll see how generous I've really been. You have a bed here and food. Neither of which come for free."

Adlai didn't answer. She couldn't. Penna's hand gently pressed down, reminding her again to stay calm.

"You're very good to us, Mother," Penna said. "I'll have those cakes warm and ready."

Mother Henson nodded. "You're a good one," she said. "I know if I extended your stay here, you'd appreciate it."

She took a last appraising look around the room and then at Gilly, whispering something final to the girl before leaving.

After the door shut, the air seemed to thin out between them and all three girls relaxed. Then a boy rushed past the window and tapped on the glass making them jump. He laughed and stuck his tongue out at Gilly.